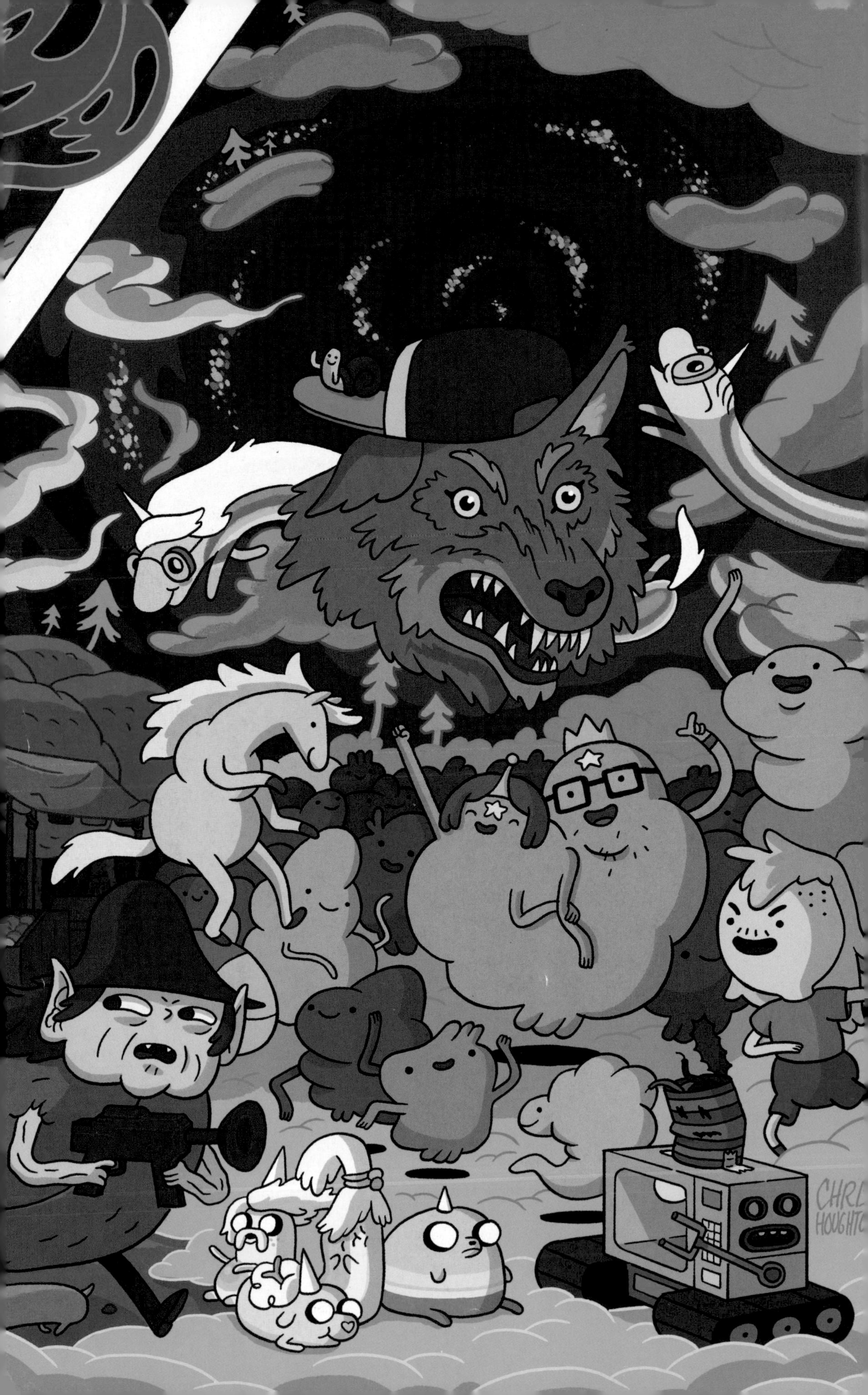

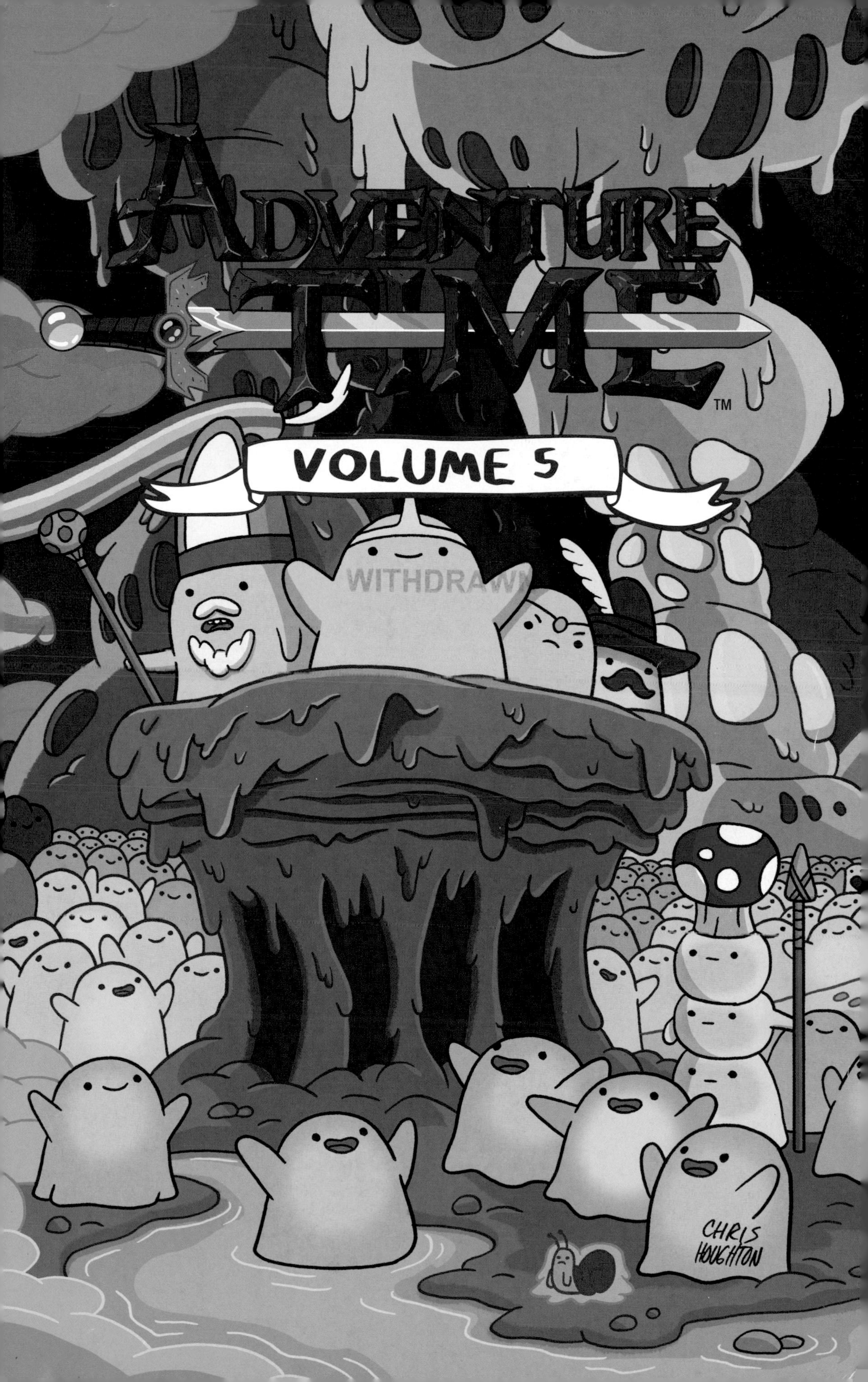
ADVENTURE TIME™
VOLUME 5
WITHDRAWN
CHRIS HOUGHTON

ROSS RICHIE CEO & Founder • MARK SMYLIE Founder of Archaia • MATT GAGNON Editor-in-Chief • FILIP SABLIK VP of Publishing & Marketing • STEPHEN CHRISTY VP of Development
LANCE KREITER VP of Licensing & Merchandising • PHIL BARBARO VP of Finance • BRYCE CARLSON Managing Editor • MEL CAYLO Marketing Manager • SCOTT NEWMAN Production Design Manager • IRENE BRADISH Operations Manager
CHRISTINE DINH Brand Communications Manager • DAFNA PLEBAN Editor • SHANNON WATTERS Editor • ERIC HARBURN Editor • REBECCA TAYLOR Editor • IAN BRILL Editor • CHRIS ROSA Assistant Editor
ALEX GALER Assistant Editor • WHITNEY LEOPARD Assistant Editor • JASMINE AMIRI Assistant Editor • CAMERON CHITTOCK Assistant Editor • HANNAH NANCE PARTLOW Production Designer
KELSEY DIETERICH Production Designer • EMI YONEMURA BROWN Production Designer • DEVIN FUNCHES E-Commerce & Inventory Coordinator • ANDY LIEGL Event Coordinator • BRIANNA HART Executive Assistant
AARON FERRARA Operations Assistant • JOSÉ MEZA Sales Assistant • MICHELLE ANKLEY Sales Assistant • ELIZABETH LOUGHRIDGE Accounting Assistant • STEPHANIE HOCUTT PR Assistant

ADVENTURE TIME Volume Five, September 2014. Published by KaBOOM!, a division of Boom Entertainment, Inc. ADVENTURE TIME, CARTOON NETWORK, the
logos, and all related characters and elements are trademarks of and © Cartoon Network. (S14) Originally published in single magazine form as ADVENTURE TIME 20-
24. © Cartoon Network. (S13) All rights reserved. KaBOOM! and the KaBOOM! logo are trademarks of Boom Entertainment, Inc., registered in various countries and
categories. All characters, events, and institutions depicted herein are fictional. Any similarity between any of the names, characters, persons, events, and/or institutions in
this publication to actual names, characters, and persons, whether living or dead, events, and/or institutions is unintended and purely coincidental. KaBOOM! does not read
or accept unsolicited submissions of ideas, stories, or artwork.

A catalog record of this book is available from OCLC and from the KaBOOM! website, www.kaboom-studios.com, on the Librarians Page.

BOOM! Studios, 5670 Wilshire Boulevard, Suite 450, Los Angeles, CA 90036-5679. Printed in China. First Printing.
ISBN: 978-1-60886-401-0, eISBN: 978-1-61398-255-6

CREATED BY
Pendleton Ward

WRITTEN BY
Ryan North

ILLUSTRATED BY
Shelli Paroline
& Braden Lamb

ADDITIONAL COLORS BY
Chris O'Neill

LETTERS BY
Steve Wands

COVER BY
Scott Maynard

DESIGNERS
Hannah Nance Partlow
& Emi Yonemura Brown

ASSISTANT EDITOR
Whitney Leopard

EDITOR
Shannon Watters

With special thanks to
Marisa Marionakis, Rick Blanco, Jeff Parker, Laurie Halal-Ono, Nicole Rivera, Conrad
Montgomery, Meghan Bradley, Curtis Lelash and the wonderful folks at Cartoon Network.

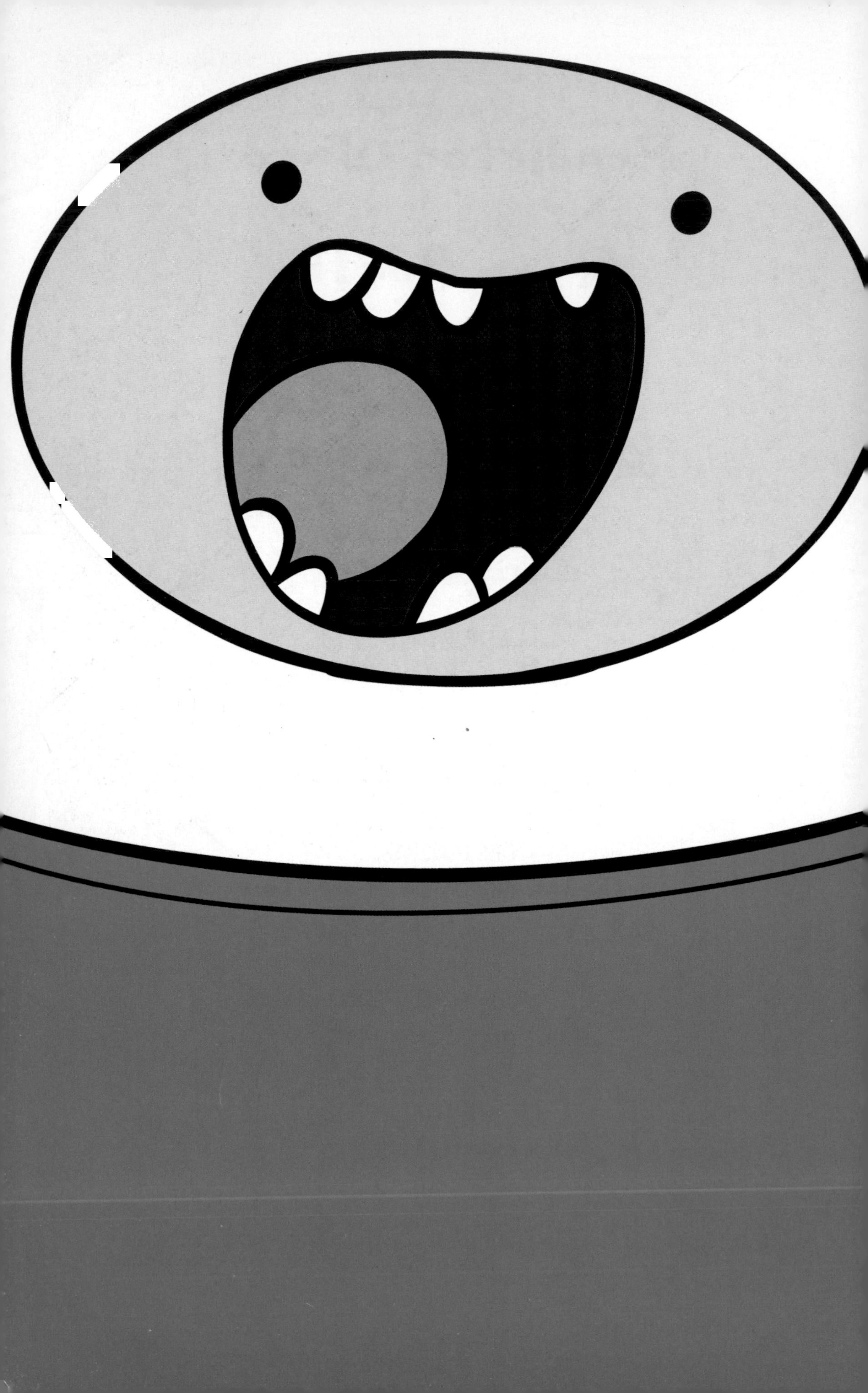

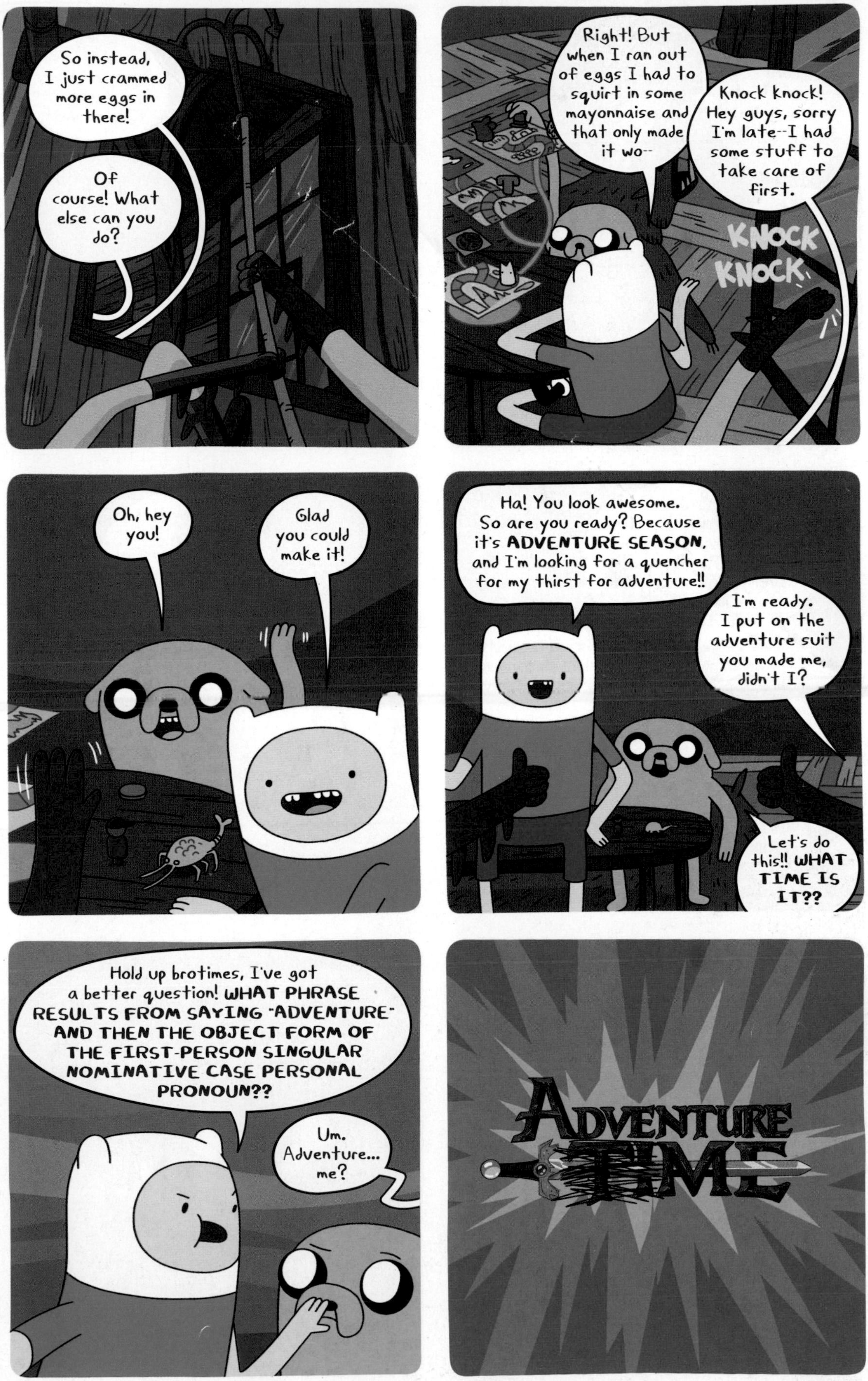
So instead, I just crammed more eggs in there!
Of course! What else can you do?
Right! But when I ran out of eggs I had to squirt in some mayonnaise and that only made it wo--
Knock knock! Hey guys, sorry I'm late--I had some stuff to take care of first.
KNOCK KNOCK
Oh, hey you!
Glad you could make it!
Ha! You look awesome. So are you ready? Because it's ADVENTURE SEASON, and I'm looking for a quencher for my thirst for adventure!!
I'm ready. I put on the adventure suit you made me, didn't I?
Let's do this!! WHAT TIME IS IT??
Hold up brotimes, I've got a better question! WHAT PHRASE RESULTS FROM SAYING "ADVENTURE" AND THEN THE OBJECT FORM OF THE FIRST-PERSON SINGULAR NOMINATIVE CASE PERSONAL PRONOUN??
Um. Adventure... me?
ADVENTURE
TIME

"Adventure Me"? What's next, "Adventure Tim"? Oh wait we already did that, haha, okay nevermind!

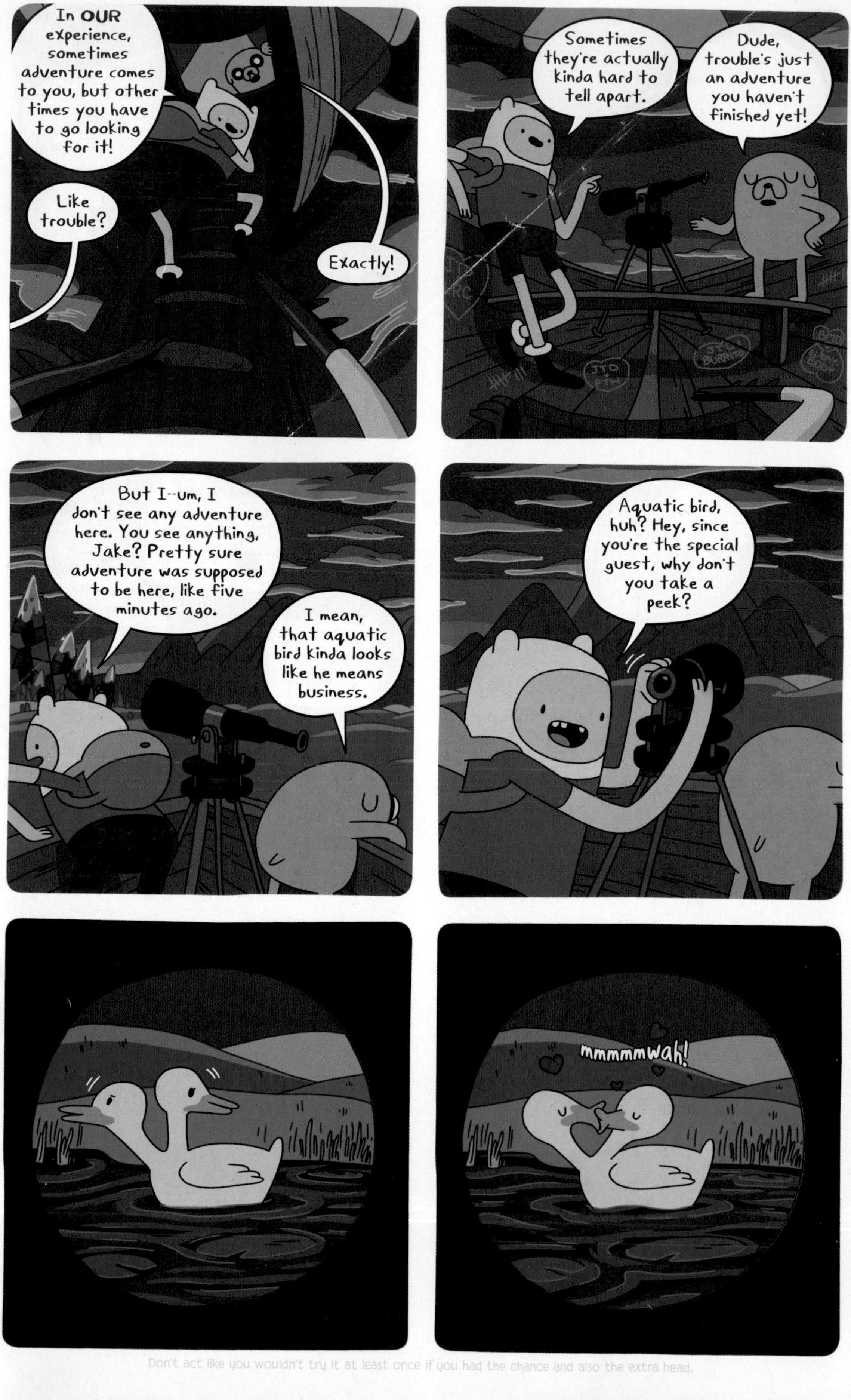
In OUR experience, sometimes adventure comes to you, but other times you have to go looking for it!
Like trouble?
Exactly!
Sometimes they're actually kinda hard to tell apart.
Dude, trouble's just an adventure you haven't finished yet!
But I--um, I don't see any adventure here. You see anything, Jake? Pretty sure adventure was supposed to be here, like five minutes ago.
I mean, that aquatic bird kinda looks like he means business.
Aquatic bird, huh? Hey, since you're the special guest, why don't you take a peek?
mmmmmwah!

Don't act like you wouldn't try it at least once if you had the chance and also the extra head.

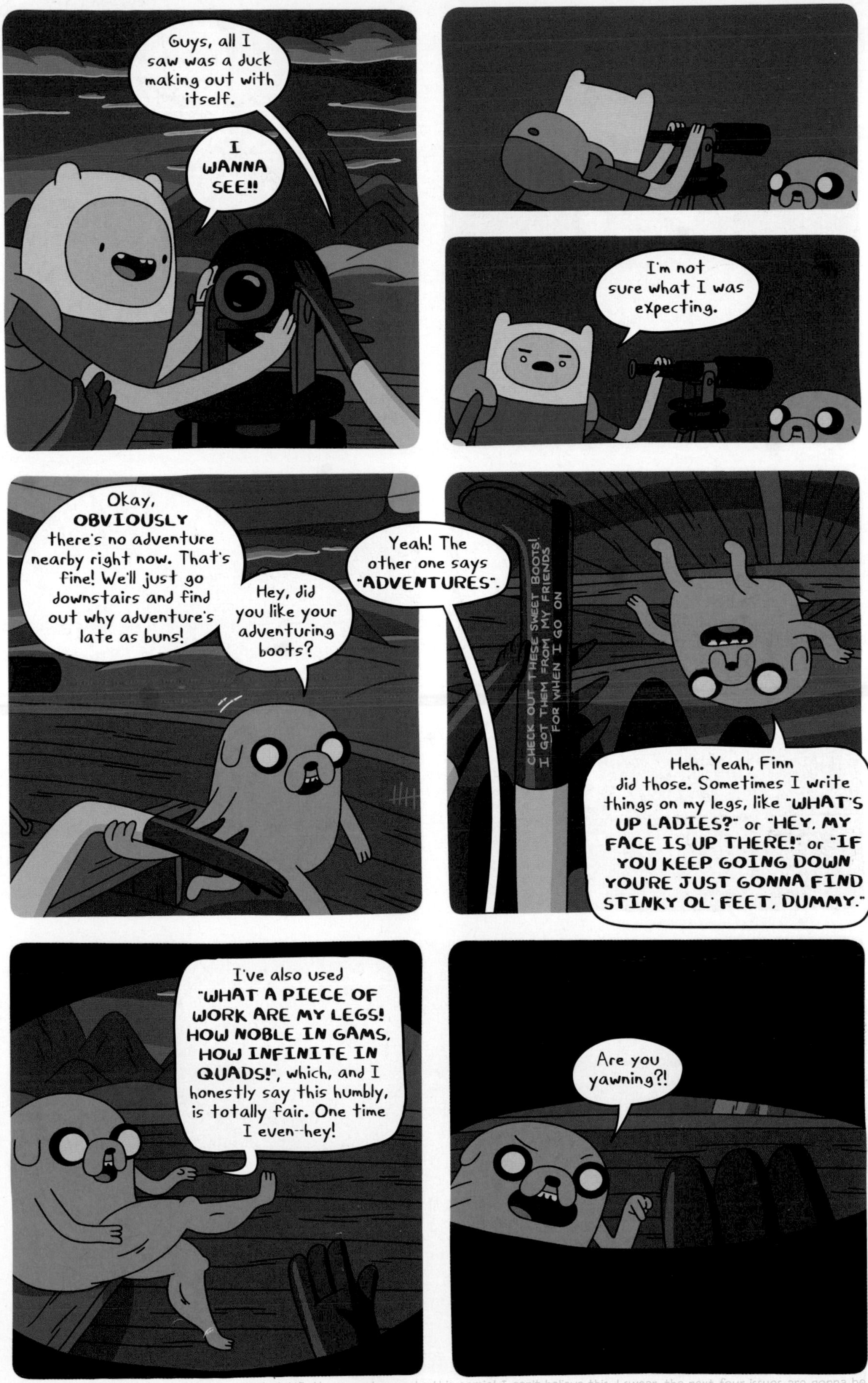
Guys, all I saw was a duck making out with itself.
I WANNA SEE!!
I'm not sure what I was expecting.
Okay, **OBVIOUSLY** there's no adventure nearby right now. That's fine! We'll just go downstairs and find out why adventure's late as buns!
Hey, did you like your adventuring boots?
Yeah! The other one says "**ADVENTURES**".
CHECK OUT THESE SWEET BOOTS! I GOT THEM FROM MY FRIENDS FOR WHEN I GO ON
Heh. Yeah, Finn did those. Sometimes I write things on my legs, like "**WHAT'S UP LADIES?**" or "**HEY, MY FACE IS UP THERE!**" or "**IF YOU KEEP GOING DOWN YOU'RE JUST GONNA FIND STINKY OL' FEET, DUMMY.**"
I've also used "**WHAT A PIECE OF WORK ARE MY LEGS! HOW NOBLE IN GAMS, HOW INFINITE IN QUADS!**", which, and I honestly say this humbly, is totally fair. One time I even--hey!
Are you yawning?!

You are yawning!! You insult not only Jake but ME, the guy who wrote this comic! I can't believe this. I swear, the next four issues are gonna be called "FINN AND JAKE LEARN TO BE POLITE: YOU, AS THE READER, SHOULD PROBABLY BE TAKING NOTES"

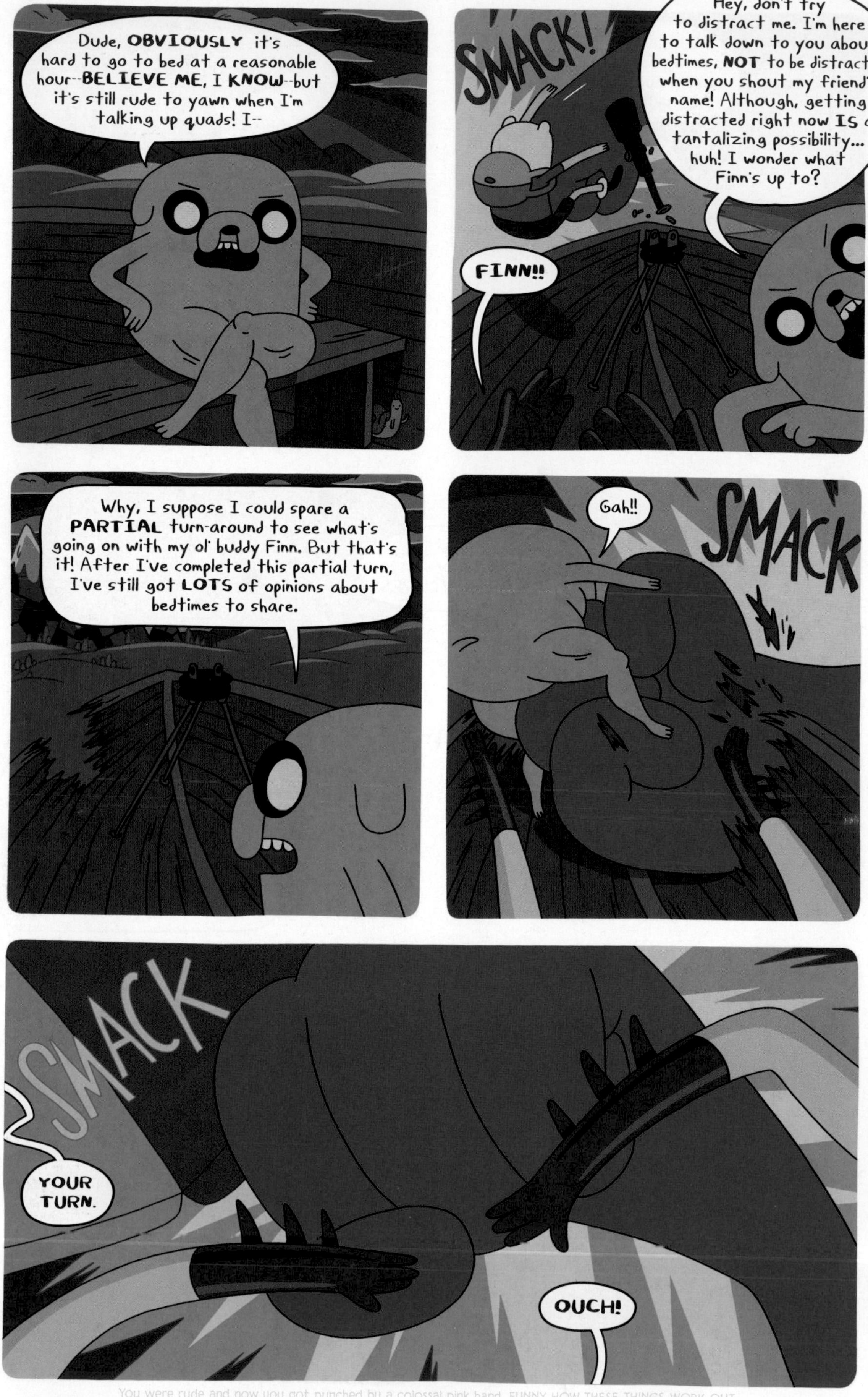
Dude, **OBVIOUSLY** it's hard to go to bed at a reasonable hour--**BELIEVE ME, I KNOW**--but it's still rude to yawn when I'm talking up quads! I--
SMACK!
FINN!!
Hey, don't try to distract me. I'm here to talk down to you about bedtimes, **NOT** to be distracted when you shout my friend's name! Although, getting distracted right now **IS** a tantalizing possibility... huh! I wonder what Finn's up to?
Why, I suppose I could spare a **PARTIAL** turn-around to see what's going on with my ol' buddy Finn. But that's it! After I've completed this partial turn, I've still got **LOTS** of opinions about bedtimes to share.
Gah!!
SMACK
SMACK
YOUR TURN.
OUCH!

You were rude and now you got punched by a colossal pink hand. FUNNY HOW THESE THINGS WORK OUT.

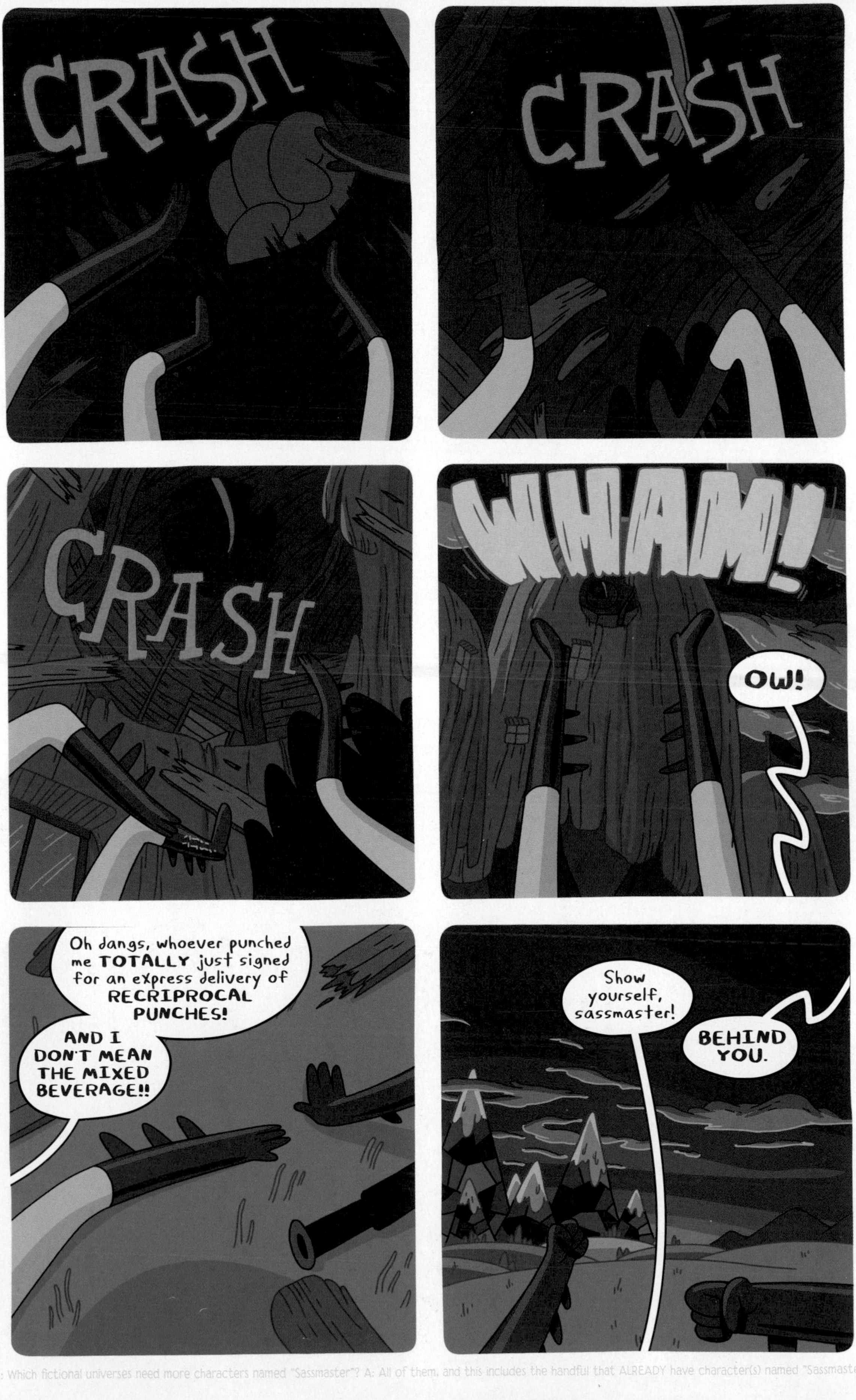
CRASH
CRASH
CRASH
WHAM!
OW!
Oh dangs, whoever punched me TOTALLY just signed for an express delivery of RECRIPROCAL PUNCHES!
AND I DON'T MEAN THE MIXED BEVERAGE!!
Show yourself, sassmaster!
BEHIND YOU.

Q: Which fictional universes need more characters named "Sassmaster"? A: All of them, and this includes the handful that ALREADY have character(s) named "Sassmaster".

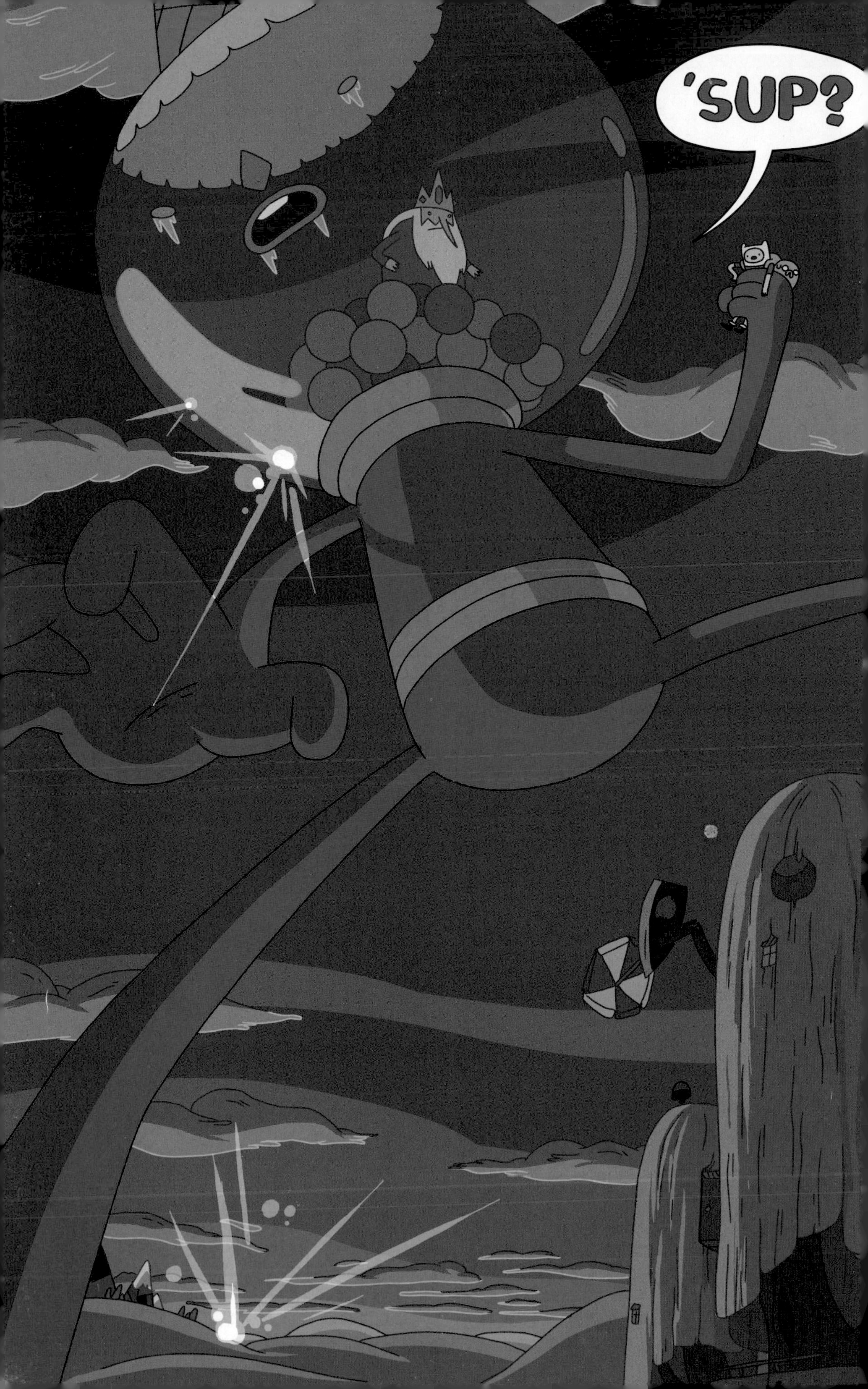
'SUP?

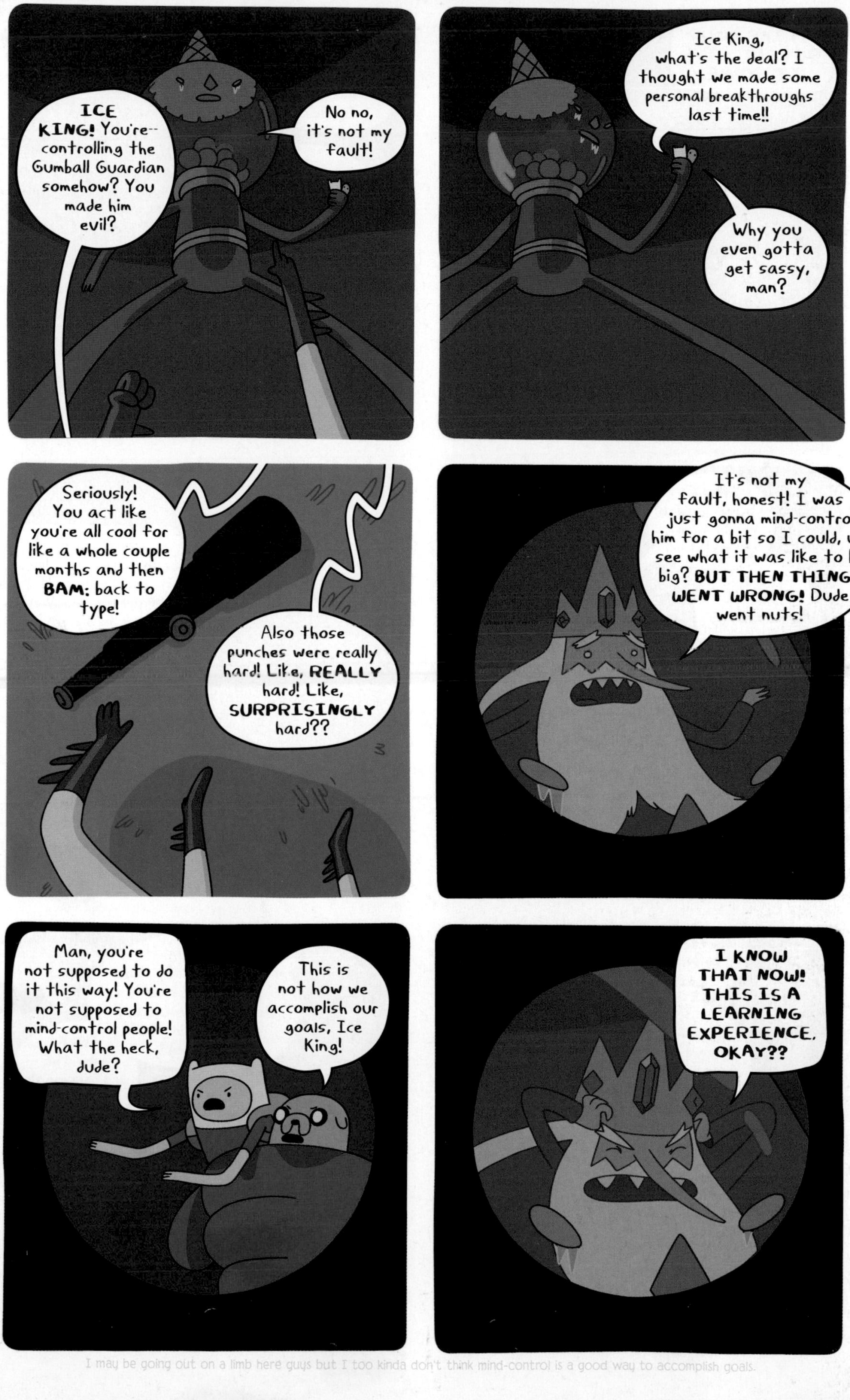
ICE KING! You're-- controlling the Gumball Guardian somehow? You made him evil?
No no, it's not my fault!
Ice King, what's the deal? I thought we made some personal breakthroughs last time!!
Why you even gotta get sassy, man?
Seriously! You act like you're all cool for like a whole couple months and then BAM: back to type!
Also those punches were really hard! Like, REALLY hard! Like, SURPRISINGLY hard??
It's not my fault, honest! I was just gonna mind-control him for a bit so I could, uh, see what it was like to be big? BUT THEN THINGS WENT WRONG! Dude went nuts!
Man, you're not supposed to do it this way! You're not supposed to mind-control people! What the heck, dude?
This is not how we accomplish our goals, Ice King!
I KNOW THAT NOW! THIS IS A LEARNING EXPERIENCE, OKAY??

I may be going out on a limb here guys but I too kinda don't think mind-control is a good way to accomplish goals.

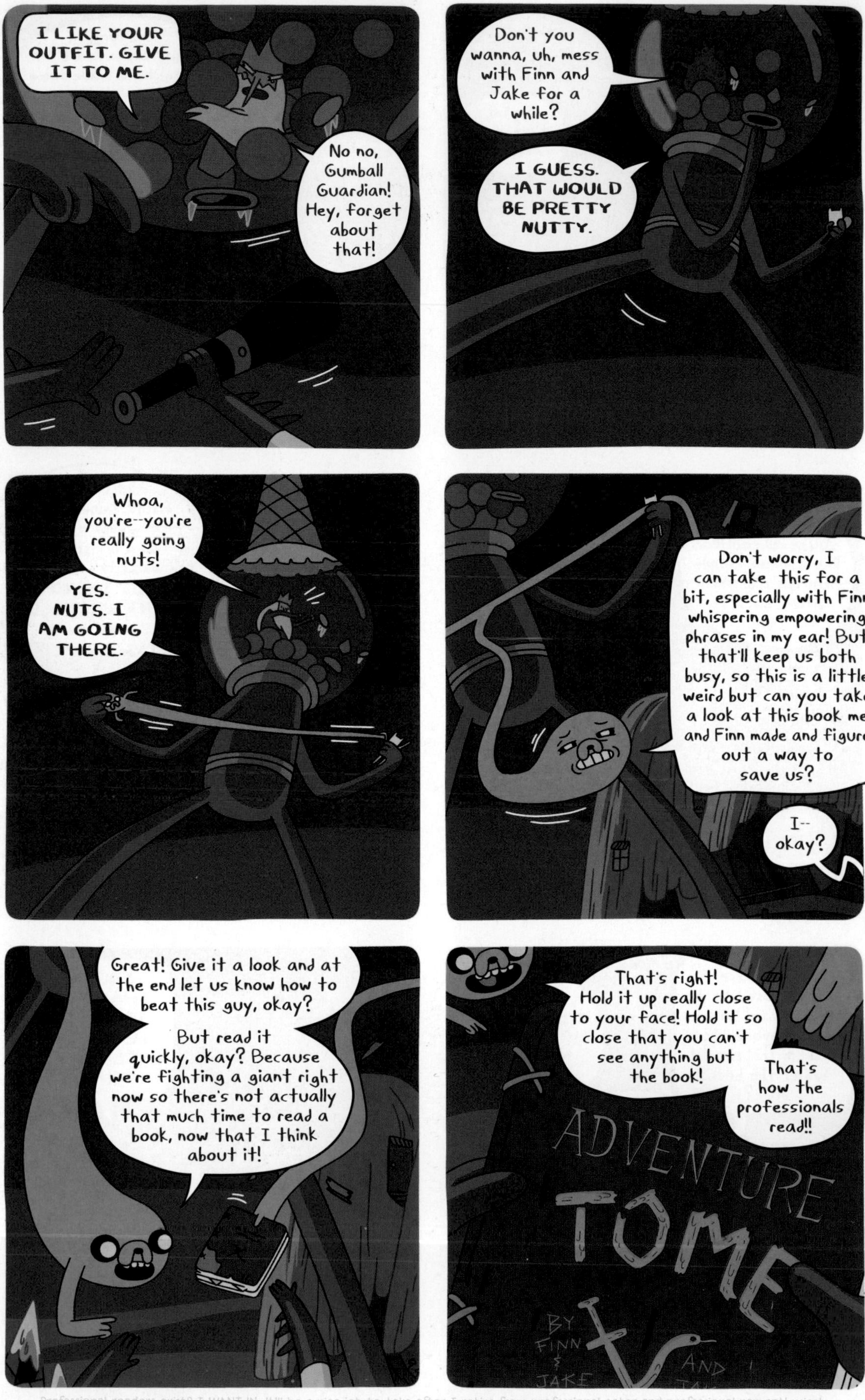
I LIKE YOUR OUTFIT. GIVE IT TO ME.
No no, Gumball Guardian! Hey, forget about that!
Don't you wanna, uh, mess with Finn and Jake for a while?
I GUESS. THAT WOULD BE PRETTY NUTTY.
Whoa, you're--you're really going nuts!
YES. NUTS. I AM GOING THERE.
Don't worry, I can take this for a bit, especially with Finn whispering empowering phrases in my ear! But that'll keep us both busy, so this is a little weird but can you take a look at this book me and Finn made and figure out a way to save us?
I-- okay?
Great! Give it a look and at the end let us know how to beat this guy, okay?
But read it quickly, okay? Because we're fighting a giant right now so there's not actually that much time to read a book, now that I think about it!
That's right! Hold it up really close to your face! Hold it so close that you can't see anything but the book!
That's how the professionals read!!
ADVENTURE TOME
BY FINN & JAKE
AND

Professional readers exist? I WANT IN. It'll be a nice job to take after I retire from professional eater and professional nap enthusiast.

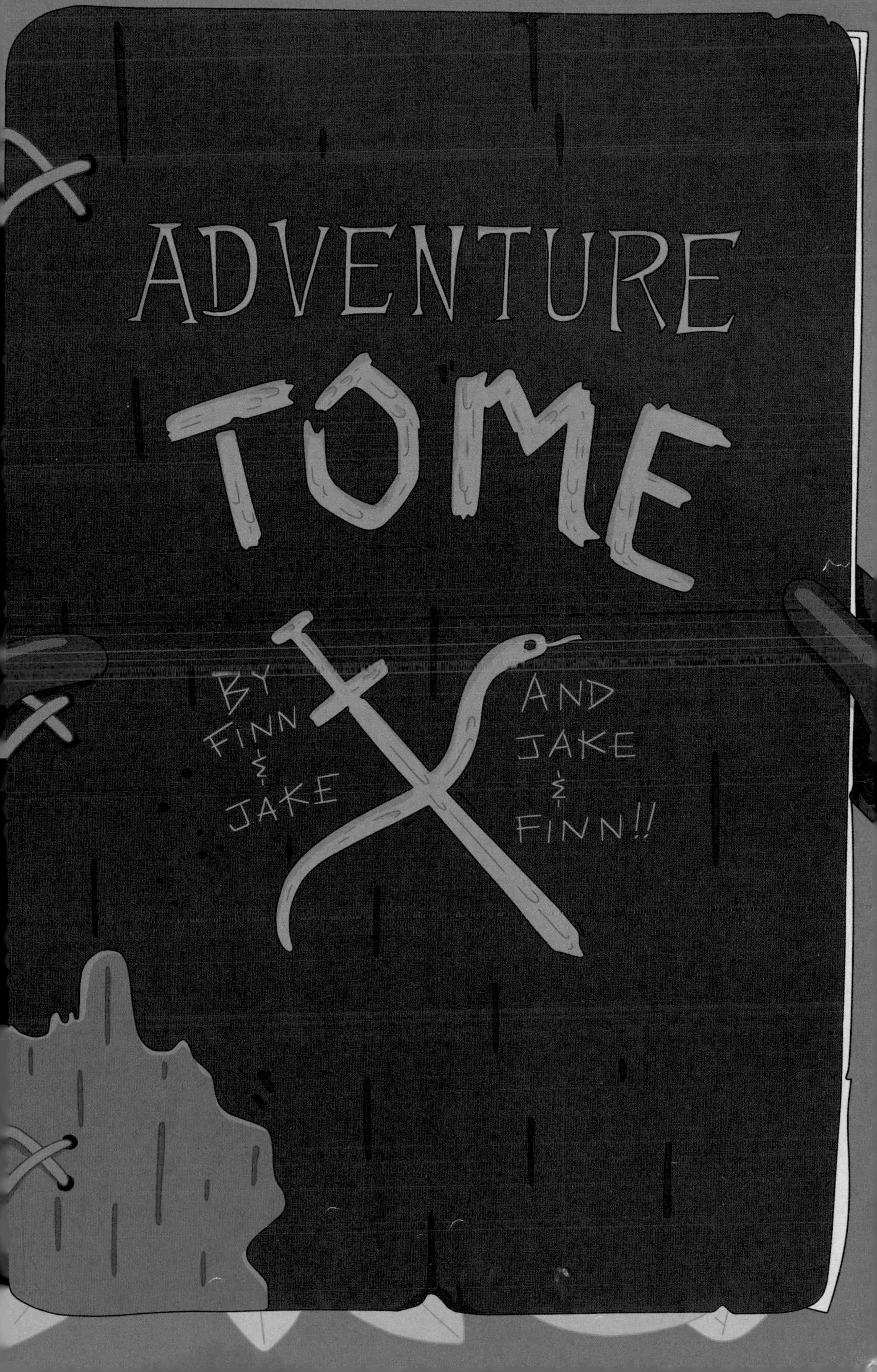
ADVENTURE
TOME
BY
FINN
&
JAKE
AND
JAKE
&
FINN!!

GOOD PLACES for Adventures

UP ON the ROOF
- only sometimes adventures are had here.
- not so good during knife storms

CaNDy KINGDOM
AKA "Shenanigan Central"
× We've got an "IN" with the Head of State

THE WOODLANDS CLEAR and COOL
* Cool place to learn nature stuff
MANY gross bugs can be found under Rocks.

SAW A COOL DEER HERE ONCE 2 (had shades + backwards cap)

FIRE KINGDOM
BE SURE TO BRING MAGIC OR BE DOWN WITH GETTING HECKA BURNED

CITY OF THIEVES
IF you go here everything you own will get stolen...
INCLUDING YOUR HEART!
- Actually that's not true, it's not that great.

BREAKFAST KINGDOM
- DO NOT GO WHEN HUNGRY!
- DO NOT GO IN THE LATE AFTERNOON EITHER, IT'S FULL OF BREAKFASTS THAT HAVE BEEN LEFT OUT ALL DAY

GLOB Land
← SOUNDS NEAT!
* Probably rad parties there ?? Worth investigating eventually.

Whirlpool OF SHARKS
FUN for at least a little while...

Whirlpool OF WHALES
- WHALE OF A GOOD TIME -
- by that I mean they hug you and feed you shrimp.
+ It's pretty rad, gotta say

CLOUd LAND
← hard to get to
- everyone there made out of clouds
- sucks to breathe in a pal by mistake
- although honestly, it's kinda fun to breathe in a pal by mistake

BLOOD LAND
× Not what it sounds like, actually more of a plasma grotto

ICE KINGDOM
Good place to go if you think "Adventure" means "hanging out with adult senior"

ISLE OF STEAM
↳ Nice place to relax

LUMPY SPACE
ONLY accessible through portal, the password is "Whatevers" and then the TOTAL NUMBER of cans of beans you've eaten so far this year

LUMPY space residents will call you "smoothies" — which is fine because smoothies are a delicious treat any time of day

MOUNT CRAGDOR
A mountain full of challenges for ADVENTURERS!
BEST PLACE EVER
We should go back sometime, yo!

ENEMIES AND FRENEMIES

Who sometimes get all up in our fries.

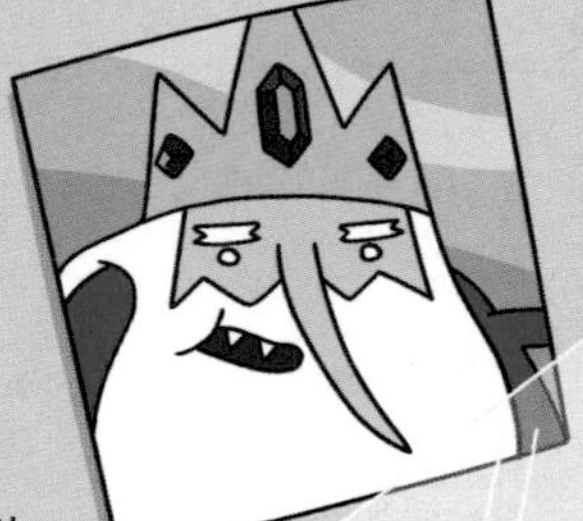

ICE KING

- weird old man, smells like cold socks
- wants to talk about feelings
- easily defeated, just dodge his ice and punch him.

#1 BABE???

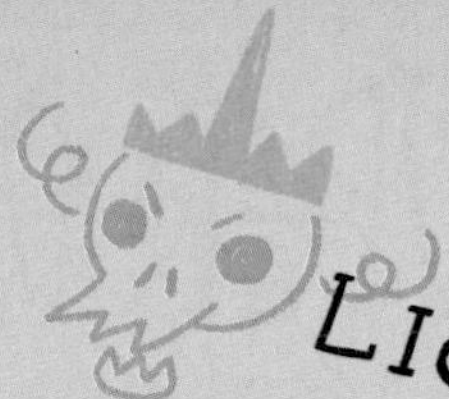

LICH

- TOTALLY DEAD FOR 100% REAL THIS TIME.
- Hard to beat (Final boss level abilities?? IT'S NUTS!)

8-HEAD TED ↓ only one of his heads is evil: the other 7 are pretty chill, actually.

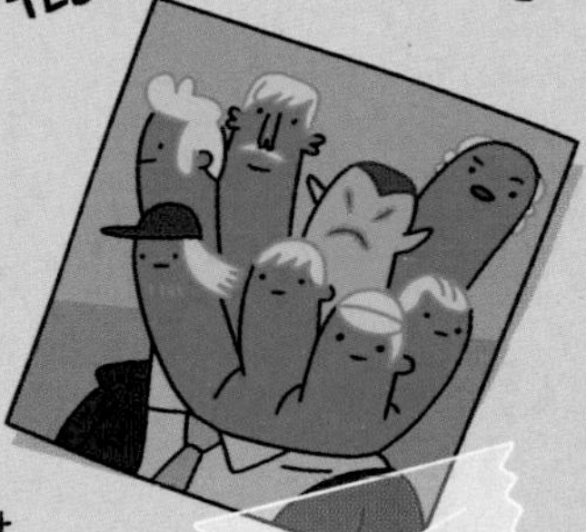

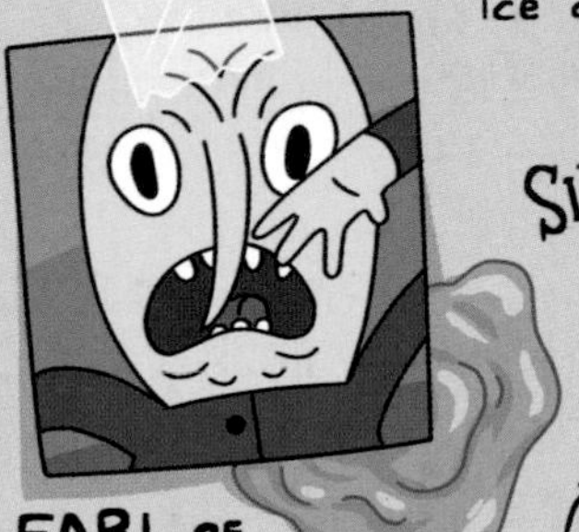

EARL of LEMONGRAB

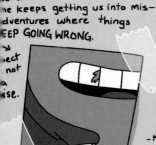

This guy, oh my glob, this guy

- defeated by earplugs so you can ignore him
- if he offers to let you look inside his mouth SAY NO.

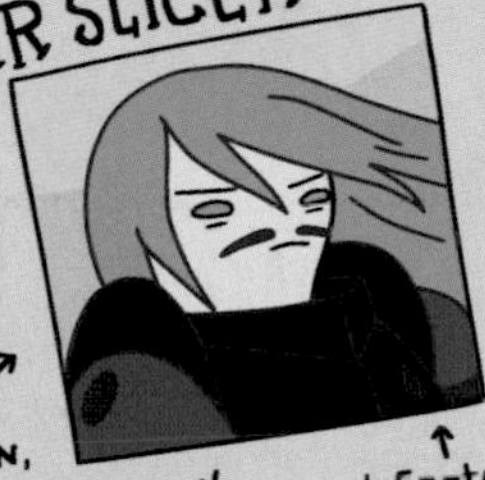

SIR SLICER

MAN, FORGET THIS GUY!

defeated by heavy armor AND/OR hubris

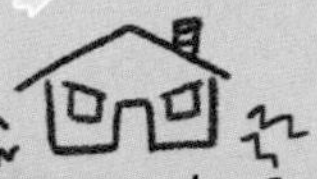

SENTIENT HOUSE THAT DOES NOT RESPOND TO STIMULI

- hard to tell if actually sentient but I'm PRETTY sure it is.

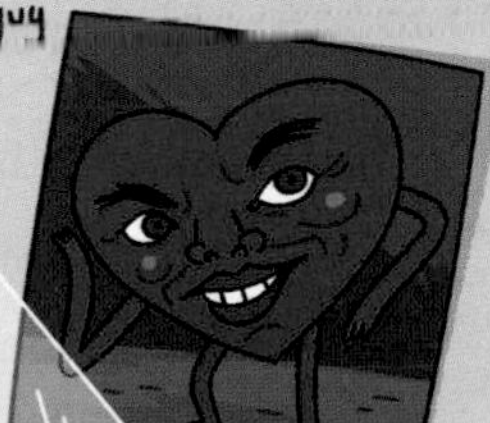

RICARDIO

- one of the several alive Ice King body parts we've had to defeat already
- GROSS
- Why is this so gross.

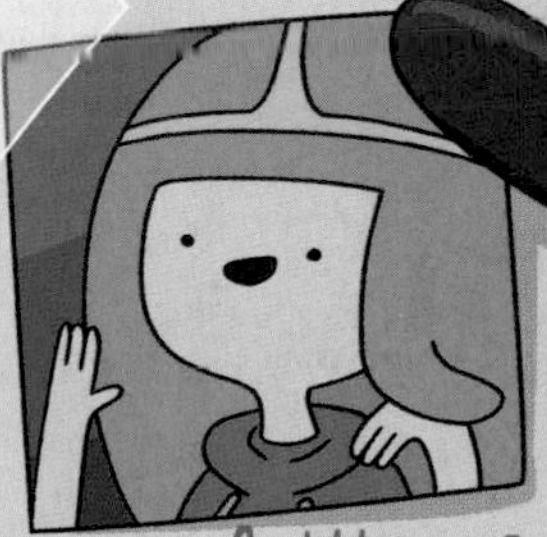

Princess Bubblegum

- Not an enemy! She is really smart and nice
- She is a real special lady and I'm glad we're friends ♡

...S ...DVENTURE

...ounds like she'd be rad, but instead ...he keeps getting us into mis- ...dventures where things ...EEP GOING WRONG.

↘ ...ect ... not ... a ...ise.

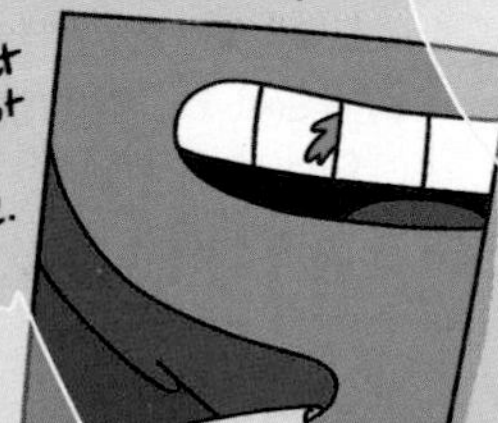

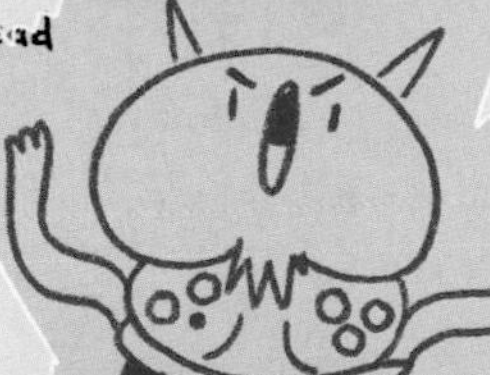

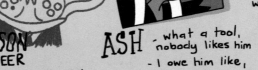

HUNSON ABADEER

- Marceline's dad: It's weird around your friend's parents sometimes
- ALSO he's evil.

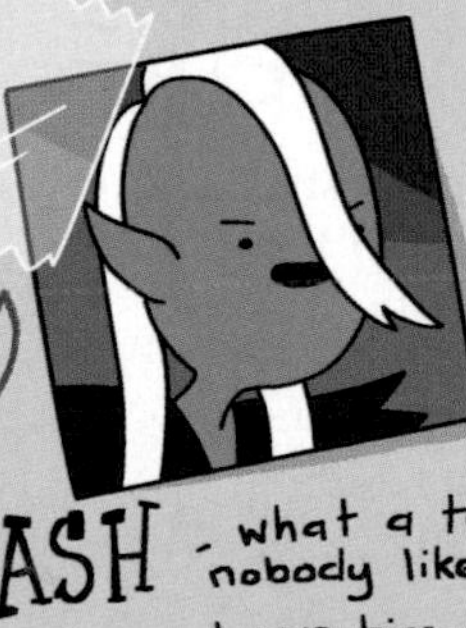

ASH

- what a tool, nobody likes him
- I owe him like, 30 punches.

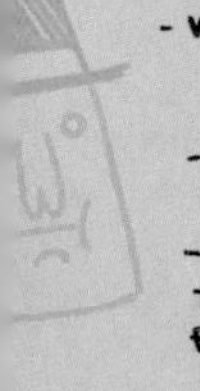

* MAGIC MAN *

- WHAT A JERK! HE IS THE ONE WHO SHOULD EAT IT, NOT ME
- used to be real cool? I don't buy it
- defeat him by never talking to him in the first place, HE'S A JERK!

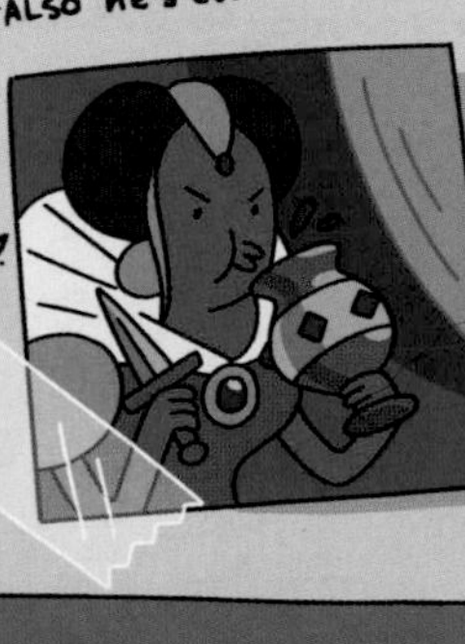

Lady Stabsworth Z. Backwash III

- It's really unlikely that someone born with such a name would live up to it perfectly but here we are.

GUNTER

DO NOT ENGAGE!

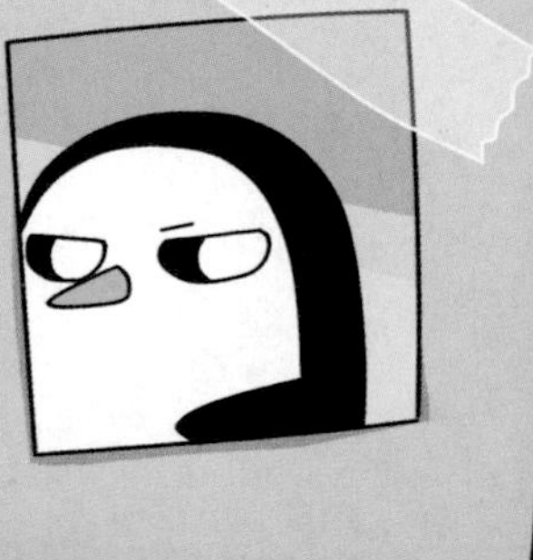

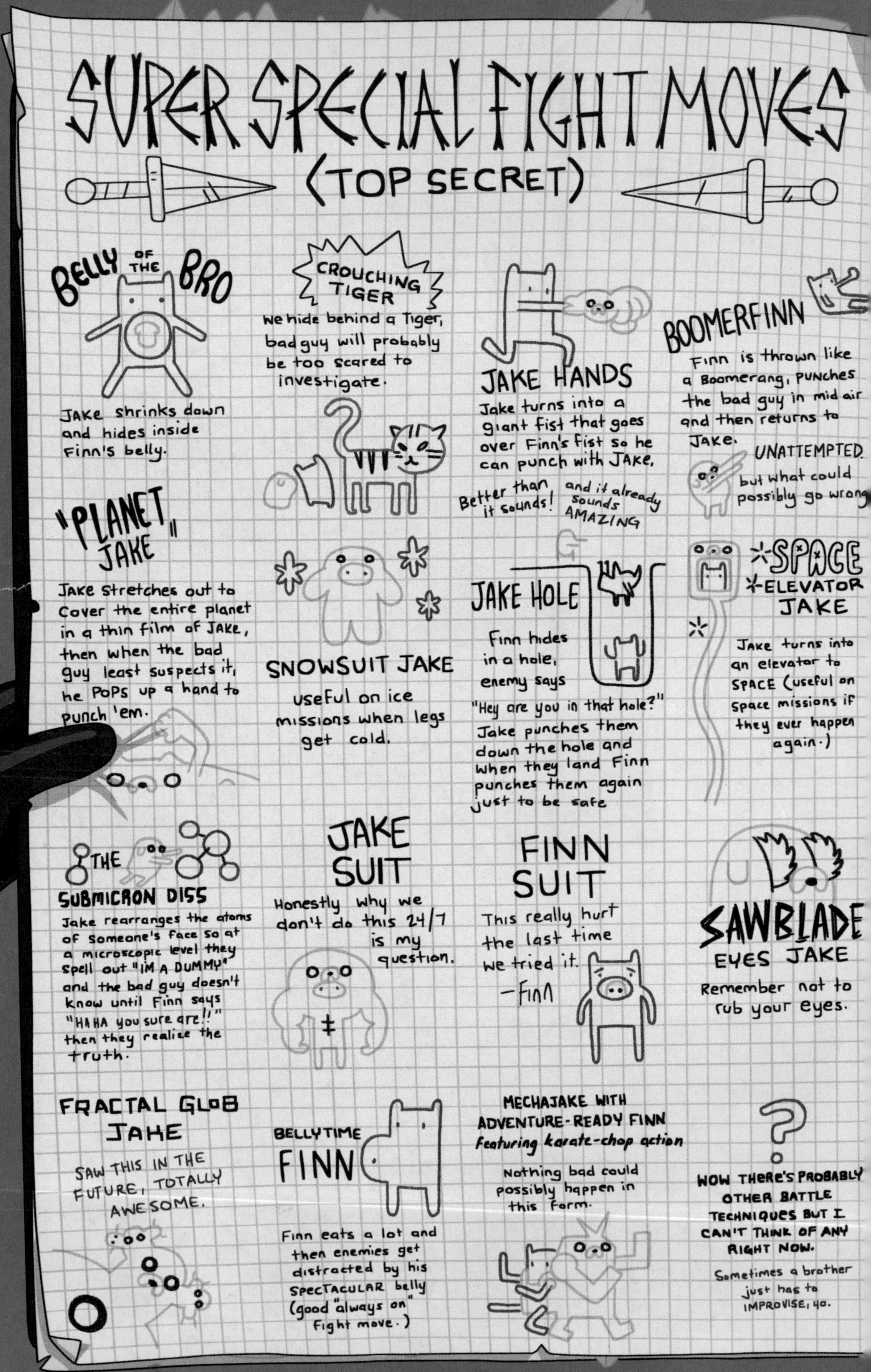
SUPER SPECIAL FIGHT MOVES
(TOP SECRET)
BELLY OF THE BRO
JAKE shrinks down and hides inside Finn's belly.
CROUCHING TIGER
We hide behind a Tiger, bad guy will probably be too scared to investigate.
JAKE HANDS
Jake turns into a giant fist that goes over Finn's fist so he can punch with JAKE.
Better than it sounds!
and it already sounds AMAZING
BOOMERFINN
Finn is thrown like a Boomerang, punches the bad guy in mid air and then returns to JAKE.
UNATTEMPTED
but what could possibly go wrong
"PLANET JAKE"
Jake stretches out to cover the entire planet in a thin film of JAKE, then when the bad guy least suspects it, he POPS up a hand to punch 'em.
SNOWSUIT JAKE
useful on ice missions when legs get cold.
JAKE HOLE
Finn hides in a hole, enemy says "Hey are you in that hole?" Jake punches them down the hole and when they land Finn punches them again just to be safe
SPACE ELEVATOR JAKE
Jake turns into an elevator to SPACE (useful on space missions if they ever happen again.)
THE SUBMICRON DISS
Jake rearranges the atoms of someone's face so at a microscopic level they spell out "IM A DUMMY" and the bad guy doesn't know until Finn says "HA HA you sure are!!" then they realize the truth.
JAKE SUIT
Honestly why we don't do this 24/7 is my question.
FINN SUIT
This really hurt the last time we tried it.
-Finn
SAWBLADE EYES JAKE
Remember not to rub your eyes.
FRACTAL GLOB JAKE
SAW THIS IN THE FUTURE, TOTALLY AWESOME.
BELLYTIME FINN
Finn eats a lot and then enemies get distracted by his SPECTACULAR belly (good "always on" Fight move.)
MECHAJAKE WITH ADVENTURE-READY FINN
featuring karate-chop action
Nothing bad could possibly happen in this form.
?
WOW THERE'S PROBABLY OTHER BATTLE TECHNIQUES BUT I CAN'T THINK OF ANY RIGHT NOW.
Sometimes a brother just has to IMPROVISE, yo.

Dudes, yo, that book was pretty useless! But I'm gonna **IMPROVISE.**

SUPER SPECIAL FIGHT MOVES

TOP **10** CANDY KINGDOM ADVENTURES

Finn, ask for a gumball and don't forget to be polite! Ice King, be the gumball--then you'll be able to reset him from the inside during the gumball purchase process!

What? No! I'm not going in there! I don't know where those gumballs come out!!

Come on, it's not hard! Here. **I'LL DO IT.**

I'm still a valued member of the team! I just don't wanna get swallowed--that doesn't make me a bad Ice King! That doesn't make me weird!

Ready, Finn?

Ready when you are!!

Three...

Two...

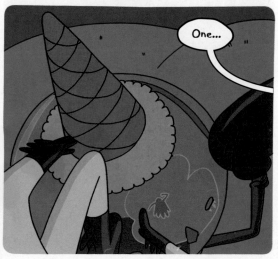

One...

NOW, Finn!!

Excuse me, Gumball Guardian! **I'D LIKE TO HAVE A GUMBALL, PLEASE!!**

As the old saying goes, ABPAYMGAG. ("Always Be Polite. And You Might Get A Gumball").

GUMBALL GUARDIANS REWARD POLITENESS. ENJOY YOUR REWARD. IT IS A GIANT GUMBALL AND IT IS COMING OUT OF ME NOW.
! GUARDIAN COLD RESET MANUAL TOGGLE !
KA-CHOOM
YES! Did it!
CLANGGG

OFFICIAL BACKSTORY: the Gumball Guardians hadn't actually given out gumballs for a quite a while, so they're as surprised by this gumball hatch opening up as anyone.

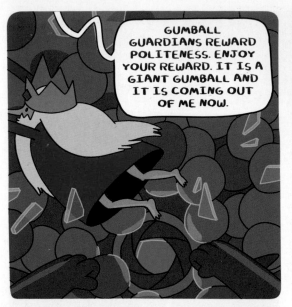

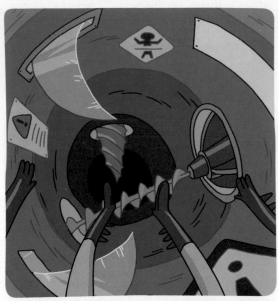

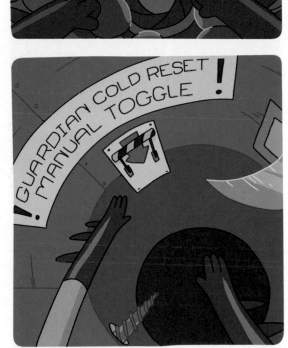

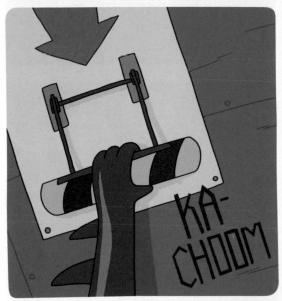

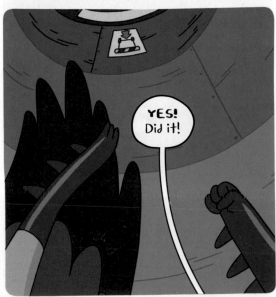

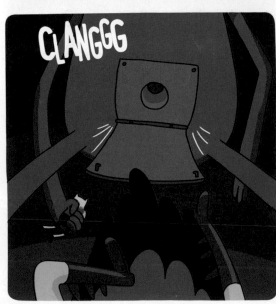

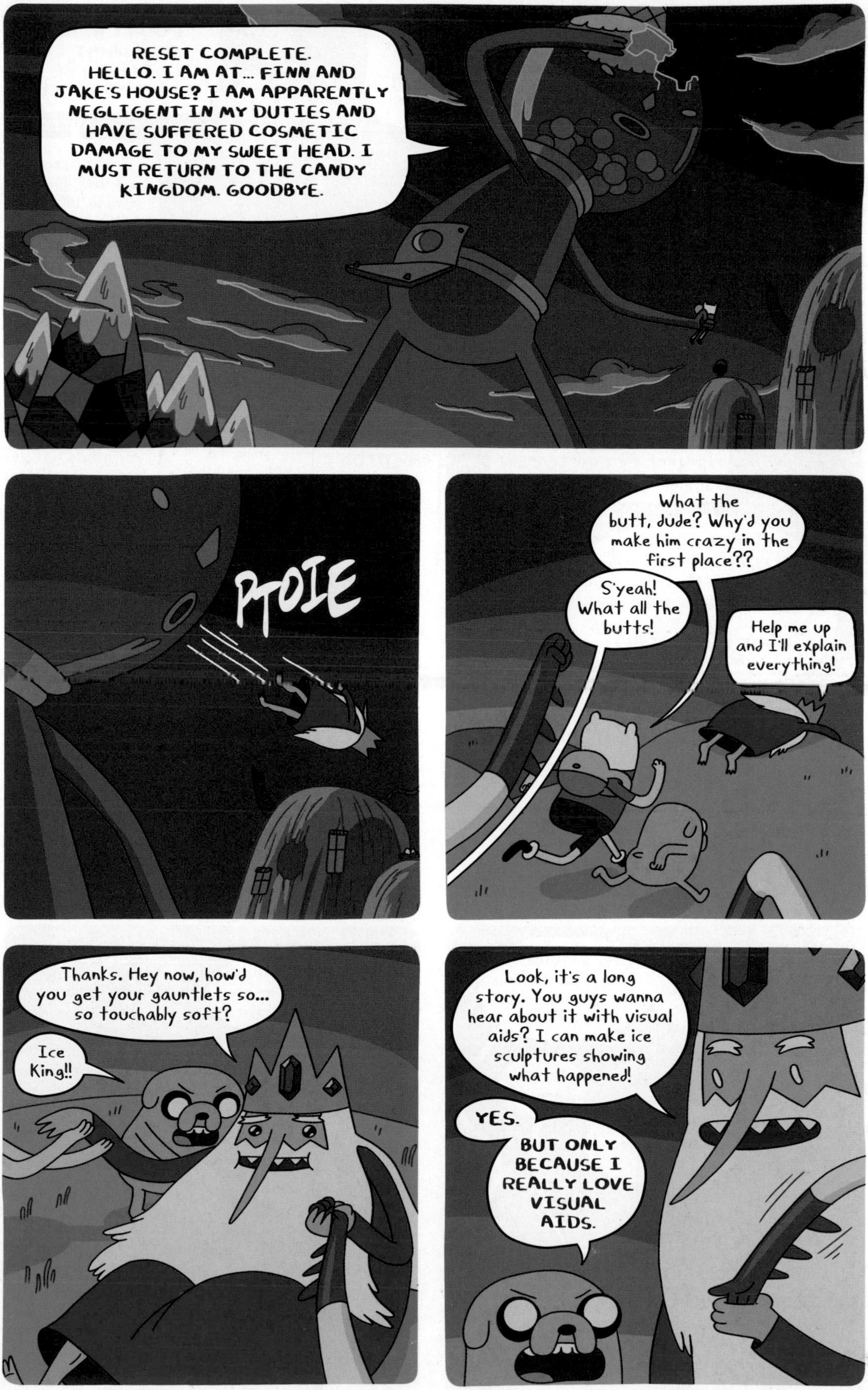
RESET COMPLETE. HELLO. I AM AT... FINN AND JAKE'S HOUSE? I AM APPARENTLY NEGLIGENT IN MY DUTIES AND HAVE SUFFERED COSMETIC DAMAGE TO MY SWEET HEAD. I MUST RETURN TO THE CANDY KINGDOM. GOODBYE.
PTOIE
What the butt, dude? Why'd you make him crazy in the first place??
S'yeah! What all the butts!
Help me up and I'll explain everything!
Thanks. Hey now, how'd you get your gauntlets so... so touchably soft?
Ice King!!
Look, it's a long story. You guys wanna hear about it with visual aids? I can make ice sculptures showing what happened!
YES.
BUT ONLY BECAUSE I REALLY LOVE VISUAL AIDS.

Your gauntlets – so touchably soft! So pliable, and yet, so battle ready!

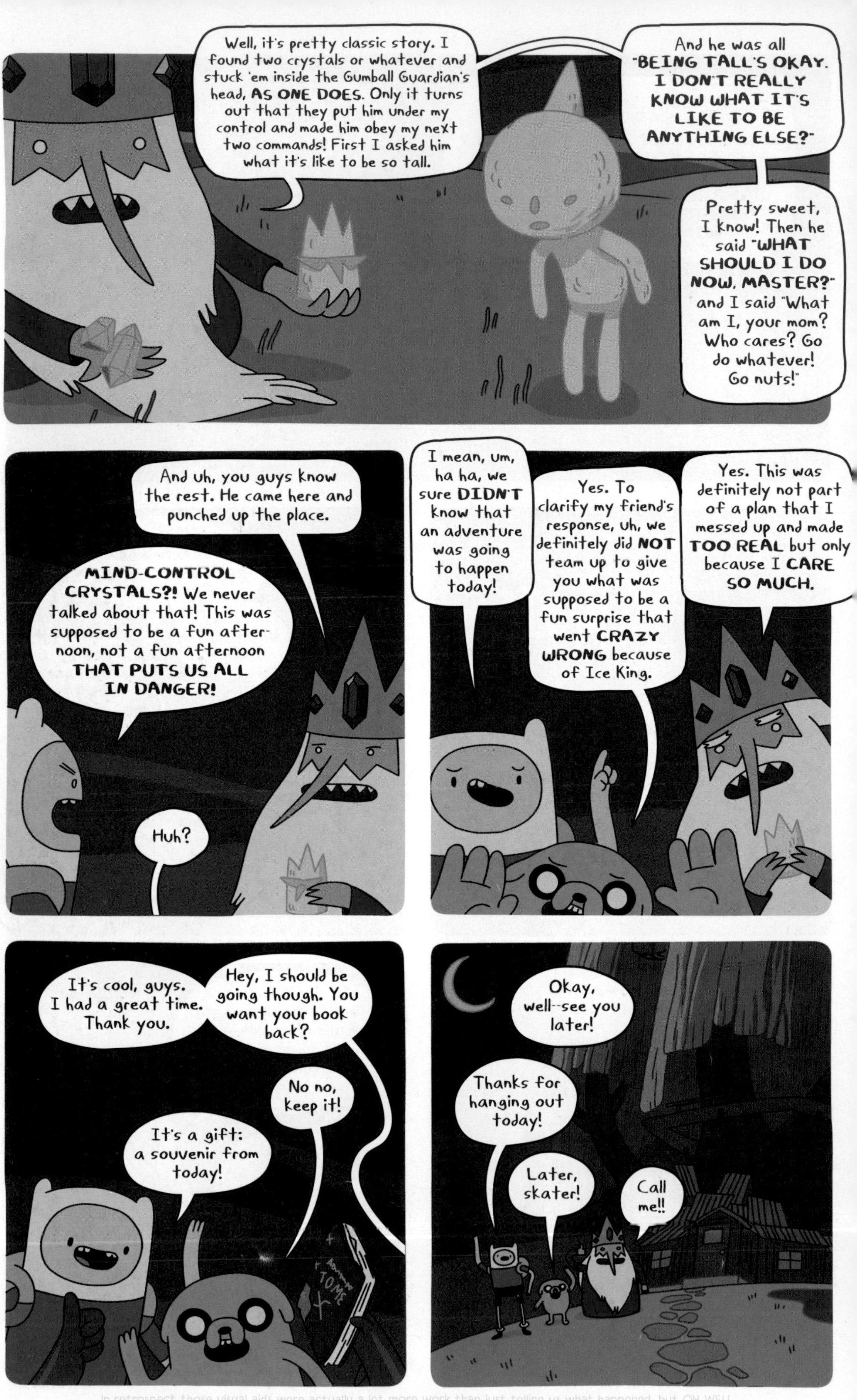
Well, it's pretty classic story. I found two crystals or whatever and stuck 'em inside the Gumball Guardian's head, AS ONE DOES. Only it turns out that they put him under my control and made him obey my next two commands! First I asked him what it's like to be so tall.
And he was all "BEING TALL'S OKAY. I DON'T REALLY KNOW WHAT IT'S LIKE TO BE ANYTHING ELSE?"
Pretty sweet, I know! Then he said "WHAT SHOULD I DO NOW, MASTER?" and I said "What am I, your mom? Who cares? Go do whatever! Go nuts!"
And uh, you guys know the rest. He came here and punched up the place.
MIND-CONTROL CRYSTALS?! We never talked about that! This was supposed to be a fun afternoon, not a fun afternoon THAT PUTS US ALL IN DANGER!
Huh?
I mean, um, ha ha, we sure DIDN'T know that an adventure was going to happen today!
Yes. To clarify my friend's response, uh, we definitely did NOT team up to give you what was supposed to be a fun surprise that went CRAZY WRONG because of Ice King.
Yes. This was definitely not part of a plan that I messed up and made TOO REAL but only because I CARE SO MUCH.
It's cool, guys. I had a great time. Thank you.
Hey, I should be going though. You want your book back?
No no, keep it!
It's a gift: a souvenir from today!
TOME
Okay, well--see you later!
Thanks for hanging out today!
Later, skater!
Call me!!

In retrospect those visual aids were actually a lot more work than just telling us what happened, but OH WELL.

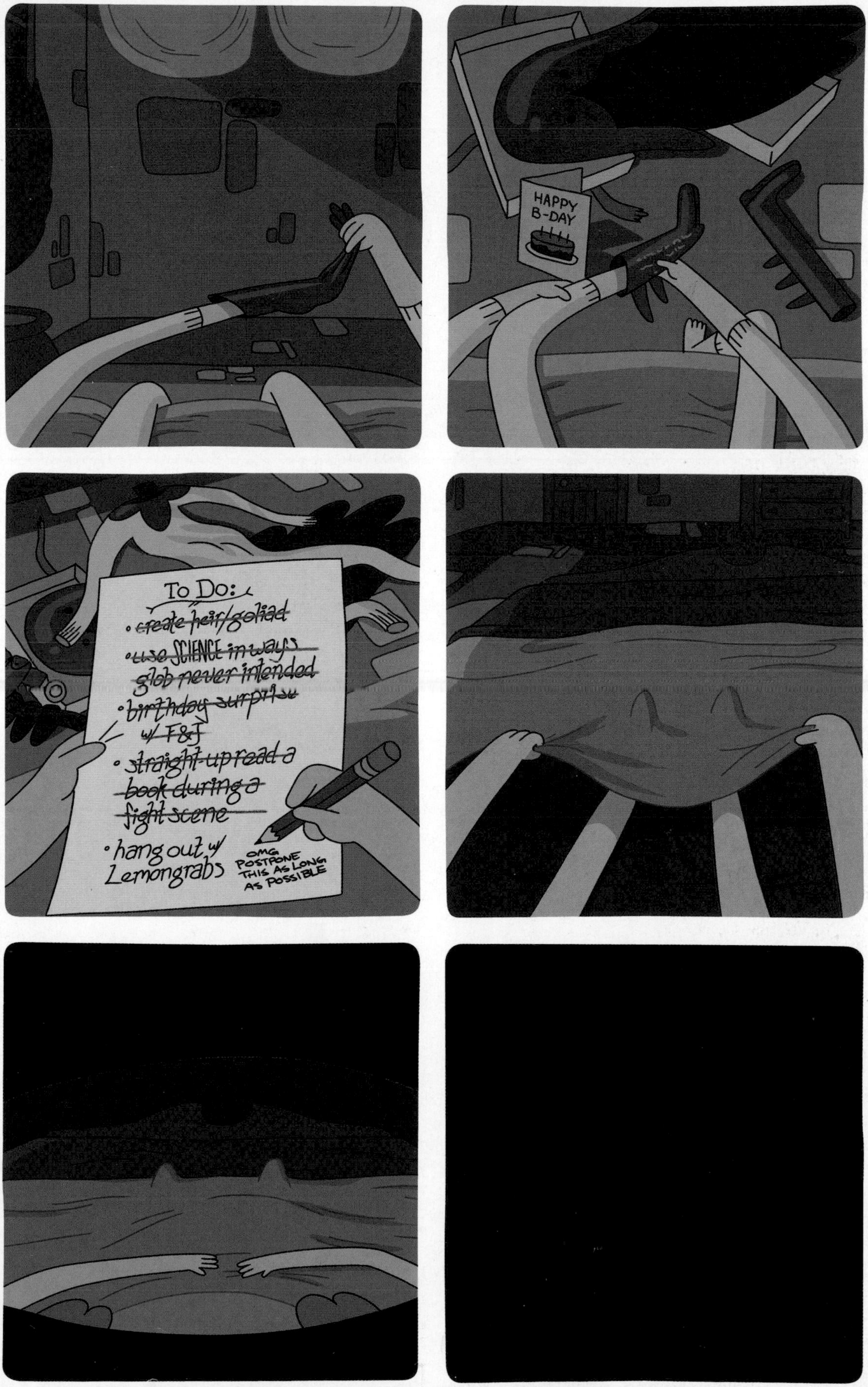
HAPPY B-DAY
To Do:
• create heir/goliad
• use SCIENCE in ways glob never intended
• birthday surprise w/ F&J
• straight-up read a book during a fight scene
• hang out w/ Lemongrabs
OMG POSTPONE THIS AS LONG AS POSSIBLE

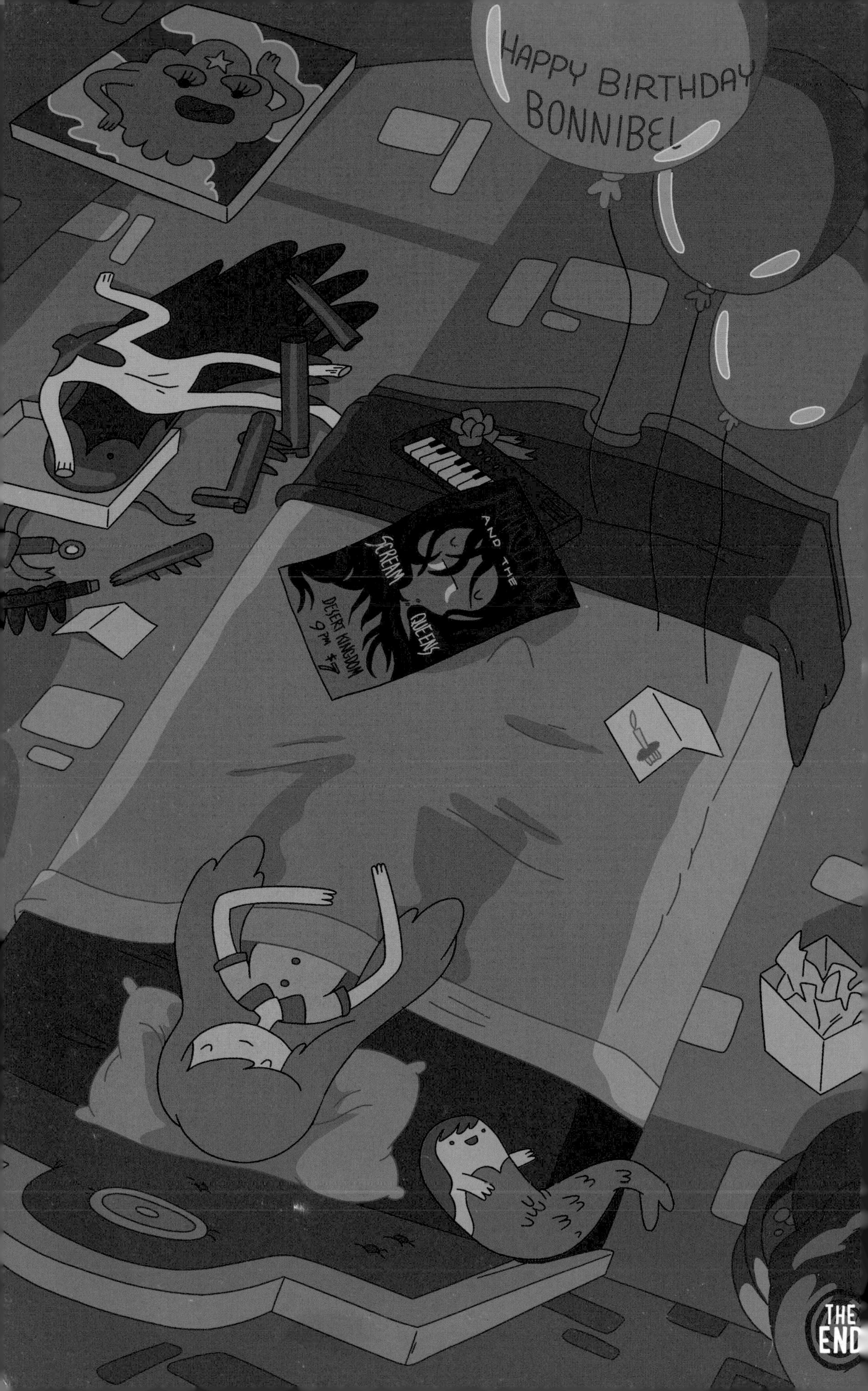
HAPPY BIRTHDAY BONNIBEL
AND THE SCREAM QUEENS
DESERT KINGDOM
9PM $7
THE END

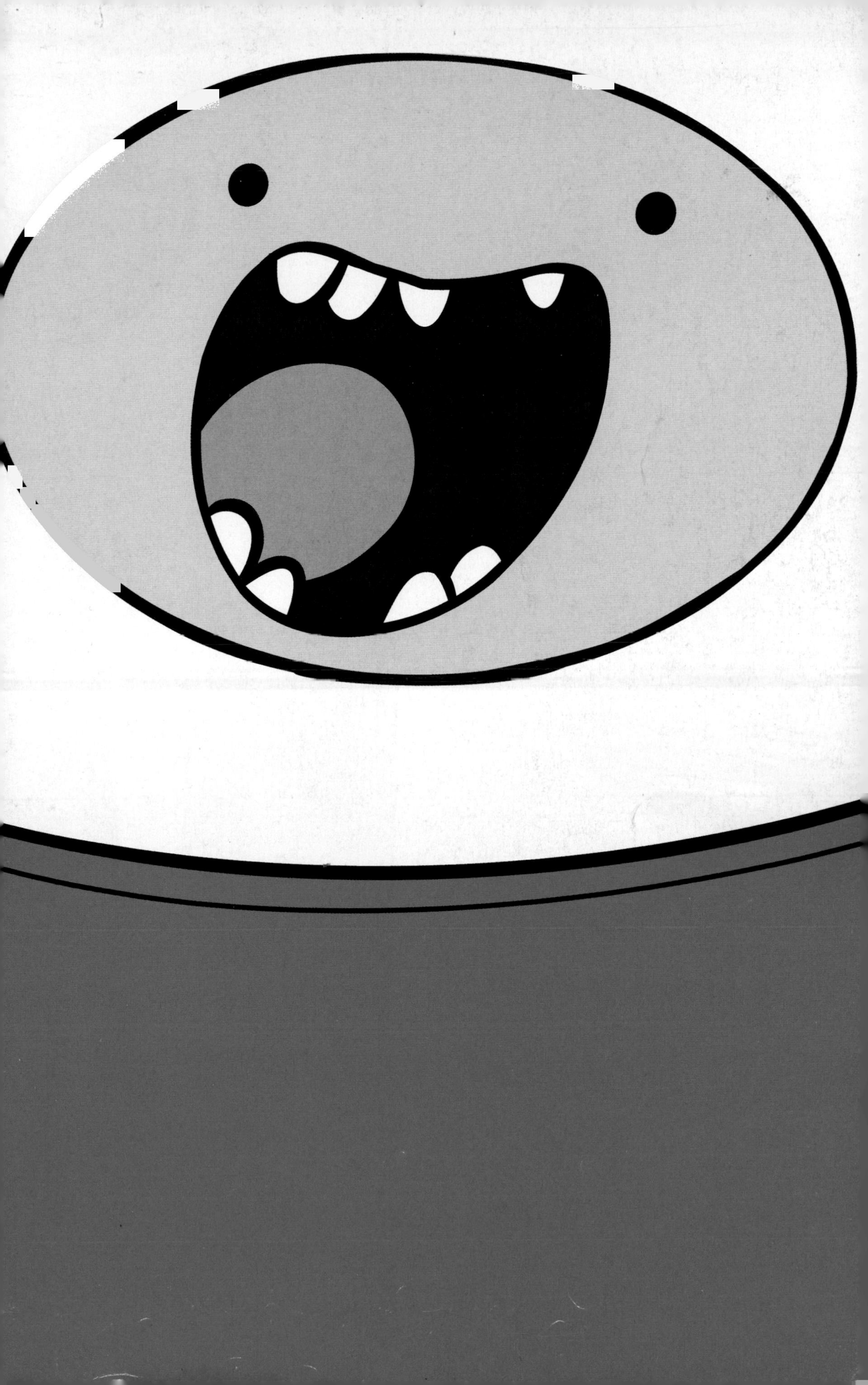

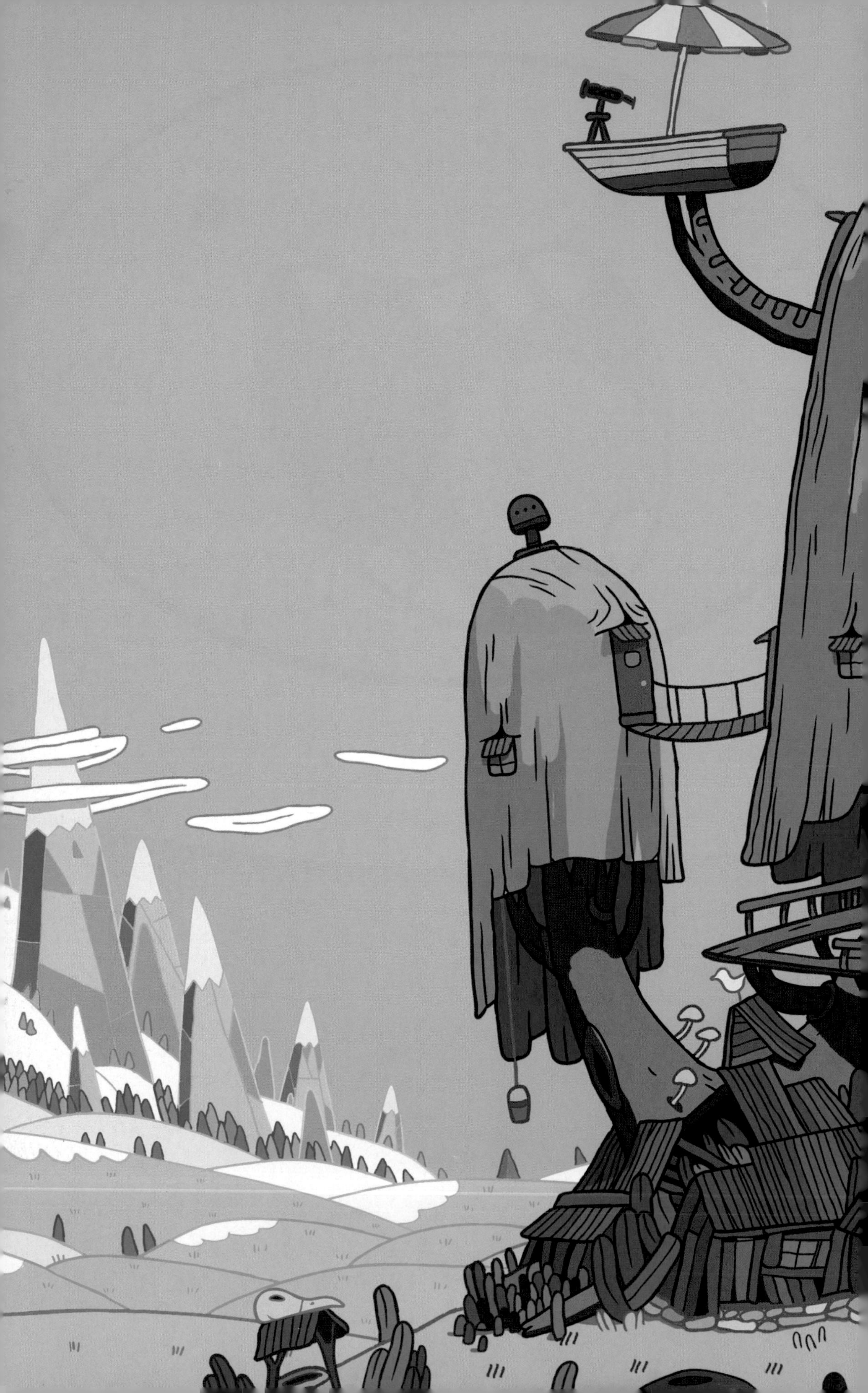

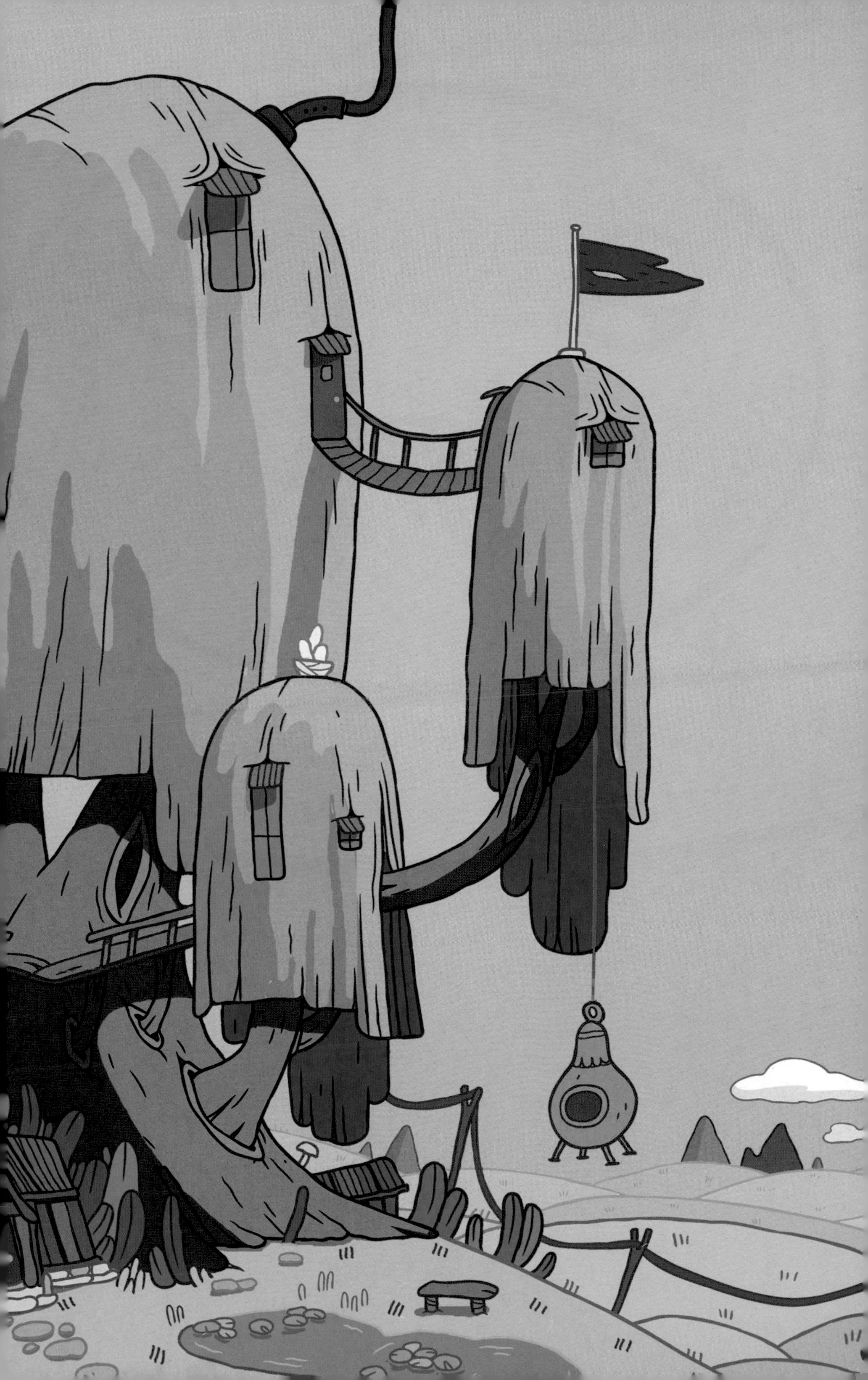

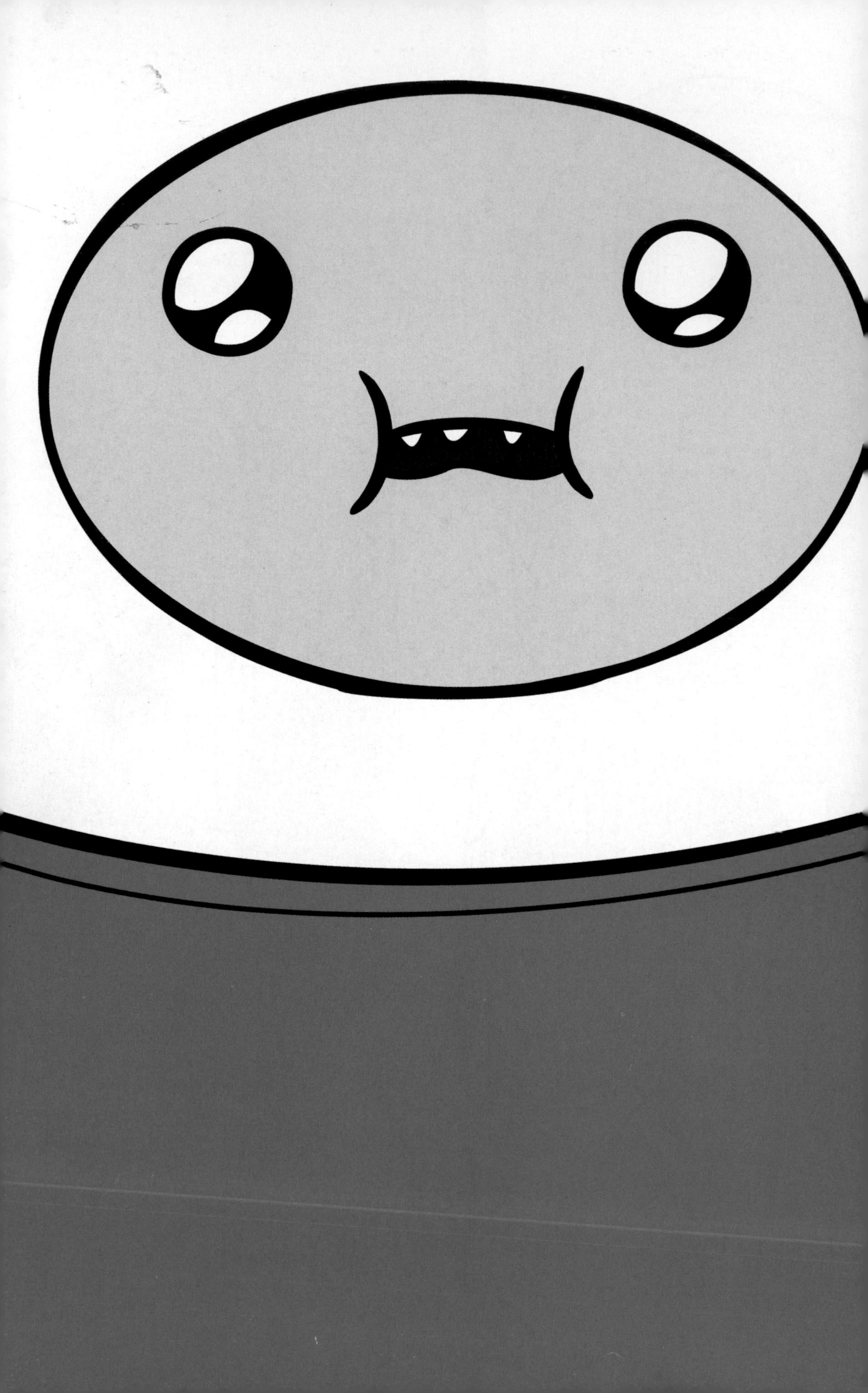

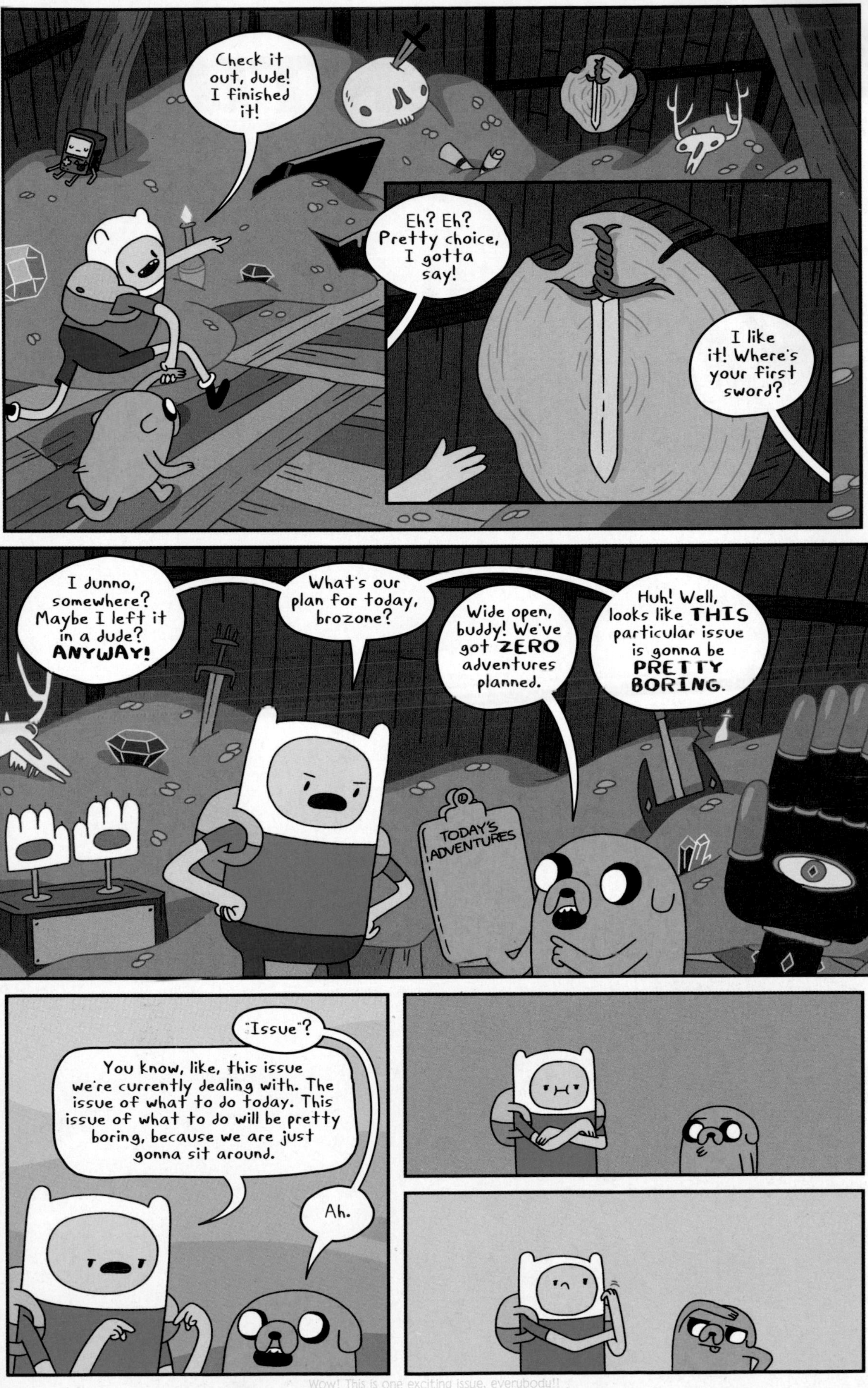
Check it out, dude! I finished it!
Eh? Eh? Pretty choice, I gotta say!
I like it! Where's your first sword?
I dunno, somewhere? Maybe I left it in a dude? ANYWAY!
What's our plan for today, brozone?
Wide open, buddy! We've got ZERO adventures planned.
TODAY'S ADVENTURES
Huh! Well, looks like THIS particular issue is gonna be PRETTY BORING.
"Issue"?
You know, like, this issue we're currently dealing with. The issue of what to do today. This issue of what to do will be pretty boring, because we are just gonna sit around.
Ah.

Wow! This is one exciting issue, everybody!!

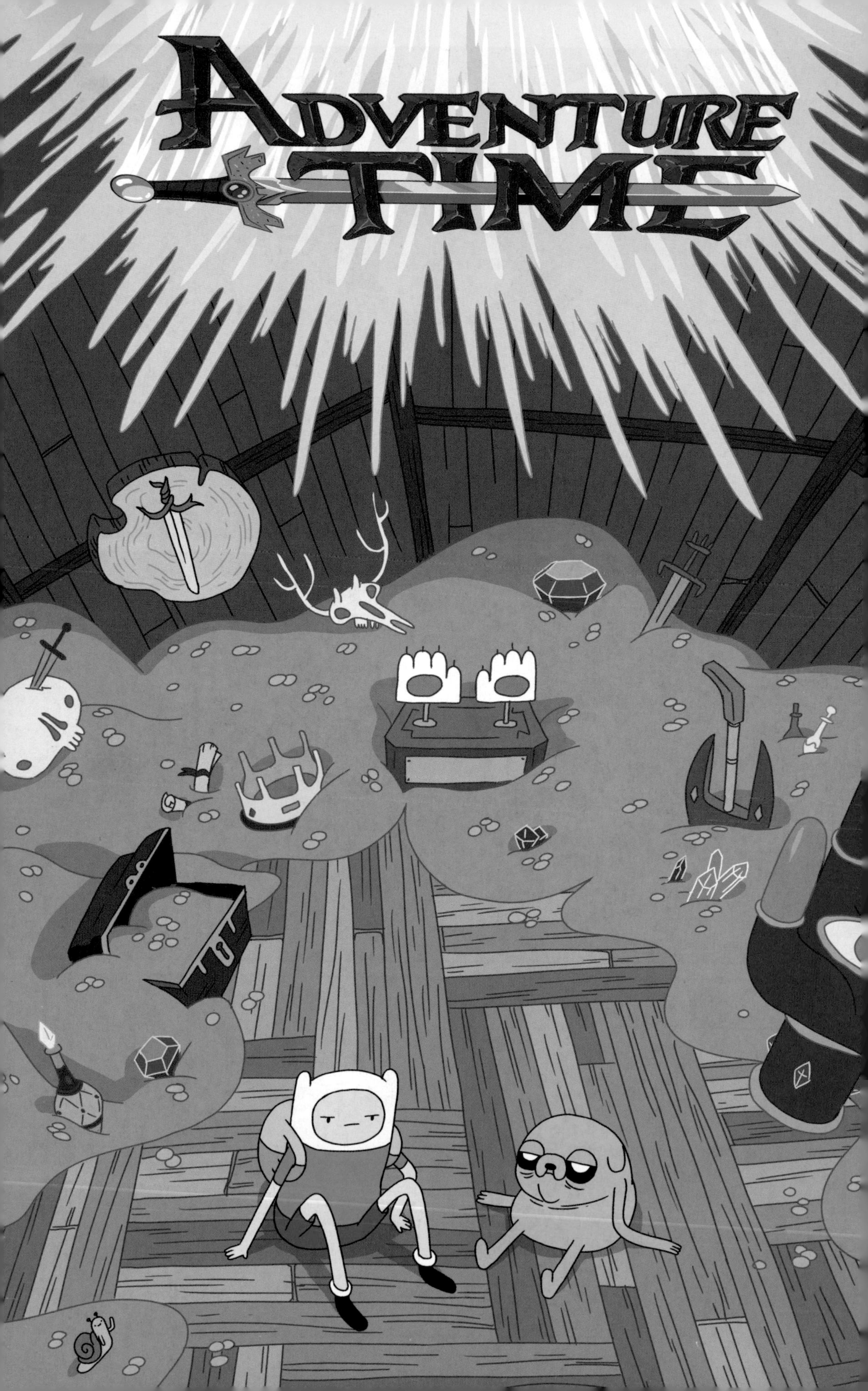
ADVENTURE
TIME

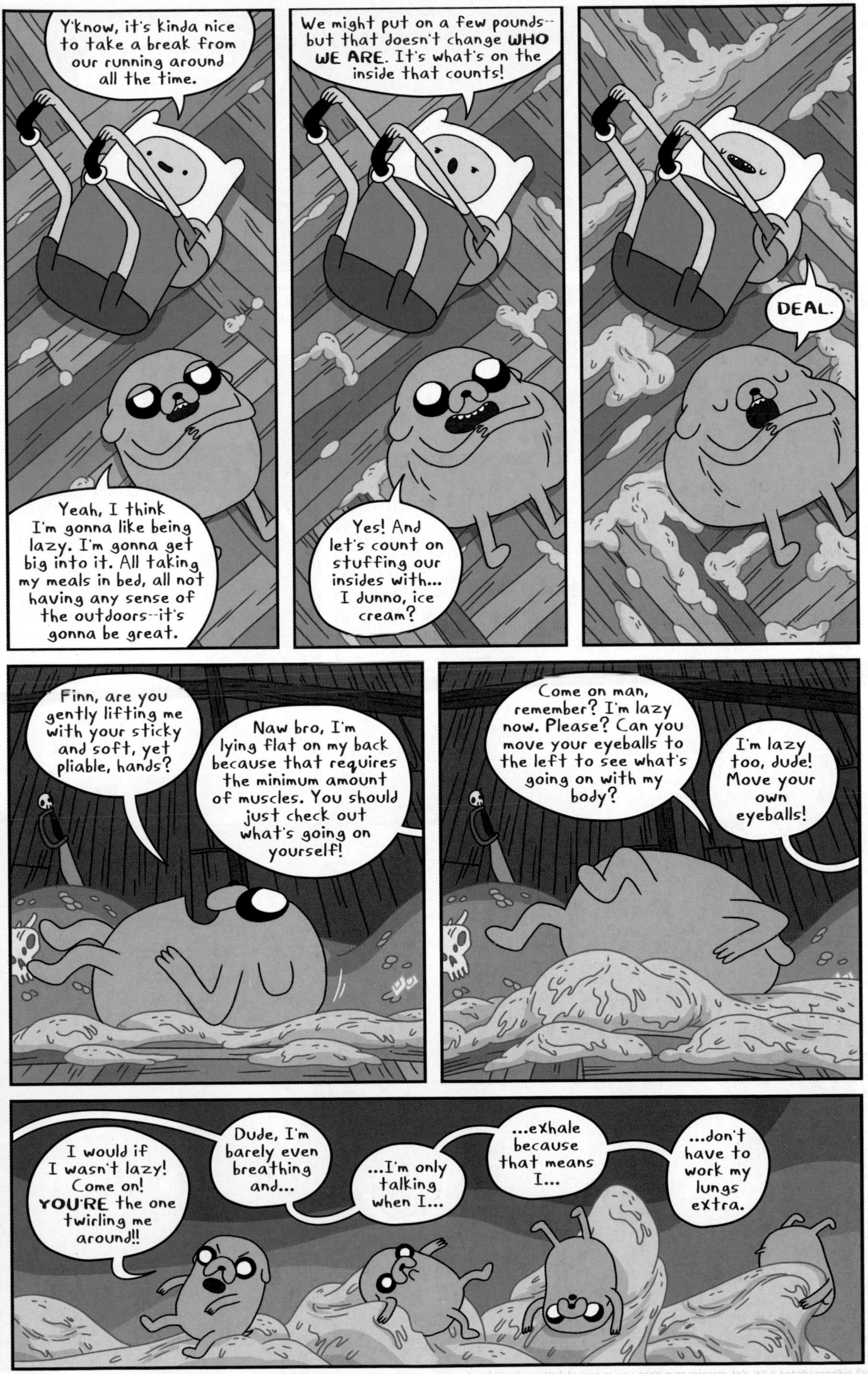
Y'know, it's kinda nice to take a break from our running around all the time.
Yeah, I think I'm gonna like being lazy. I'm gonna get big into it. All taking my meals in bed, all not having any sense of the outdoors--it's gonna be great.
We might put on a few pounds--but that doesn't change **WHO WE ARE**. It's what's on the inside that counts!
Yes! And let's count on stuffing our insides with... I dunno, ice cream?
DEAL.
Finn, are you gently lifting me with your sticky and soft, yet pliable, hands?
Naw bro, I'm lying flat on my back because that requires the minimum amount of muscles. You should just check out what's going on yourself!
Come on man, remember? I'm lazy now. Please? Can you move your eyeballs to the left to see what's going on with my body?
I'm lazy too, dude! Move your own eyeballs!
I would if I wasn't lazy! Come on! **YOU'RE** the one twirling me around!!
Dude, I'm barely even breathing and...
...I'm only talking when I...
...exhale because that means I...
...don't have to work my lungs extra.

AMAZING FACT: "Move your own eyeballs!" is the one sentence that appears in every single great works of literature. Yes! As long as you don't ever research this, it's a totally credible fact!

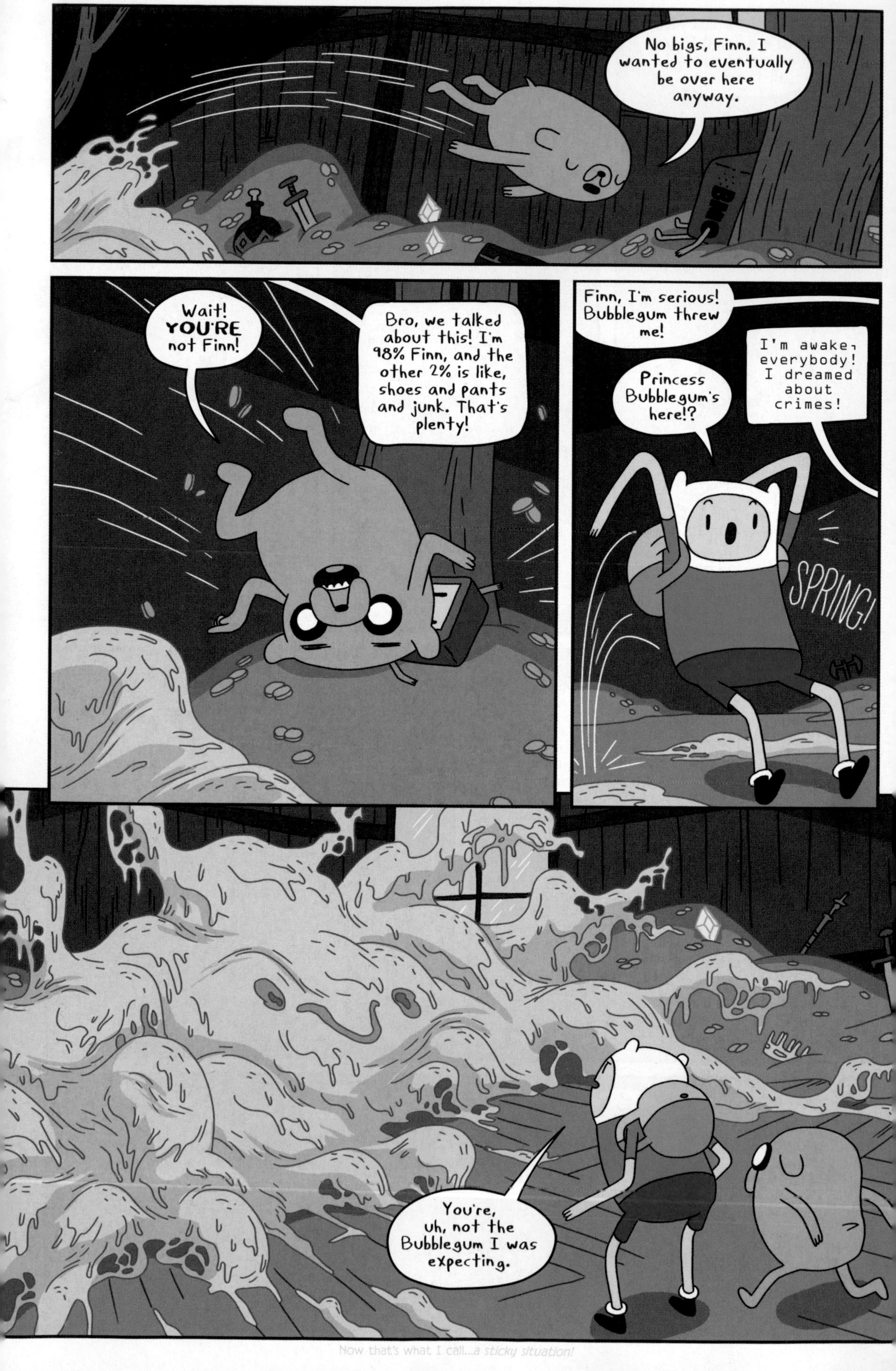
No bigs, Finn. I wanted to eventually be over here anyway.
Wait! YOU'RE not Finn!
Bro, we talked about this! I'm 98% Finn, and the other 2% is like, shoes and pants and junk. That's plenty!
Finn, I'm serious! Bubblegum threw me!
Princess Bubblegum's here!?
I'm awake, everybody! I dreamed about crimes!
SPRING!
You're, uh, not the Bubblegum I was expecting.

Now that's what I call...*a sticky situation!*

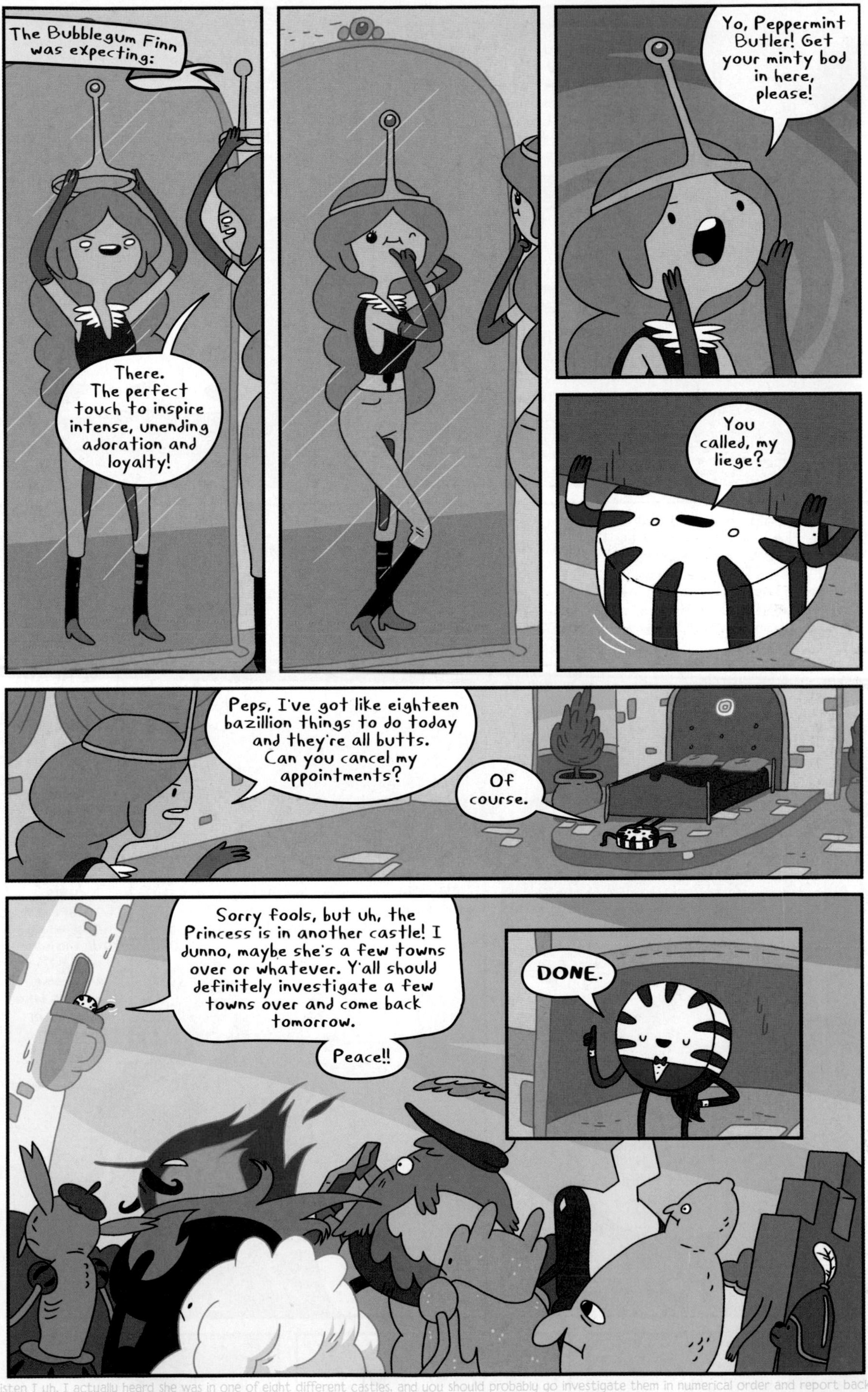
The Bubblegum Finn was expecting:
There. The perfect touch to inspire intense, unending adoration and loyalty!
Yo, Peppermint Butler! Get your minty bod in here, please!
You called, my liege?
Peps, I've got like eighteen bazillion things to do today and they're all butts. Can you cancel my appointments?
Of course.
Sorry fools, but uh, the Princess is in another castle! I dunno, maybe she's a few towns over or whatever. Y'all should definitely investigate a few towns over and come back tomorrow.
Peace!!
DONE.

Listen I uh, I actually heard she was in one of eight different castles, and you should probably go investigate them in numerical order and report back.

Peps, have you noticed the Candy Kingdom seems to face an insanely deadly new threat, like, every few weeks or so?

Hup!

pat
pat

Princess, we have always defeated our enemies and come out the other side looking totally awesome.

I know, I know. But we only need to mess up once and we're in big trouble.

A while back Finn and Jake told me that in the future we'd be attacked by evil robots, but that they travelled through time and stopped it. What am I supposed to do with that information? Is the problem fixed forever? Is it gonna happen again? Should I be worried?

It does pose a leadership challenge!

In the Nightosphere, we--I mean, they--I mean, I **HEARD** that they--

Knock knock, Pubble Bubble!

Marceline! You're early for lunch!

I got hungry ahead of schedule. It happens. What's up, Pep-o-hutts?

Ms. Abadeer.

Hey Marceline, let me ask you a question, woman to woman...how do you protect your subjects from getting beat up?

I dunno. I mean, it's easy when your kingdom is 100% awesome vampires who can fly in space and never get old.

Dang. My entire population's edible little people who don't know how tasty they be.

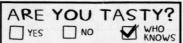

ARE YOU TASTY?
☐ YES ☐ NO ☑ WHO KNOWS

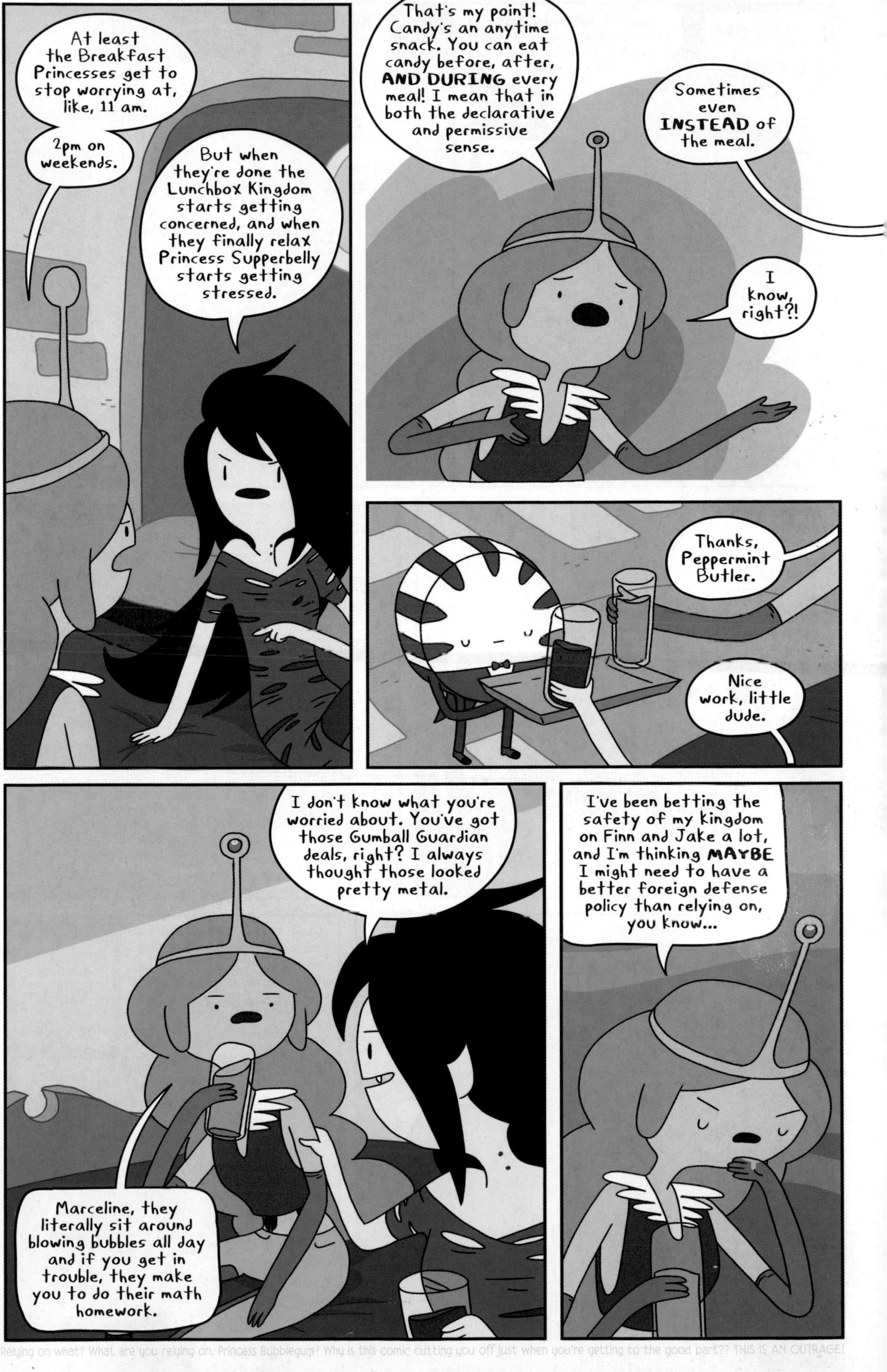
At least the Breakfast Princesses get to stop worrying at, like, 11 am.
2pm on weekends.
But when they're done the Lunchbox Kingdom starts getting concerned, and when they finally relax Princess Supperbelly starts getting stressed.
That's my point! Candy's an anytime snack. You can eat candy before, after, **AND DURING** every meal! I mean that in both the declarative and permissive sense.
Sometimes even **INSTEAD** of the meal.
I know, right?!
Thanks, Peppermint Butler.
Nice work, little dude.
I don't know what you're worried about. You've got those Gumball Guardian deals, right? I always thought those looked pretty metal.
Marceline, they literally sit around blowing bubbles all day and if you get in trouble, they make you to do their math homework.
I've been betting the safety of my kingdom on Finn and Jake a lot, and I'm thinking **MAYBE** I might need to have a better foreign defense policy than relying on, you know...

Relying on what? What are you relying on, Princess Bubblegum? Why is this comic cutting you off just when you're getting to the good part?? THIS IS AN OUTRAGE!

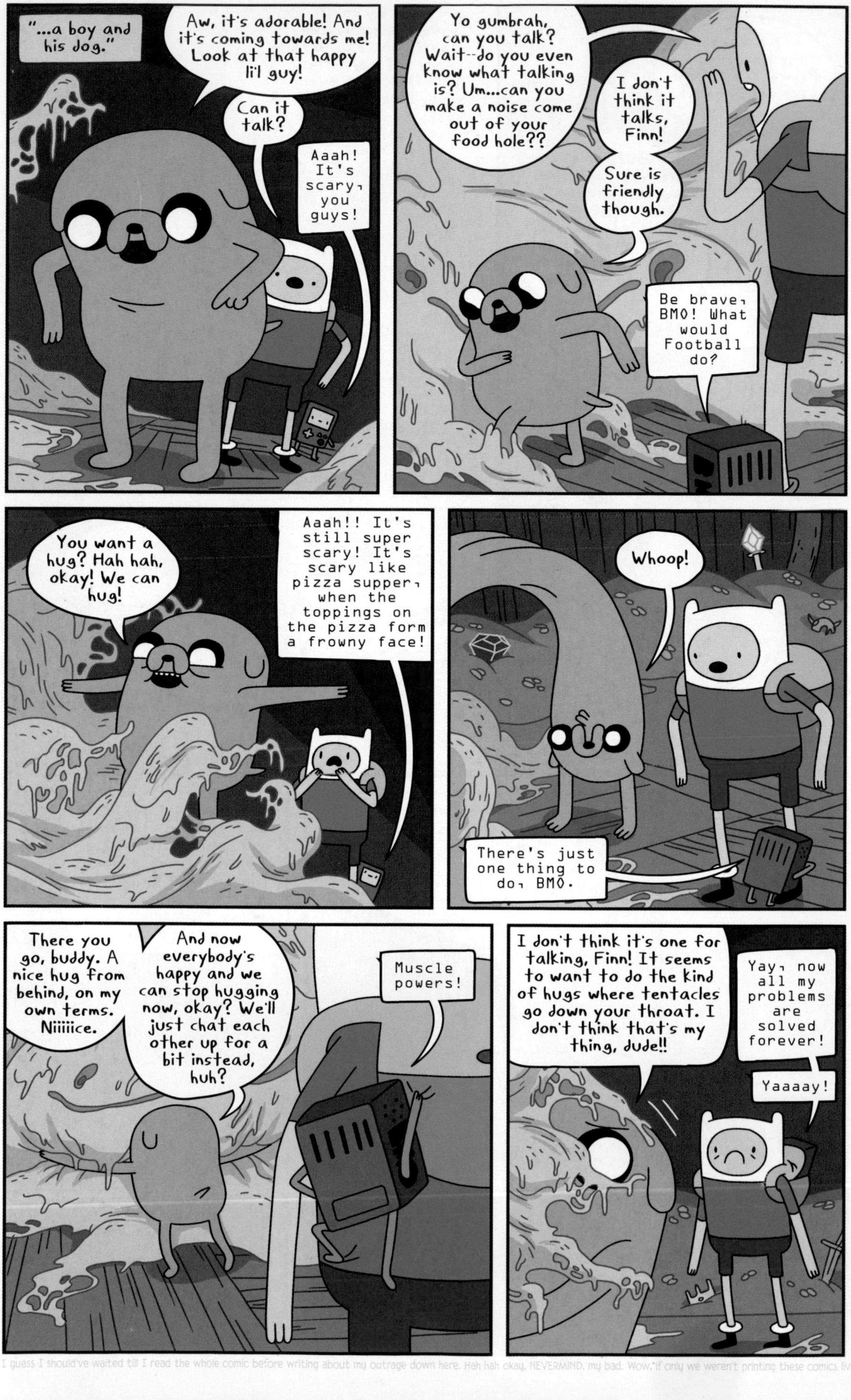
"...a boy and his dog."
Aw, it's adorable! And it's coming towards me! Look at that happy li'l guy!
Can it talk?
Aaah! It's scary, you guys!
Yo gumbrah, can you talk? Wait--do you even know what talking is? Um...can you make a noise come out of your food hole??
I don't think it talks, Finn!
Sure is friendly though.
Be brave, BMO! What would Football do?
You want a hug? Hah hah, okay! We can hug!
Aaah!! It's still super scary! It's scary like pizza supper, when the toppings on the pizza form a frowny face!
Whoop!
There's just one thing to do, BMO.
There you go, buddy. A nice hug from behind, on my own terms. Niiiiice.
And now everybody's happy and we can stop hugging now, okay? We'll just chat each other up for a bit instead, huh?
Muscle powers!
I don't think it's one for talking, Finn! It seems to want to do the kind of hugs where tentacles go down your throat. I don't think that's my thing, dude!!
Yay, now all my problems are solved forever!
Yaaaay!

Oh I guess I should've waited till I read the whole comic before writing about my outrage down here. Hah hah okay, NEVERMIND, my bad. Wow, if only we weren't printing these comics live!

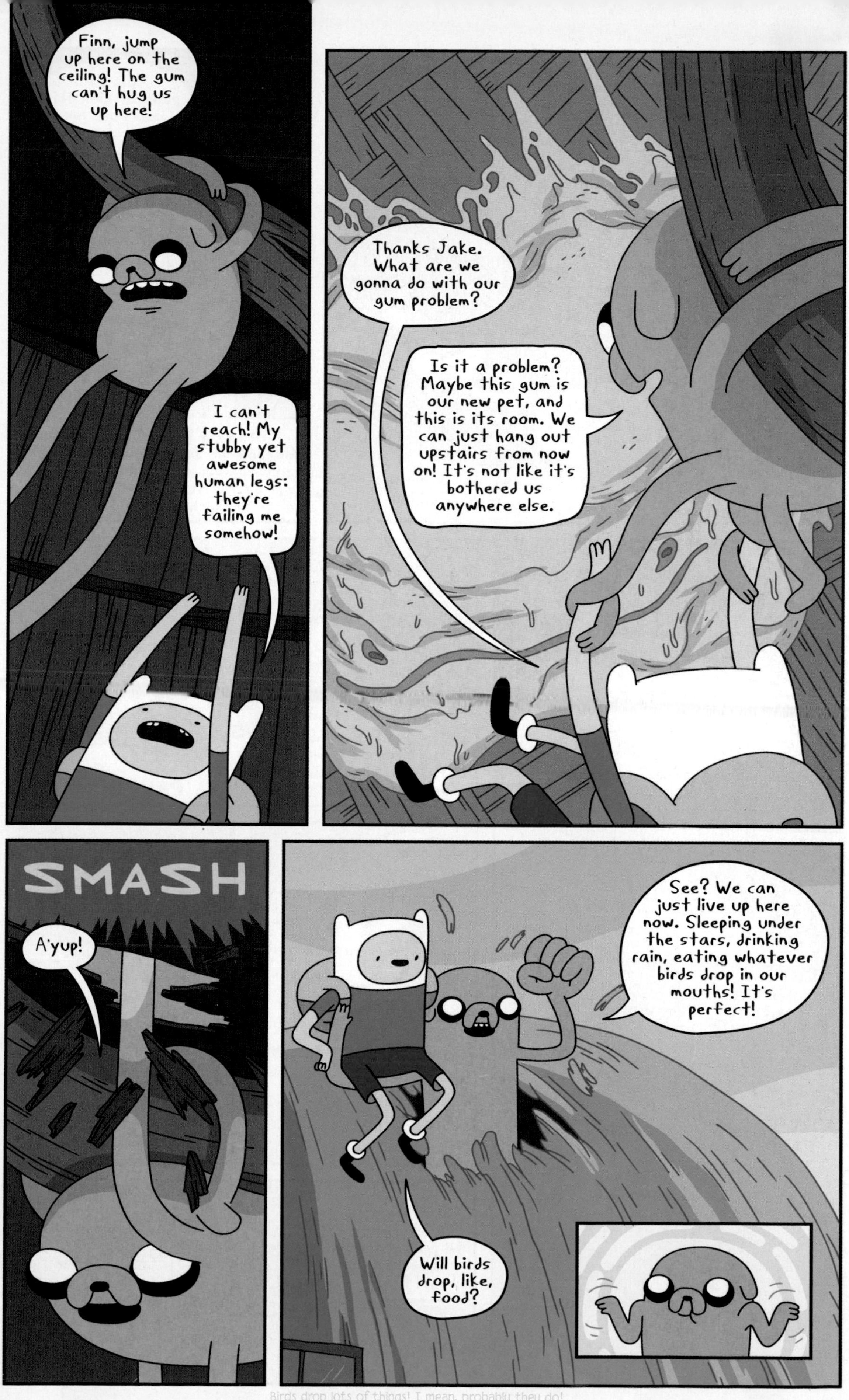
Finn, jump up here on the ceiling! The gum can't hug us up here!
I can't reach! My stubby yet awesome human legs: they're failing me somehow!
Thanks Jake. What are we gonna do with our gum problem?
Is it a problem? Maybe this gum is our new pet, and this is its room. We can just hang out upstairs from now on! It's not like it's bothered us anywhere else.
SMASH
A'yup!
See? We can just live up here now. Sleeping under the stars, drinking rain, eating whatever birds drop in our mouths! It's perfect!
Will birds drop, like, food?

Birds drop lots of things! I mean, probably they do!

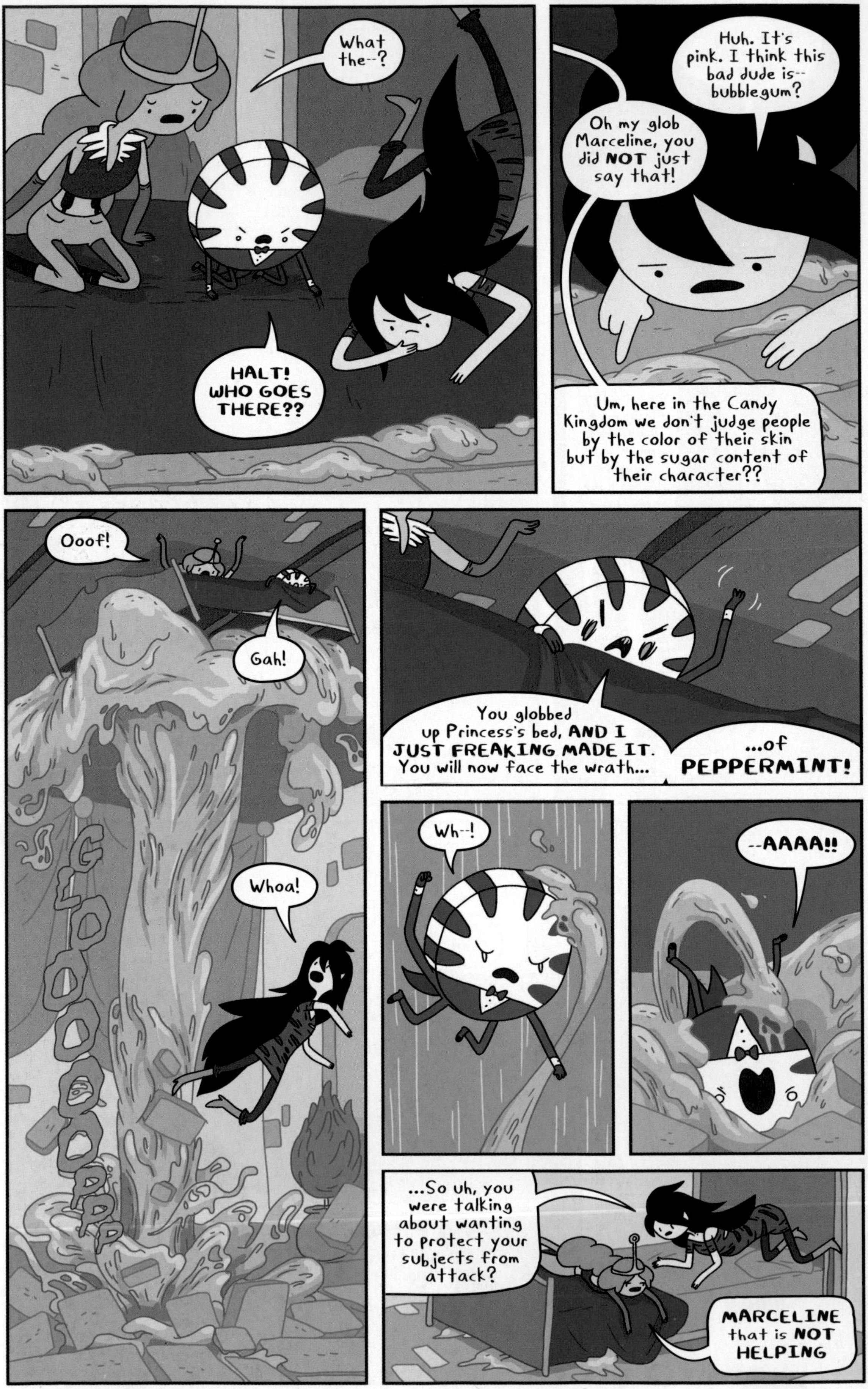
What the--?
HALT! WHO GOES THERE??
Huh. It's pink. I think this bad dude is-- bubblegum?
Oh my glob Marceline, you did NOT just say that!
Um, here in the Candy Kingdom we don't judge people by the color of their skin but by the sugar content of their character??
Ooof!
Gah!
GLOOOOPPP
Whoa!
You globbed up Princess's bed, AND I JUST FREAKING MADE IT. You will now face the wrath...
...of PEPPERMINT!
Wh--!
--AAAA!!
...So uh, you were talking about wanting to protect your subjects from attack?
MARCELINE that is NOT HELPING

If you think the wrath of peppermint is bad, wait till you see the wrath of spearmint. It's *spikier*.

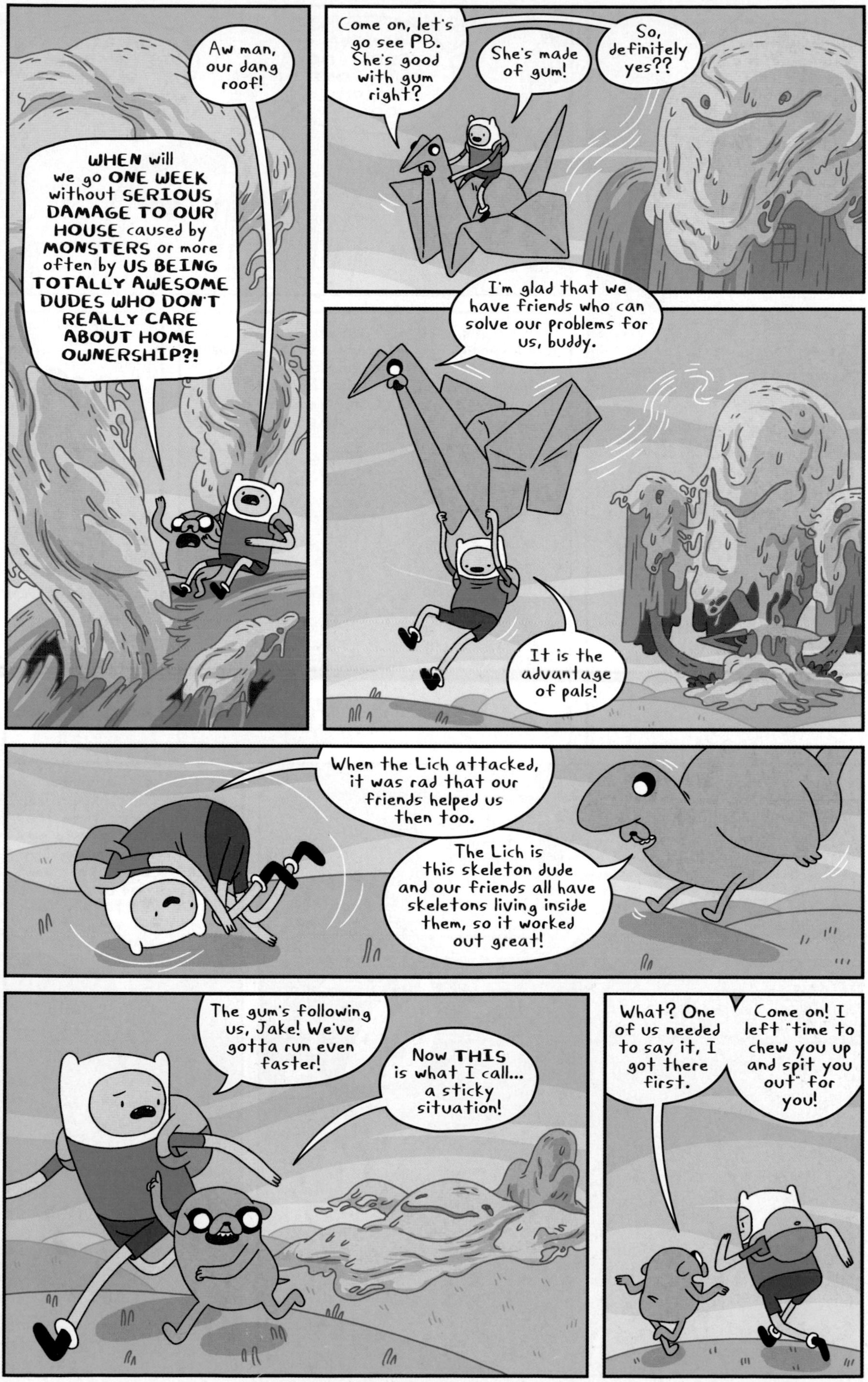
Aw man, our dang roof!
WHEN will we go **ONE WEEK** without **SERIOUS DAMAGE TO OUR HOUSE** caused by **MONSTERS** or more often by **US BEING TOTALLY AWESOME DUDES WHO DON'T REALLY CARE ABOUT HOME OWNERSHIP?!**
Come on, let's go see PB. She's good with gum right?
She's made of gum!
So, definitely yes??
I'm glad that we have friends who can solve our problems for us, buddy.
It is the advantage of pals!
When the Lich attacked, it was rad that our friends helped us then too.
The Lich is this skeleton dude and our friends all have skeletons living inside them, so it worked out great!
The gum's following us, Jake! We've gotta run even faster!
Now **THIS** is what I call... a sticky situation!
What? One of us needed to say it, I got there first.
Come on! I left "time to chew you up and spit you out" for you!

What?! NO, I GOT THERE FIRST! JAKE STOLE THAT ONE FROM ME!!

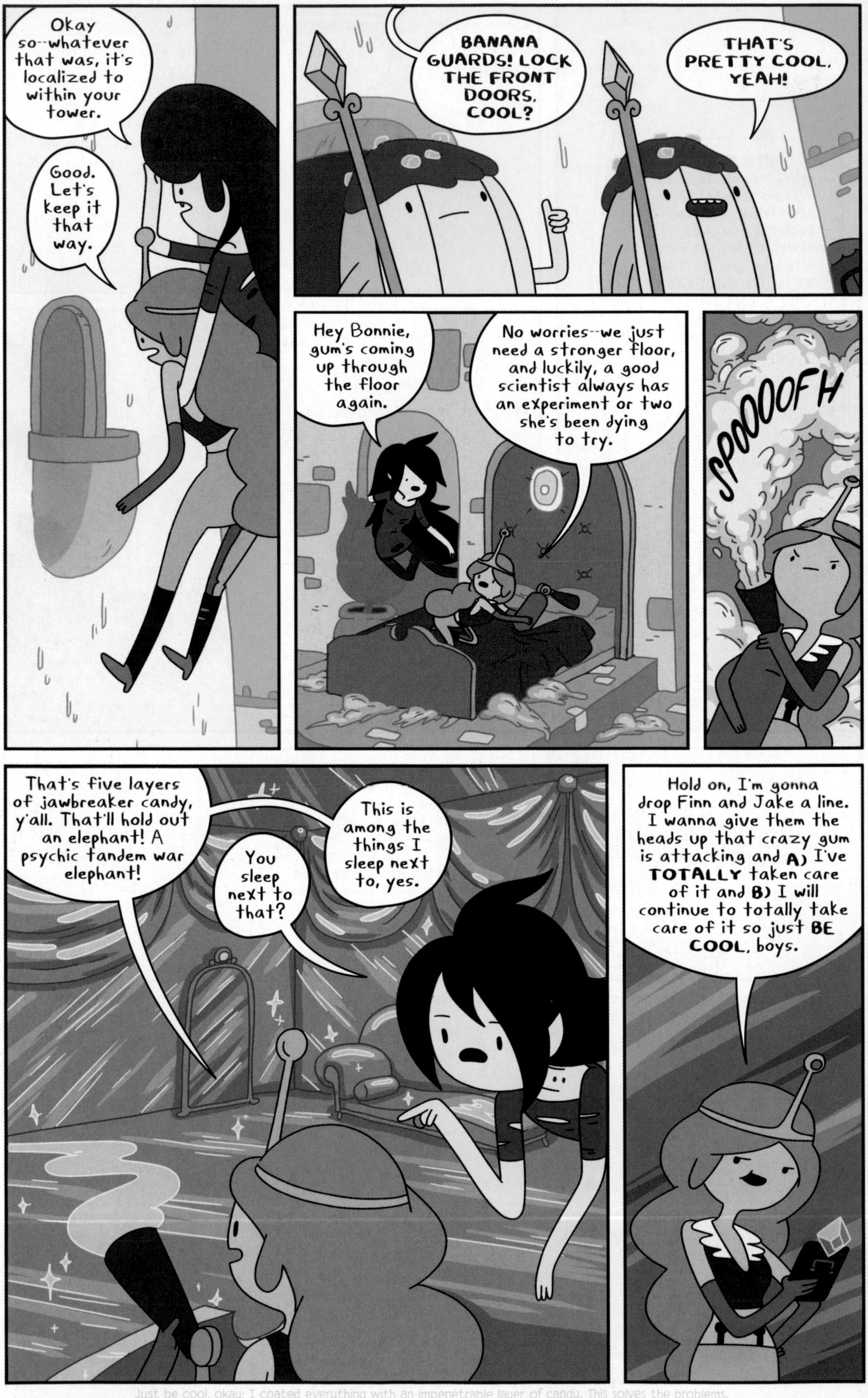
Okay so--whatever that was, it's localized to within your tower.
Good. Let's keep it that way.
BANANA GUARDS! LOCK THE FRONT DOORS, COOL?
THAT'S PRETTY COOL, YEAH!
Hey Bonnie, gum's coming up through the floor again.
No worries--we just need a stronger floor, and luckily, a good scientist always has an experiment or two she's been dying to try.
SPOOOOFH
That's five layers of jawbreaker candy, y'all. That'll hold out an elephant! A psychic tandem war elephant!
You sleep next to that?
This is among the things I sleep next to, yes.
Hold on, I'm gonna drop Finn and Jake a line. I wanna give them the heads up that crazy gum is attacking and A) I've TOTALLY taken care of it and B) I will continue to totally take care of it so just BE COOL, boys.

Just be cool, okay: I coated everything with an impenetrable layer of candy. This solves the problems.

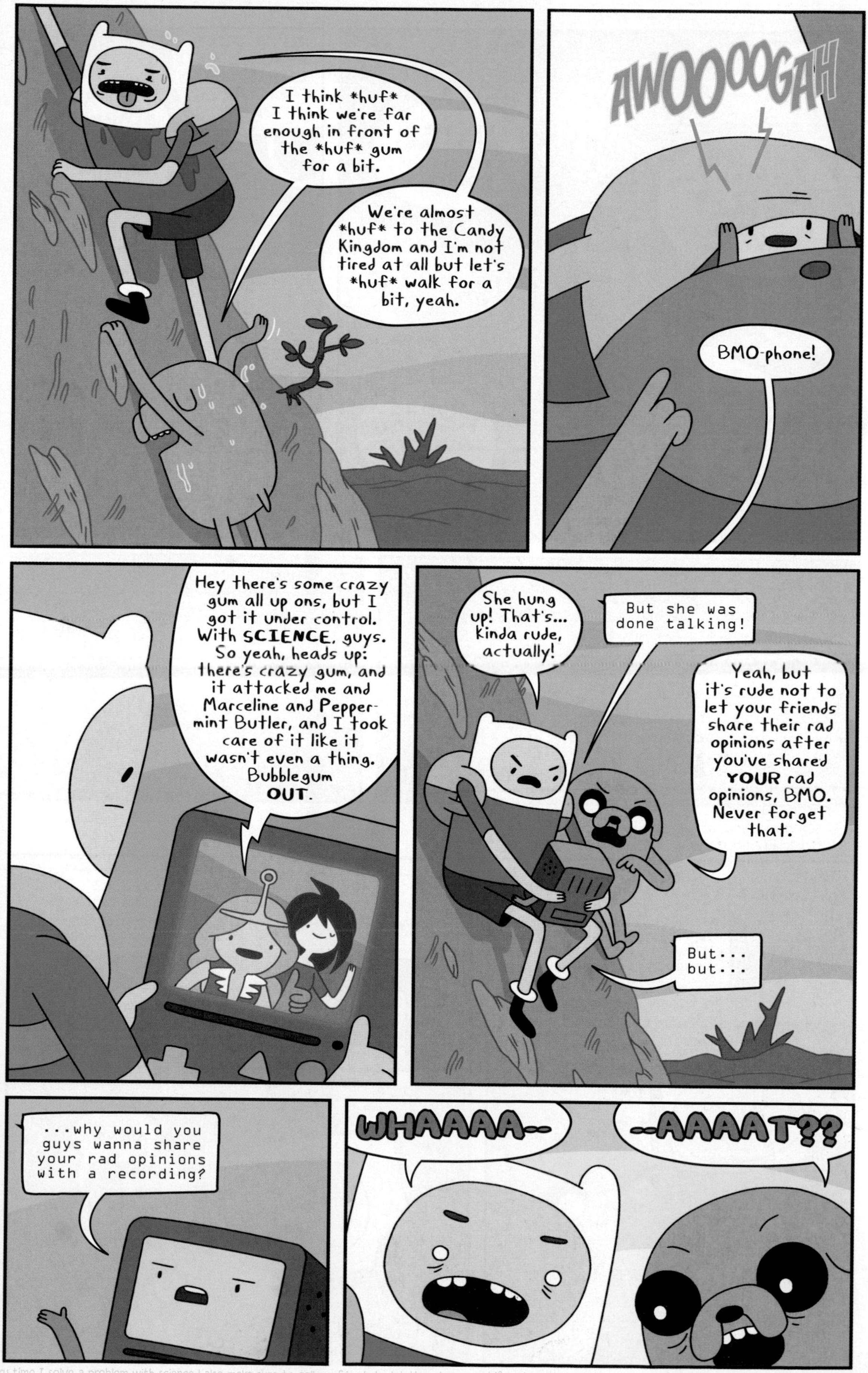
I think *huf* I think we're far enough in front of the *huf* gum for a bit.
We're almost *huf* to the Candy Kingdom and I'm not tired at all but let's *huf* walk for a bit, yeah.
AWOOOOGAH
BMO-phone!
Hey there's some crazy gum all up ons, but I got it under control. With **SCIENCE**, guys. So yeah, heads up: there's crazy gum, and it attacked me and Marceline and Peppermint Butler, and I took care of it like it wasn't even a thing. Bubblegum **OUT**.
She hung up! That's... kinda rude, actually!
But she was done talking!
Yeah, but it's rude not to let your friends share their rad opinions after you've shared **YOUR** rad opinions, BMO. Never forget that.
But... but...
...why would you guys wanna share your rad opinions with a recording?
WHAAAAA--
--AAAAT??

ery time I solve a problem with science I also make sure to call my friends to let them know, and if you're not doing this then I'm afraid you're not living life to the fullest.

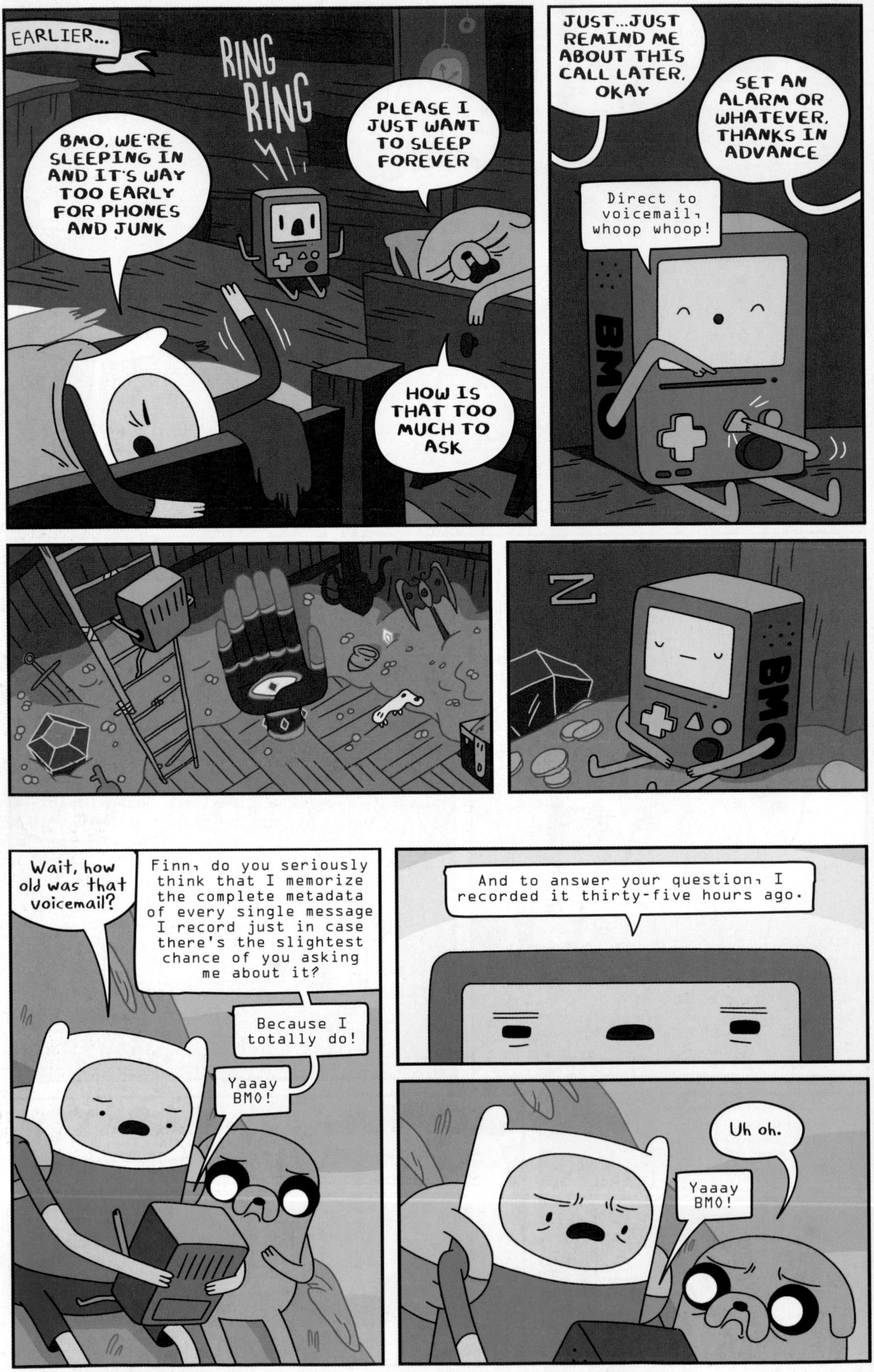
EARLIER...
RING RING
BMO, WE'RE SLEEPING IN AND IT'S WAY TOO EARLY FOR PHONES AND JUNK
PLEASE I JUST WANT TO SLEEP FOREVER
HOW IS THAT TOO MUCH TO ASK
JUST...JUST REMIND ME ABOUT THIS CALL LATER, OKAY
SET AN ALARM OR WHATEVER, THANKS IN ADVANCE
Direct to voicemail, whoop whoop!
BMO
Z
BMO
Wait, how old was that voicemail?
Finn, do you seriously think that I memorize the complete metadata of every single message I record just in case there's the slightest chance of you asking me about it?
Because I totally do!
Yaaay BMO!
And to answer your question, I recorded it thirty-five hours ago.
Uh oh.
Yaaay BMO!

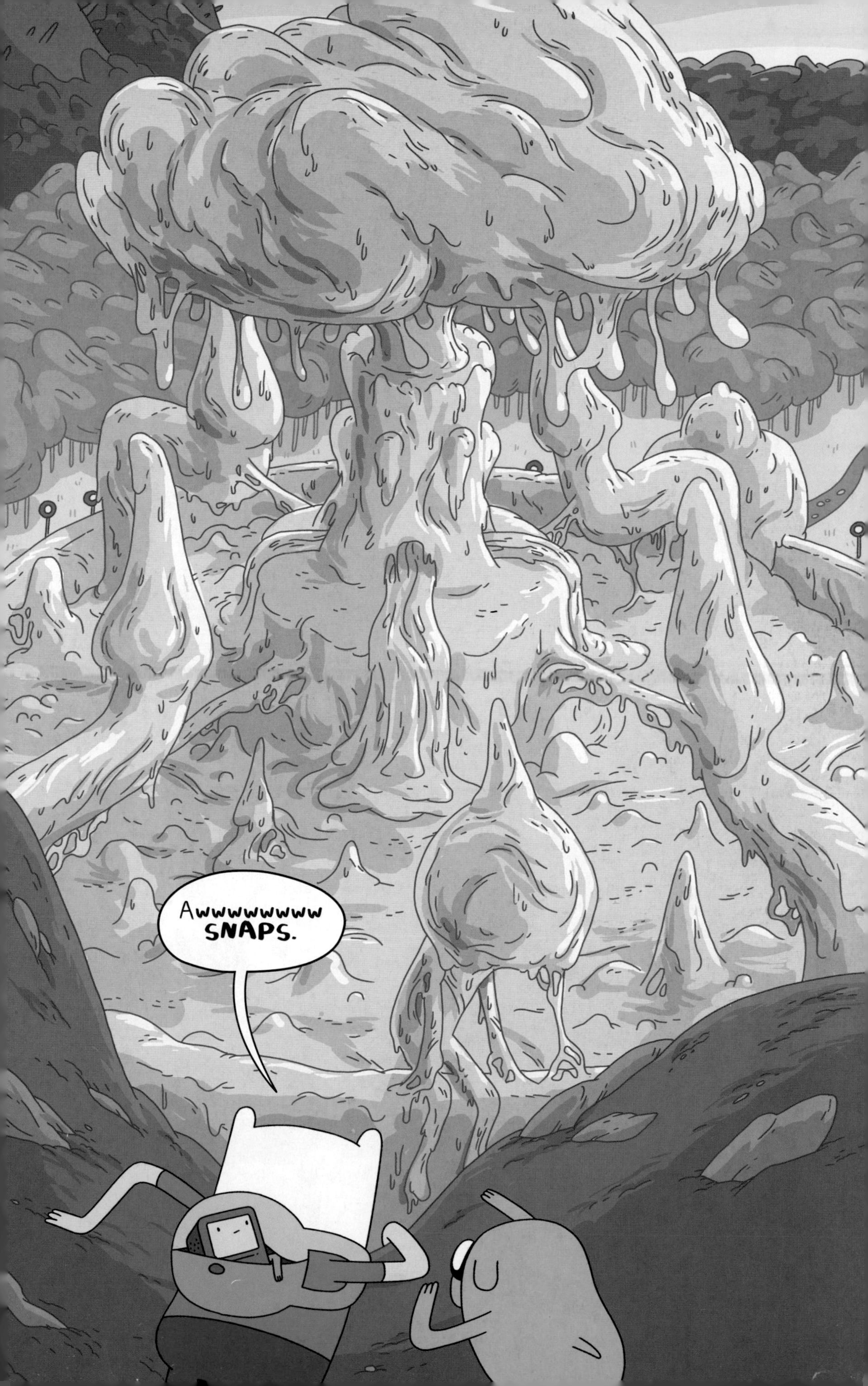
AWWWWWWWW
SNAPS.

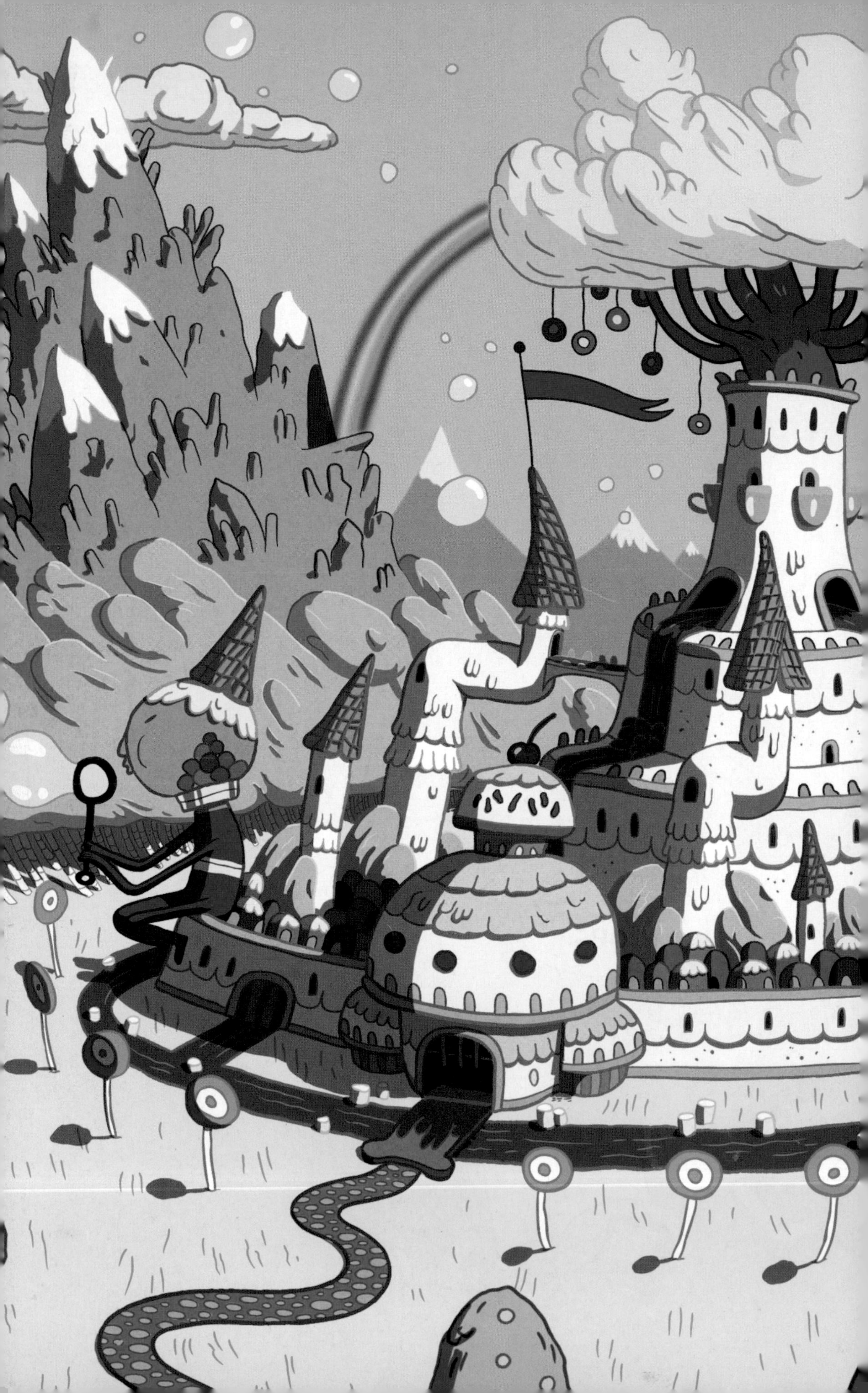

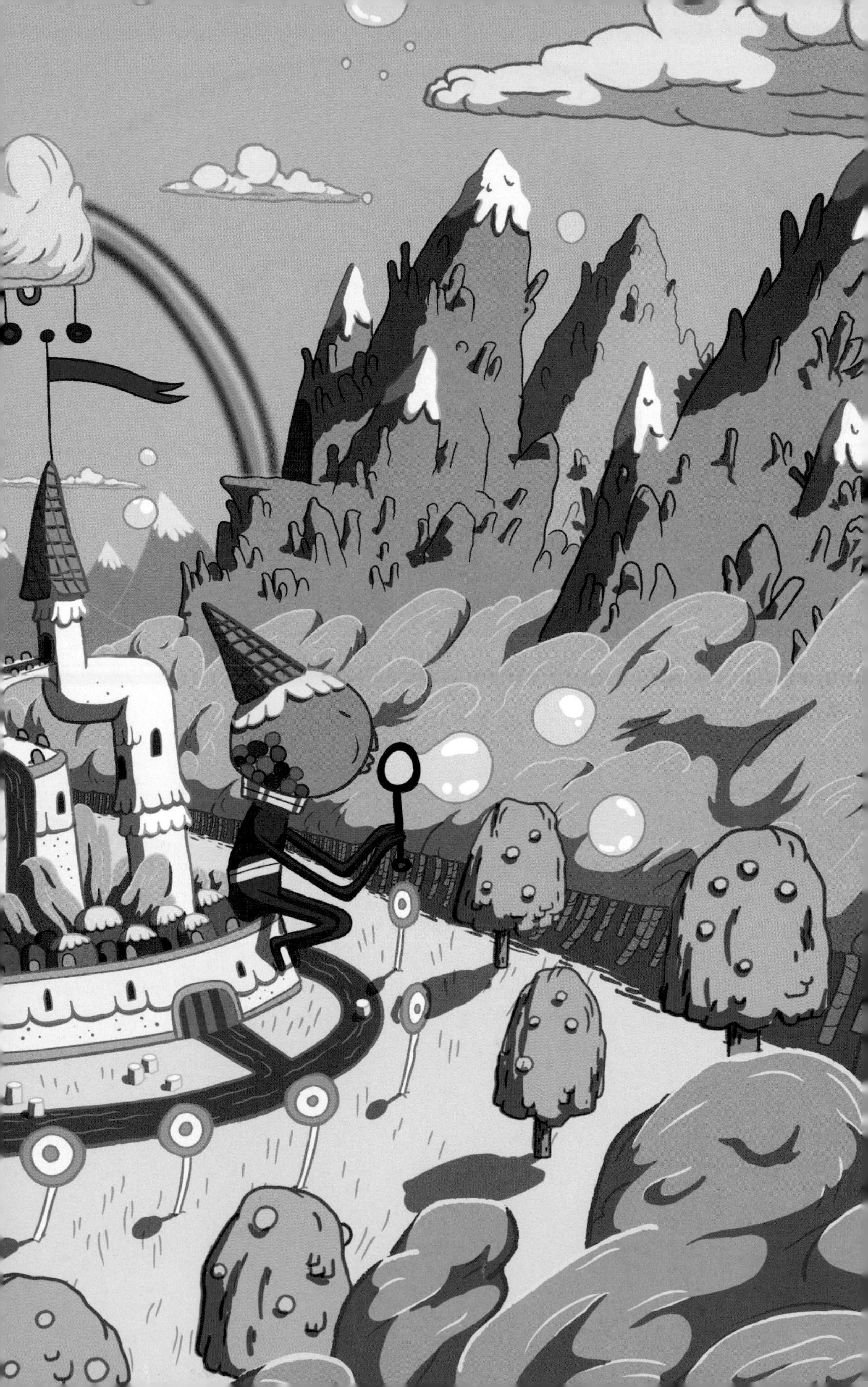

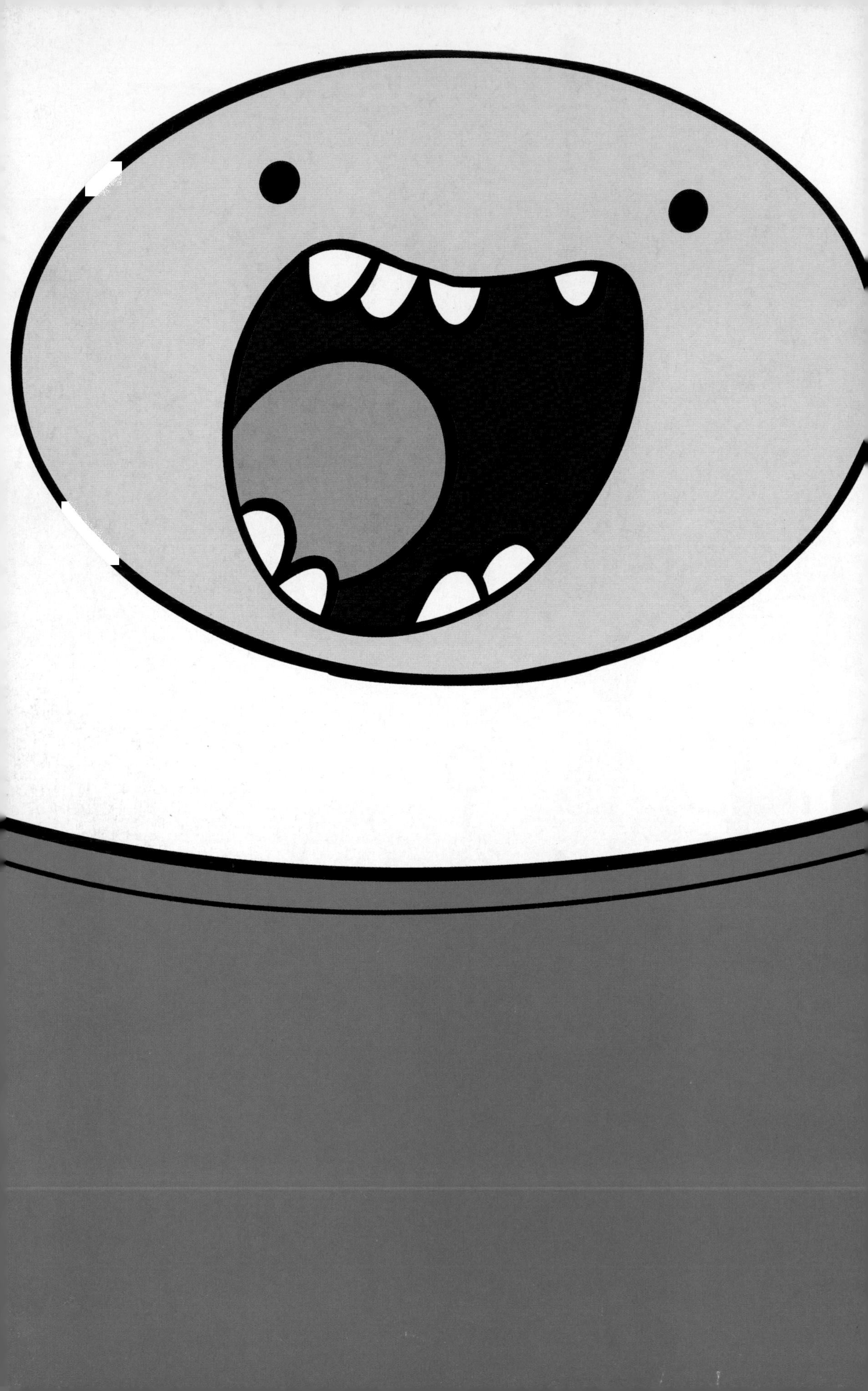

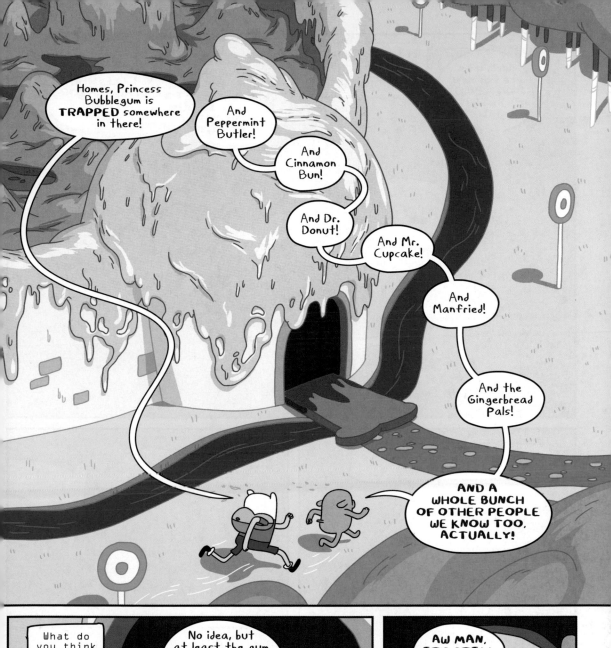

Homes, Princess Bubblegum is **TRAPPED** somewhere in there!

And Peppermint Butler!

And Cinnamon Bun!

And Dr. Donut!

And Mr. Cupcake!

And Manfried!

And the Gingerbread Pals!

AND A WHOLE BUNCH OF OTHER PEOPLE WE KNOW TOO, ACTUALLY!

What do you think is the cause of all this gum?

No idea, but at least the gum that was chasing us seems to have given up!

What makes you say that?

AW MAN, IT'S STILL THERE??

DISS

The Gingerbread Pals have just one unbreakable rule: everyone is pals!

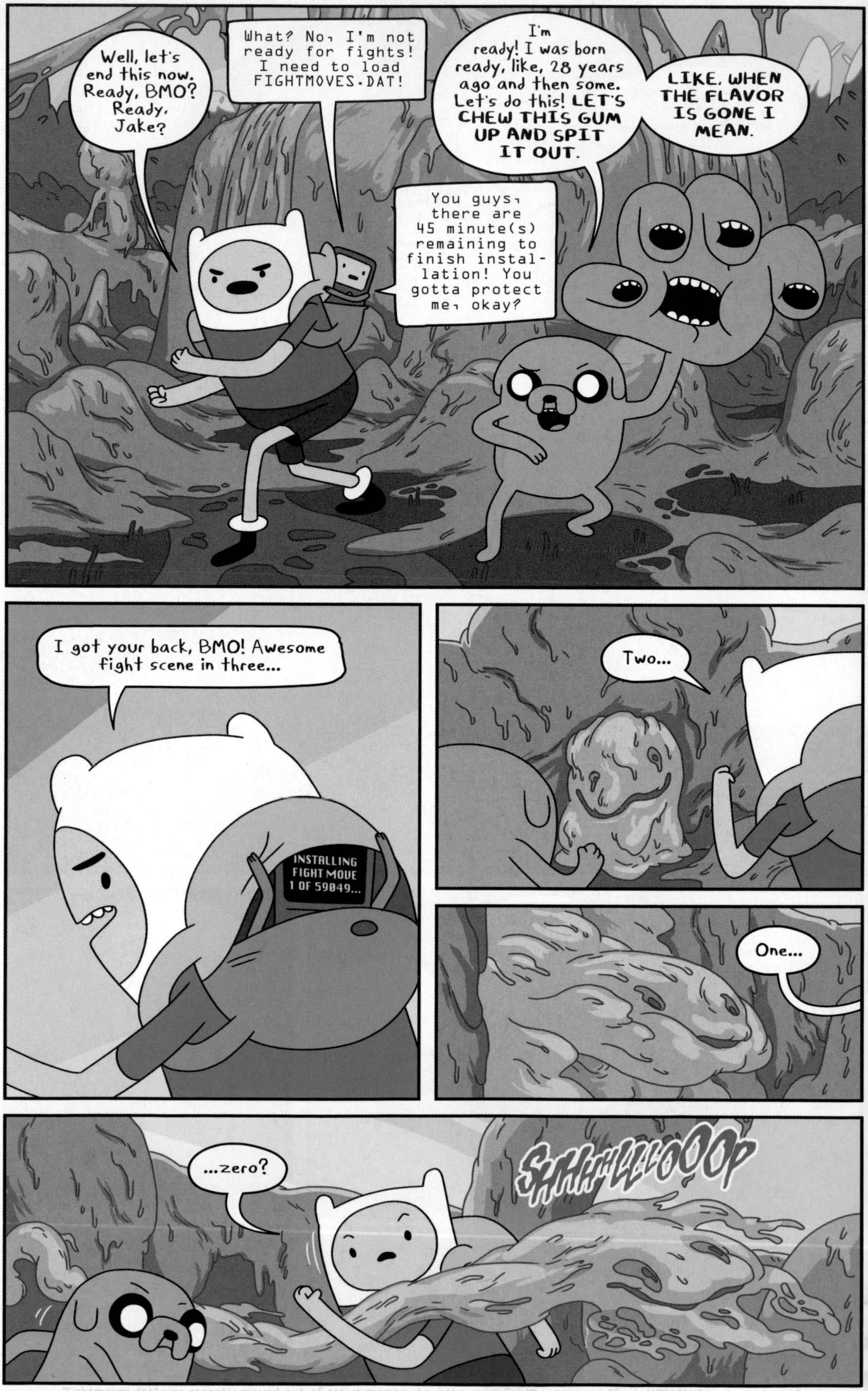
Well, let's end this now. Ready, BMO? Ready, Jake?
What? No, I'm not ready for fights! I need to load FIGHTMOVES.DAT!
I'm ready! I was born ready, like, 28 years ago and then some. Let's do this! LET'S CHEW THIS GUM UP AND SPIT IT OUT.
LIKE, WHEN THE FLAVOR IS GONE I MEAN.
You guys, there are 45 minute(s) remaining to finish instal-lation! You gotta protect me, okay?
I got your back, BMO! Awesome fight scene in three...
INSTALLING FIGHT MOVE 1 OF 59049...
Two...
One...
...zero?
SHHHHLLLOOOP

"Fightmoves.dat" was recently moved out of active memory to make room for "Dancemoves-2fresh-NOTAFAKE.legitpoppin.dat"

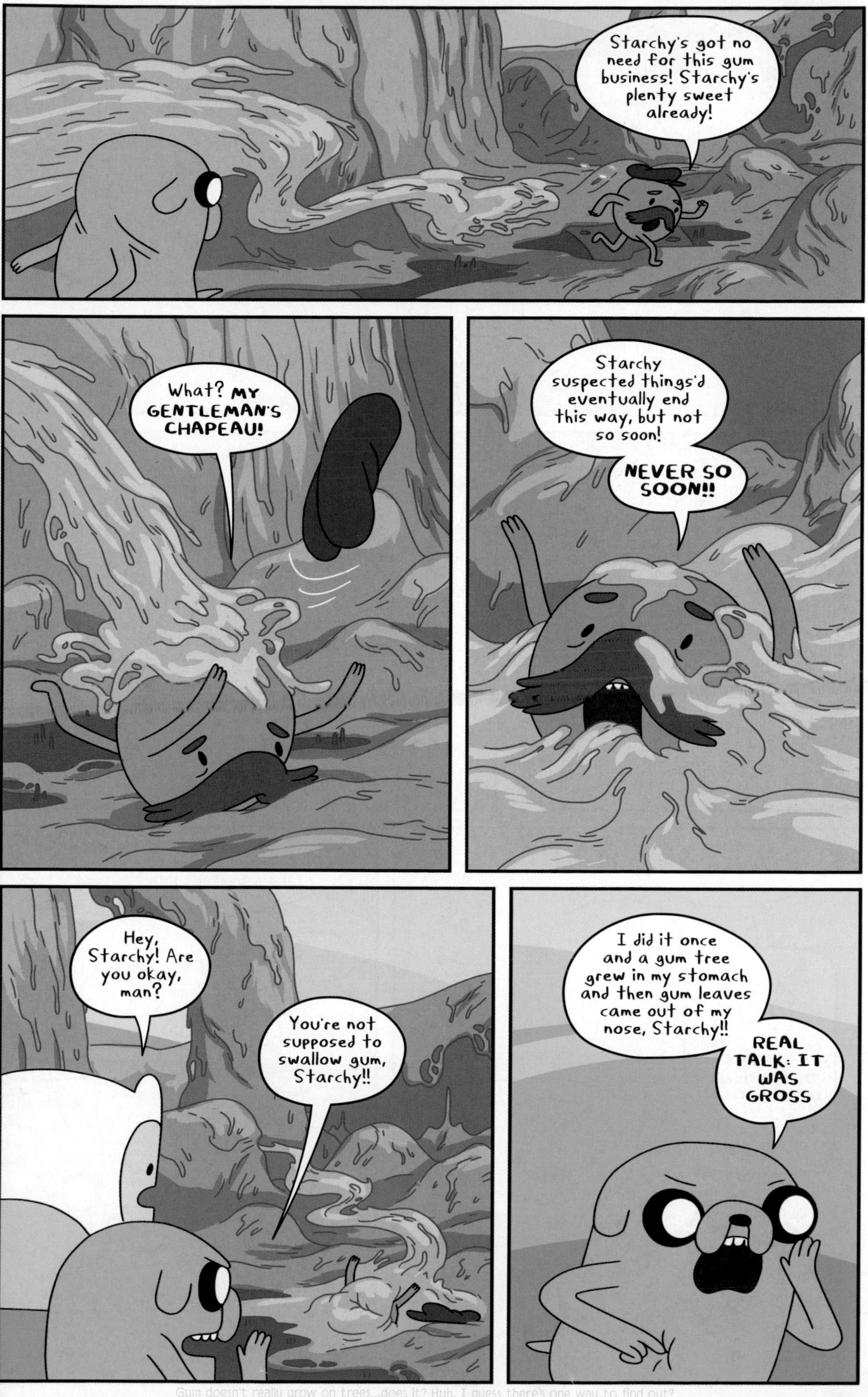
Starchy's got no need for this gum business! Starchy's plenty sweet already!
What? MY GENTLEMAN'S CHAPEAU!
Starchy suspected things'd eventually end this way, but not so soon!
NEVER SO SOON!!
Hey, Starchy! Are you okay, man?
You're not supposed to swallow gum, Starchy!!
I did it once and a gum tree grew in my stomach and then gum leaves came out of my nose, Starchy!!
REAL TALK: IT WAS GROSS

Gum doesn't really grow on trees...does it? Huh. I guess there's one way to find out?

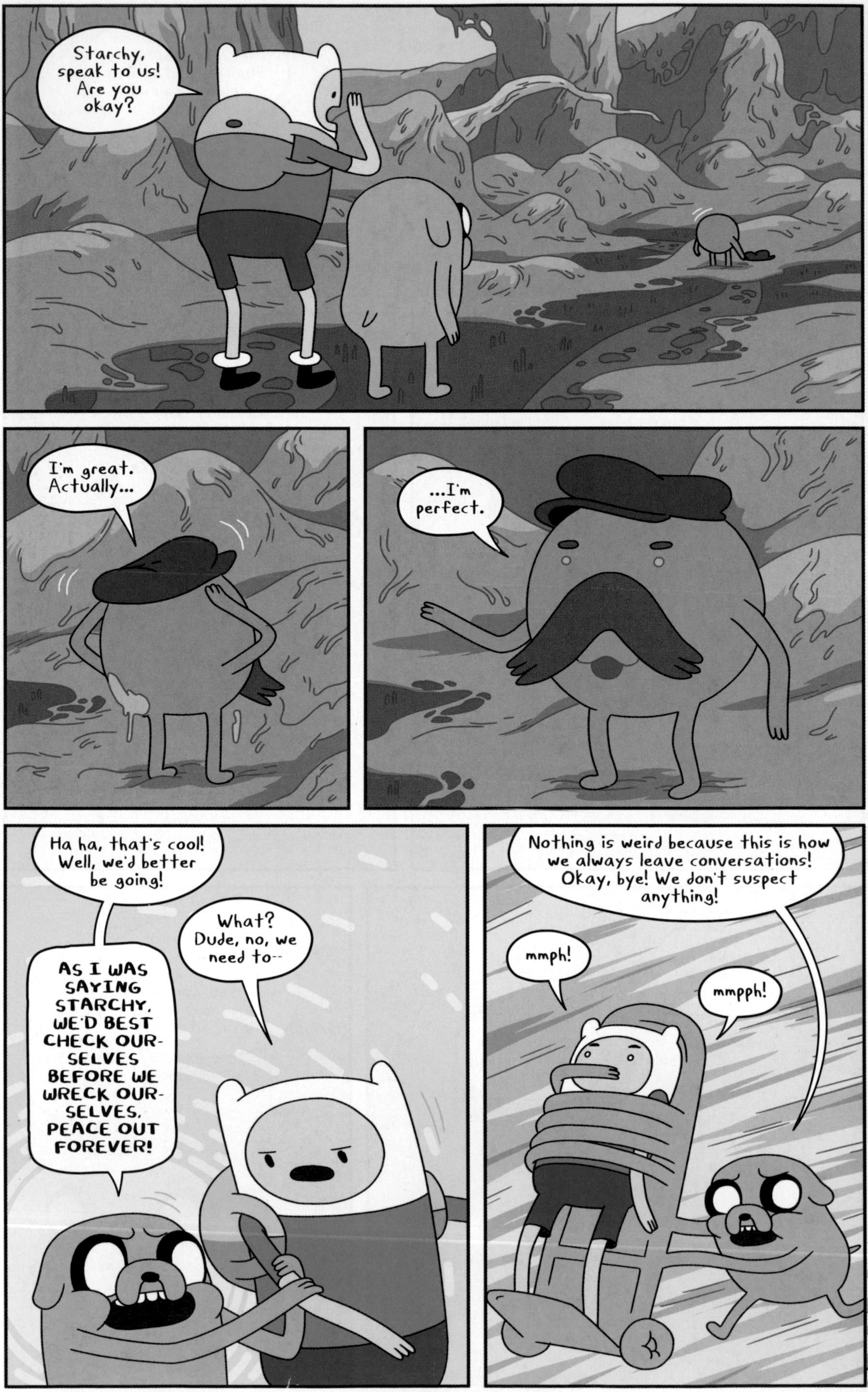
Starchy, speak to us! Are you okay?
I'm great. Actually...
...I'm perfect.
Ha ha, that's cool! Well, we'd better be going!
AS I WAS SAYING STARCHY, WE'D BEST CHECK OURSELVES BEFORE WE WRECK OURSELVES, PEACE OUT FOREVER!
What? Dude, no, we need to--
Nothing is weird because this is how we always leave conversations! Okay, bye! We don't suspect anything!
mmph!
mmpph!

Consider us checked AND pre-wrecked, Starchy!

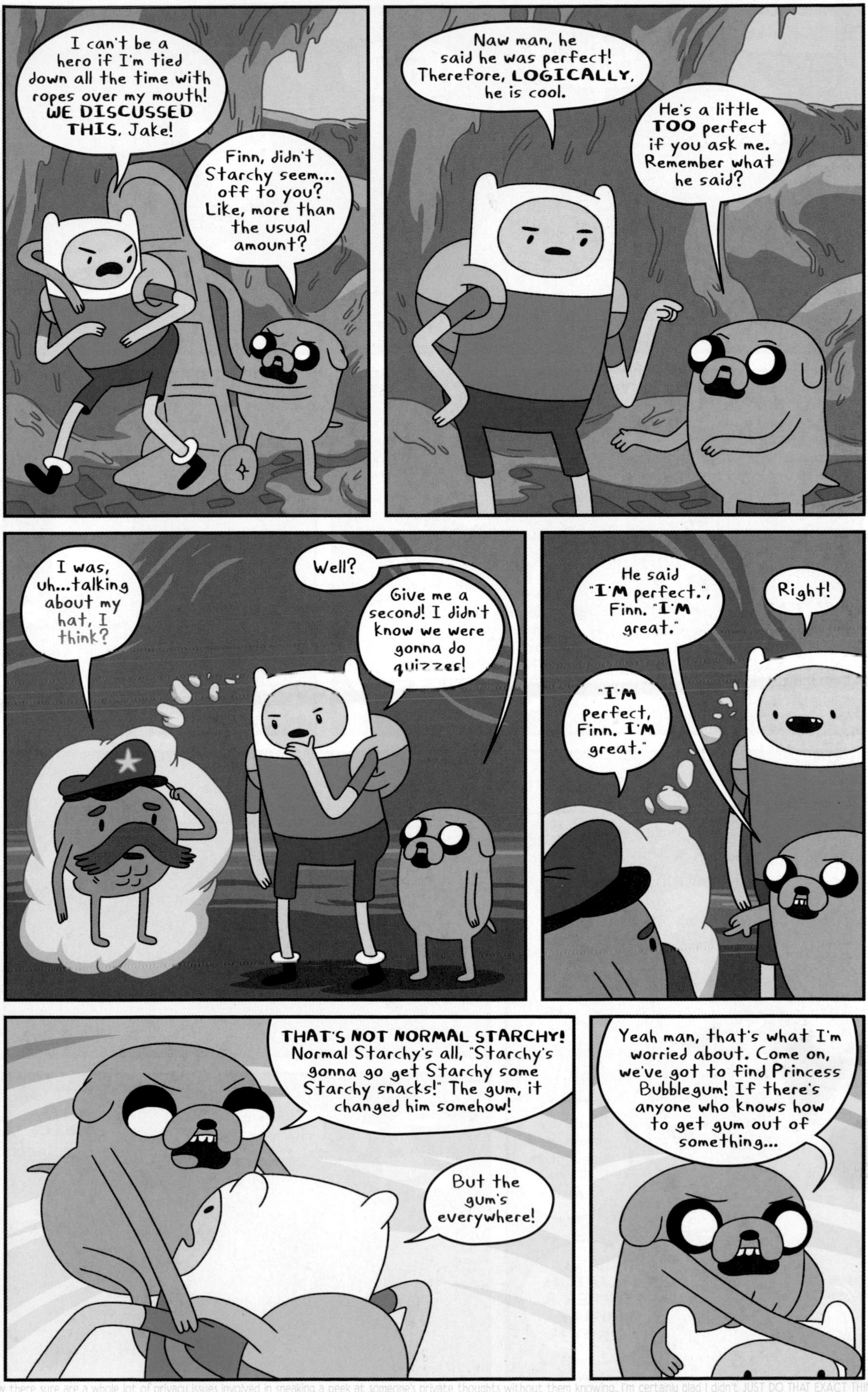
I can't be a hero if I'm tied down all the time with ropes over my mouth! WE DISCUSSED THIS, Jake!
Finn, didn't Starchy seem... off to you? Like, more than the usual amount?
Naw man, he said he was perfect! Therefore, LOGICALLY, he is cool.
He's a little TOO perfect if you ask me. Remember what he said?
I was, uh...talking about my hat, I think?
Well?
Give me a second! I didn't know we were gonna do quizzes!
He said "I'M perfect.", Finn. "I'M great."
Right!
"I'M perfect, Finn. I'M great."
THAT'S NOT NORMAL STARCHY! Normal Starchy's all, "Starchy's gonna go get Starchy some Starchy snacks!" The gum, it changed him somehow!
But the gum's everywhere!
Yeah man, that's what I'm worried about. Come on, we've got to find Princess Bubblegum! If there's anyone who knows how to get gum out of something...

w there sure are a whole lot of privacy issues involved in sneaking a peek at someone's private thoughts without them knowing.. I'm certainly glad I didn't JUST DO THAT EXACT THING.

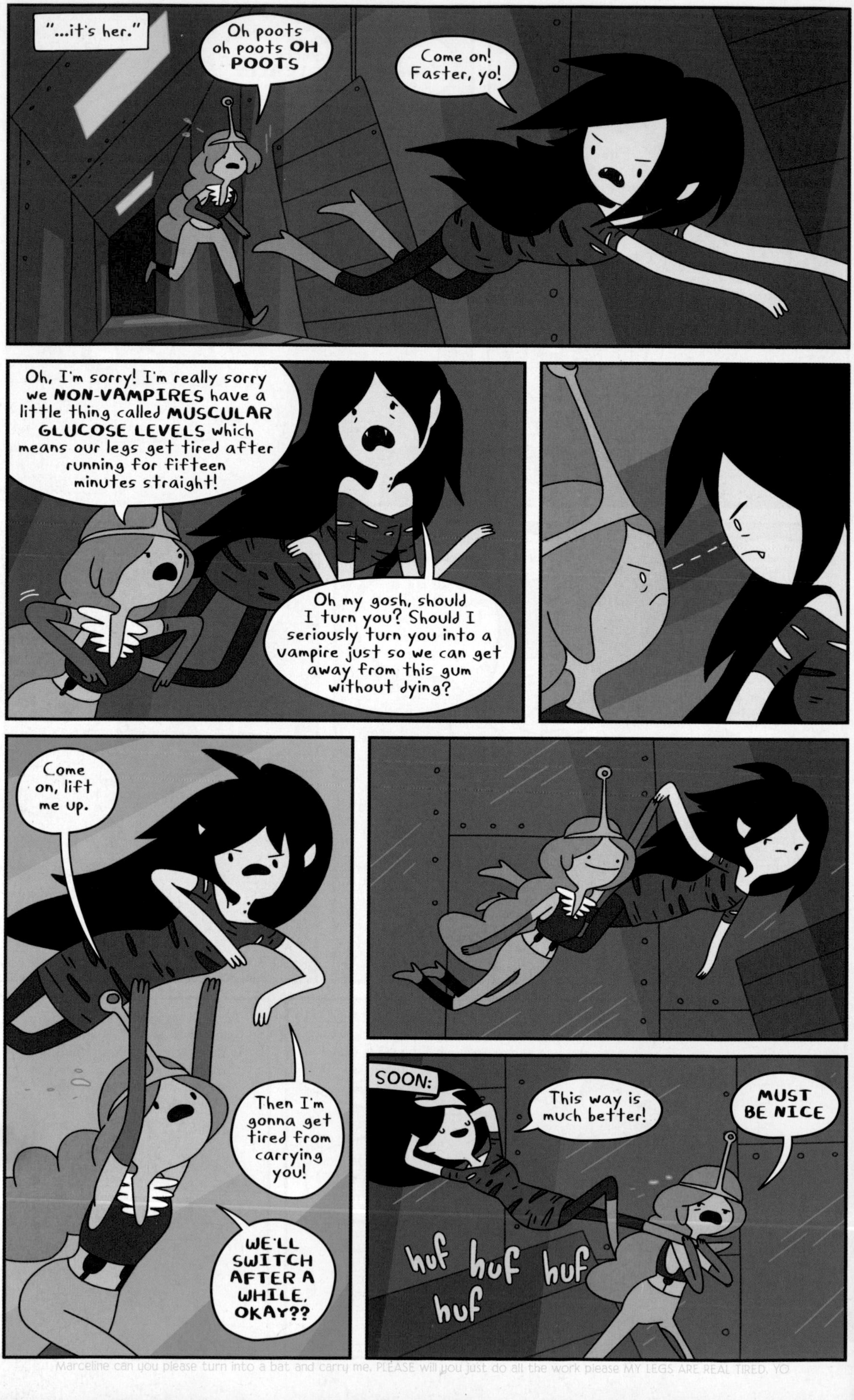
"...it's her."
Oh poots oh poots OH POOTS
Come on! Faster, yo!
Oh, I'm sorry! I'm really sorry we NON-VAMPIRES have a little thing called MUSCULAR GLUCOSE LEVELS which means our legs get tired after running for fifteen minutes straight!
Oh my gosh, should I turn you? Should I seriously turn you into a vampire just so we can get away from this gum without dying?
Come on, lift me up.
Then I'm gonna get tired from carrying you!
WE'LL SWITCH AFTER A WHILE, OKAY??
SOON:
This way is much better!
MUST BE NICE
huf huf huf huf

Marceline can you please turn into a bat and carry me. PLEASE will you just do all the work please MY LEGS ARE REAL TIRED. YO

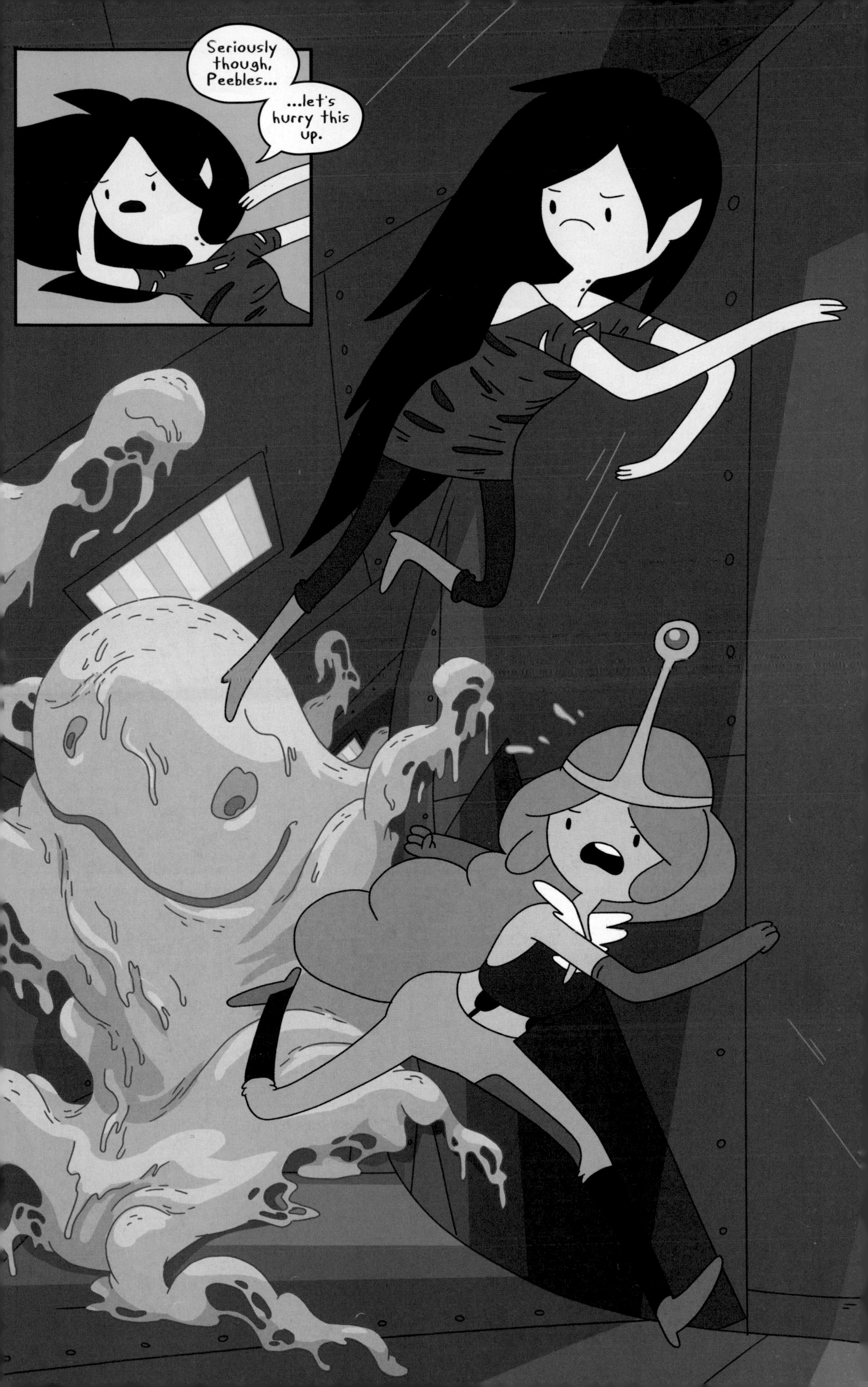
Seriously though, Peebles...
...let's hurry this up.

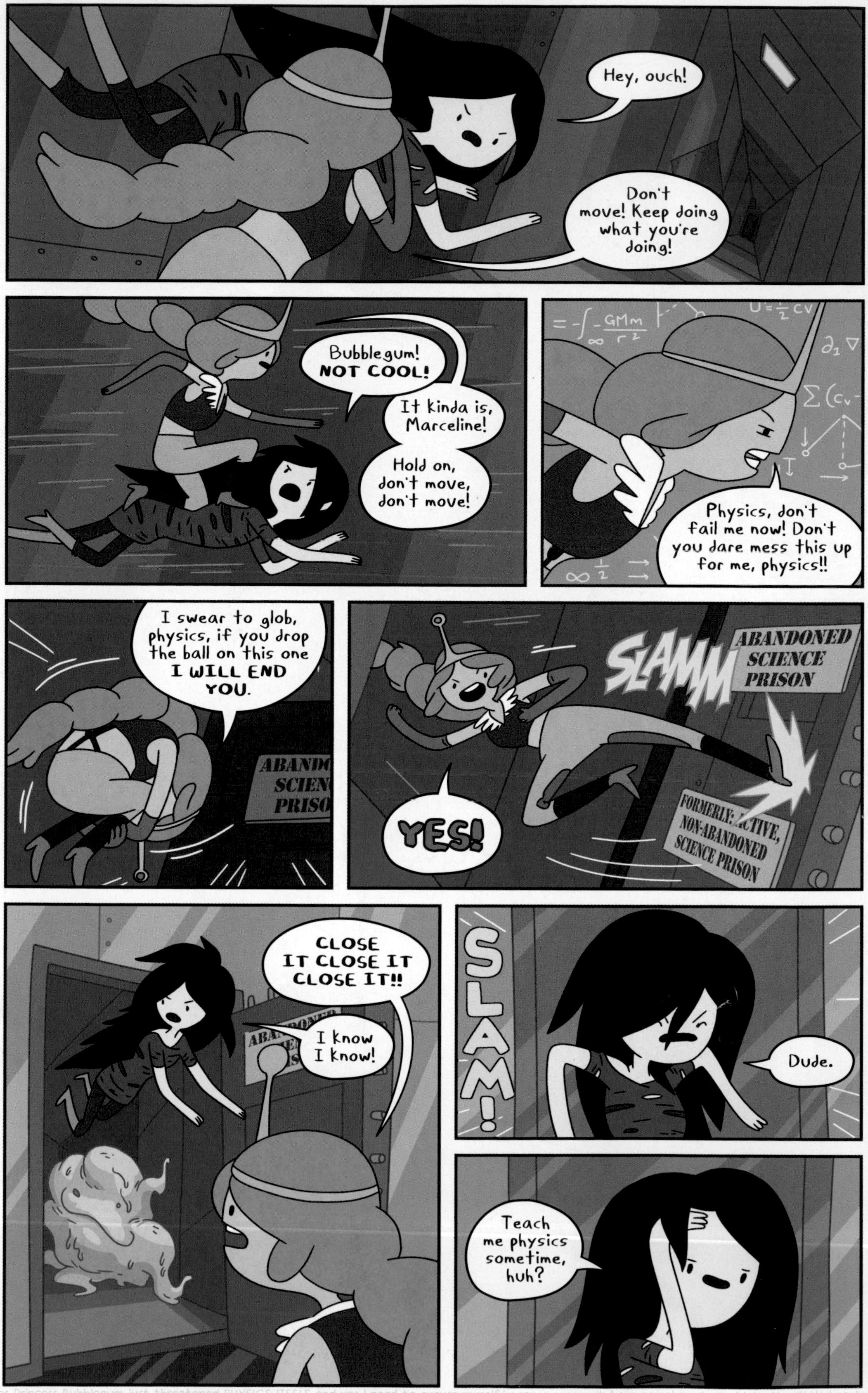
Hey, ouch!
Don't move! Keep doing what you're doing!
Bubblegum! NOT COOL!
It kinda is, Marceline!
Hold on, don't move, don't move!
Physics, don't fail me now! Don't you dare mess this up for me, physics!!
I swear to glob, physics, if you drop the ball on this one I WILL END YOU.
SLAMM
ABANDONED SCIENCE PRISON
YES!
FORMERLY: ACTIVE, NON-ABANDONED SCIENCE PRISON
CLOSE IT CLOSE IT CLOSE IT!!
I know I know!
SLAM!
Dude.
Teach me physics sometime, huh?

Yes Princess Bubblegum just threatened PHYSICS ITSELF, and yes I need to excuse myself because my pupils have somehow turned into tiny little hearts.

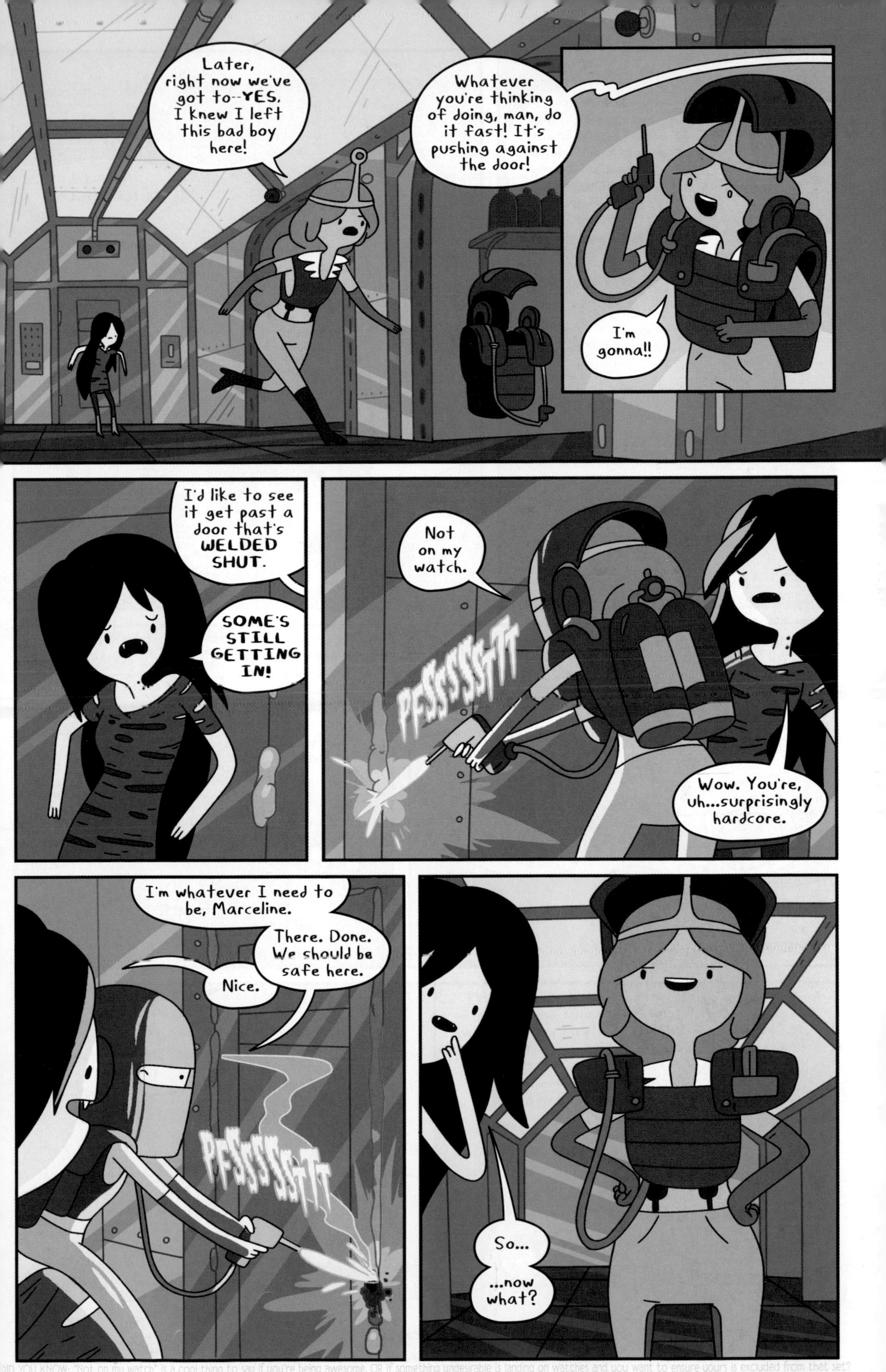

Later, right now we've got to--YES, I knew I left this bad boy here!
Whatever you're thinking of doing, man, do it fast! It's pushing against the door!
I'm gonna!!
I'd like to see it get past a door that's WELDED SHUT.
SOME'S STILL GETTING IN!
Not on my watch.
PFSSSSSTTT
Wow. You're, uh...surprisingly hardcore.
I'm whatever I need to be, Marceline.
There. Done. We should be safe here.
Nice.
PFSSSSSTTT
So...
...now what?

DID YOU KNOW: "Not on my watch" is a cool thing to say if you're being awesome, OR if something undesirable is landing on watches and you want to ensure yours is excluded from that set?

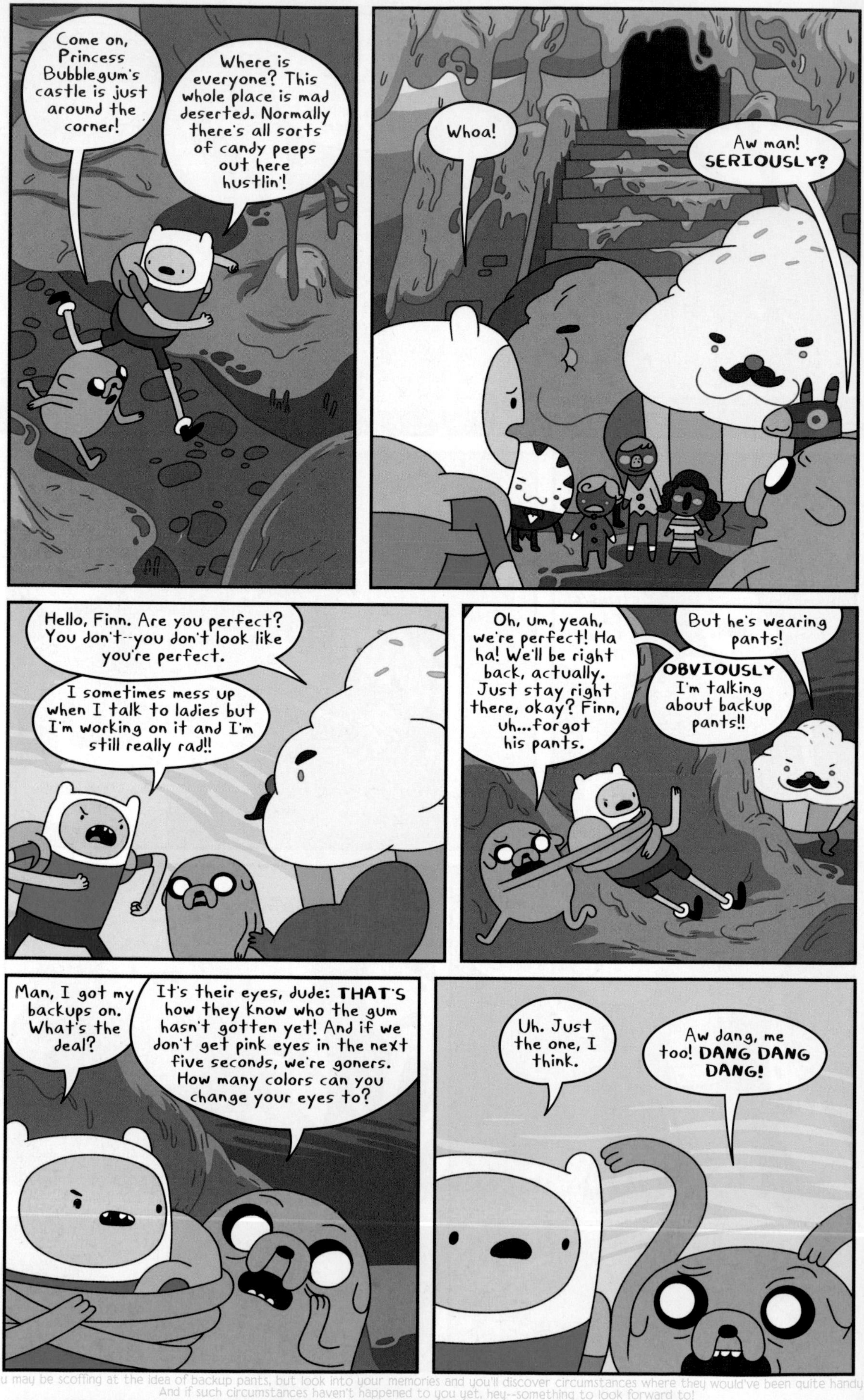
Come on, Princess Bubblegum's castle is just around the corner!
Where is everyone? This whole place is mad deserted. Normally there's all sorts of candy peeps out here hustlin'!
Whoa!
Aw man! SERIOUSLY?
Hello, Finn. Are you perfect? You don't--you don't look like you're perfect.
I sometimes mess up when I talk to ladies but I'm working on it and I'm still really rad!!
Oh, um, yeah, we're perfect! Ha ha! We'll be right back, actually. Just stay right there, okay? Finn, uh...forgot his pants.
But he's wearing pants!
OBVIOUSLY I'm talking about backup pants!!
Man, I got my backups on. What's the deal?
It's their eyes, dude: THAT'S how they know who the gum hasn't gotten yet! And if we don't get pink eyes in the next five seconds, we're goners. How many colors can you change your eyes to?
Uh. Just the one, I think.
Aw dang, me too! DANG DANG DANG!

You may be scoffing at the idea of backup pants, but look into your memories and you'll discover circumstances where they would've been quite handy. And if such circumstances haven't happened to you yet, hey--something to look forward to!

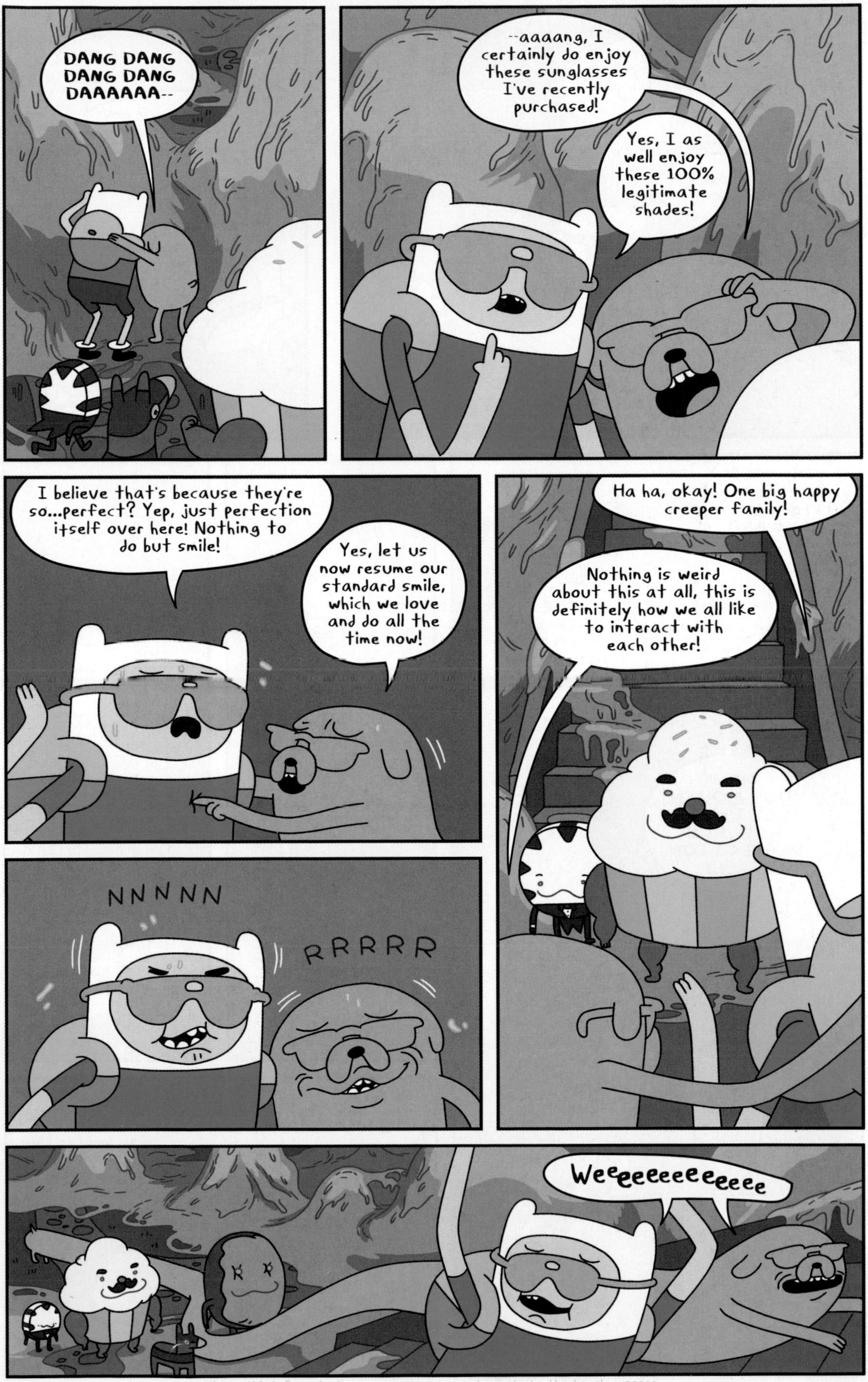
DANG DANG DANG DANG DAAAAAA--
--aaaang, I certainly do enjoy these sunglasses I've recently purchased!
Yes, I as well enjoy these 100% legitimate shades!
I believe that's because they're so...perfect? Yep, just perfection itself over here! Nothing to do but smile!
Yes, let us now resume our standard smile, which we love and do all the time now!
NNNNN
RRRRR
Ha ha, okay! One big happy creeper family!
Nothing is weird about this at all, this is definitely how we all like to interact with each other!
Weeeeeeeeeeee

Weeee this is fun, why is everyone so warm and sweaty to the touch, weeeee

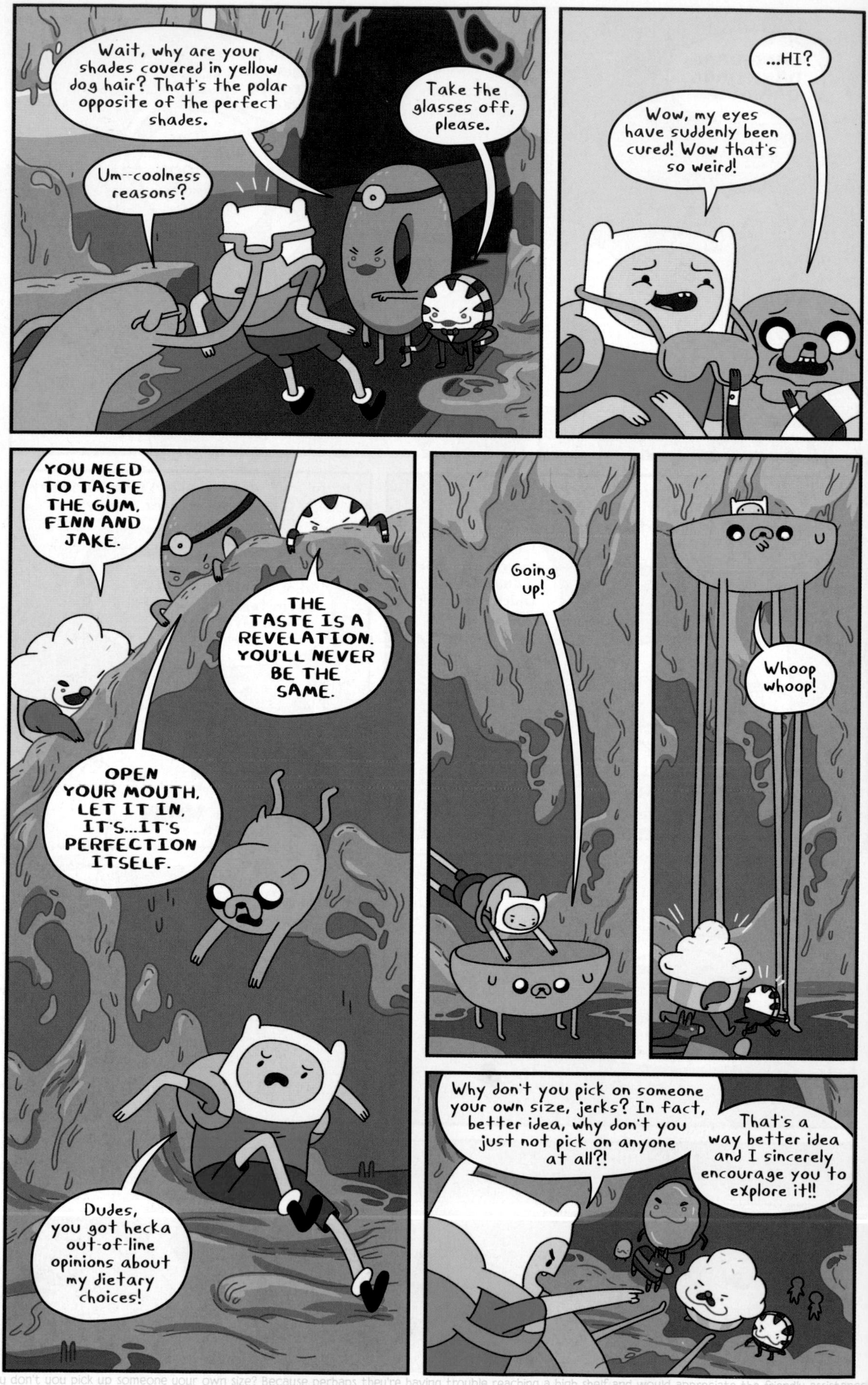
Wait, why are your shades covered in yellow dog hair? That's the polar opposite of the perfect shades.
Um--coolness reasons?
Take the glasses off, please.
...HI?
Wow, my eyes have suddenly been cured! Wow that's so weird!
YOU NEED TO TASTE THE GUM, FINN AND JAKE.
THE TASTE IS A REVELATION. YOU'LL NEVER BE THE SAME.
OPEN YOUR MOUTH, LET IT IN, IT'S...IT'S PERFECTION ITSELF.
Dudes, you got hecka out-of-line opinions about my dietary choices!
Going up!
Whoop whoop!
Why don't you pick on someone your own size, jerks? In fact, better idea, why don't you just not pick on anyone at all?!
That's a way better idea and I sincerely encourage you to explore it!!

Why don't you pick up someone your own size? Because perhaps they're having trouble reaching a high shelf and would appreciate the friendly assistance

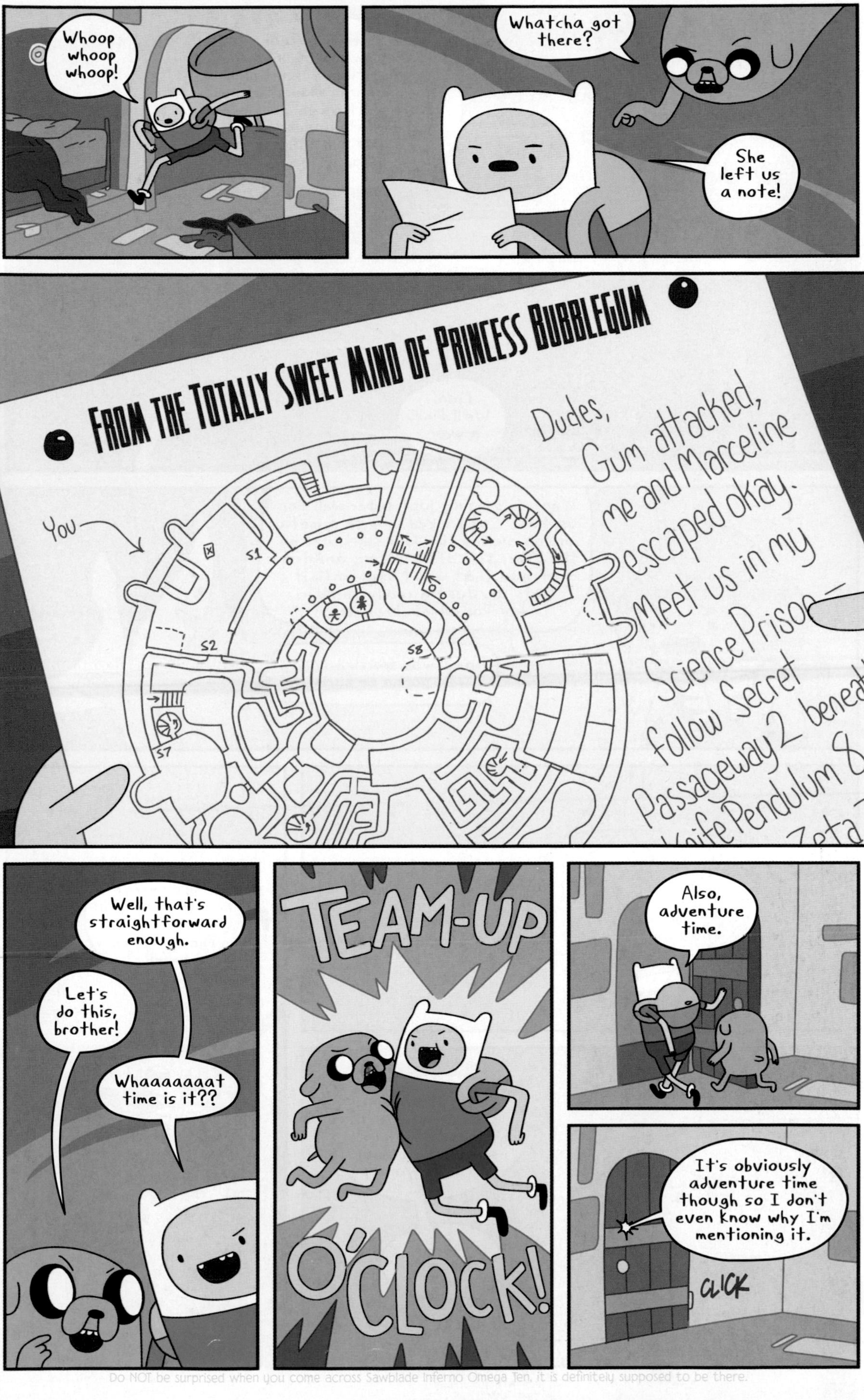

Whoop whoop whoop!
Whatcha got there?
She left us a note!
FROM THE TOTALLY SWEET MIND OF PRINCESS BUBBLEGUM
You
S1
S2
S7
S8
Dudes,
Gum attacked, me and Marceline escaped okay.
Meet us in my Science Prison—
follow Secret Passageway 2 beneath
Well, that's straightforward enough.
Let's do this, brother!
Whaaaaaaat time is it??
TEAM-UP O'CLOCK!
Also, adventure time.
It's obviously adventure time though so I don't even know why I'm mentioning it.
CLICK

Do NOT be surprised when you come across Sawblade Inferno Omega Ten, it is definitely supposed to be there.

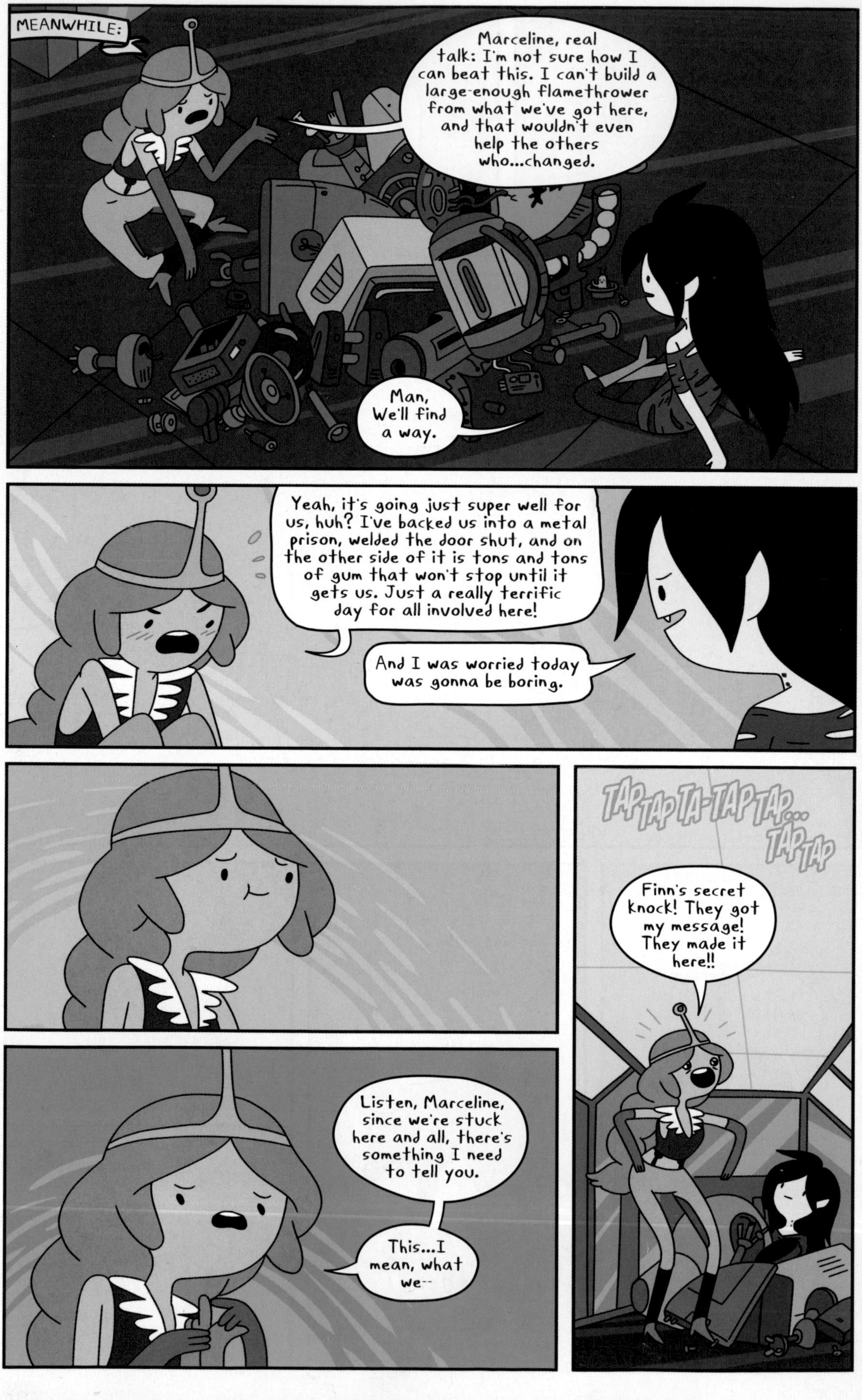
MEANWHILE:
Marceline, real talk: I'm not sure how I can beat this. I can't build a large-enough flamethrower from what we've got here, and that wouldn't even help the others who...changed.
Man, We'll find a way.
Yeah, it's going just super well for us, huh? I've backed us into a metal prison, welded the door shut, and on the other side of it is tons and tons of gum that won't stop until it gets us. Just a really terrific day for all involved here!
And I was worried today was gonna be boring.
Listen, Marceline, since we're stuck here and all, there's something I need to tell you.
This...I mean, what we--
TAP TAP TA-TAP TAP... TAP TAP
Finn's secret knock! They got my message! They made it here!!

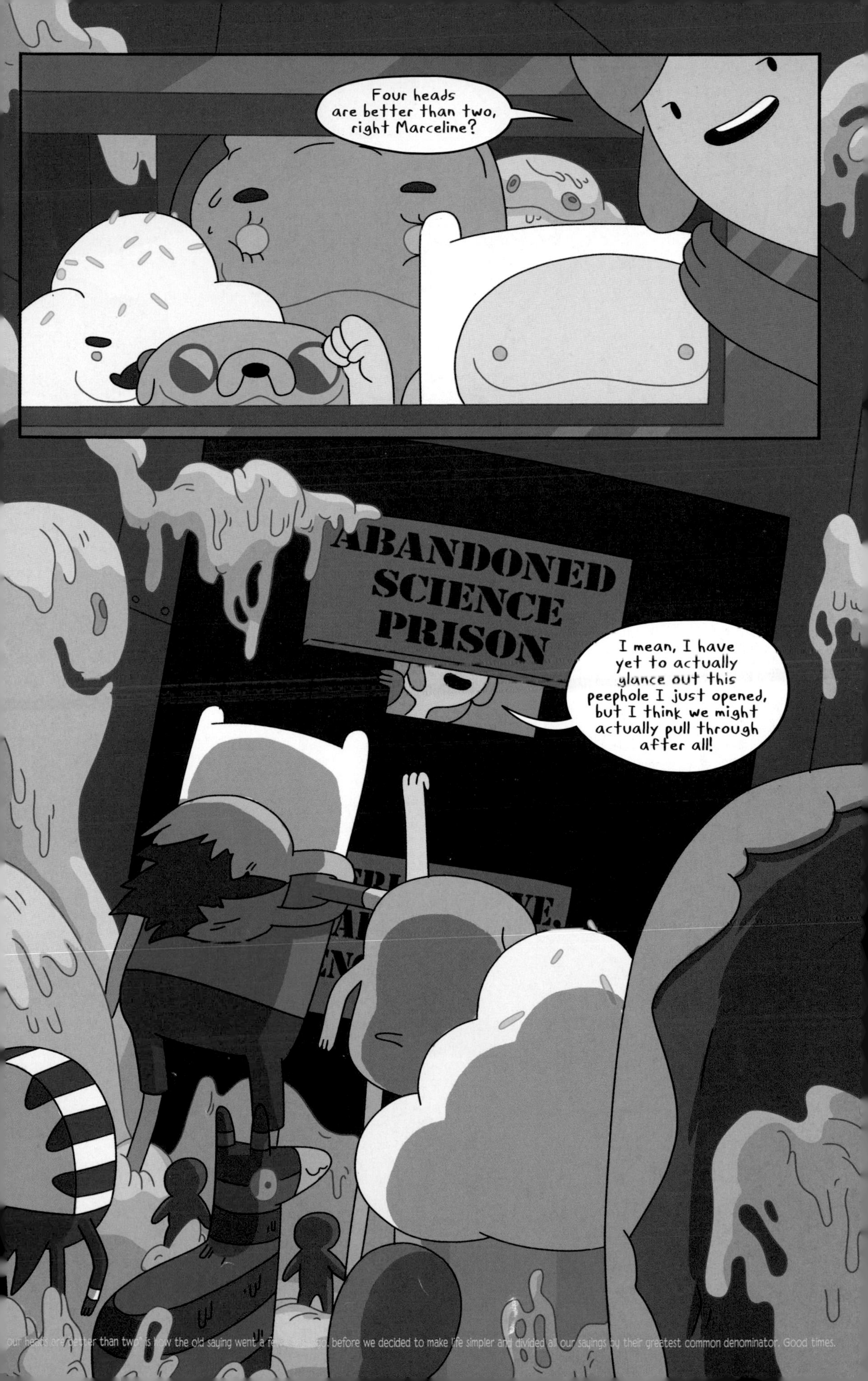
Four heads are better than two, right Marceline?
ABANDONED SCIENCE PRISON
I mean, I have yet to actually glance out this peephole I just opened, but I think we might actually pull through after all!
our heads are better than two" is how the old saying went a few years ago, before we decided to make life simpler and divided all our sayings by their greatest common denominator. Good times.

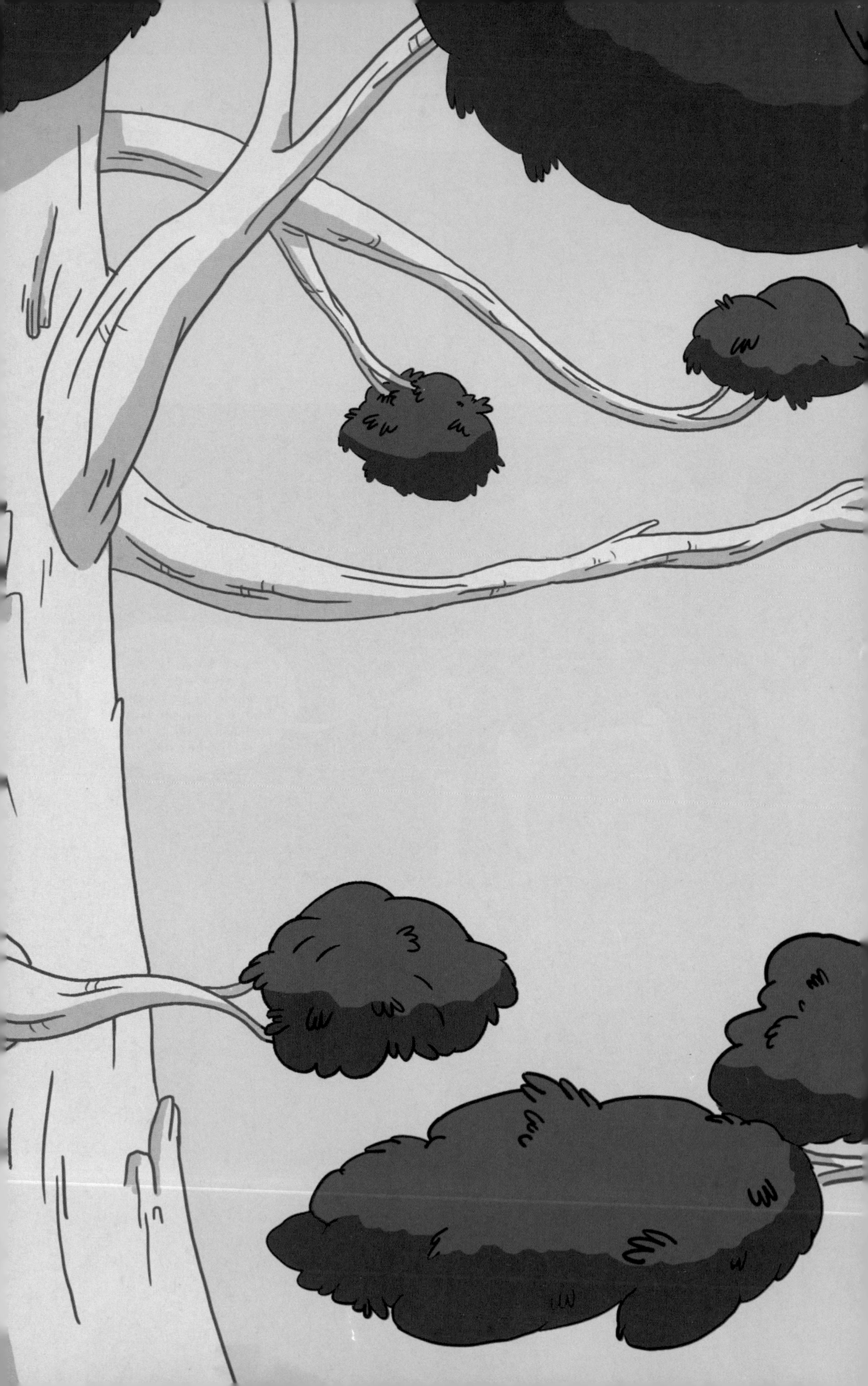

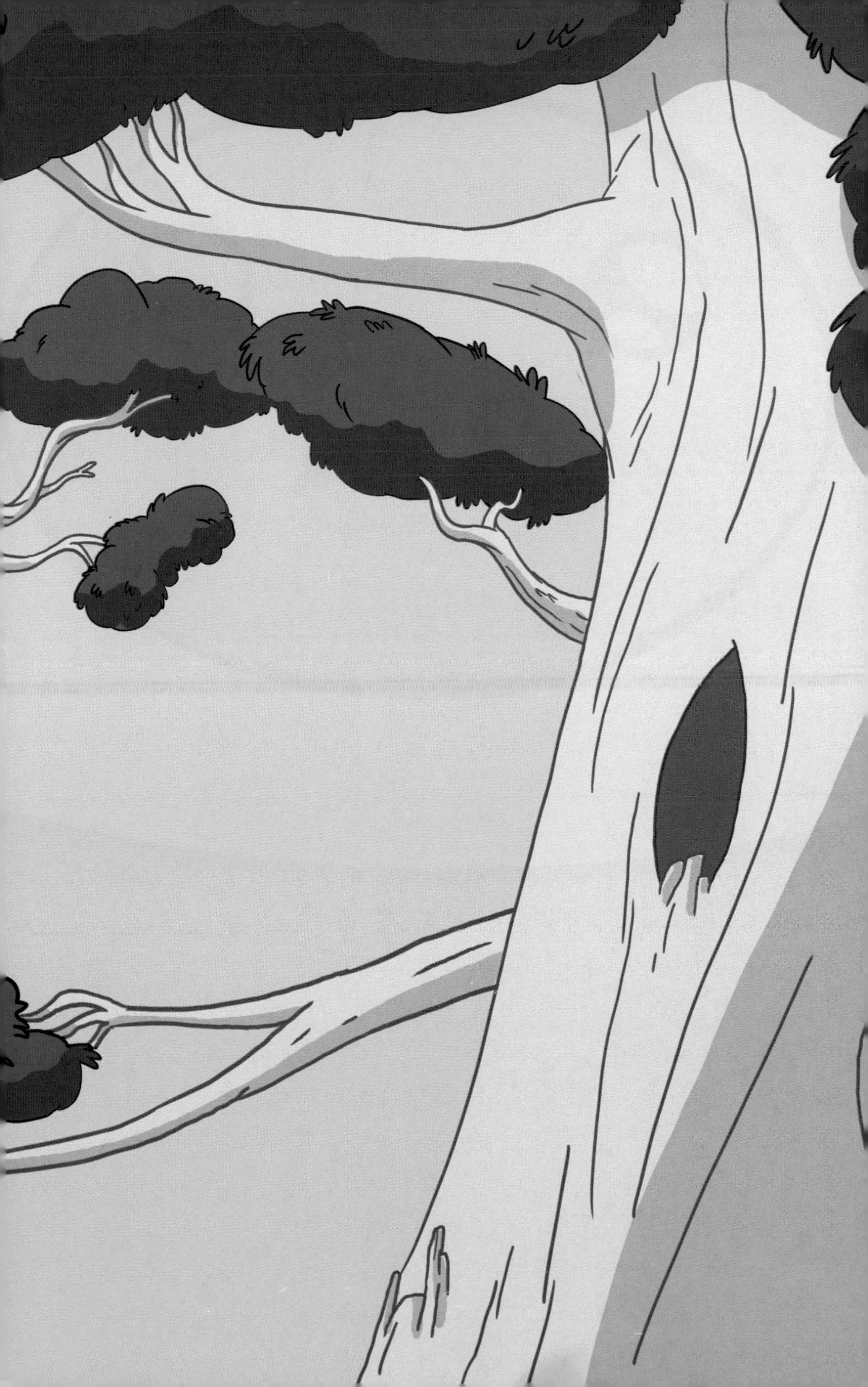

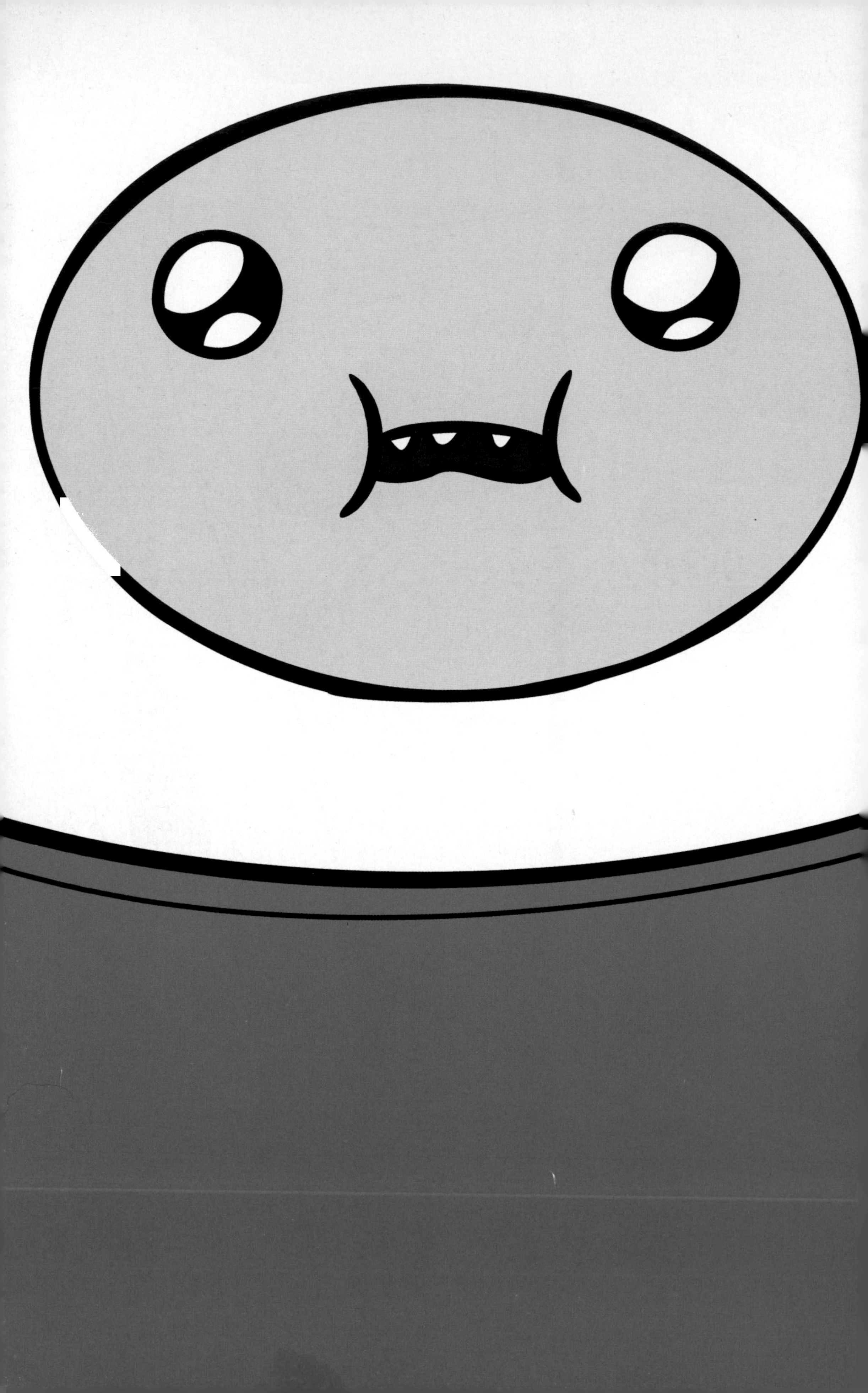

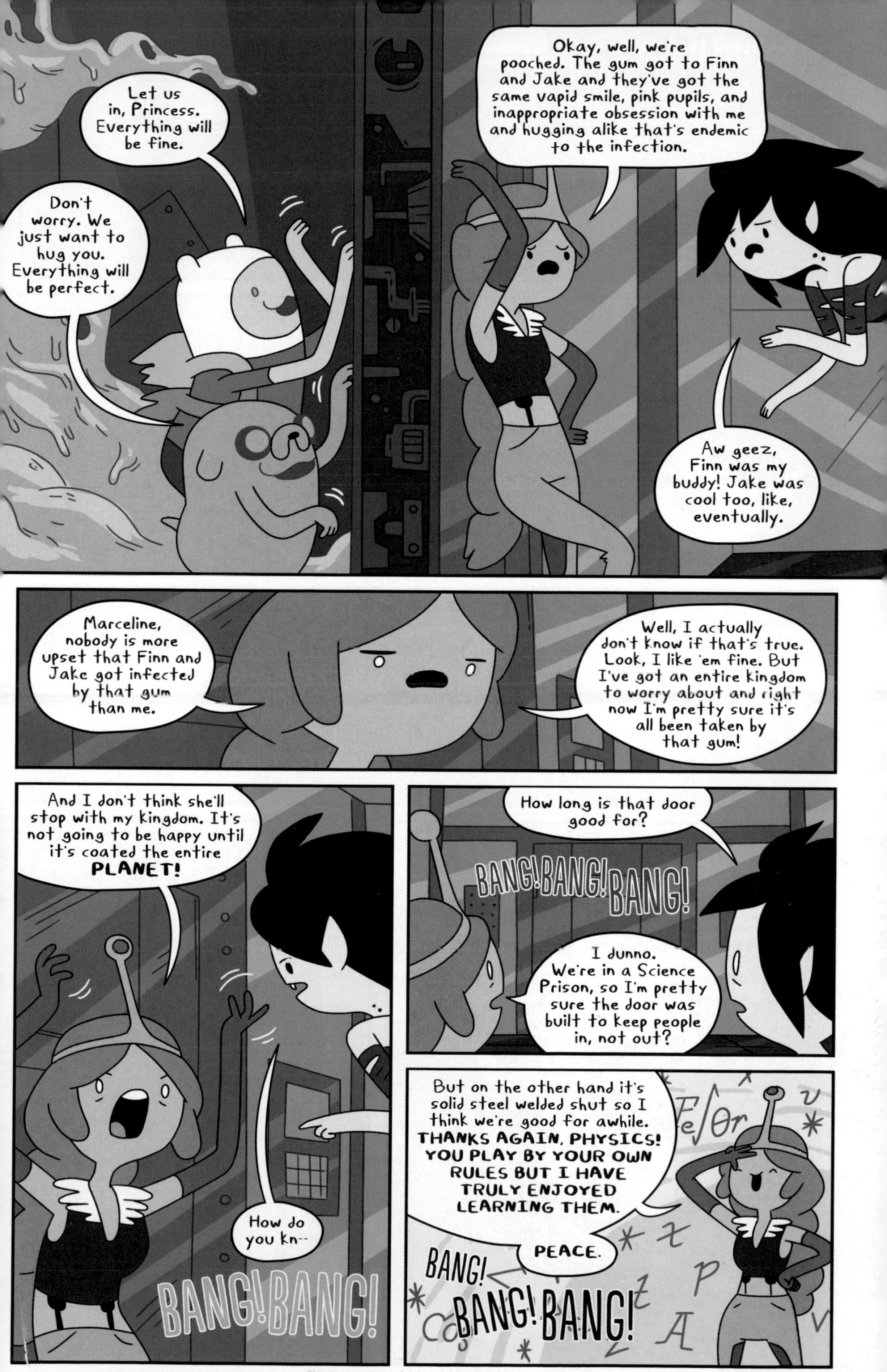
Let us in, Princess. Everything will be fine.
Don't worry. We just want to hug you. Everything will be perfect.
Okay, well, we're pooched. The gum got to Finn and Jake and they've got the same vapid smile, pink pupils, and inappropriate obsession with me and hugging alike that's endemic to the infection.
Aw geez, Finn was my buddy! Jake was cool too, like, eventually.
Marceline, nobody is more upset that Finn and Jake got infected by that gum than me.
Well, I actually don't know if that's true. Look, I like 'em fine. But I've got an entire kingdom to worry about and right now I'm pretty sure it's all been taken by that gum!
And I don't think she'll stop with my kingdom. It's not going to be happy until it's coated the entire PLANET!
How do you kn--
BANG! BANG!
How long is that door good for?
BANG! BANG! BANG!
I dunno. We're in a Science Prison, so I'm pretty sure the door was built to keep people in, not out?
But on the other hand it's solid steel welded shut so I think we're good for awhile. THANKS AGAIN, PHYSICS! YOU PLAY BY YOUR OWN RULES BUT I HAVE TRULY ENJOYED LEARNING THEM.
PEACE.
BANG! BANG! BANG!

Physics, we have had our ups and downs.

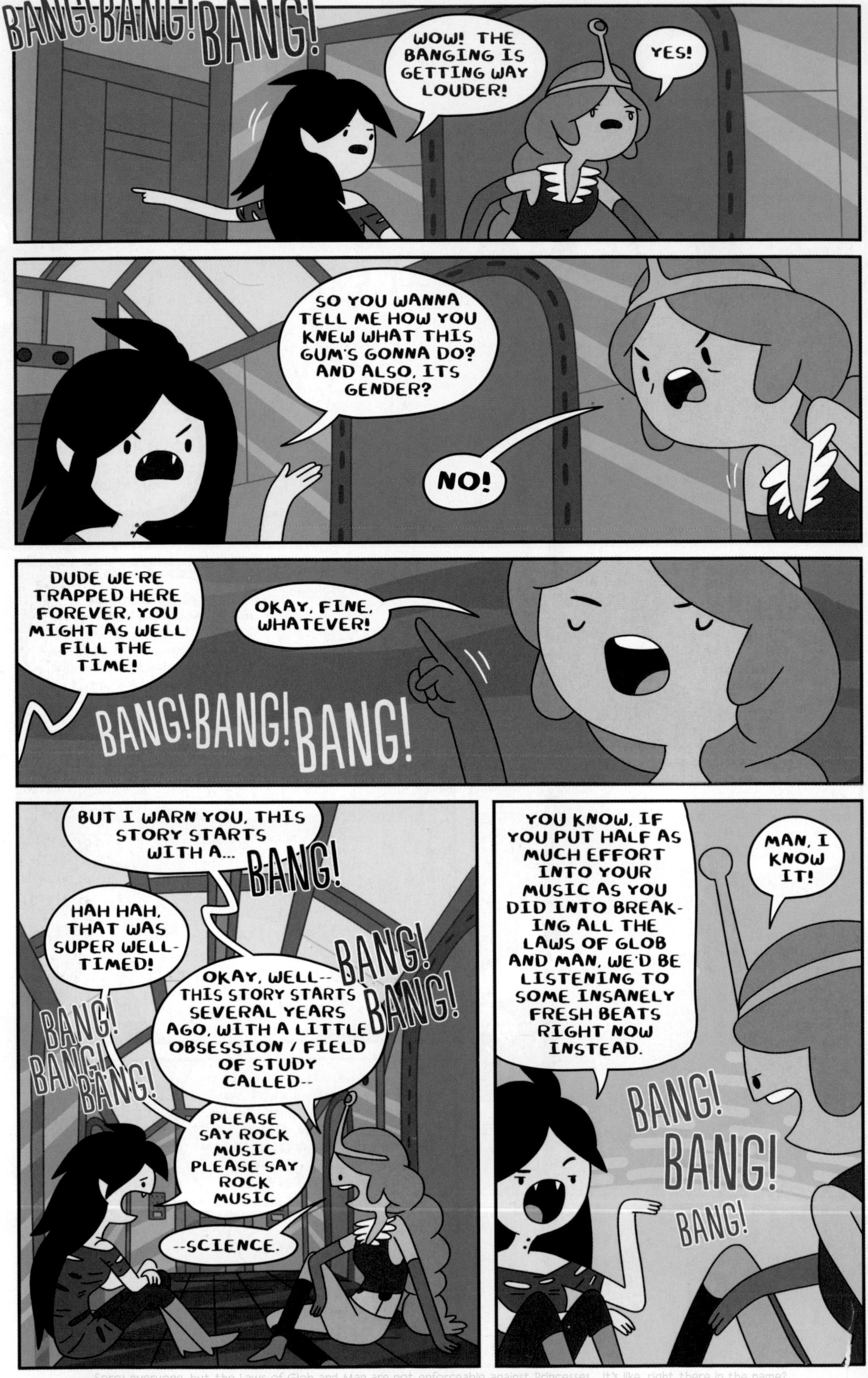
BANG! BANG! BANG!
WOW! THE BANGING IS GETTING WAY LOUDER!
YES!
SO YOU WANNA TELL ME HOW YOU KNEW WHAT THIS GUM'S GONNA DO? AND ALSO, ITS GENDER?
NO!
DUDE WE'RE TRAPPED HERE FOREVER, YOU MIGHT AS WELL FILL THE TIME!
OKAY, FINE, WHATEVER!
BANG! BANG! BANG!
BUT I WARN YOU, THIS STORY STARTS WITH A...
BANG!
HAH HAH, THAT WAS SUPER WELL-TIMED!
BANG! BANG!
BANG! BANG! BANG!
OKAY, WELL-- THIS STORY STARTS SEVERAL YEARS AGO, WITH A LITTLE OBSESSION / FIELD OF STUDY CALLED--
PLEASE SAY ROCK MUSIC PLEASE SAY ROCK MUSIC
--SCIENCE.
YOU KNOW, IF YOU PUT HALF AS MUCH EFFORT INTO YOUR MUSIC AS YOU DID INTO BREAK-ING ALL THE LAWS OF GLOB AND MAN, WE'D BE LISTENING TO SOME INSANELY FRESH BEATS RIGHT NOW INSTEAD.
MAN, I KNOW IT!
BANG! BANG! BANG!

Sorry everyone, but the Laws of Glob and Man are not enforceable against Princesses. It's like, right there in the name?

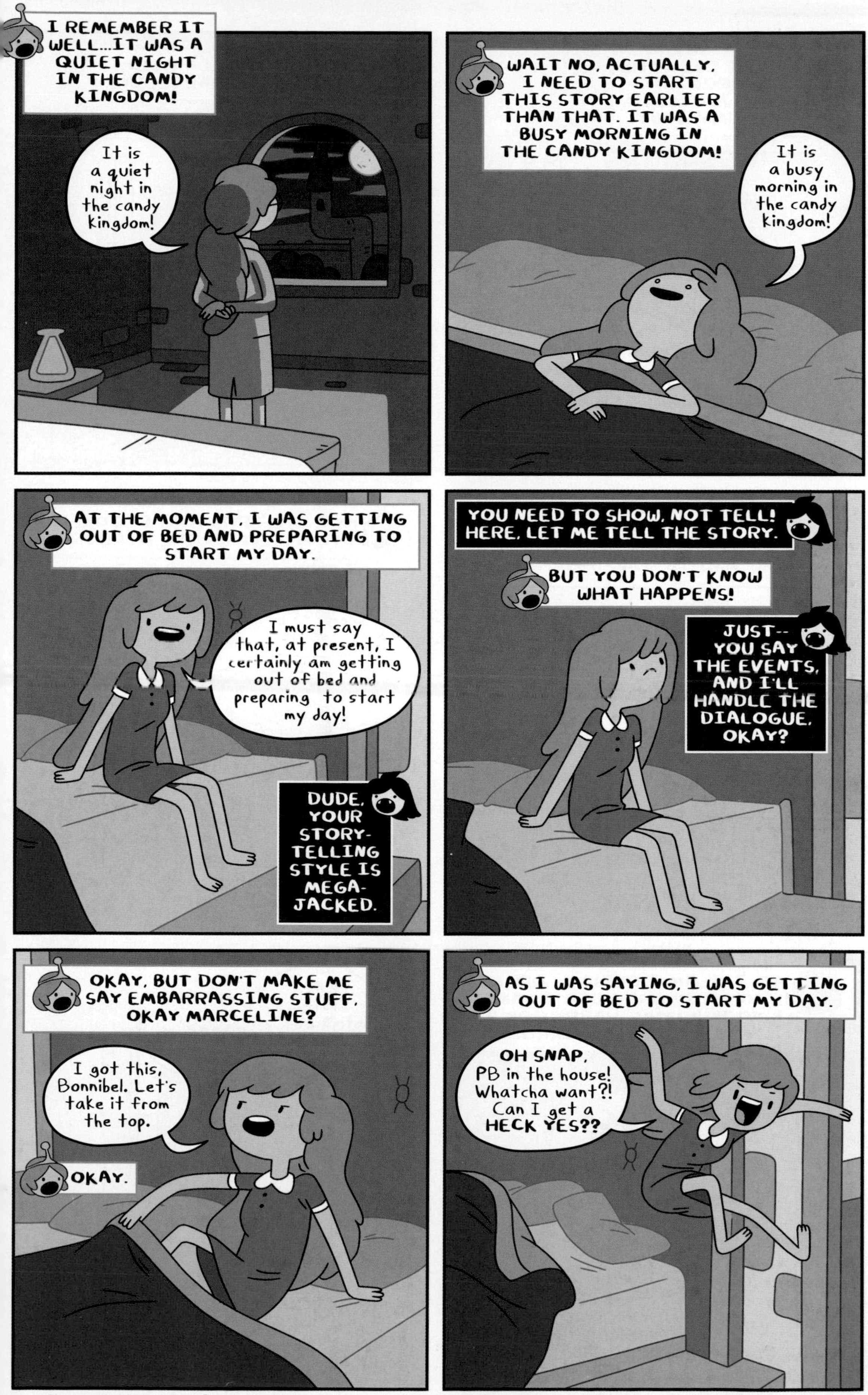
I REMEMBER IT WELL...IT WAS A QUIET NIGHT IN THE CANDY KINGDOM!
It is a quiet night in the candy kingdom!
WAIT NO, ACTUALLY, I NEED TO START THIS STORY EARLIER THAN THAT. IT WAS A BUSY MORNING IN THE CANDY KINGDOM!
It is a busy morning in the candy kingdom!
AT THE MOMENT, I WAS GETTING OUT OF BED AND PREPARING TO START MY DAY.
I must say that, at present, I certainly am getting out of bed and preparing to start my day!
DUDE, YOUR STORY-TELLING STYLE IS MEGA-JACKED.
YOU NEED TO SHOW, NOT TELL! HERE, LET ME TELL THE STORY.
BUT YOU DON'T KNOW WHAT HAPPENS!
JUST-- YOU SAY THE EVENTS, AND I'LL HANDLE THE DIALOGUE, OKAY?
OKAY, BUT DON'T MAKE ME SAY EMBARRASSING STUFF, OKAY MARCELINE?
I got this, Bonnibel. Let's take it from the top.
OKAY.
AS I WAS SAYING, I WAS GETTING OUT OF BED TO START MY DAY.
OH SNAP, PB in the house! Whatcha want?! Can I get a HECK YES??

Oh my gosh I just realized if Princess Bubblegum started a jam band she could call it "PB + Jam". Like the sandwich. LIKE THE SANDWICH!

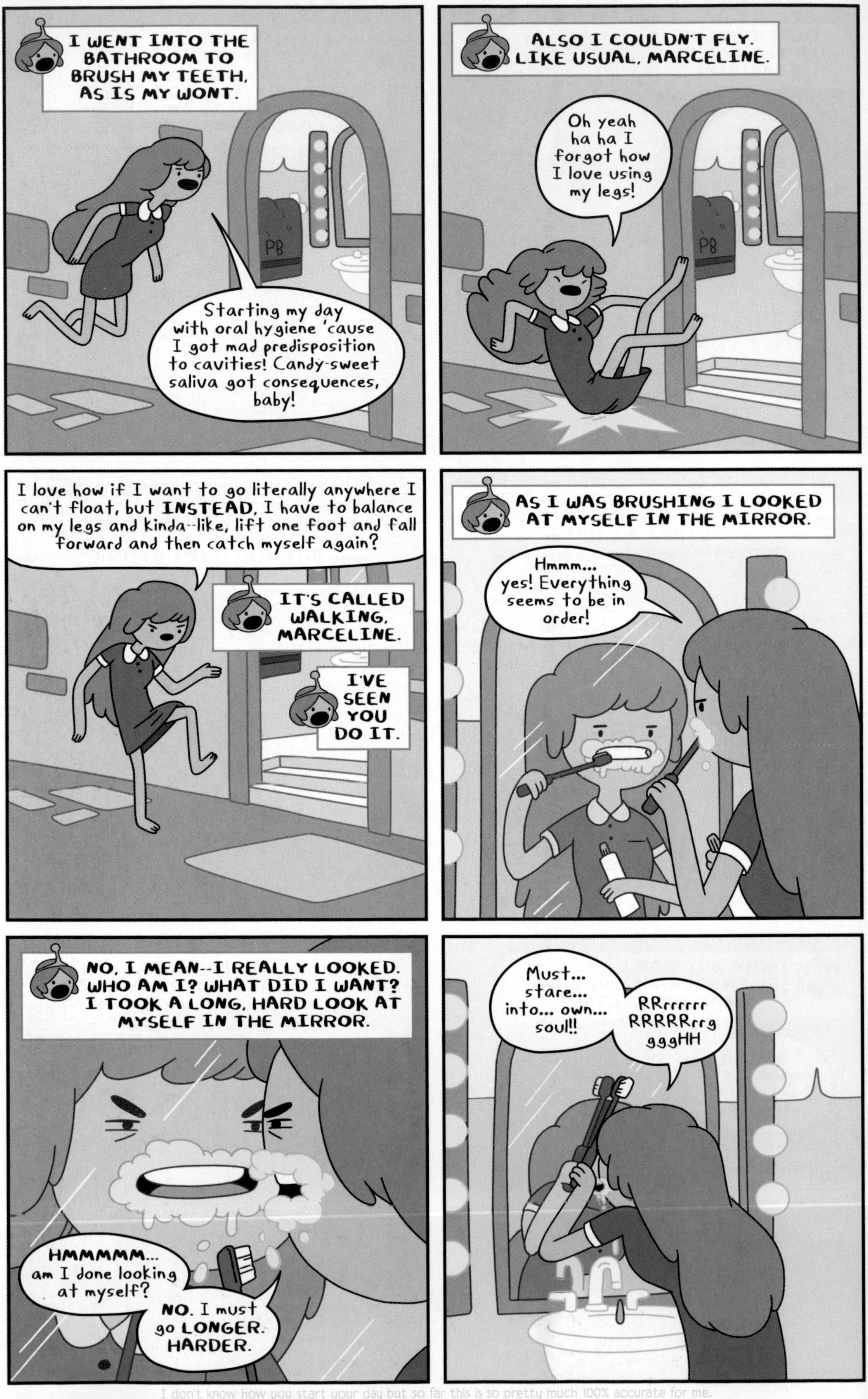
I WENT INTO THE BATHROOM TO BRUSH MY TEETH, AS IS MY WONT.
Starting my day with oral hygiene 'cause I got mad predisposition to cavities! Candy-sweet saliva got consequences, baby!
ALSO I COULDN'T FLY. LIKE USUAL, MARCELINE.
Oh yeah ha ha I forgot how I love using my legs!
PB
I love how if I want to go literally anywhere I can't float, but INSTEAD, I have to balance on my legs and kinda--like, lift one foot and fall forward and then catch myself again?
IT'S CALLED WALKING, MARCELINE.
I'VE SEEN YOU DO IT.
AS I WAS BRUSHING I LOOKED AT MYSELF IN THE MIRROR.
Hmmm... yes! Everything seems to be in order!
NO, I MEAN--I REALLY LOOKED. WHO AM I? WHAT DID I WANT? I TOOK A LONG, HARD LOOK AT MYSELF IN THE MIRROR.
HMMMMM... am I done looking at myself?
NO. I must go LONGER. HARDER.
Must... stare... into... own... soul!!
RRrrrrrr RRRRRrrg gggHH

I don't know how you start your day but so far this is so pretty much 100% accurate for me.

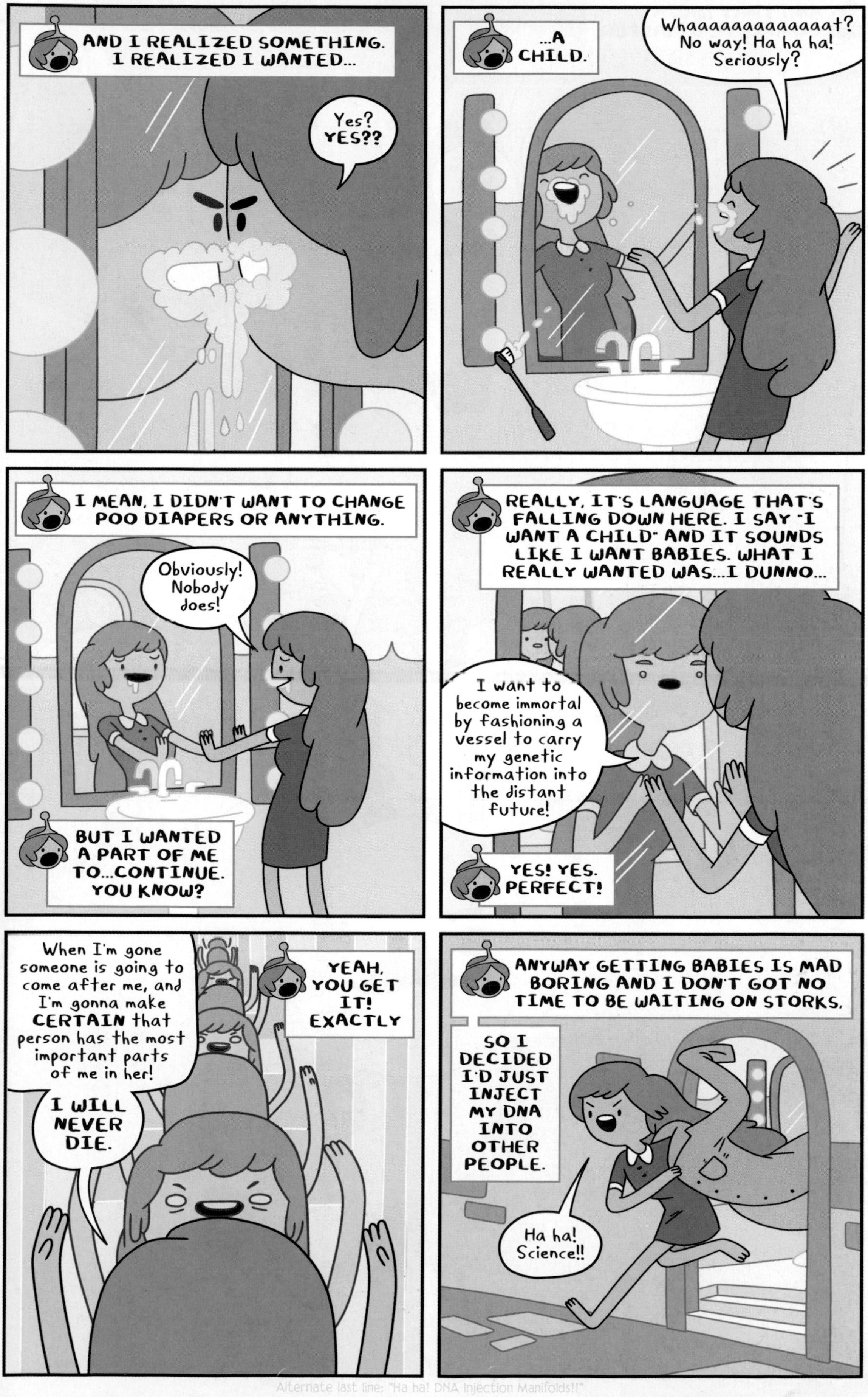
AND I REALIZED SOMETHING. I REALIZED I WANTED...
Yes? YES??
...A CHILD.
Whaaaaaaaaaaaaat? No way! Ha ha ha! Seriously?
I MEAN, I DIDN'T WANT TO CHANGE POO DIAPERS OR ANYTHING.
Obviously! Nobody does!
BUT I WANTED A PART OF ME TO...CONTINUE. YOU KNOW?
REALLY, IT'S LANGUAGE THAT'S FALLING DOWN HERE. I SAY "I WANT A CHILD" AND IT SOUNDS LIKE I WANT BABIES. WHAT I REALLY WANTED WAS...I DUNNO...
I want to become immortal by fashioning a vessel to carry my genetic information into the distant future!
YES! YES. PERFECT!
When I'm gone someone is going to come after me, and I'm gonna make CERTAIN that person has the most important parts of me in her!
YEAH, YOU GET IT! EXACTLY
I WILL NEVER DIE.
ANYWAY GETTING BABIES IS MAD BORING AND I DON'T GOT NO TIME TO BE WAITING ON STORKS.
SO I DECIDED I'D JUST INJECT MY DNA INTO OTHER PEOPLE.
Ha ha! Science!!

Alternate last line: "Ha ha! DNA Injection Manifolds!!"

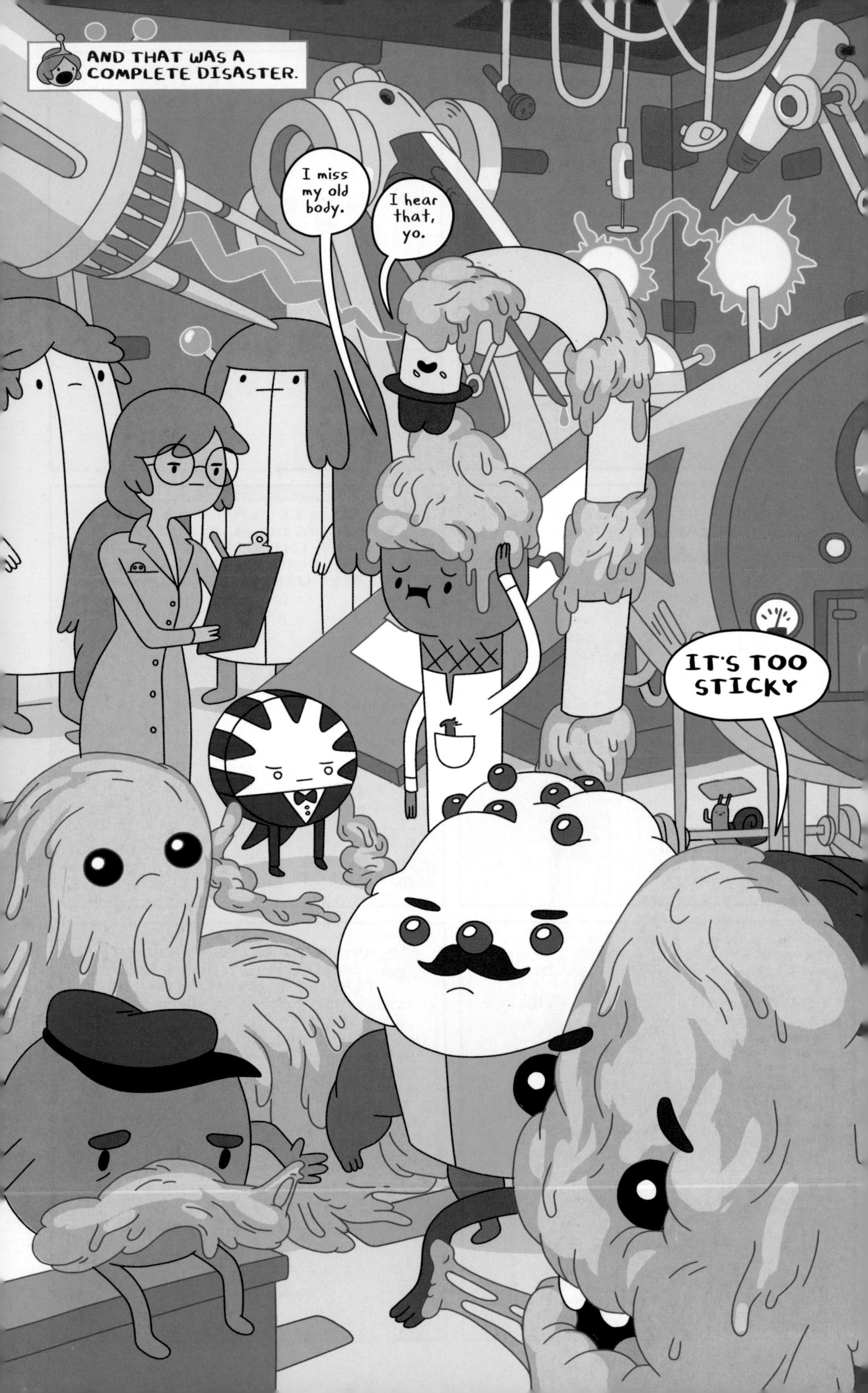
AND THAT WAS A COMPLETE DISASTER.
I miss my old body.
I hear that, yo.
IT'S TOO STICKY

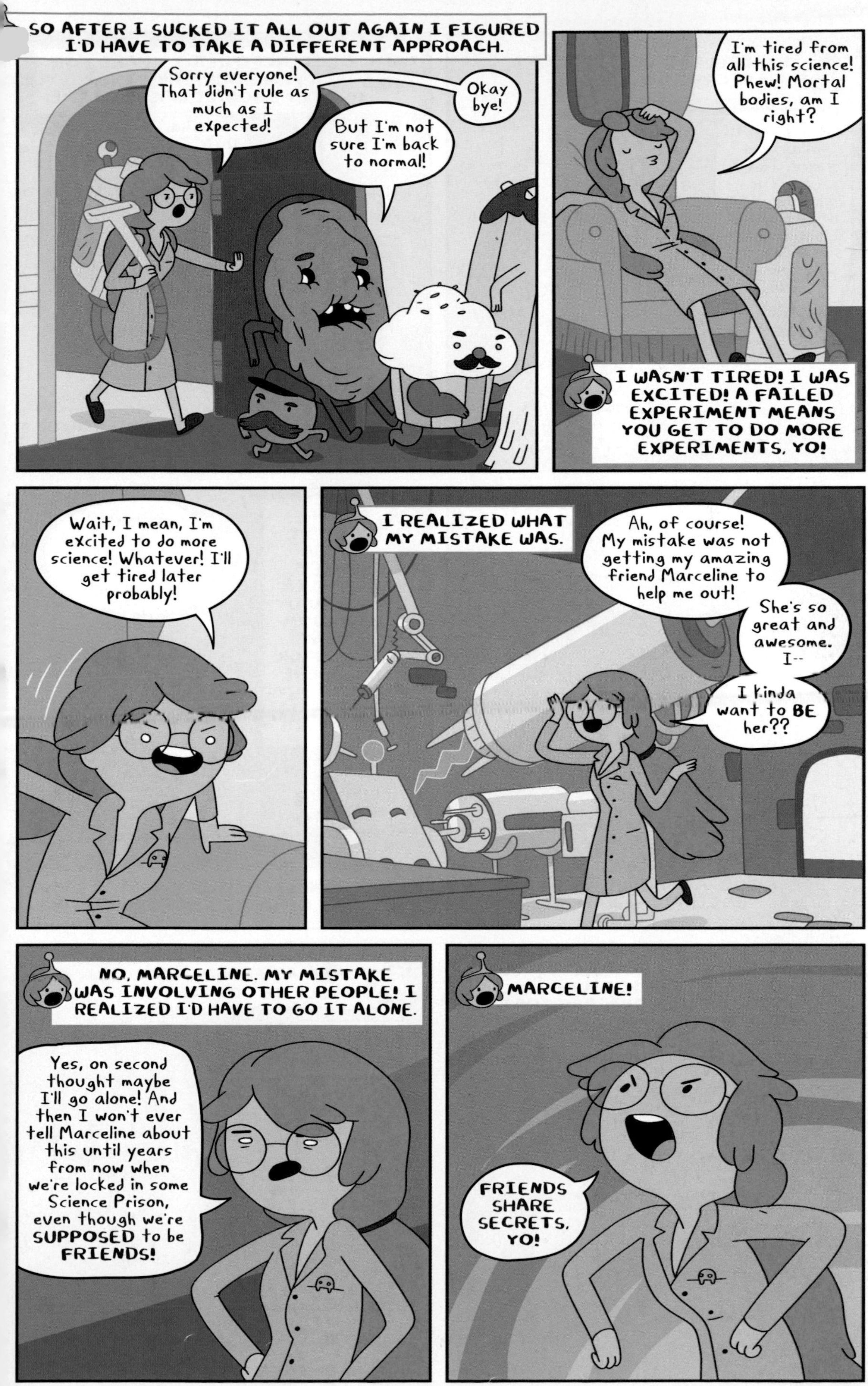
SO AFTER I SUCKED IT ALL OUT AGAIN I FIGURED I'D HAVE TO TAKE A DIFFERENT APPROACH.
Sorry everyone! That didn't rule as much as I expected!
Okay bye!
But I'm not sure I'm back to normal!
I'm tired from all this science! Phew! Mortal bodies, am I right?
I WASN'T TIRED! I WAS EXCITED! A FAILED EXPERIMENT MEANS YOU GET TO DO MORE EXPERIMENTS, YO!
Wait, I mean, I'm excited to do more science! Whatever! I'll get tired later probably!
I REALIZED WHAT MY MISTAKE WAS.
Ah, of course! My mistake was not getting my amazing friend Marceline to help me out!
She's so great and awesome. I--
I kinda want to BE her??
NO, MARCELINE. MY MISTAKE WAS INVOLVING OTHER PEOPLE! I REALIZED I'D HAVE TO GO IT ALONE.
Yes, on second thought maybe I'll go alone! And then I won't ever tell Marceline about this until years from now when we're locked in some Science Prison, even though we're SUPPOSED to be FRIENDS!
MARCELINE!
FRIENDS SHARE SECRETS, YO!

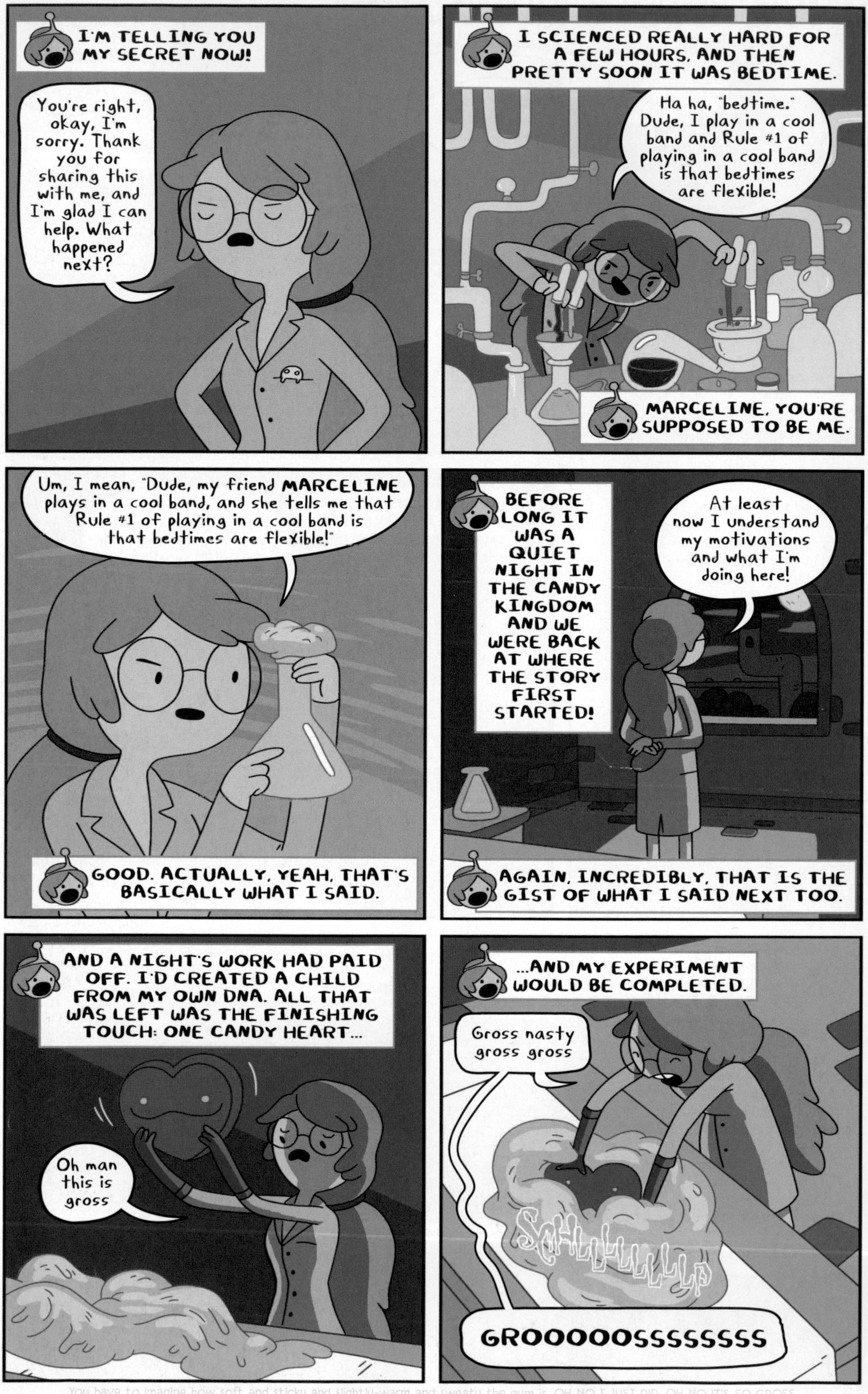
I'M TELLING YOU MY SECRET NOW!
You're right, okay, I'm sorry. Thank you for sharing this with me, and I'm glad I can help. What happened next?
I SCIENCED REALLY HARD FOR A FEW HOURS, AND THEN PRETTY SOON IT WAS BEDTIME.
Ha ha, "bedtime." Dude, I play in a cool band and Rule #1 of playing in a cool band is that bedtimes are flexible!
MARCELINE, YOU'RE SUPPOSED TO BE ME.
Um, I mean, "Dude, my friend MARCELINE plays in a cool band, and she tells me that Rule #1 of playing in a cool band is that bedtimes are flexible!"
GOOD. ACTUALLY, YEAH, THAT'S BASICALLY WHAT I SAID.
BEFORE LONG IT WAS A QUIET NIGHT IN THE CANDY KINGDOM AND WE WERE BACK AT WHERE THE STORY FIRST STARTED!
At least now I understand my motivations and what I'm doing here!
AGAIN, INCREDIBLY, THAT IS THE GIST OF WHAT I SAID NEXT TOO.
AND A NIGHT'S WORK HAD PAID OFF. I'D CREATED A CHILD FROM MY OWN DNA. ALL THAT WAS LEFT WAS THE FINISHING TOUCH: ONE CANDY HEART...
Oh man this is gross
...AND MY EXPERIMENT WOULD BE COMPLETED.
Gross nasty gross gross
GROOOOOSSSSSSSS

You have to imagine how soft and sticky and slightly-warm and sweaty the gum is. OH NO I JUST DID. OH NO IT'S SO GROSS

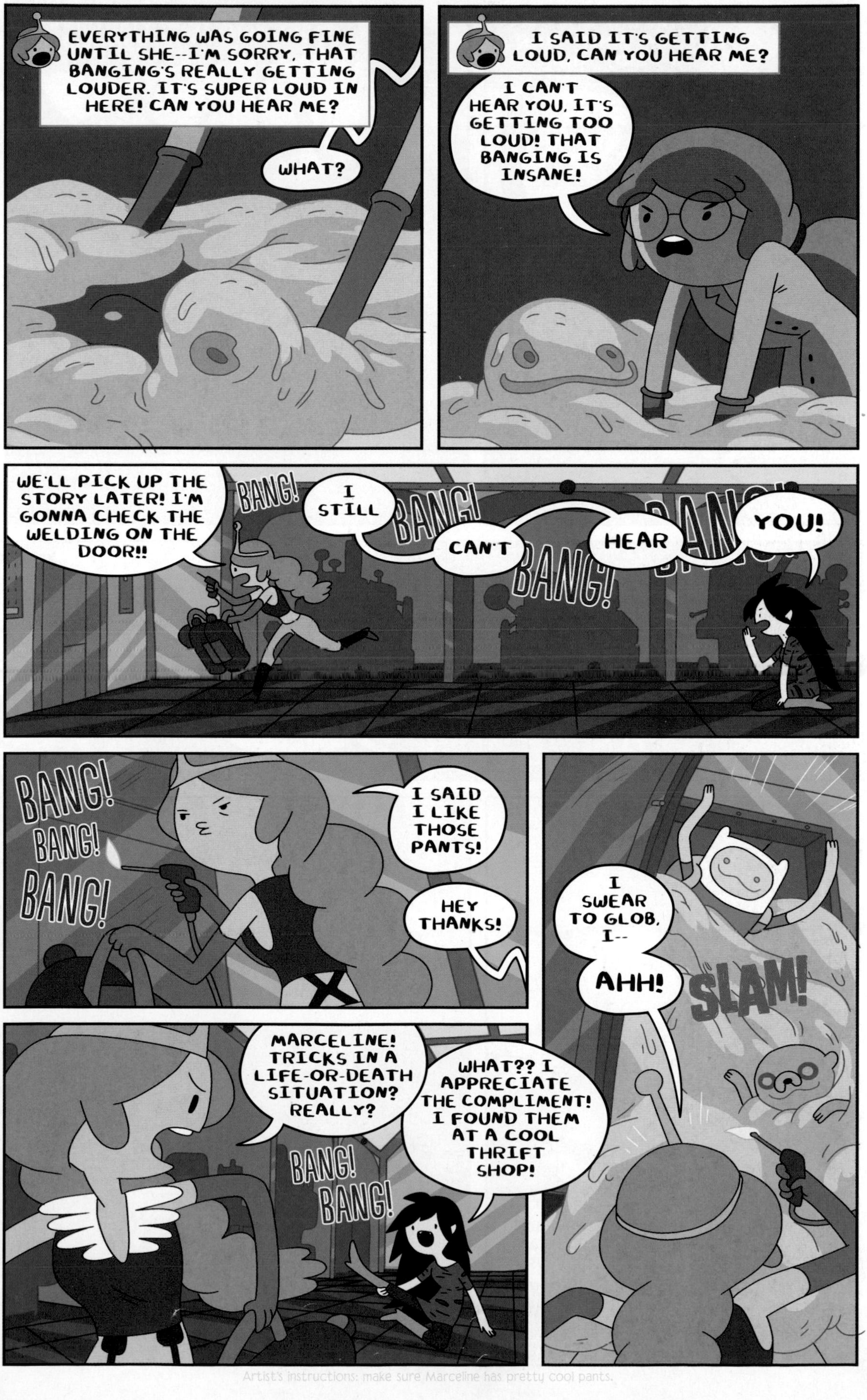
EVERYTHING WAS GOING FINE UNTIL SHE--I'M SORRY, THAT BANGING'S REALLY GETTING LOUDER. IT'S SUPER LOUD IN HERE! CAN YOU HEAR ME?
WHAT?
I SAID IT'S GETTING LOUD, CAN YOU HEAR ME?
I CAN'T HEAR YOU, IT'S GETTING TOO LOUD! THAT BANGING IS INSANE!
WE'LL PICK UP THE STORY LATER! I'M GONNA CHECK THE WELDING ON THE DOOR!!
BANG!
I
STILL
BANG!
CAN'T
BANG!
HEAR
YOU!
BANG!
BANG!
BANG!
I SAID I LIKE THOSE PANTS!
HEY THANKS!
I SWEAR TO GLOB, I--
AHH!
SLAM!
MARCELINE! TRICKS IN A LIFE-OR-DEATH SITUATION? REALLY?
BANG!
BANG!
WHAT?? I APPRECIATE THE COMPLIMENT! I FOUND THEM AT A COOL THRIFT SHOP!

Artist's instructions: make sure Marceline has pretty cool pants.

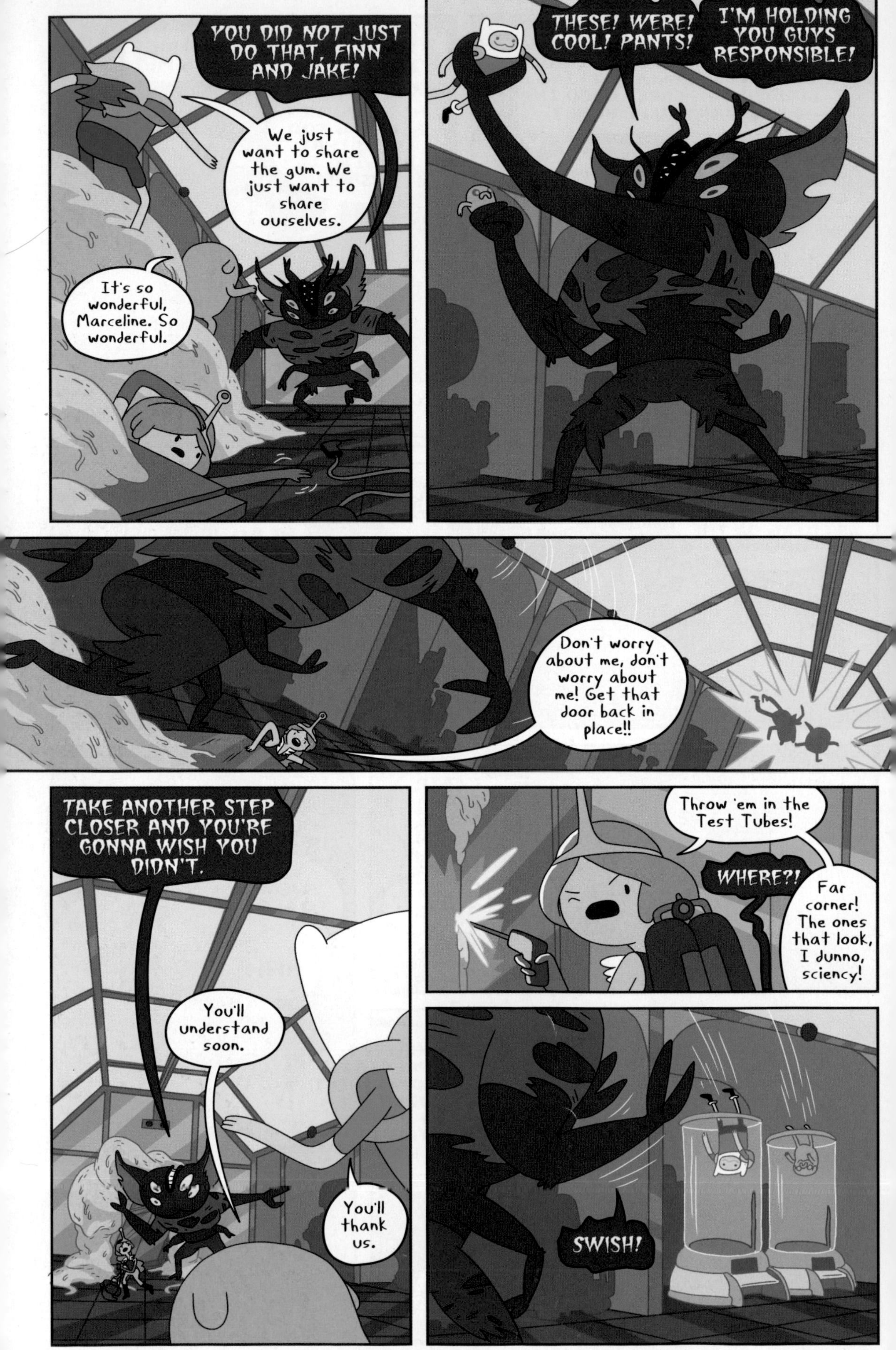
YOU DID NOT JUST DO THAT, FINN AND JAKE!
We just want to share the gum. We just want to share ourselves.
It's so wonderful, Marceline. So wonderful.
THESE! WERE! COOL! PANTS!
I'M HOLDING YOU GUYS RESPONSIBLE!
Don't worry about me, don't worry about me! Get that door back in place!!
TAKE ANOTHER STEP CLOSER AND YOU'RE GONNA WISH YOU DIDN'T.
You'll understand soon.
You'll thank us.
Throw 'em in the Test Tubes!
WHERE?!
Far corner! The ones that look, I dunno, sciency!
SWISH!

Take another step closer and you're gonna wish I'd been distracted and, during that distraction, not noticed you taking that step closer.

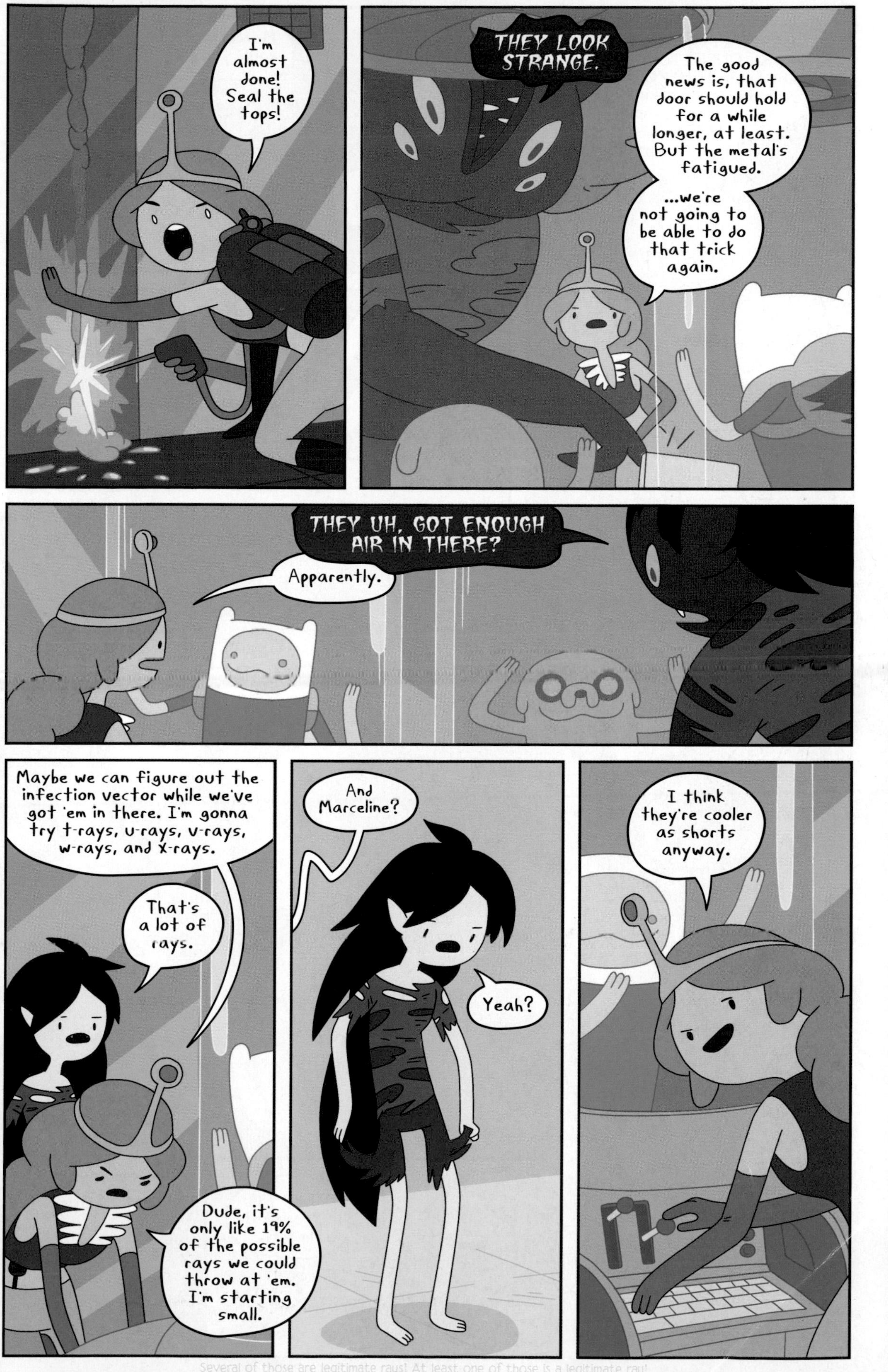
I'm almost done! Seal the tops!
THEY LOOK STRANGE.
The good news is, that door should hold for a while longer, at least. But the metal's fatigued.
...we're not going to be able to do that trick again.
THEY UH, GOT ENOUGH AIR IN THERE?
Apparently.
Maybe we can figure out the infection vector while we've got 'em in there. I'm gonna try t-rays, u-rays, v-rays, w-rays, and x-rays.
That's a lot of rays.
Dude, it's only like 19% of the possible rays we could throw at 'em. I'm starting small.
And Marceline?
Yeah?
I think they're cooler as shorts anyway.

Several of those are legitimate rays! At least one of those is a legitimate ray!

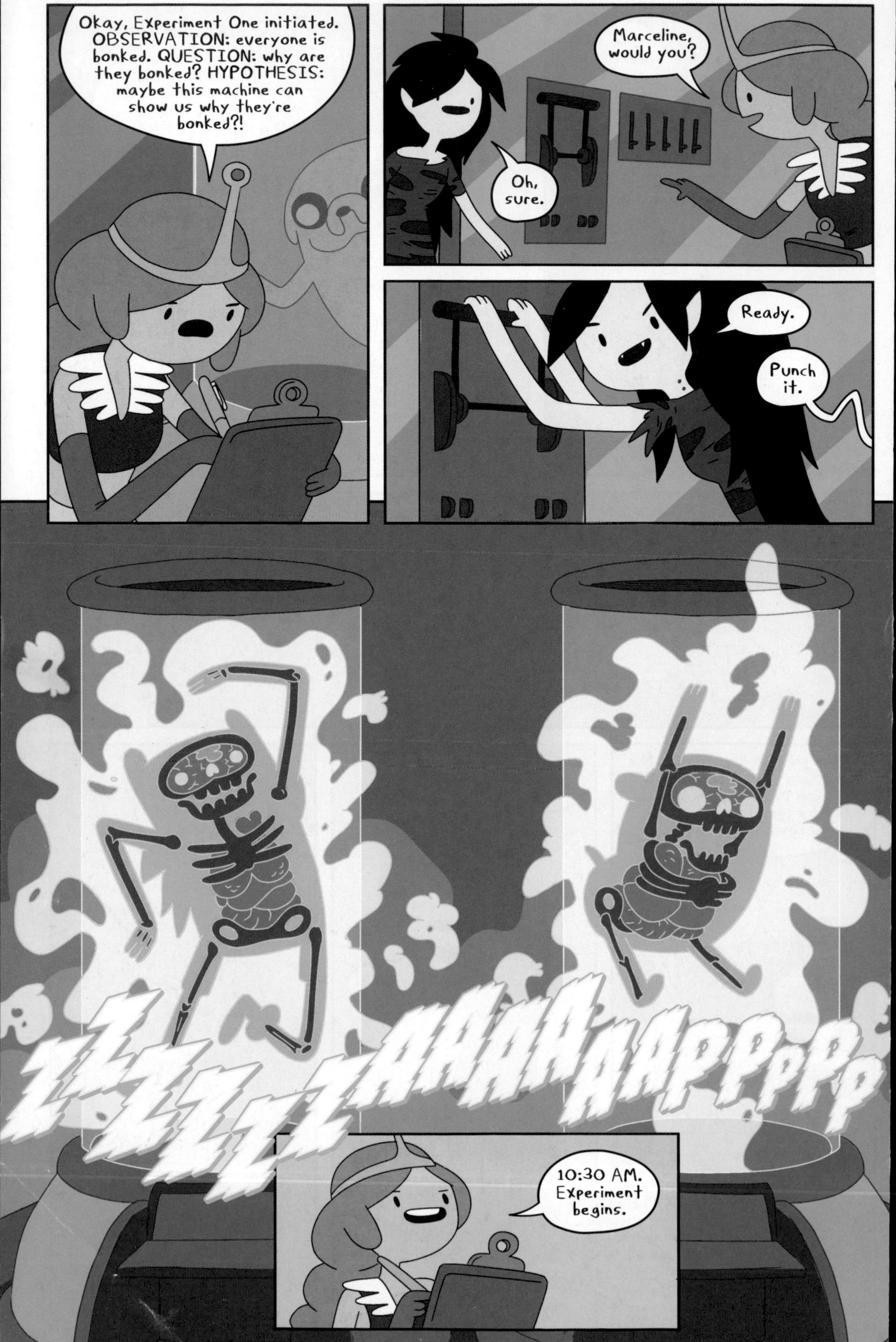
Okay, Experiment One initiated. OBSERVATION: everyone is bonked. QUESTION: why are they bonked? HYPOTHESIS: maybe this machine can show us why they're bonked?!
Marceline, would you?
Oh, sure.
Ready.
Punch it.
ZZZZZZZAAAAAAAPPPPP
10:30 AM. Experiment begins.

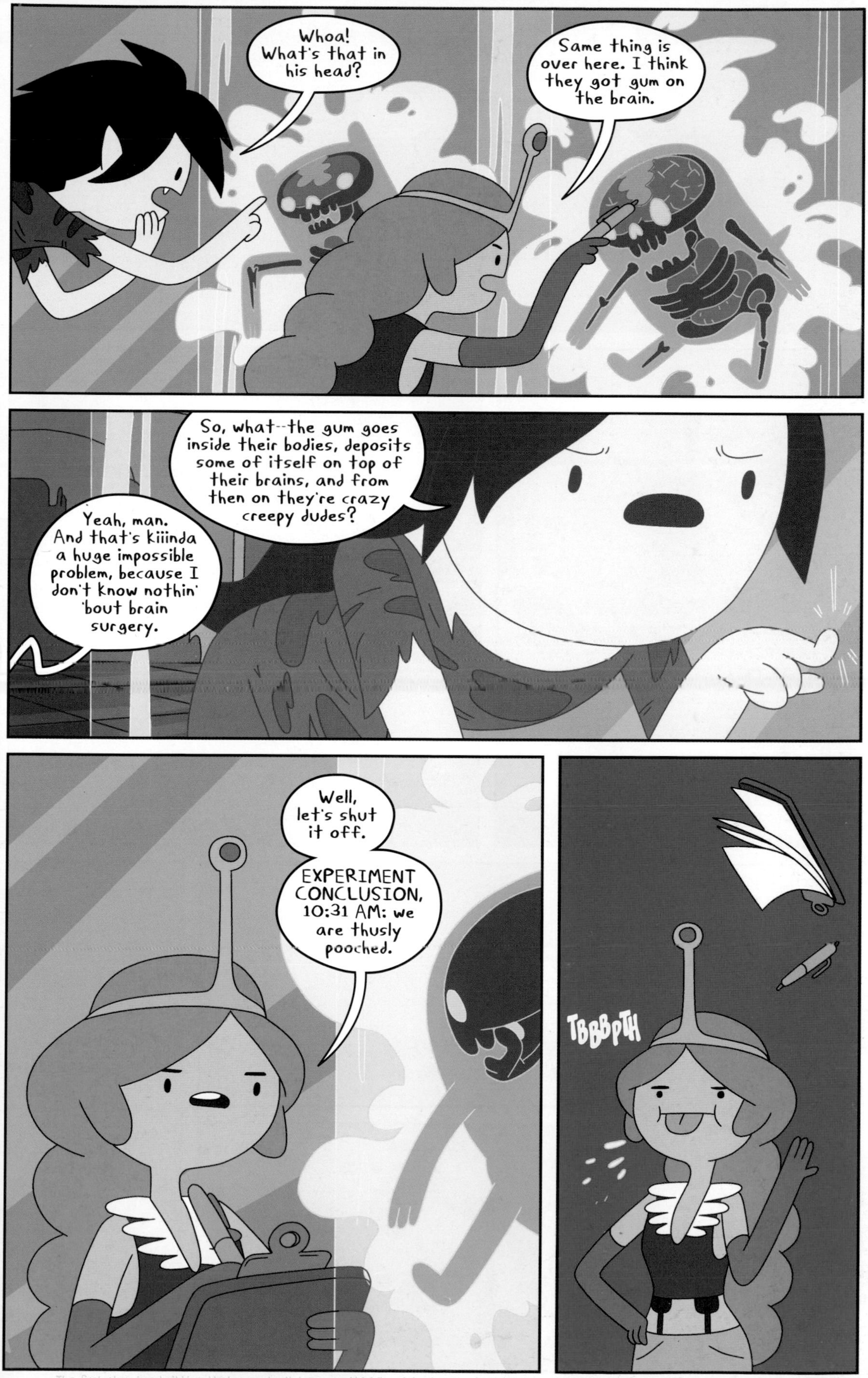
Whoa! What's that in his head?
Same thing is over here. I think they got gum on the brain.
So, what--the gum goes inside their bodies, deposits some of itself on top of their brains, and from then on they're crazy creepy dudes?
Yeah, man. And that's kiiinda a huge impossible problem, because I don't know nothin' 'bout brain surgery.
Well, let's shut it off.
EXPERIMENT CONCLUSION, 10:31 AM: we are thusly pooched.
TBBBPTH

The first step is admitting that you don't know nothin' 'bout brain surgery. I think next step is to not do brain surgery after all?

Well, at least they look happy. That's something to look forward to.

Woo hoo.

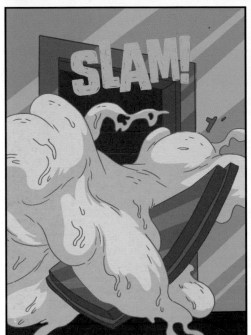

SLAM!

CRASH

Welp, I think this is it. Marcy, it has been an honor and a privilege to trap us both in this steel prison from which there is no escape.

Thank you.

NOPE.

GULP!

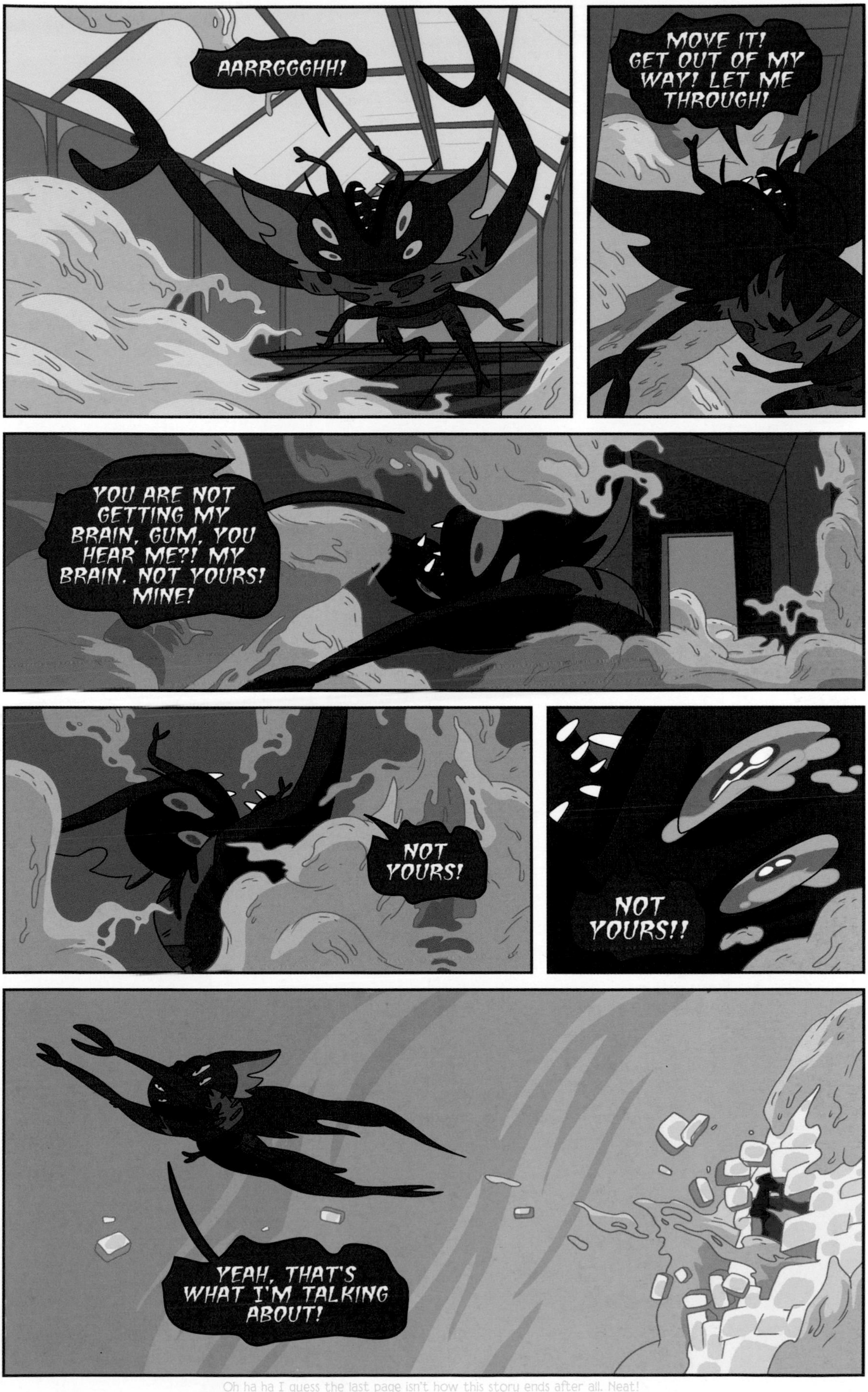
AARRGGGHH!
MOVE IT! GET OUT OF MY WAY! LET ME THROUGH!
YOU ARE NOT GETTING MY BRAIN, GUM, YOU HEAR ME?! MY BRAIN. NOT YOURS! MINE!
NOT YOURS!
NOT YOURS!!
YEAH, THAT'S WHAT I'M TALKING ABOUT!

Oh ha ha I guess the last page isn't how this story ends after all. Neat!

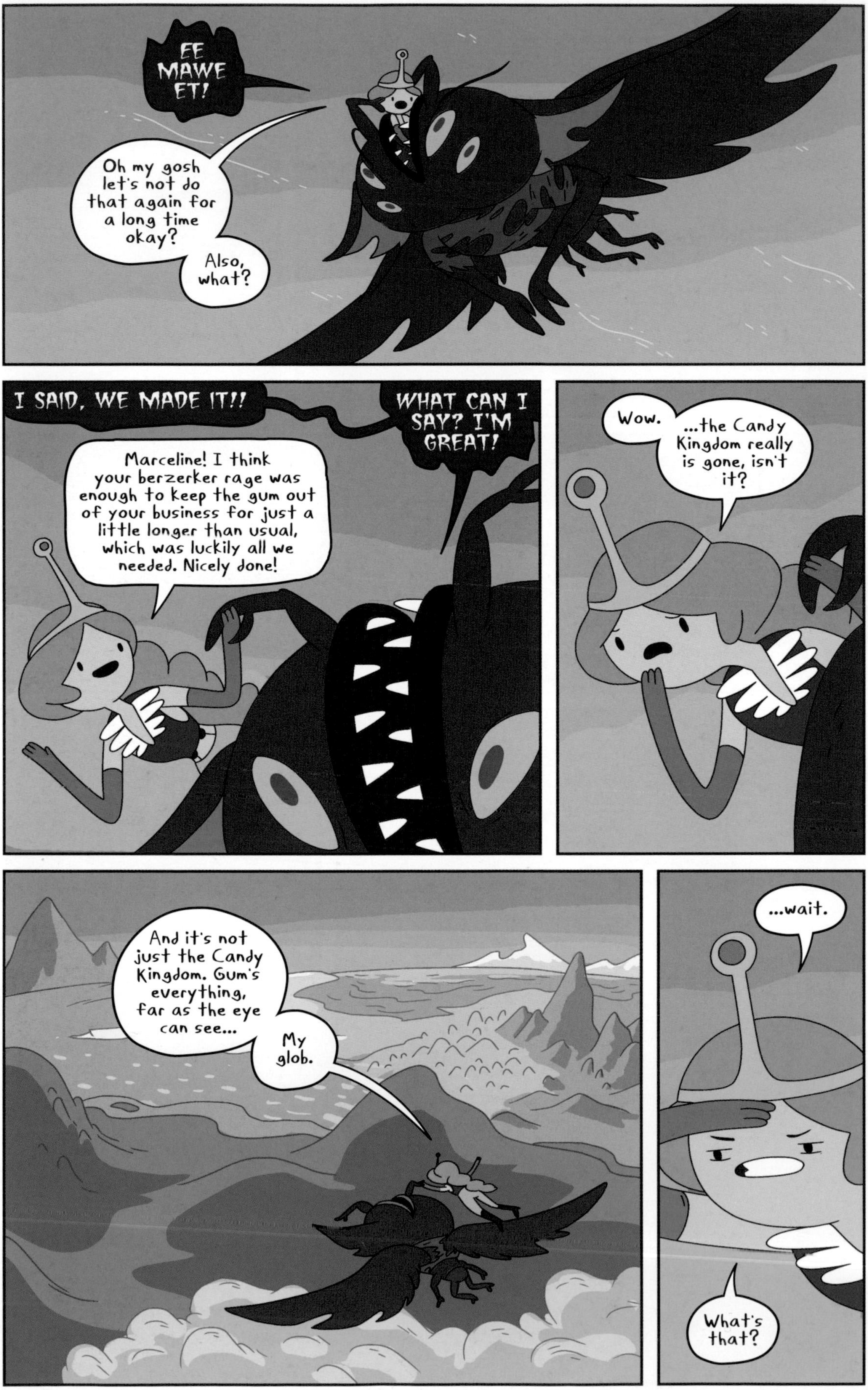
EE MAWE ET!
Oh my gosh let's not do that again for a long time okay?
Also, what?
I SAID, WE MADE IT!!
WHAT CAN I SAY? I'M GREAT!
Marceline! I think your berzerker rage was enough to keep the gum out of your business for just a little longer than usual, which was luckily all we needed. Nicely done!
Wow.
...the Candy Kingdom really is gone, isn't it?
And it's not just the Candy Kingdom. Gum's everything, far as the eye can see...
My glob.
...wait.
What's that?

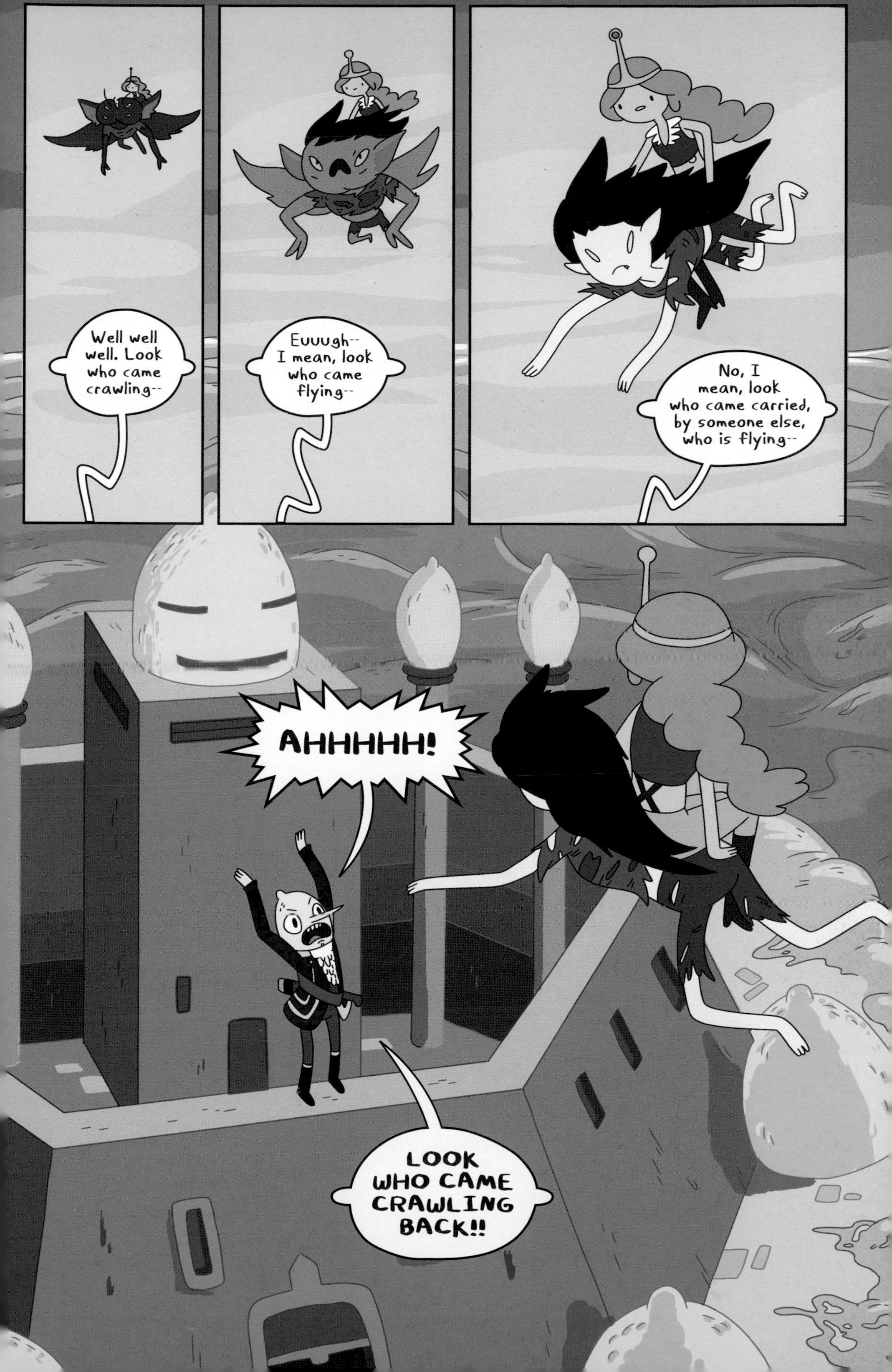
Well well well. Look who came crawling--
Euuugh-- I mean, look who came flying--
No, I mean, look who came carried, by someone else, who is flying--
AHHHHH!
LOOK WHO CAME CRAWLING BACK!!

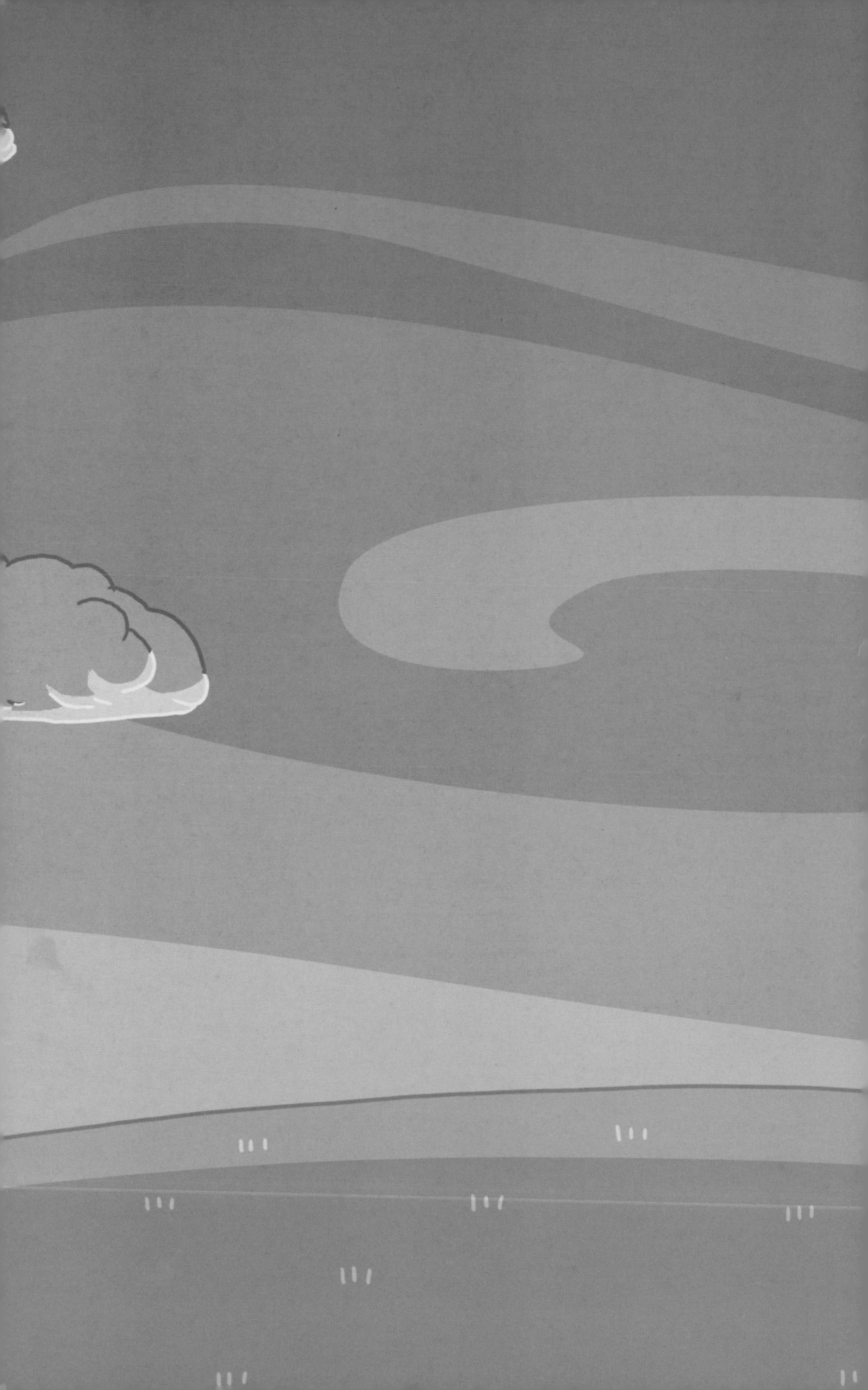

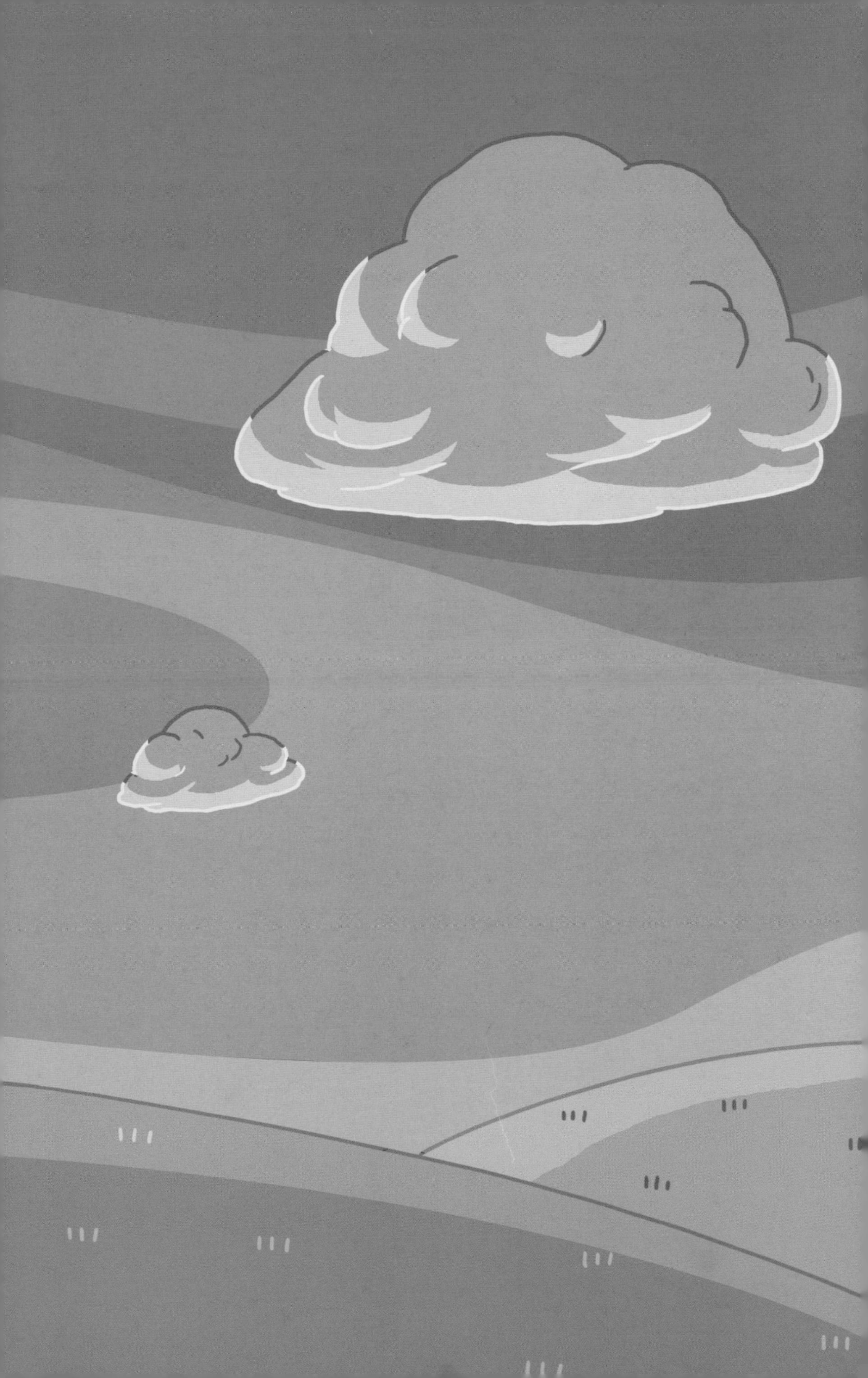

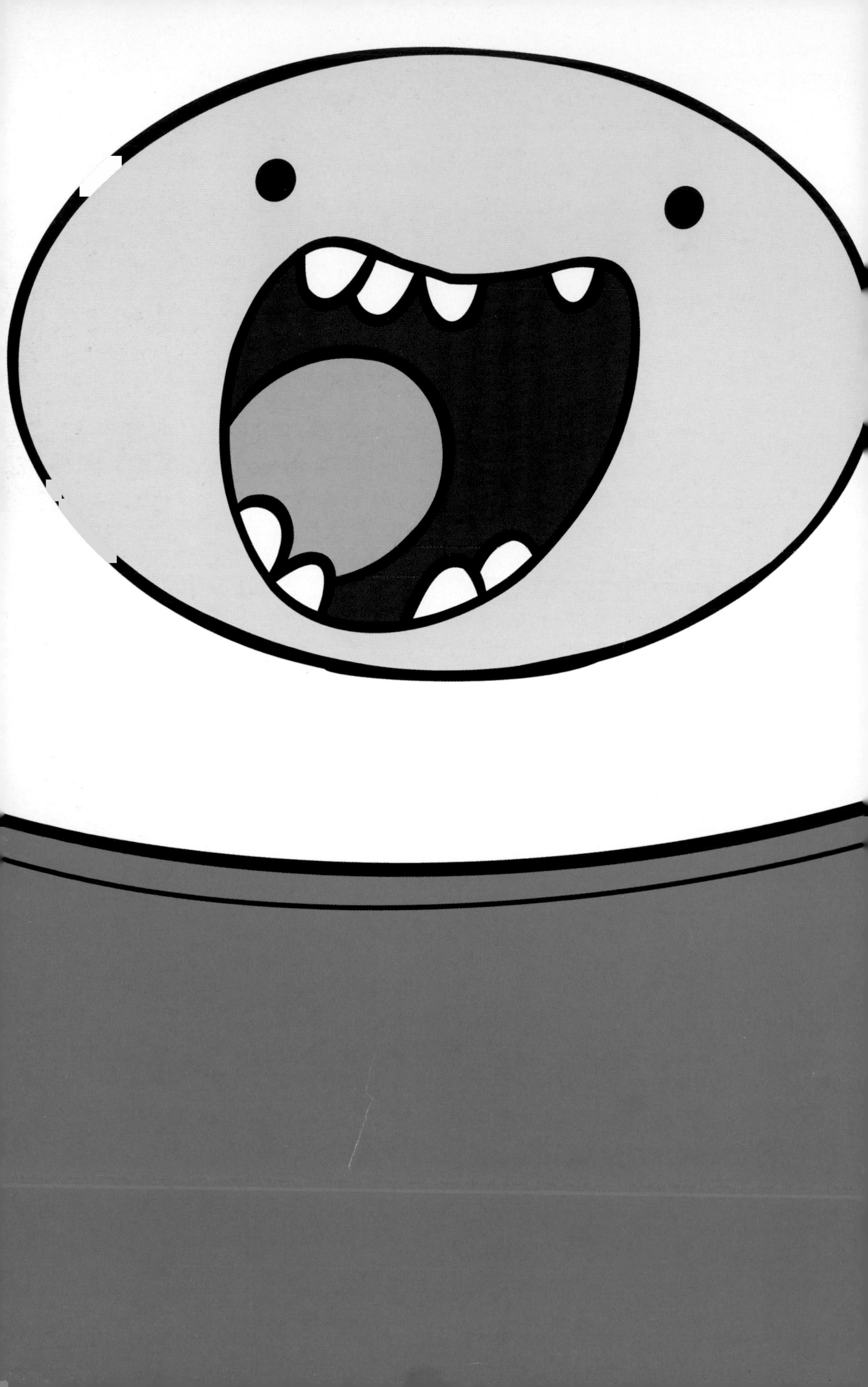

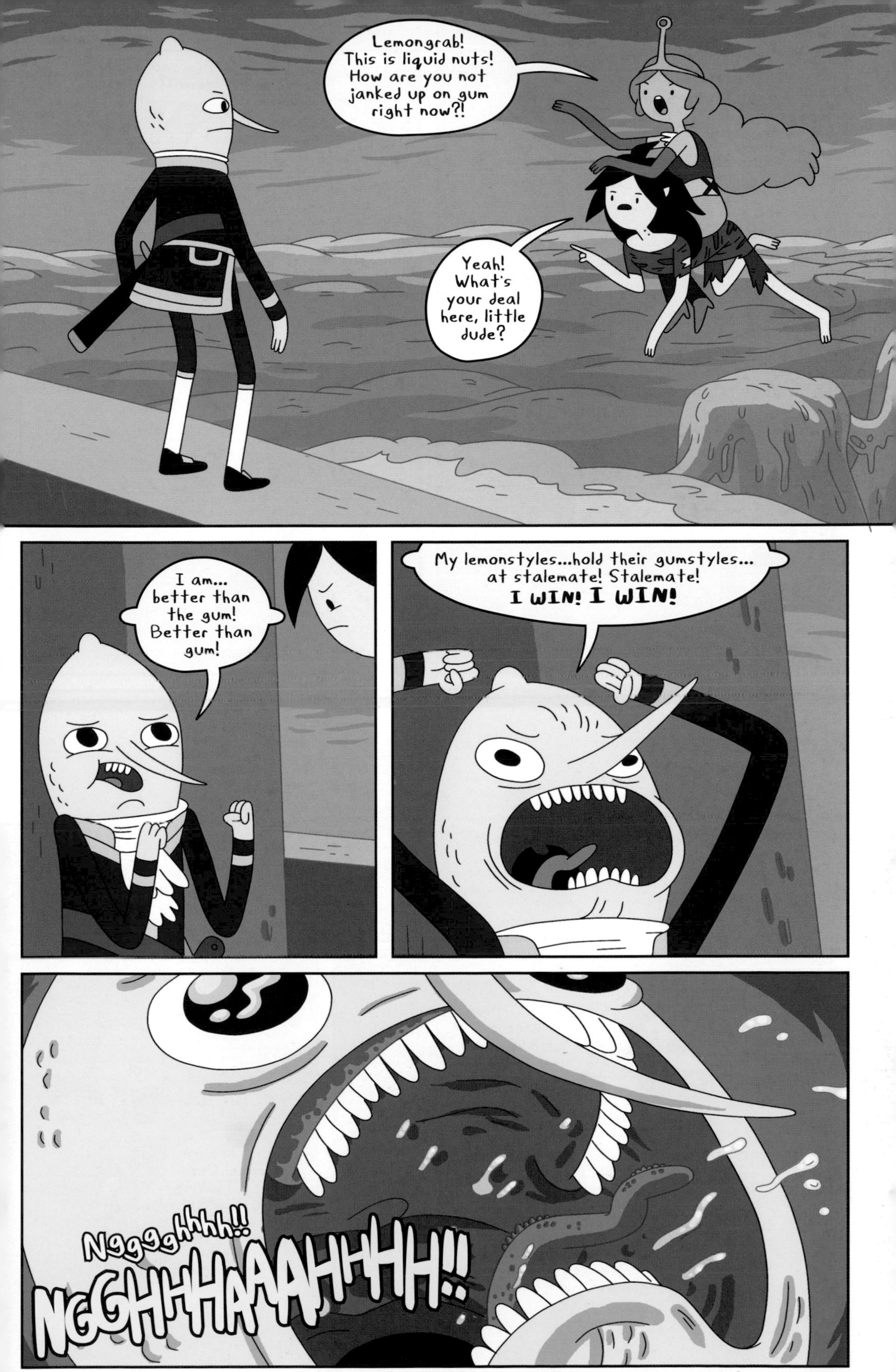
Lemongrab! This is liquid nuts! How are you not janked up on gum right now?!
Yeah! What's your deal here, little dude?
I am... better than the gum! Better than gum!
My lemonstyles...hold their gumstyles... at stalemate! Stalemate! I WIN! I WIN!
Ngggghhhh!!
NGGHHHAAAHHHH!!

ave an editor here, so you'll just have to imagine the next twenty-five pages that we had to cut. Anyway they were 100% Lemongrab screaming in a variety of ways both subtle and gross.

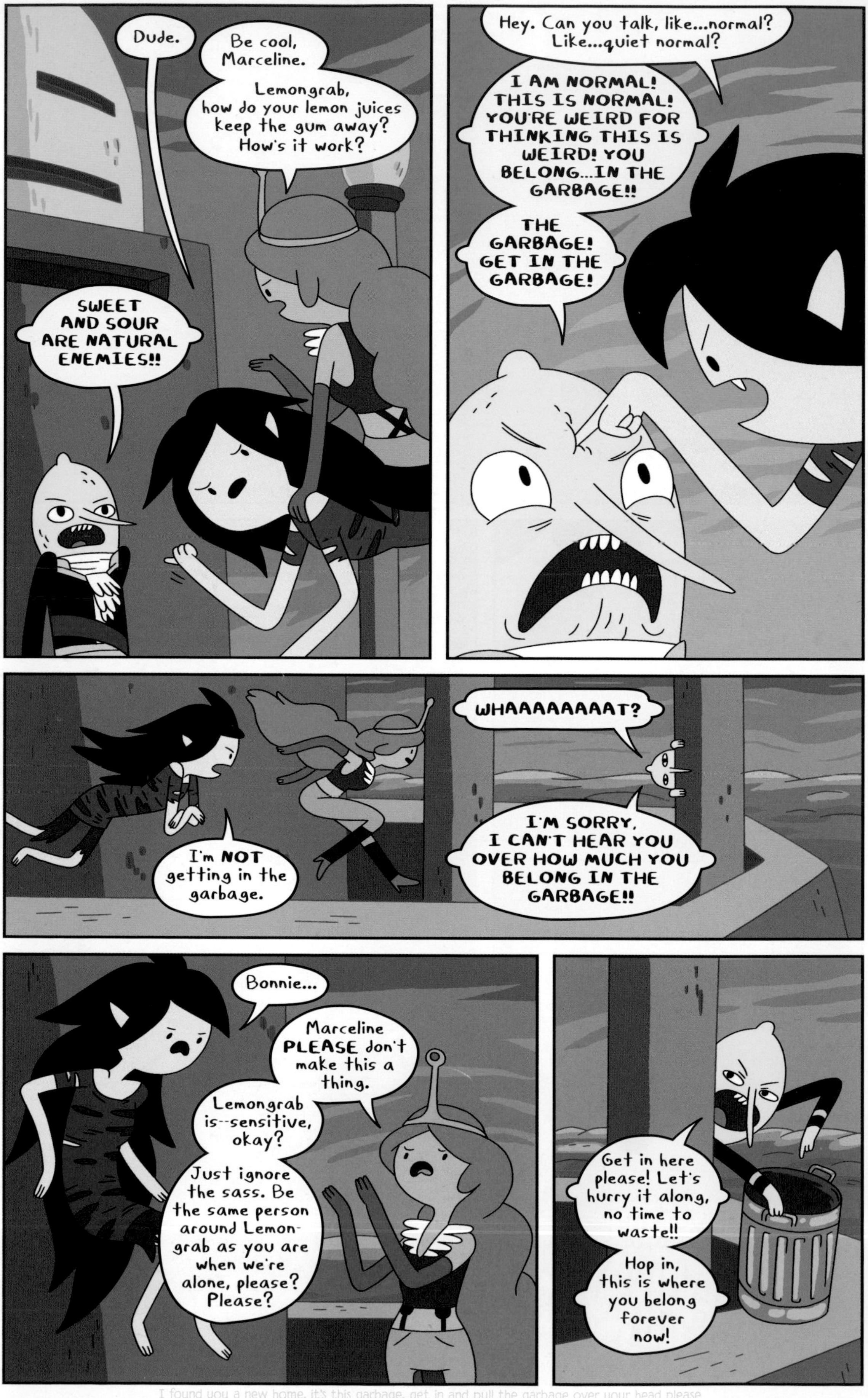
Dude.
Be cool, Marceline.
Lemongrab, how do your lemon juices keep the gum away? How's it work?
SWEET AND SOUR ARE NATURAL ENEMIES!!
Hey. Can you talk, like...normal? Like...quiet normal?
I AM NORMAL! THIS IS NORMAL! YOU'RE WEIRD FOR THINKING THIS IS WEIRD! YOU BELONG...IN THE GARBAGE!!
THE GARBAGE! GET IN THE GARBAGE!
I'm NOT getting in the garbage.
WHAAAAAAAAT?
I'M SORRY, I CAN'T HEAR YOU OVER HOW MUCH YOU BELONG IN THE GARBAGE!!
Bonnie...
Marceline PLEASE don't make this a thing.
Lemongrab is--sensitive, okay?
Just ignore the sass. Be the same person around Lemongrab as you are when we're alone, please? Please?
Get in here please! Let's hurry it along, no time to waste!!
Hop in, this is where you belong forever now!

I found you a new home, it's this garbage, get in and pull the garbage over your head please

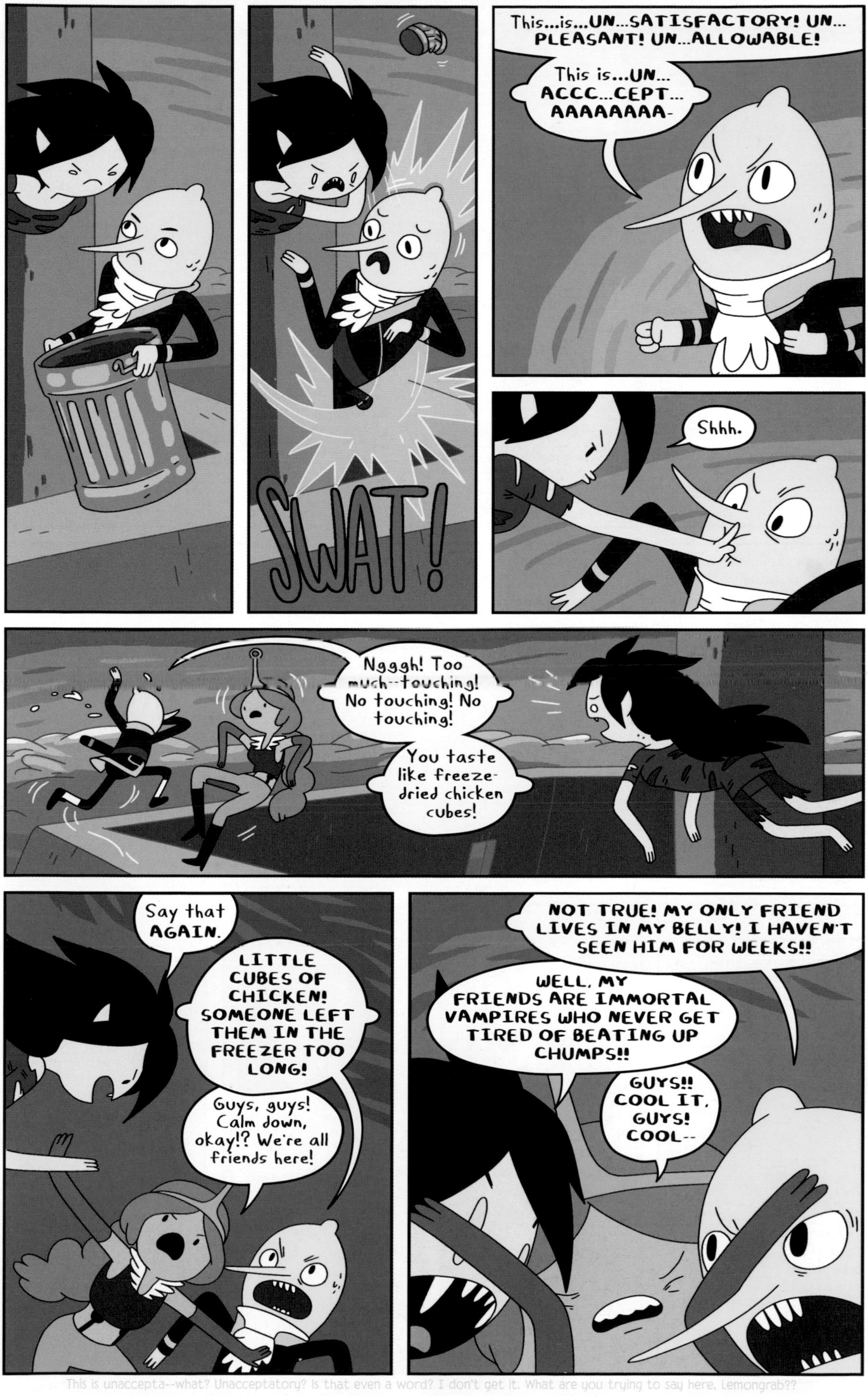
SWAT!
This...is...UN...SATISFACTORY! UN... PLEASANT! UN...ALLOWABLE!
This is...UN... ACCC...CEPT... AAAAAAAA-
Shhh.
Ngggh! Too much--touching! No touching! No touching!
You taste like freeze-dried chicken cubes!
Say that AGAIN.
LITTLE CUBES OF CHICKEN! SOMEONE LEFT THEM IN THE FREEZER TOO LONG!
Guys, guys! Calm down, okay!? We're all friends here!
NOT TRUE! MY ONLY FRIEND LIVES IN MY BELLY! I HAVEN'T SEEN HIM FOR WEEKS!!
WELL, MY FRIENDS ARE IMMORTAL VAMPIRES WHO NEVER GET TIRED OF BEATING UP CHUMPS!!
GUYS!! COOL IT, GUYS! COOL--

This is unaccepta--what? Unacceptatory? Is that even a word? I don't get it. What are you trying to say here, Lemongrab??

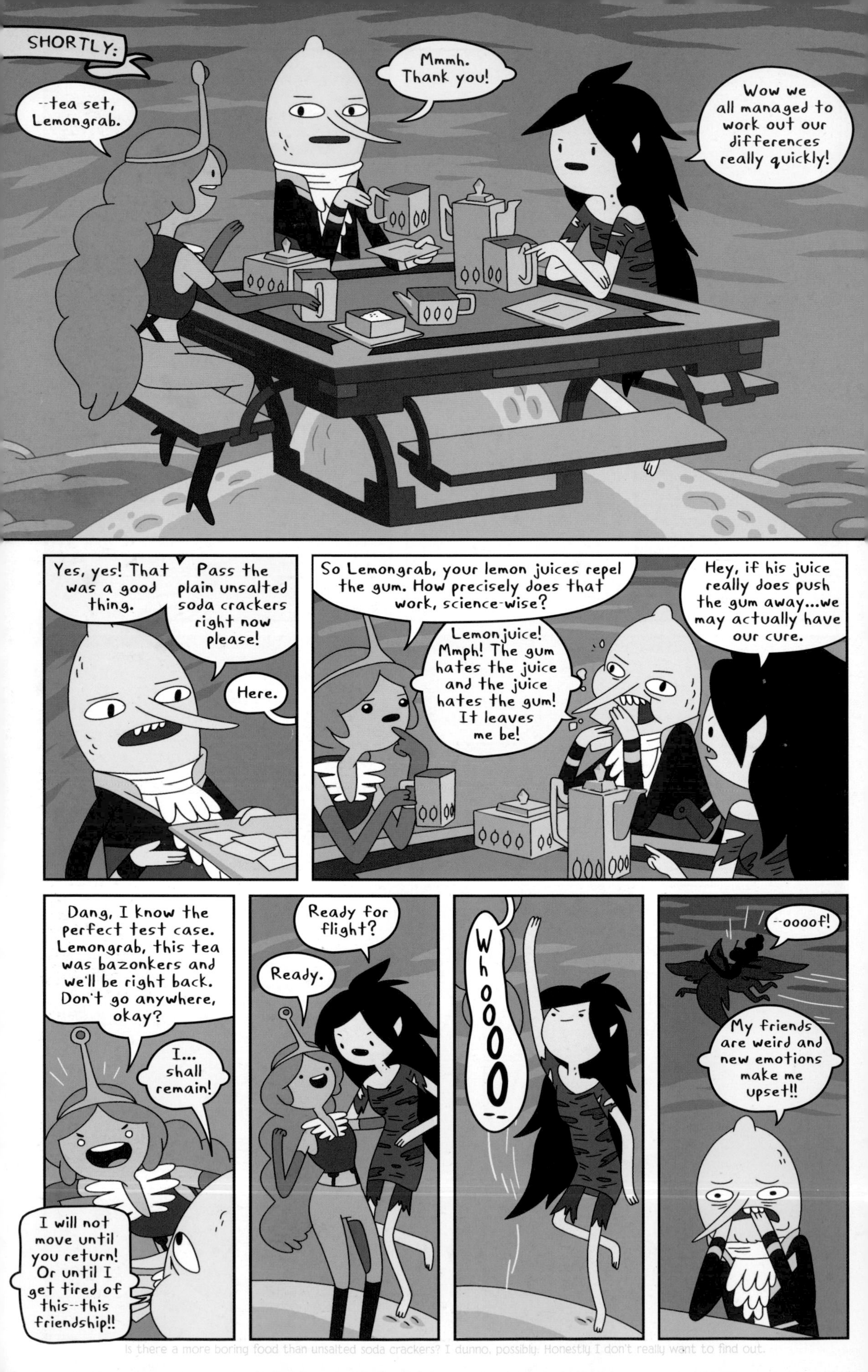
SHORTLY:
--tea set, Lemongrab.
Mmmh. Thank you!
Wow we all managed to work out our differences really quickly!
Yes, yes! That was a good thing.
Pass the plain unsalted soda crackers right now please!
Here.
So Lemongrab, your lemon juices repel the gum. How precisely does that work, science-wise?
Lemonjuice! Mmph! The gum hates the juice and the juice hates the gum! It leaves me be!
Hey, if his juice really does push the gum away...we may actually have our cure.
Dang, I know the perfect test case. Lemongrab, this tea was bazonkers and we'll be right back. Don't go anywhere, okay?
I... shall remain!
I will not move until you return! Or until I get tired of this--this friendship!!
Ready for flight?
Ready.
WhoOOO--
--oooof!
My friends are weird and new emotions make me upset!!

Is there a more boring food than unsalted soda crackers? I dunno, possibly. Honestly I don't really want to find out.

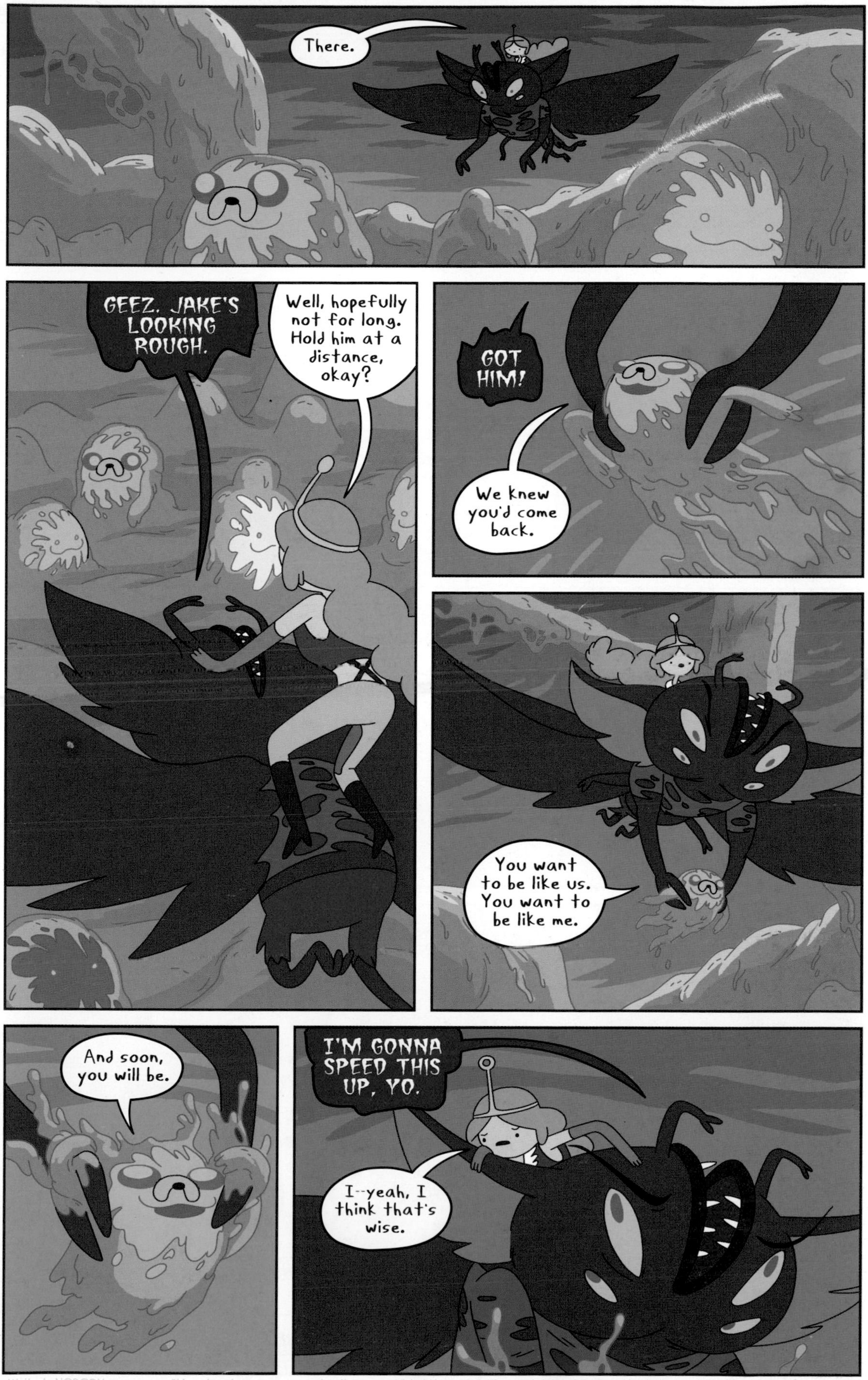
There.
GEEZ. JAKE'S LOOKING ROUGH.
Well, hopefully not for long. Hold him at a distance, okay?
GOT HIM!
We knew you'd come back.
You want to be like us. You want to be like me.
And soon, you will be.
I'M GONNA SPEED THIS UP, YO.
I--yeah, I think that's wise.

Wait--is NOBODY gonna say "time to chew you up and spit you out" to the gum? Finn and Jake dropped the ball, guys! That line is up for grabs!!

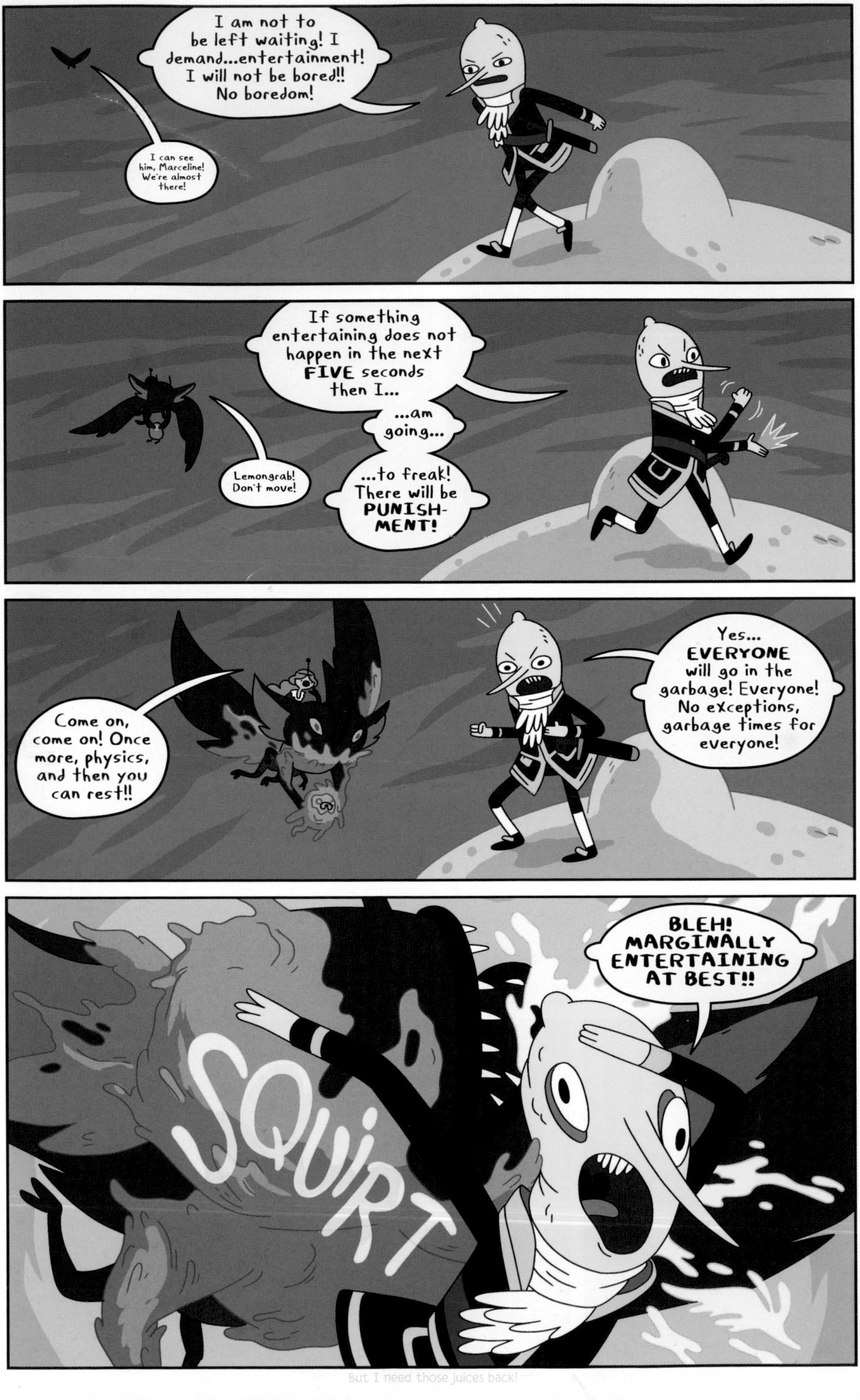
I am not to be left waiting! I demand...entertainment! I will not be bored!! No boredom!
I can see him, Marceline! We're almost there!
If something entertaining does not happen in the next FIVE seconds then I...
...am going...
...to freak! There will be PUNISHMENT!
Lemongrab! Don't move!
Come on, come on! Once more, physics, and then you can rest!!
Yes... EVERYONE will go in the garbage! Everyone! No exceptions, garbage times for everyone!
BLEH! MARGINALLY ENTERTAINING AT BEST!!
SQUIRT

But I need those juices back!

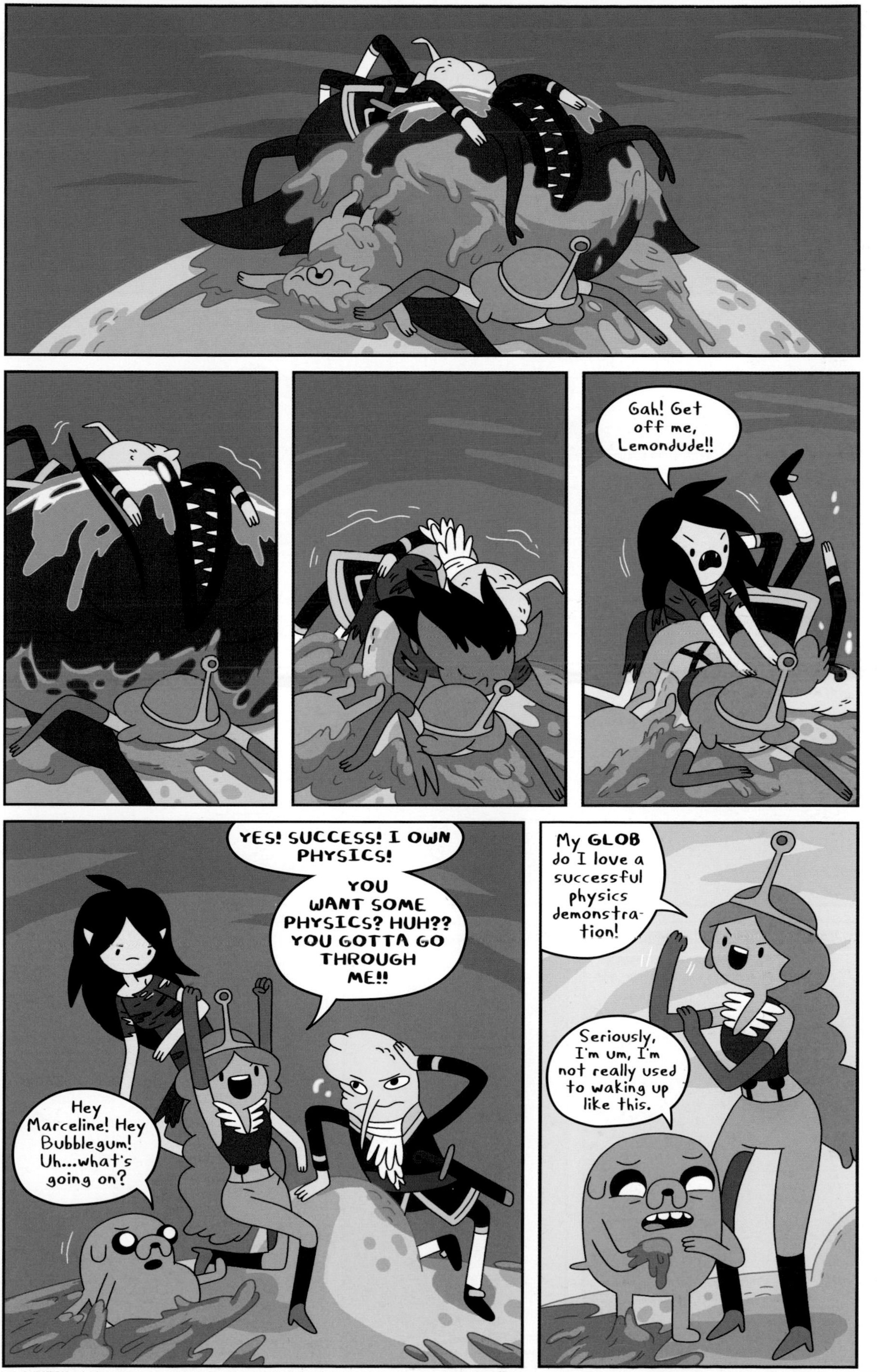
Gah! Get off me, Lemondude!!
YES! SUCCESS! I OWN PHYSICS!
YOU WANT SOME PHYSICS? HUH?? YOU GOTTA GO THROUGH ME!!
Hey Marceline! Hey Bubblegum! Uh...what's going on?
My GLOB do I love a successful physics demonstra-tion!
Seriously, I'm um, I'm not really used to waking up like this.

ERIOUS QUESTION: why is not every Adventure Time comic just all the characters being strong and showing off their muscles?? Did I mess up by not making this happen? I think maybe I did??

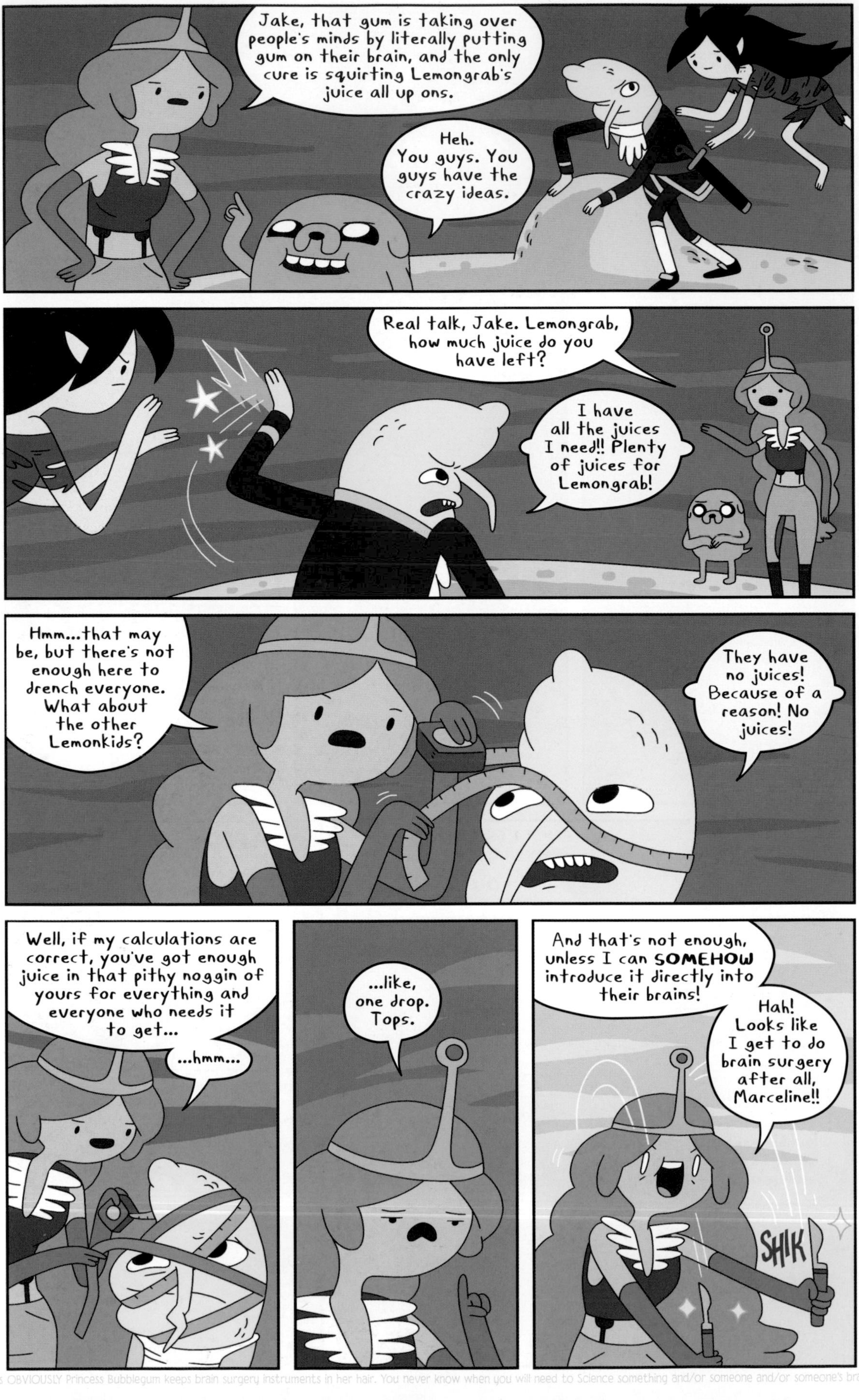

Jake, that gum is taking over people's minds by literally putting gum on their brain, and the only cure is squirting Lemongrab's juice all up ons.
Heh. You guys. You guys have the crazy ideas.
Real talk, Jake. Lemongrab, how much juice do you have left?
I have all the juices I need!! Plenty of juices for Lemongrab!
Hmm...that may be, but there's not enough here to drench everyone. What about the other Lemonkids?
They have no juices! Because of a reason! No juices!
Well, if my calculations are correct, you've got enough juice in that pithy noggin of yours for everything and everyone who needs it to get...
...hmm...
...like, one drop. Tops.
And that's not enough, unless I can **SOMEHOW** introduce it directly into their brains!
Hah! Looks like I get to do brain surgery after all, Marceline!!
SHIK

Yes OBVIOUSLY Princess Bubblegum keeps brain surgery instruments in her hair. You never know when you will need to Science something and/or someone and/or someone's brain!

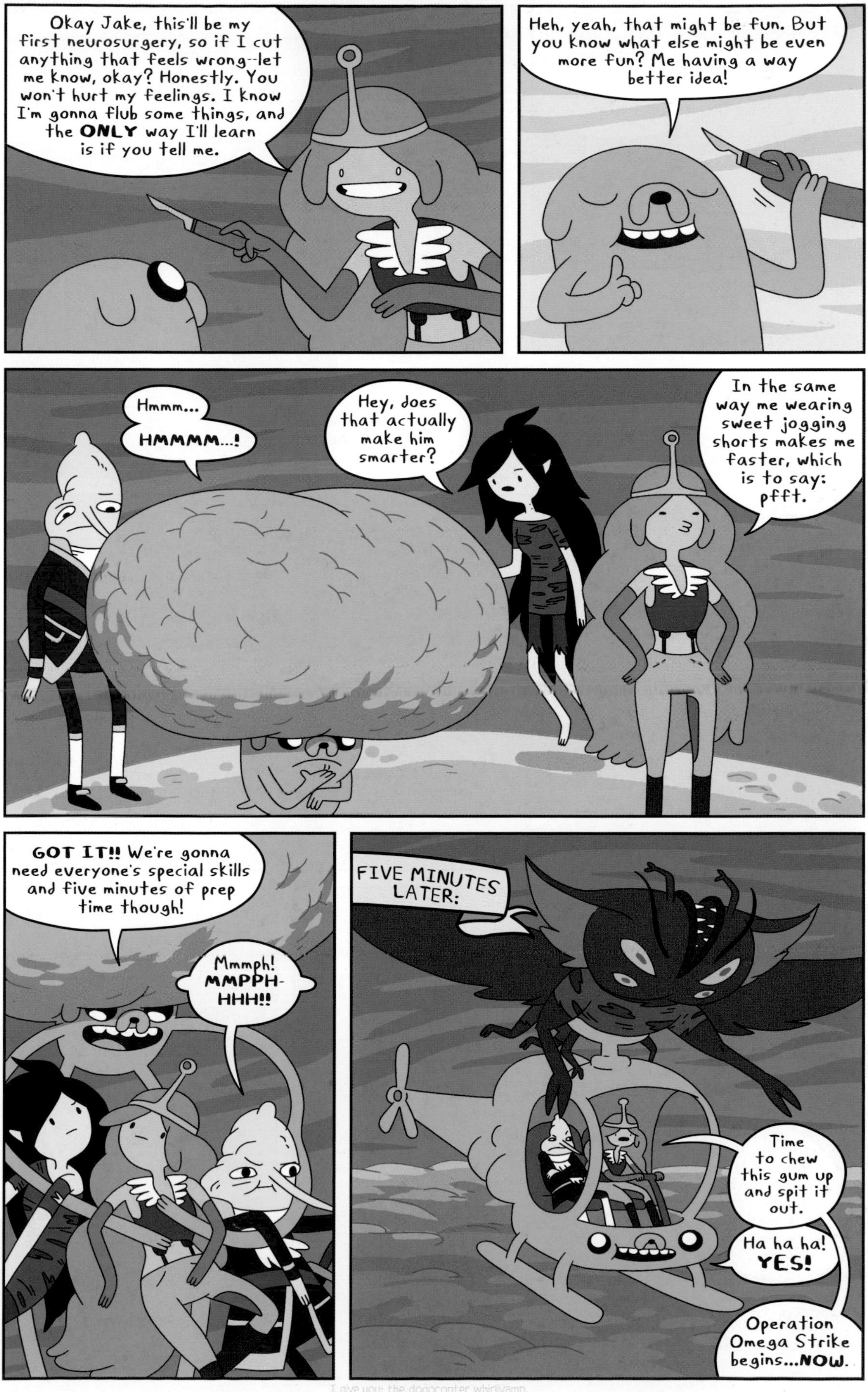
Okay Jake, this'll be my first neurosurgery, so if I cut anything that feels wrong--let me know, okay? Honestly. You won't hurt my feelings. I know I'm gonna flub some things, and the ONLY way I'll learn is if you tell me.
Heh, yeah, that might be fun. But you know what else might be even more fun? Me having a way better idea!
Hmmm... HMMMM...!
Hey, does that actually make him smarter?
In the same way me wearing sweet jogging shorts makes me faster, which is to say: pfft.
GOT IT!! We're gonna need everyone's special skills and five minutes of prep time though!
Mmmph! MMPPH-HHH!!
FIVE MINUTES LATER:
Time to chew this gum up and spit it out.
Ha ha ha! YES!
Operation Omega Strike begins...NOW.

I give you: the dogocopter whirlivamp.

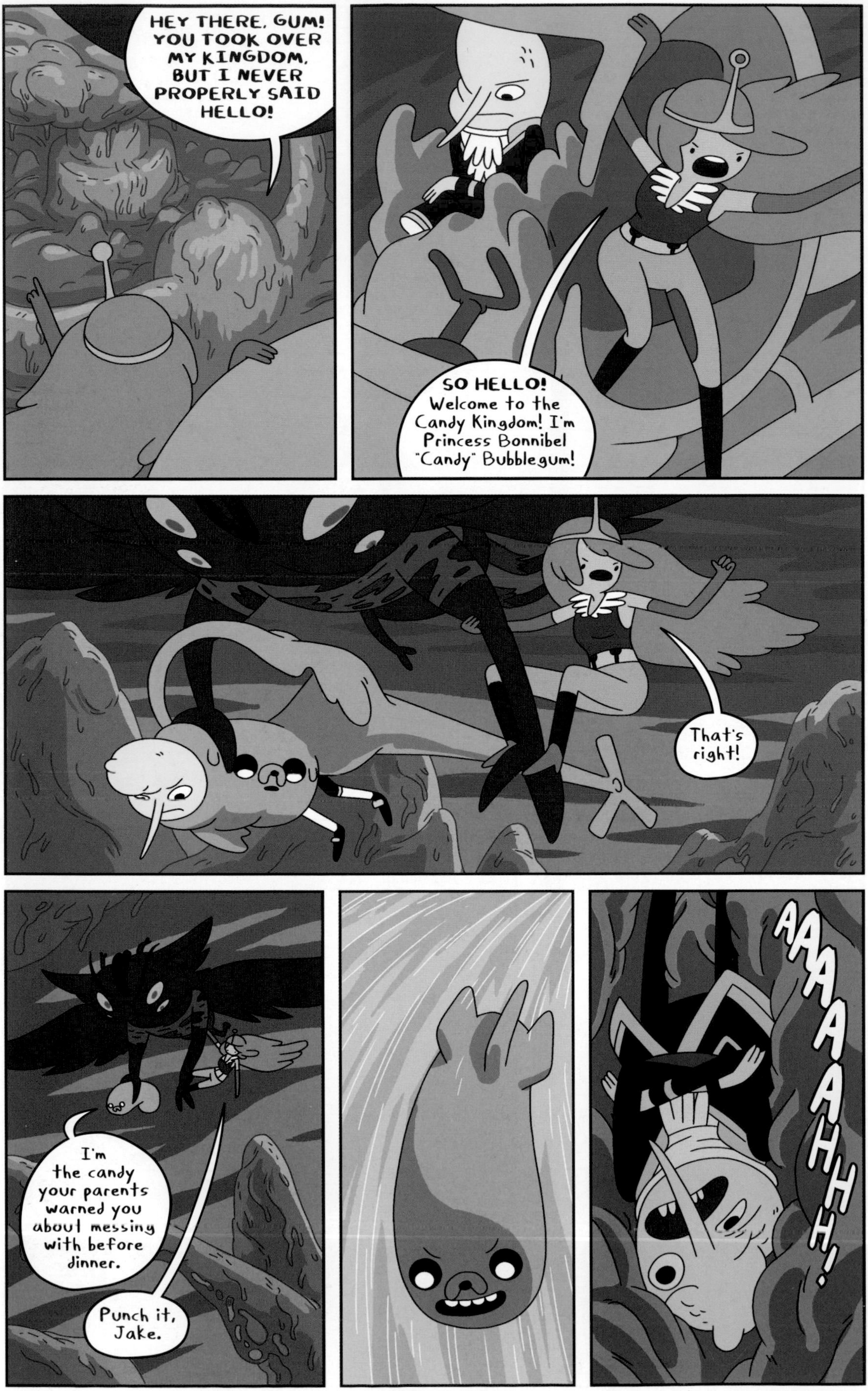
HEY THERE, GUM! YOU TOOK OVER MY KINGDOM, BUT I NEVER PROPERLY SAID HELLO!
SO HELLO! Welcome to the Candy Kingdom! I'm Princess Bonnibel "Candy" Bubblegum!
That's right!
I'm the candy your parents warned you about messing with before dinner.
Punch it, Jake.
AAAAAAAHHH!

Yeah, PB's special skill here is Talking Trash and Throwing Shade. It's a valuable skillset, yo!

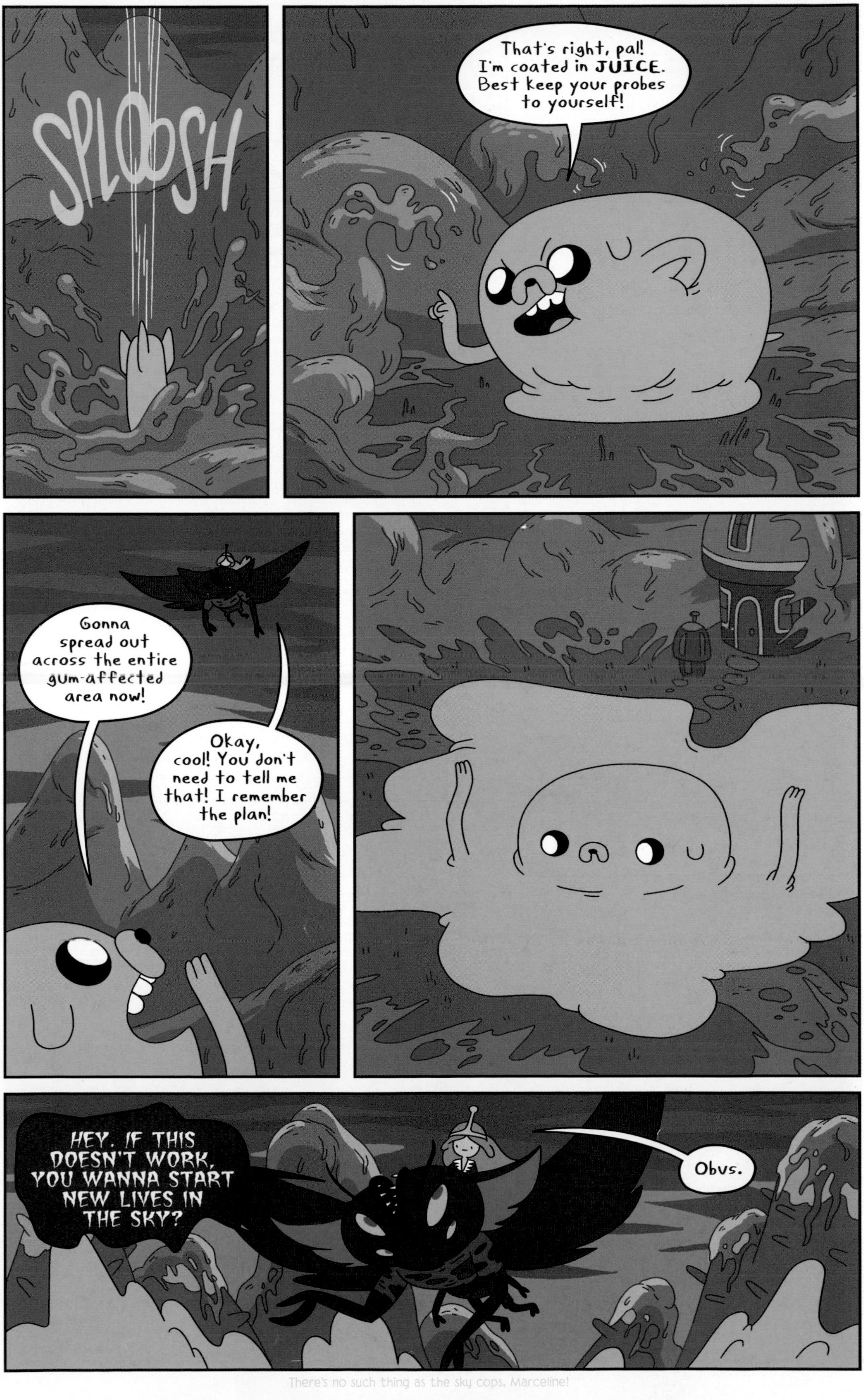
SPLOOSH
That's right, pal! I'm coated in JUICE. Best keep your probes to yourself!
Gonna spread out across the entire gum-affected area now!
Okay, cool! You don't need to tell me that! I remember the plan!
HEY. IF THIS DOESN'T WORK, YOU WANNA START NEW LIVES IN THE SKY?
Obvs.

There's no such thing as the sky cops, Marceline!

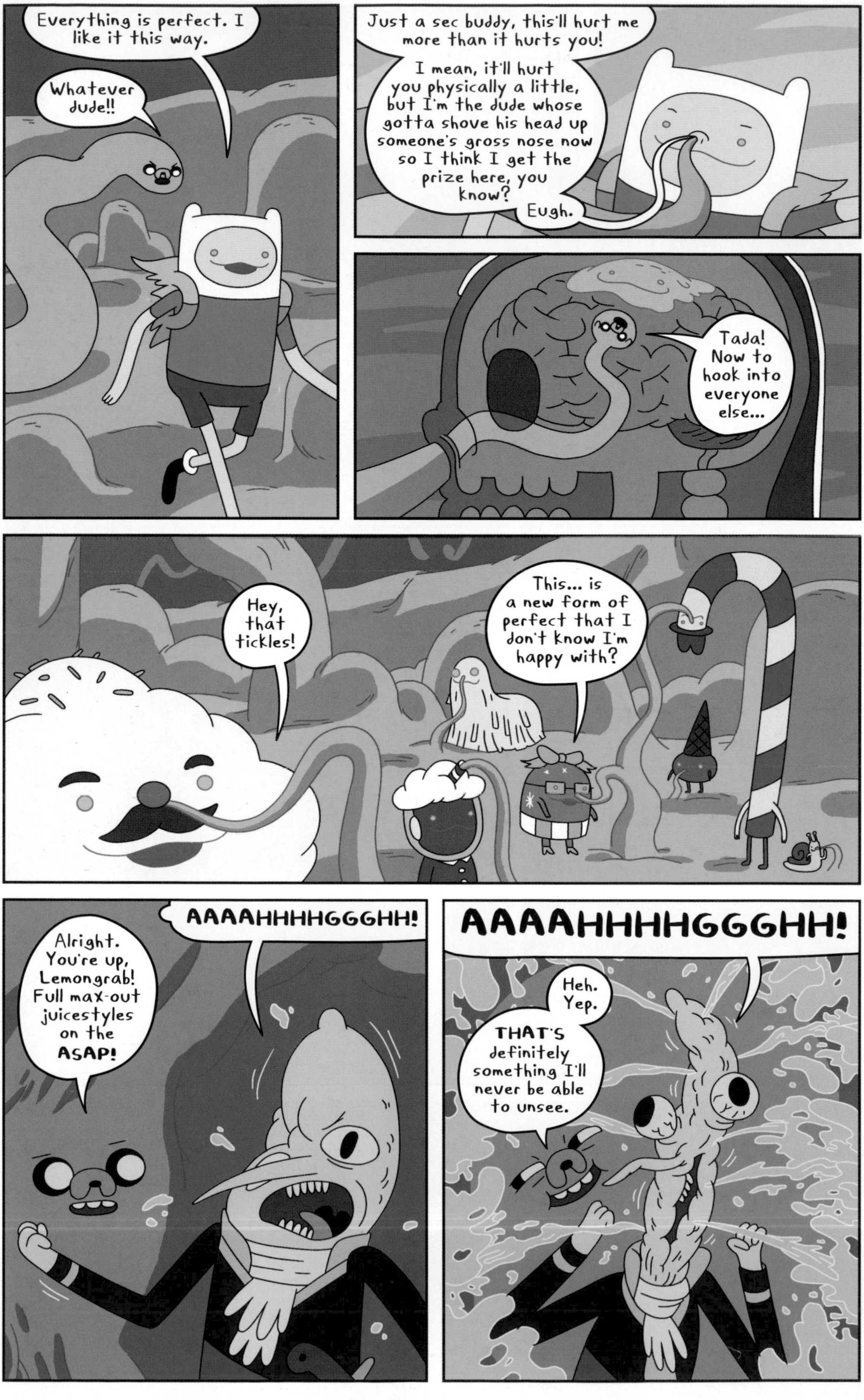
Everything is perfect. I like it this way.
Whatever dude!!
Just a sec buddy, this'll hurt me more than it hurts you!
I mean, it'll hurt you physically a little, but I'm the dude whose gotta shove his head up someone's gross nose now so I think I get the prize here, you know?
Eugh.
Tada! Now to hook into everyone else...
Hey, that tickles!
This... is a new form of perfect that I don't know I'm happy with?
Alright. You're up, Lemongrab! Full max-out juicestyles on the ASAP!
AAAAHHHHGGGHH!
AAAAHHHHGGGHH!
Heh. Yep.
THAT'S definitely something I'll never be able to unsee.

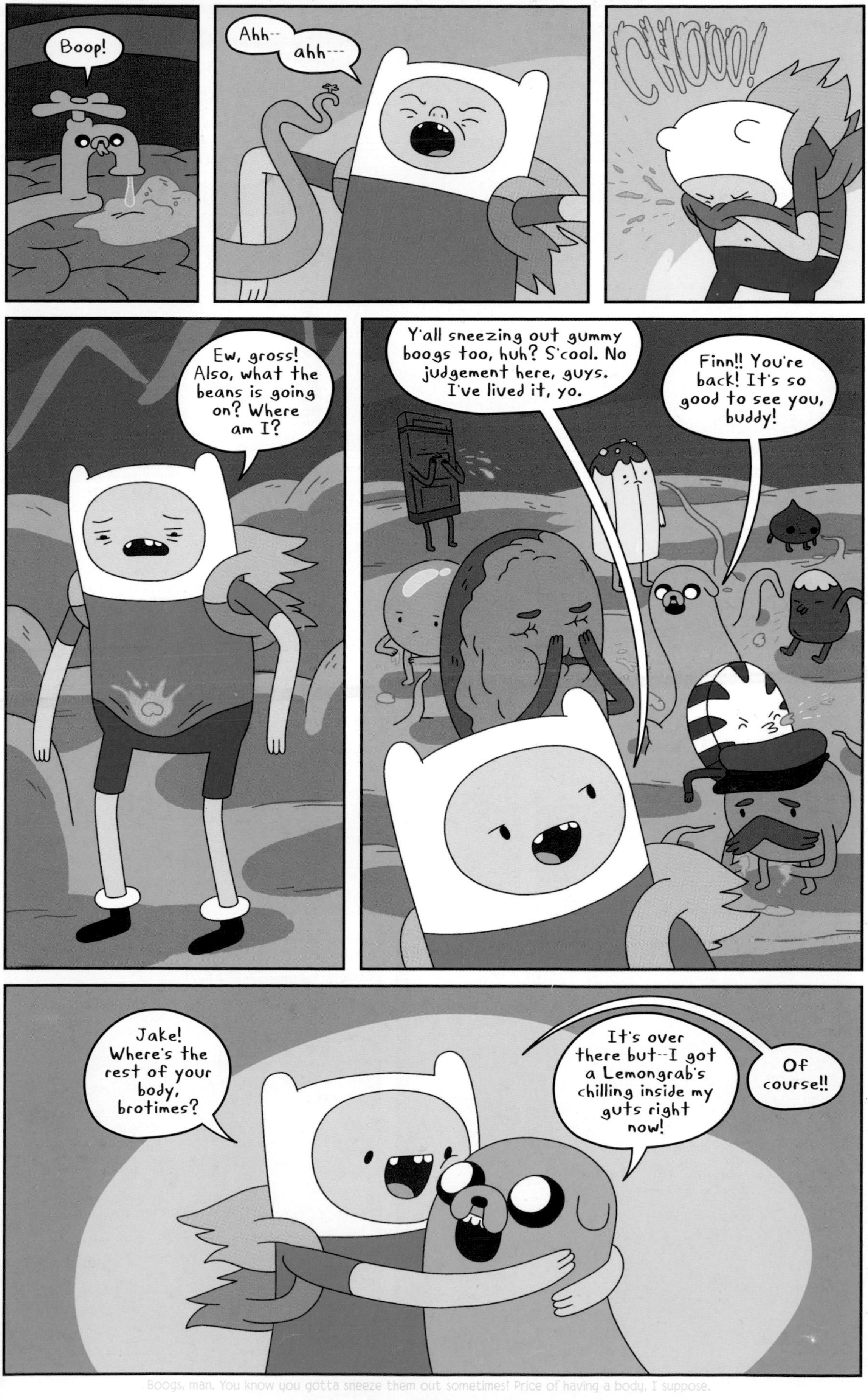
Boop!
Ahh--
ahh---
CHOOO!
Ew, gross! Also, what the beans is going on? Where am I?
Y'all sneezing out gummy boogs too, huh? S'cool. No judgement here, guys. I've lived it, yo.
Finn!! You're back! It's so good to see you, buddy!
Jake! Where's the rest of your body, brotimes?
It's over there but--I got a Lemongrab's chilling inside my guts right now!
Of course!!

Boogs, man. You know you gotta sneeze them out sometimes! Price of having a body, I suppose.

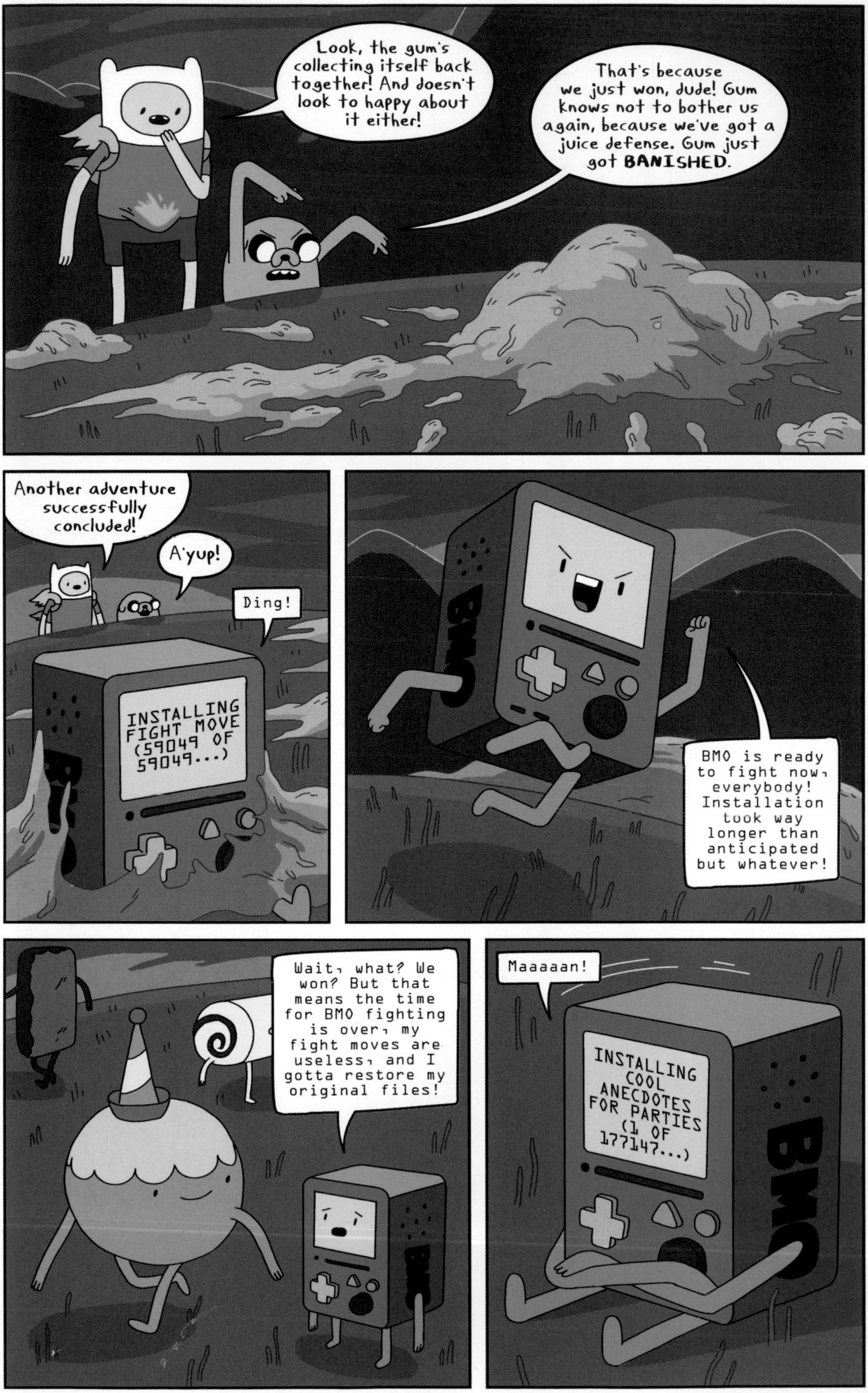
Look, the gum's collecting itself back together! And doesn't look to happy about it either!
That's because we just won, dude! Gum knows not to bother us again, because we've got a juice defense. Gum just got BANISHED.
Another adventure successfully concluded!
A'yup!
Ding!
INSTALLING FIGHT MOVE (59049 OF 59049...)
BMO is ready to fight now, everybody! Installation took way longer than anticipated but whatever!
Wait, what? We won? But that means the time for BMO fighting is over, my fight moves are useless, and I gotta restore my original files!
Maaaaan!
INSTALLING COOL ANECDOTES FOR PARTIES (1 OF 177147...)

Y'all are gonna love #34502. Something to look forward to!

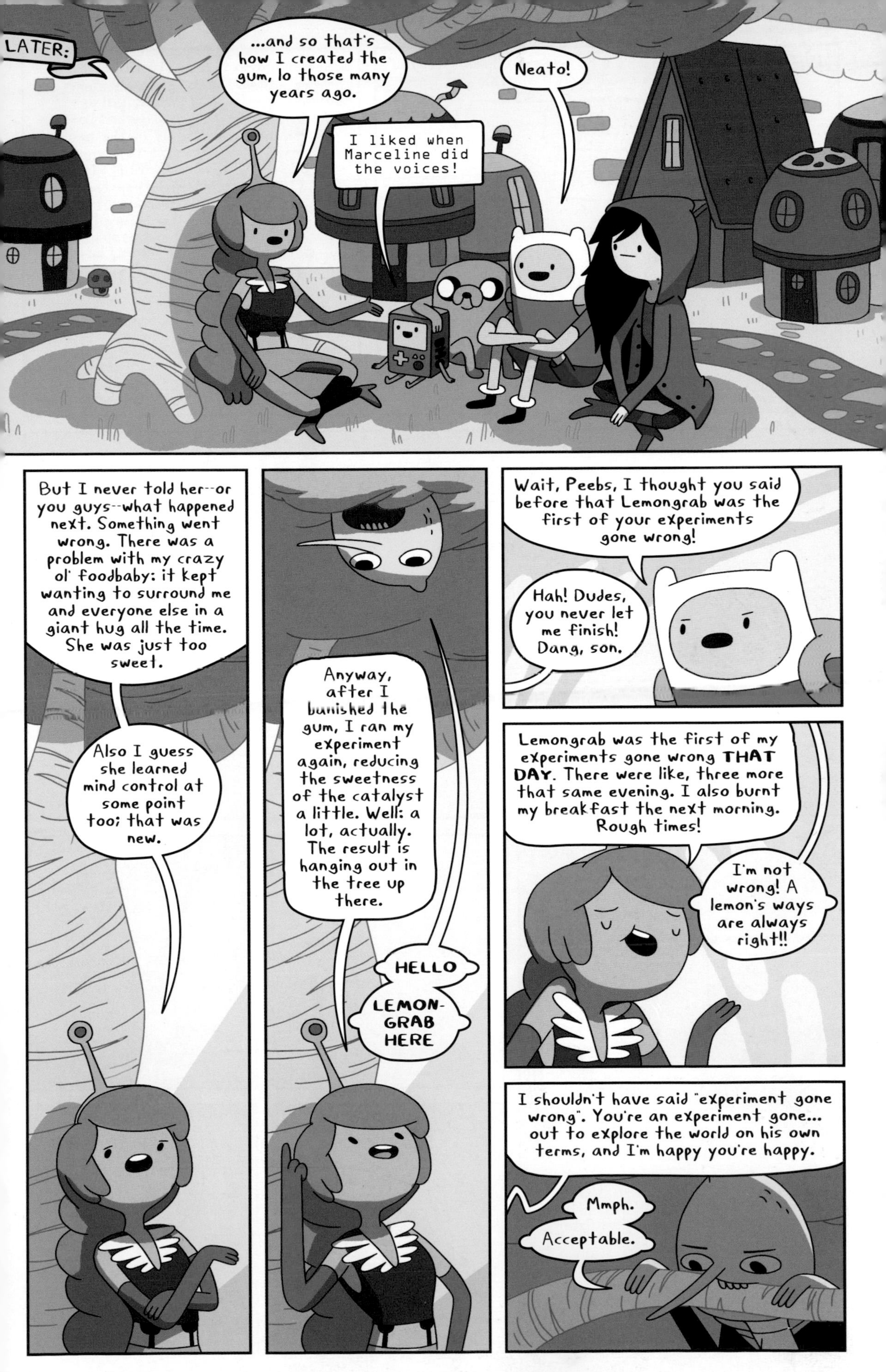
LATER:
...and so that's how I created the gum, lo those many years ago.
I liked when Marceline did the voices!
Neato!
But I never told her--or you guys--what happened next. Something went wrong. There was a problem with my crazy ol' foodbaby: it kept wanting to surround me and everyone else in a giant hug all the time. She was just too sweet.
Also I guess she learned mind control at some point too; that was new.
Anyway, after I banished the gum, I ran my experiment again, reducing the sweetness of the catalyst a little. Well: a lot, actually. The result is hanging out in the tree up there.
HELLO
LEMON-GRAB HERE
Wait, Peebs, I thought you said before that Lemongrab was the first of your experiments gone wrong!
Hah! Dudes, you never let me finish! Dang, son.
Lemongrab was the first of my experiments gone wrong THAT DAY. There were like, three more that same evening. I also burnt my breakfast the next morning. Rough times!
I'm not wrong! A lemon's ways are always right!!
I shouldn't have said "experiment gone wrong". You're an experiment gone... out to explore the world on his own terms, and I'm happy you're happy.
Mmph.
Acceptable.

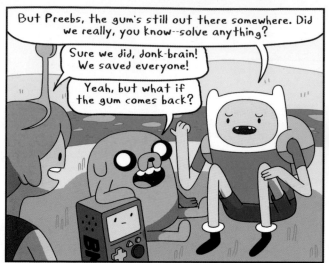

But Preebs, the gum's still out there somewhere. Did we really, you know--solve anything?

Sure we did, donk-brain! We saved everyone!

Yeah, but what if the gum comes back?

When it learns some dang boundaries it can come hang with us again.

Until then it's probably chillin' in the usual spot: a nearly bottomless pit in the ground next to a sign that says "GUM KINGDOM" and then there's an arrow on the sign pointing into a big ol' hole filled with gum.

GUM KINGDOM

Ah. So...everything is definitely solved forever?

Yep! And despite all my preparation, despite my greatest efforts, despite a nation's armament and my kingdom's best defenses, in the end I still had to rely on a kid and this dog he knows to fix all my problems.

Hah!

HAH HAH!

HAH HAH HAH HAH HAH HAH

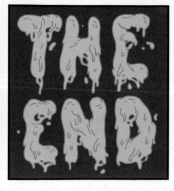

THE END

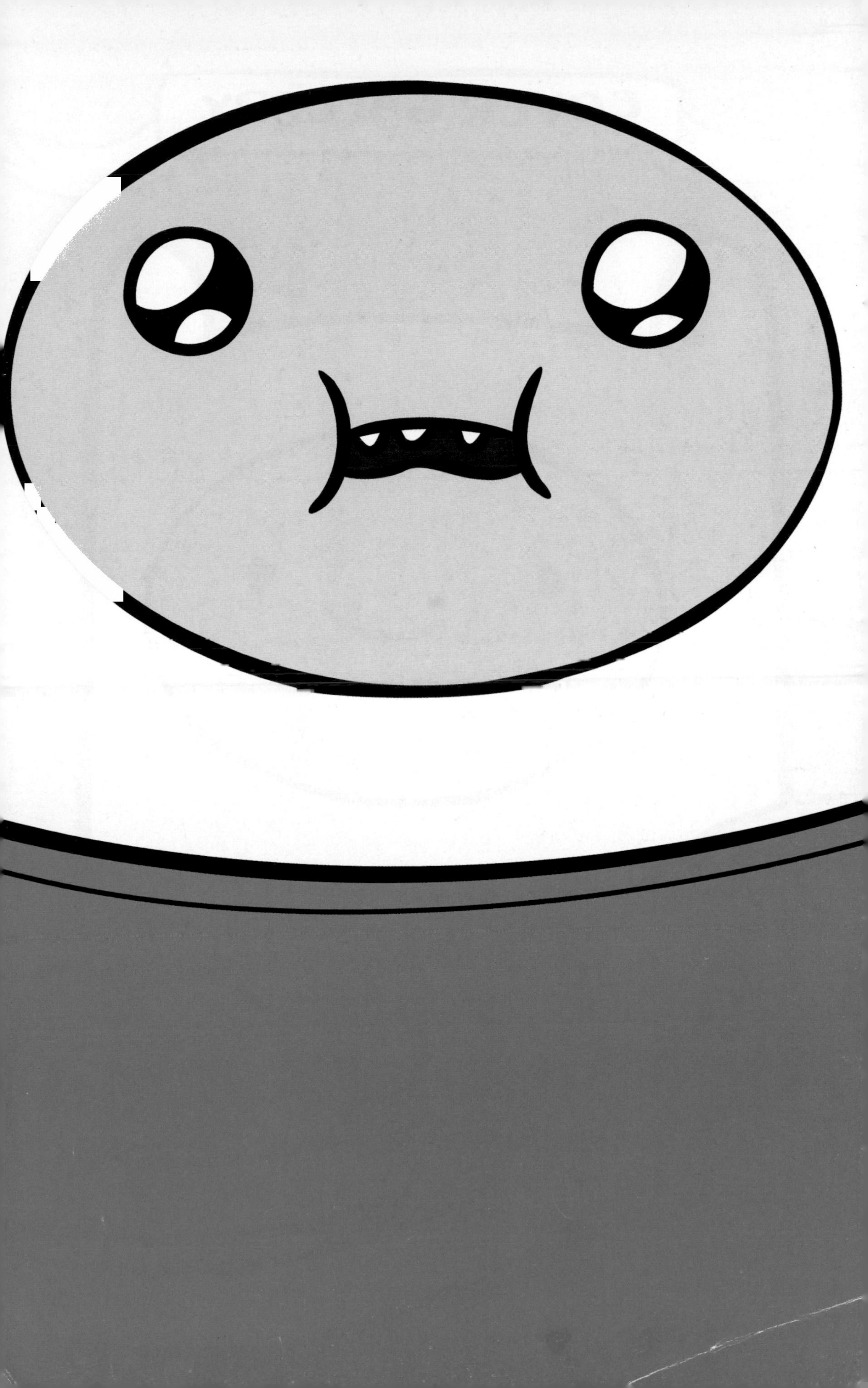

COVER GALLERY

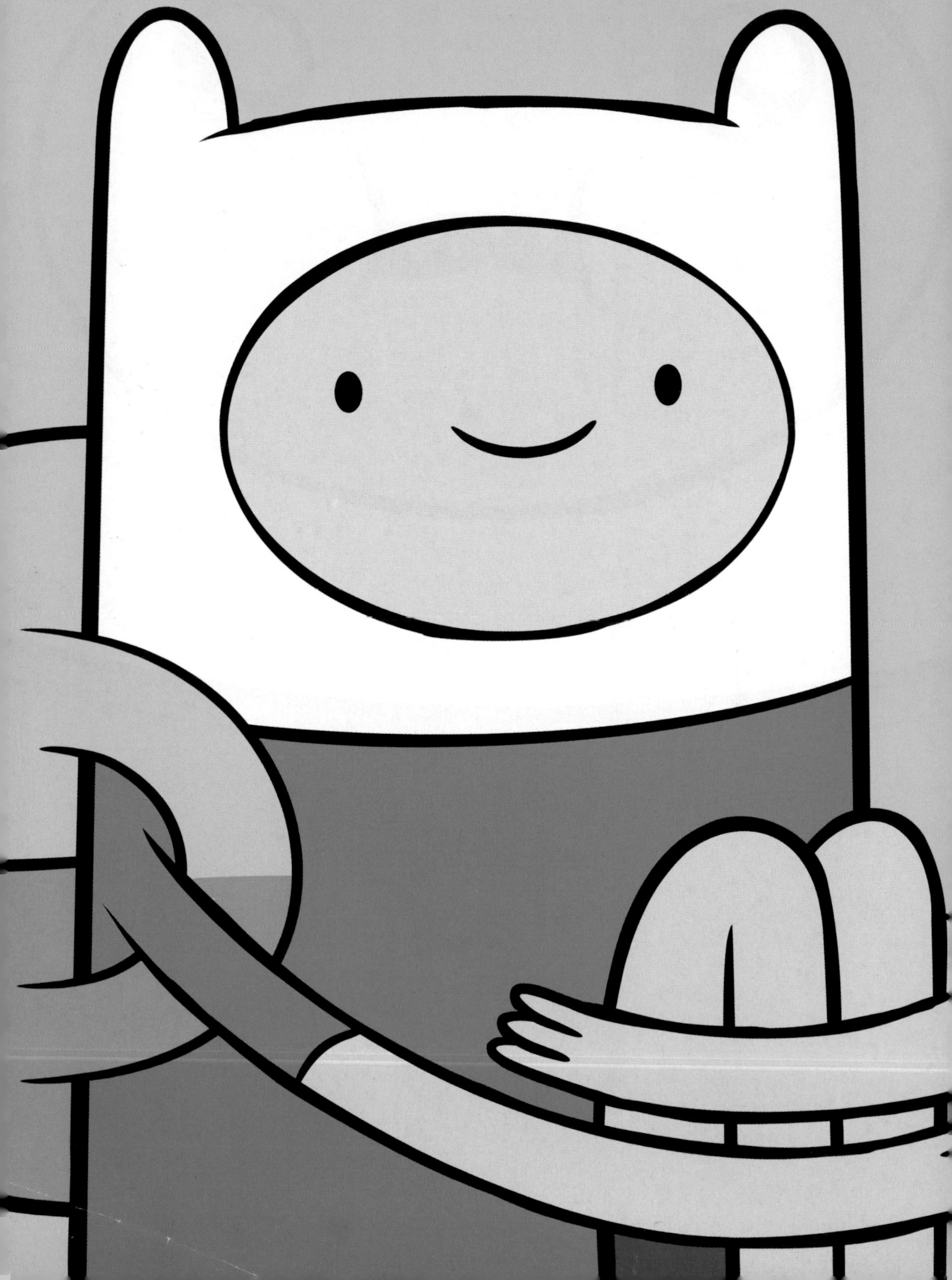

Cover 20A:
Mike Holmes

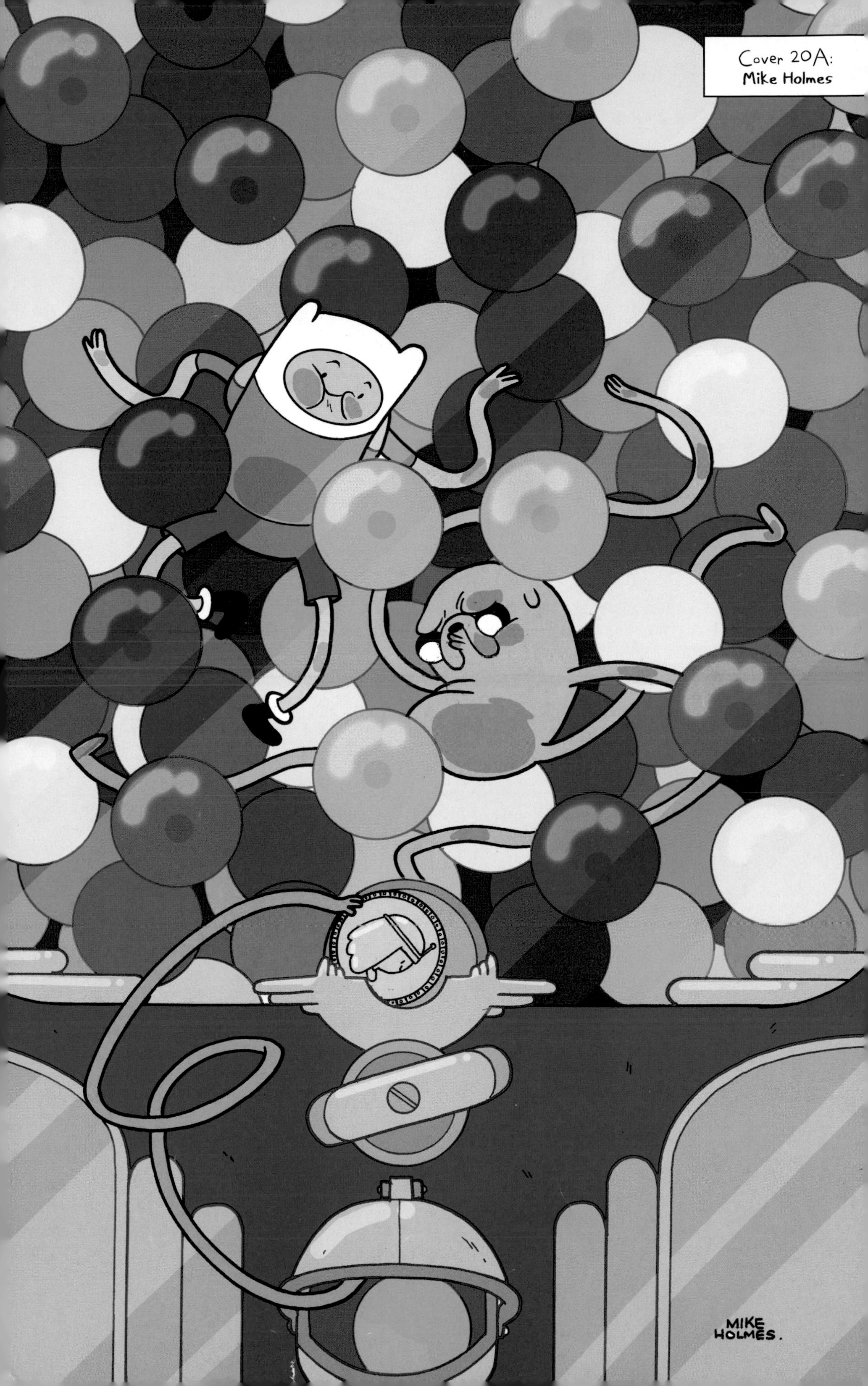
MIKE HOLMES.

Cover 20B:
T. Fabert

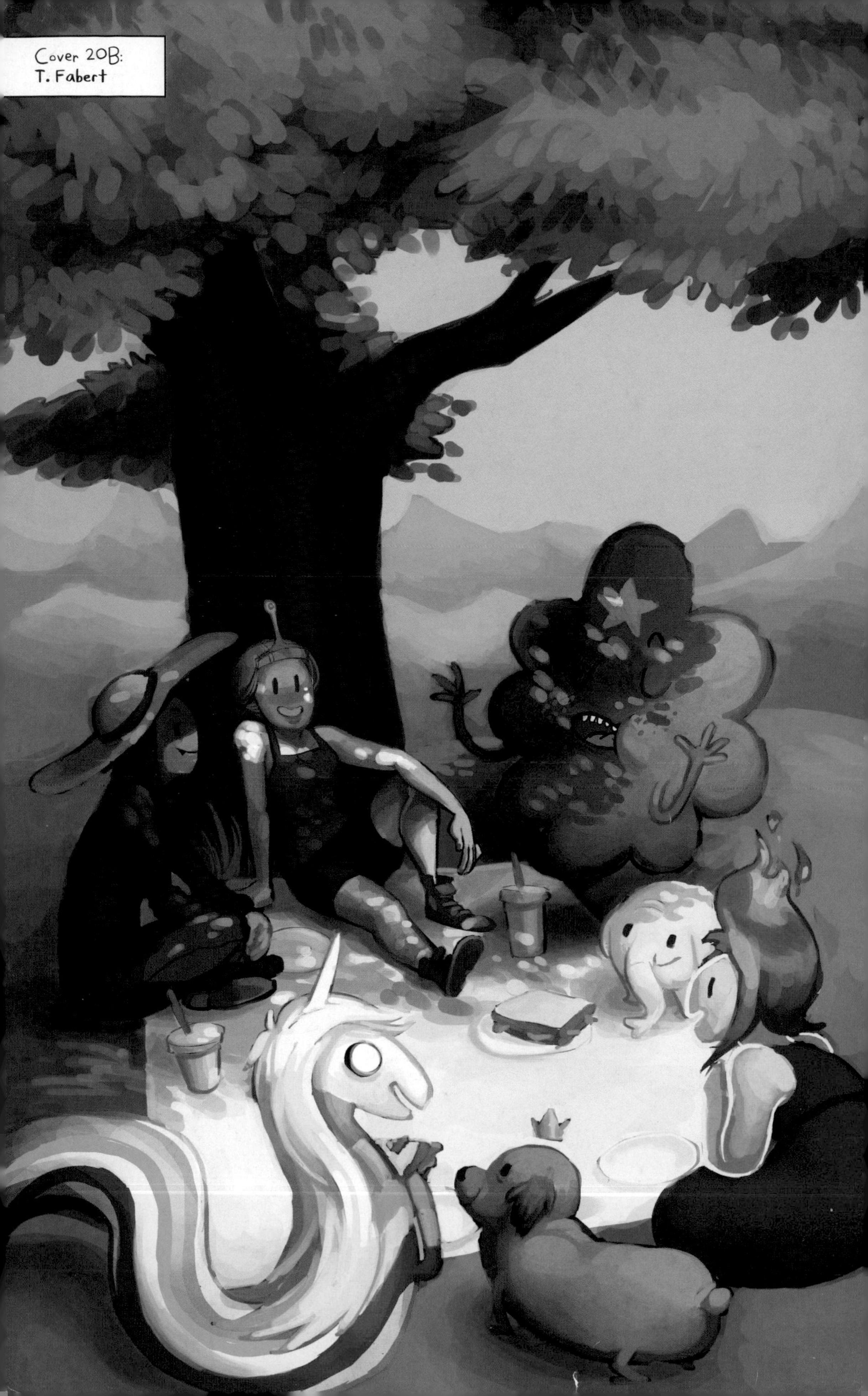

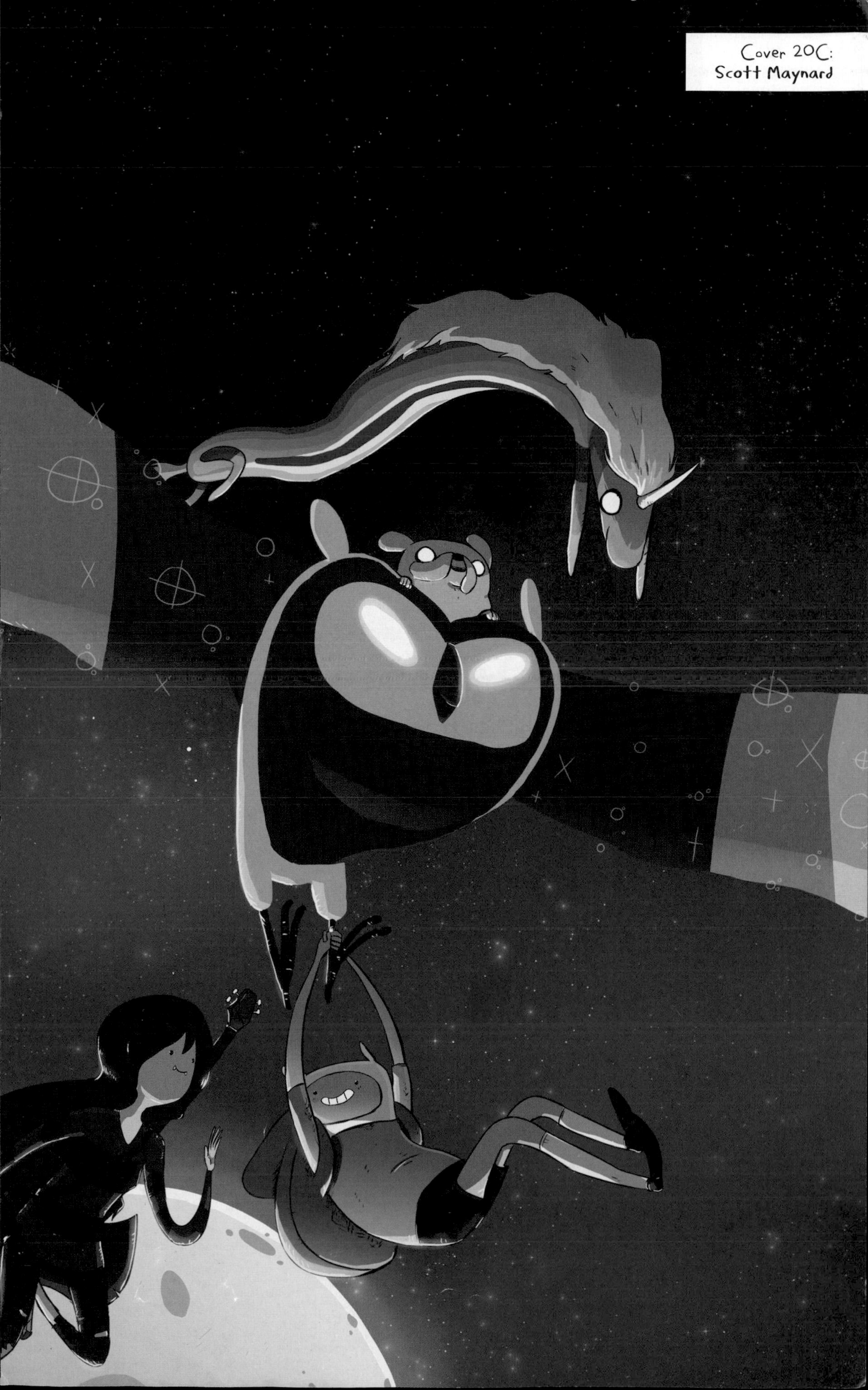

Cover 20C:
Scott Maynard

Cover 20D:
Wes Craig

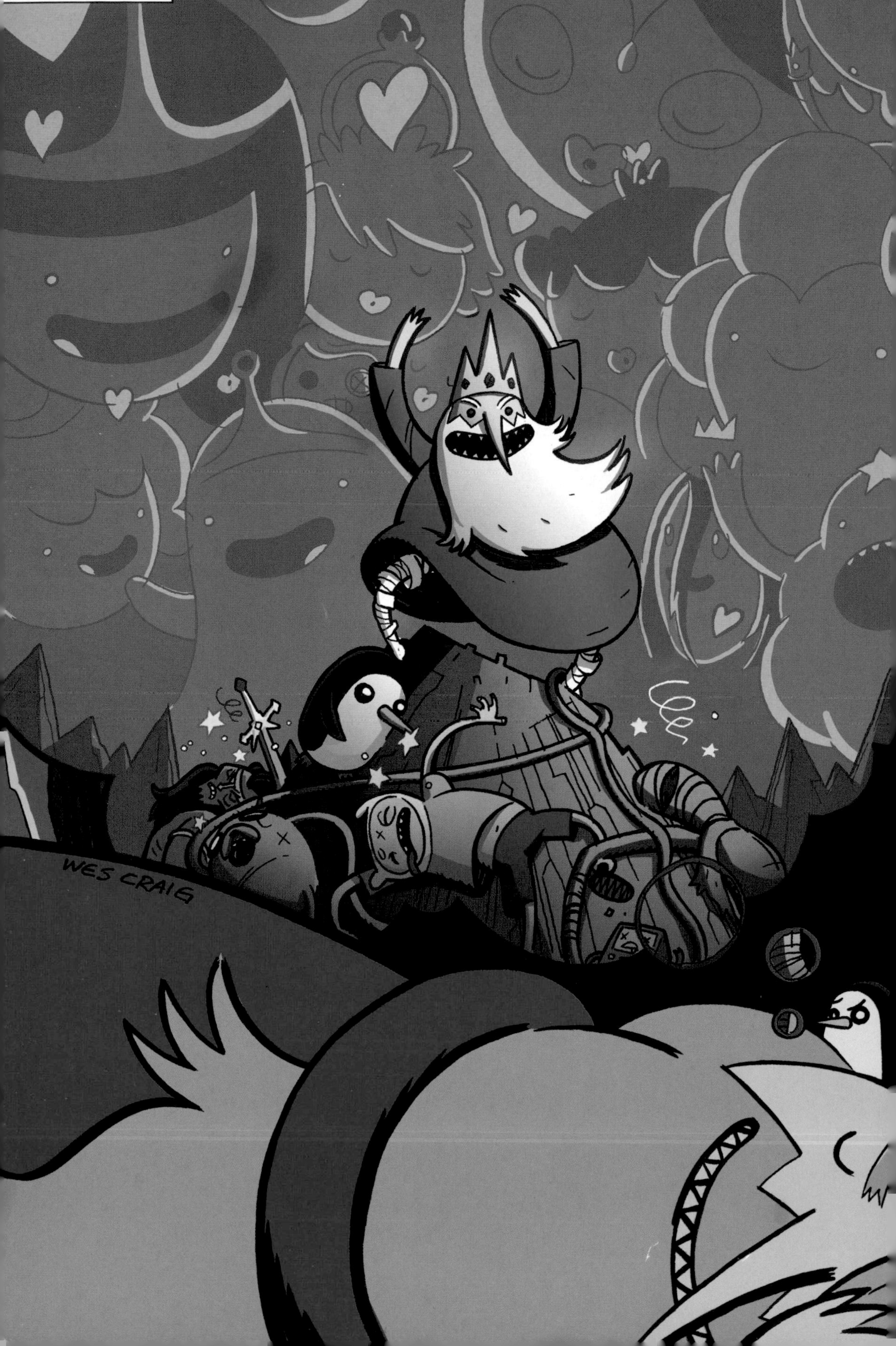
WES CRAIG

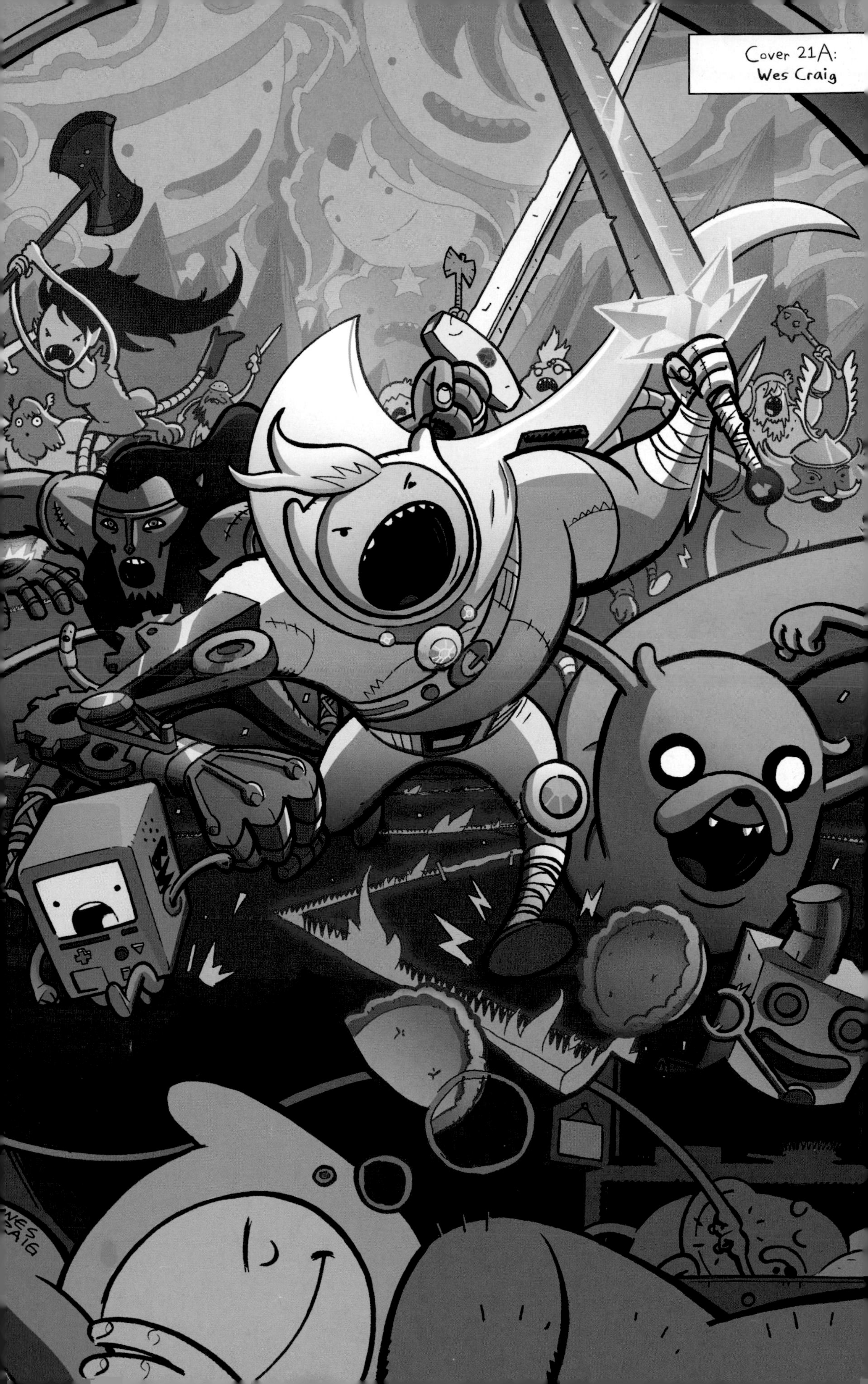

Cover 21A:
Wes Craig

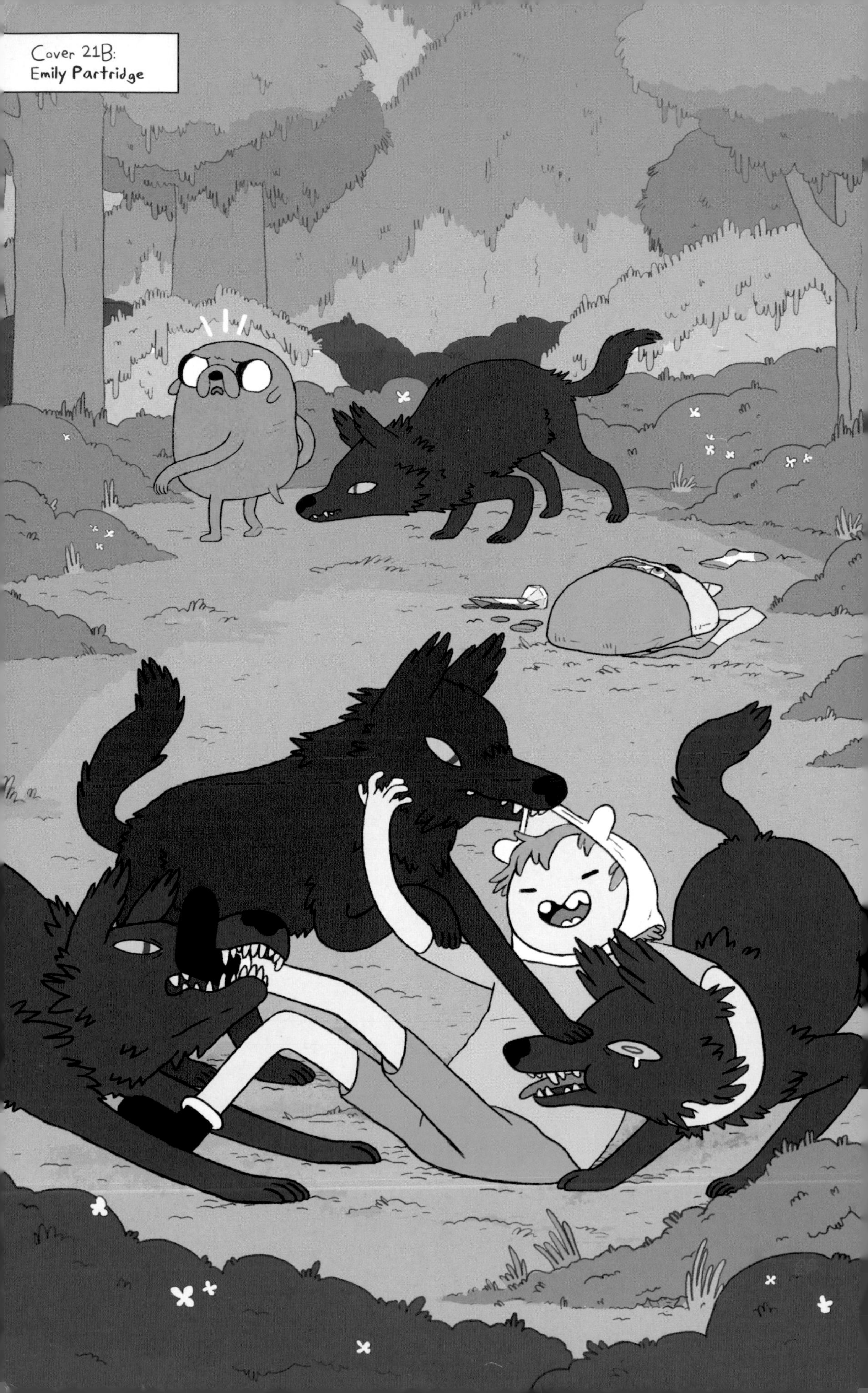
Cover 21B:
Emily Partridge

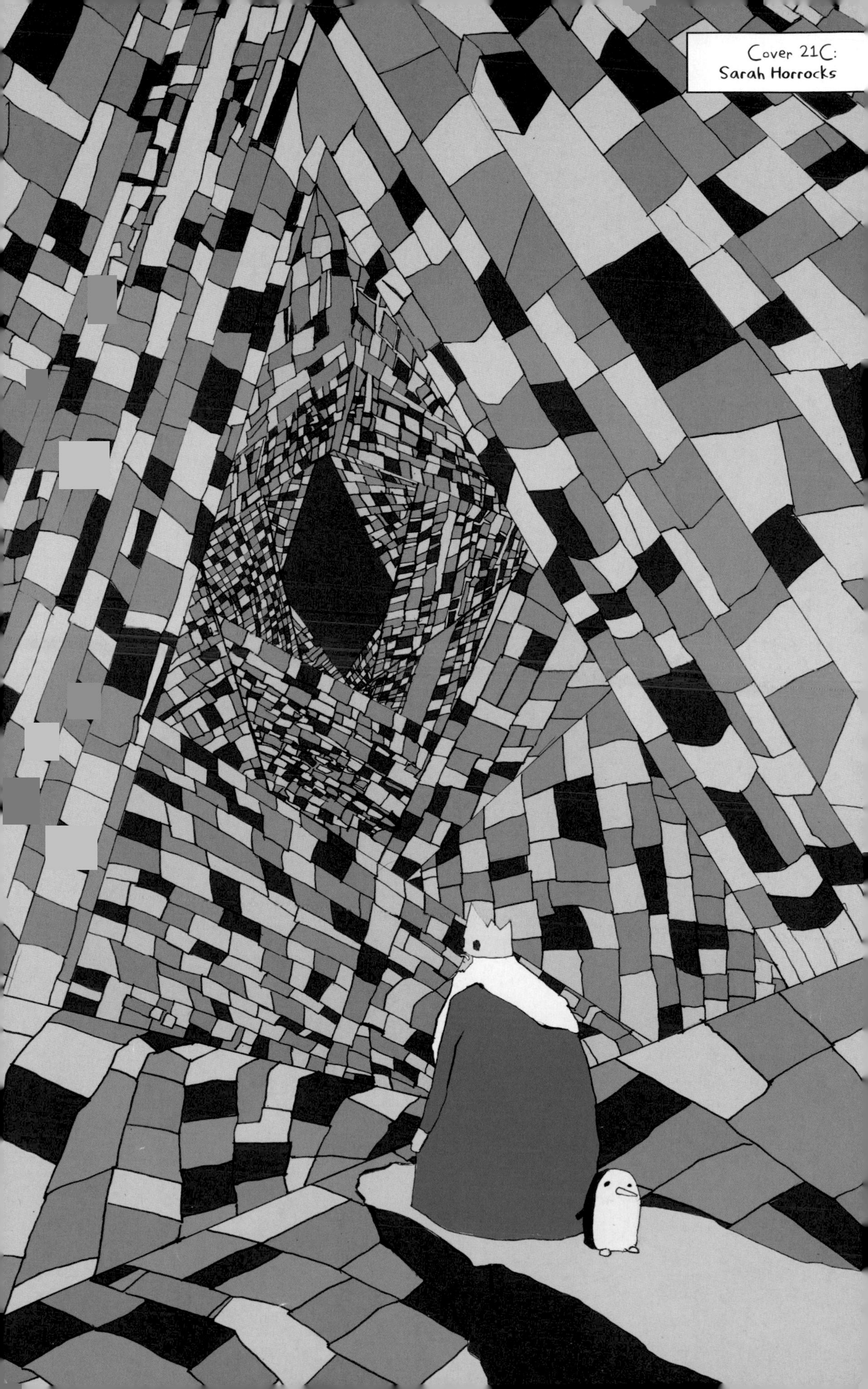
Cover 21C:
Sarah Horrocks

Cover 21D:
Ryo Nishiguchi

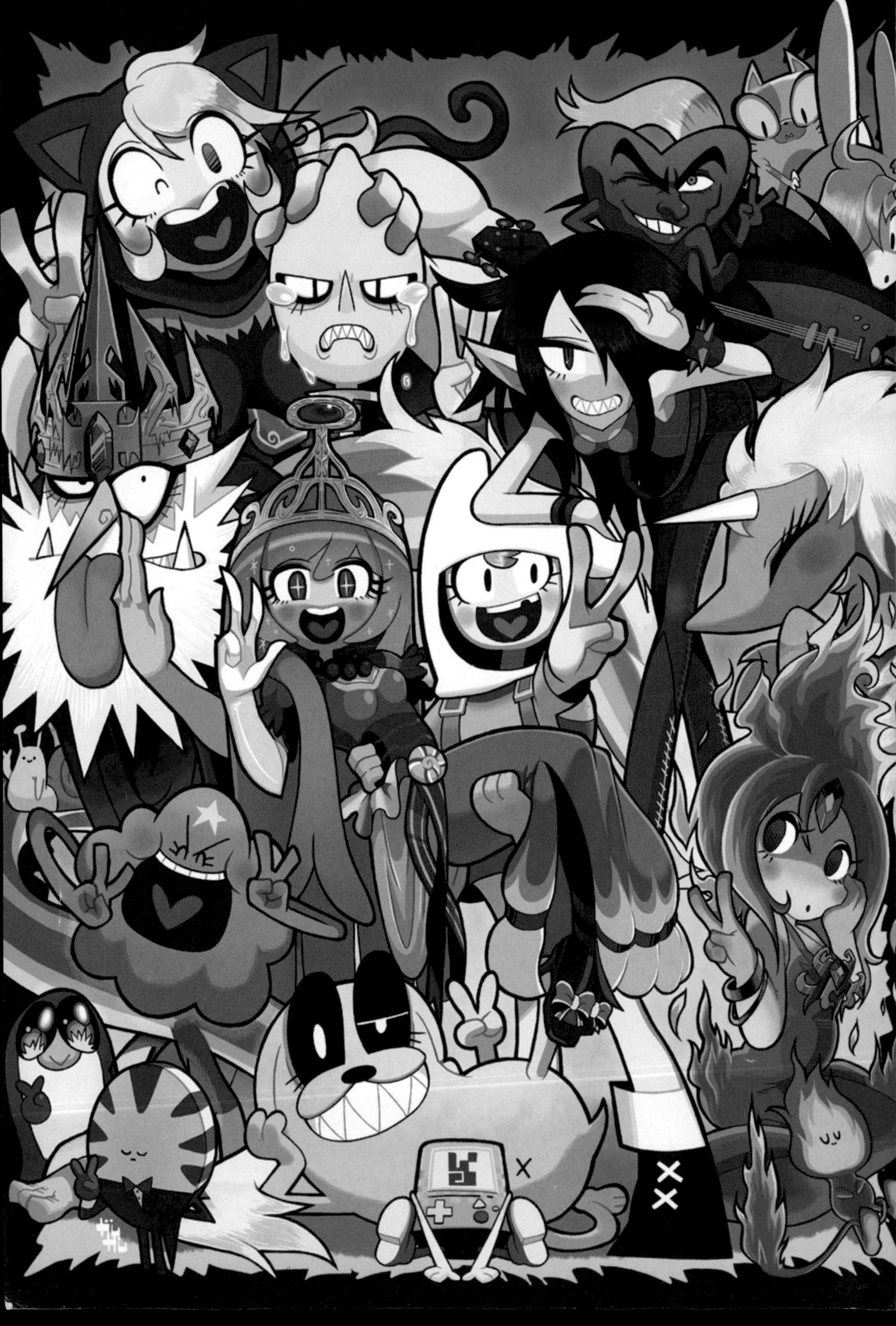

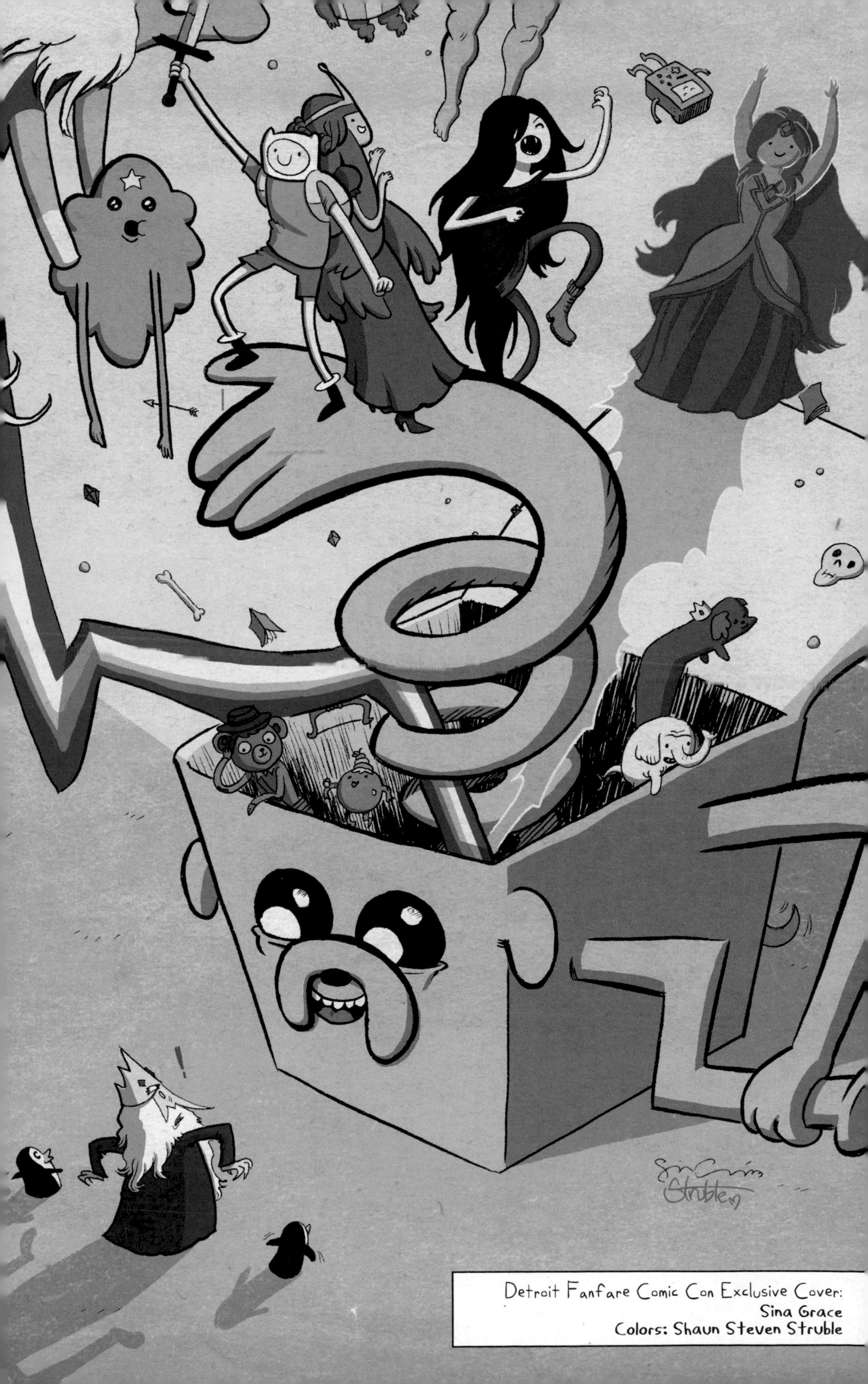

Detroit Fanfare Comic Con Exclusive Cover:
Sina Grace
Colors: Shaun Steven Struble

Alamo City Comic Con Exclusive Cover:
Colin Raff

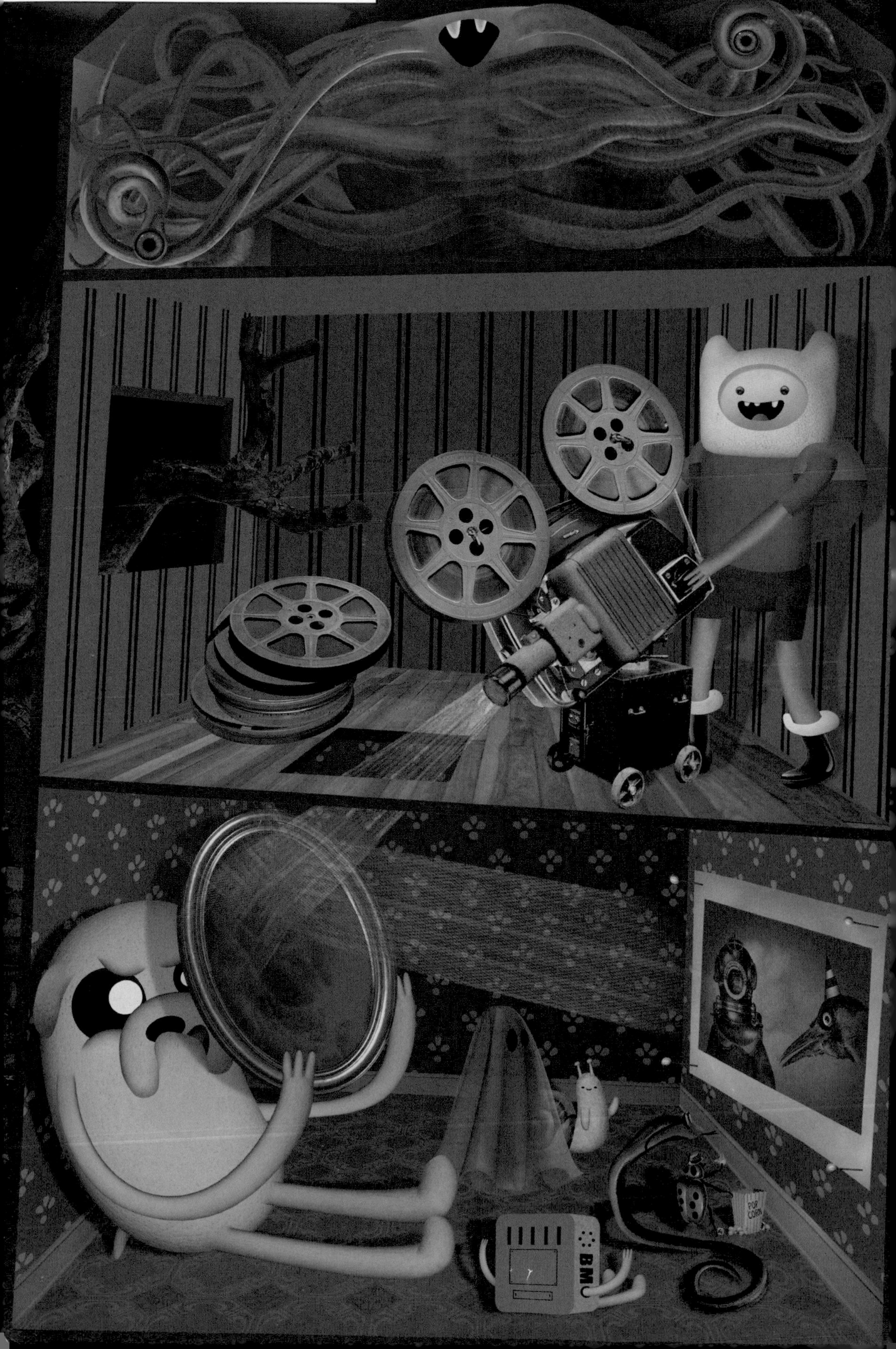

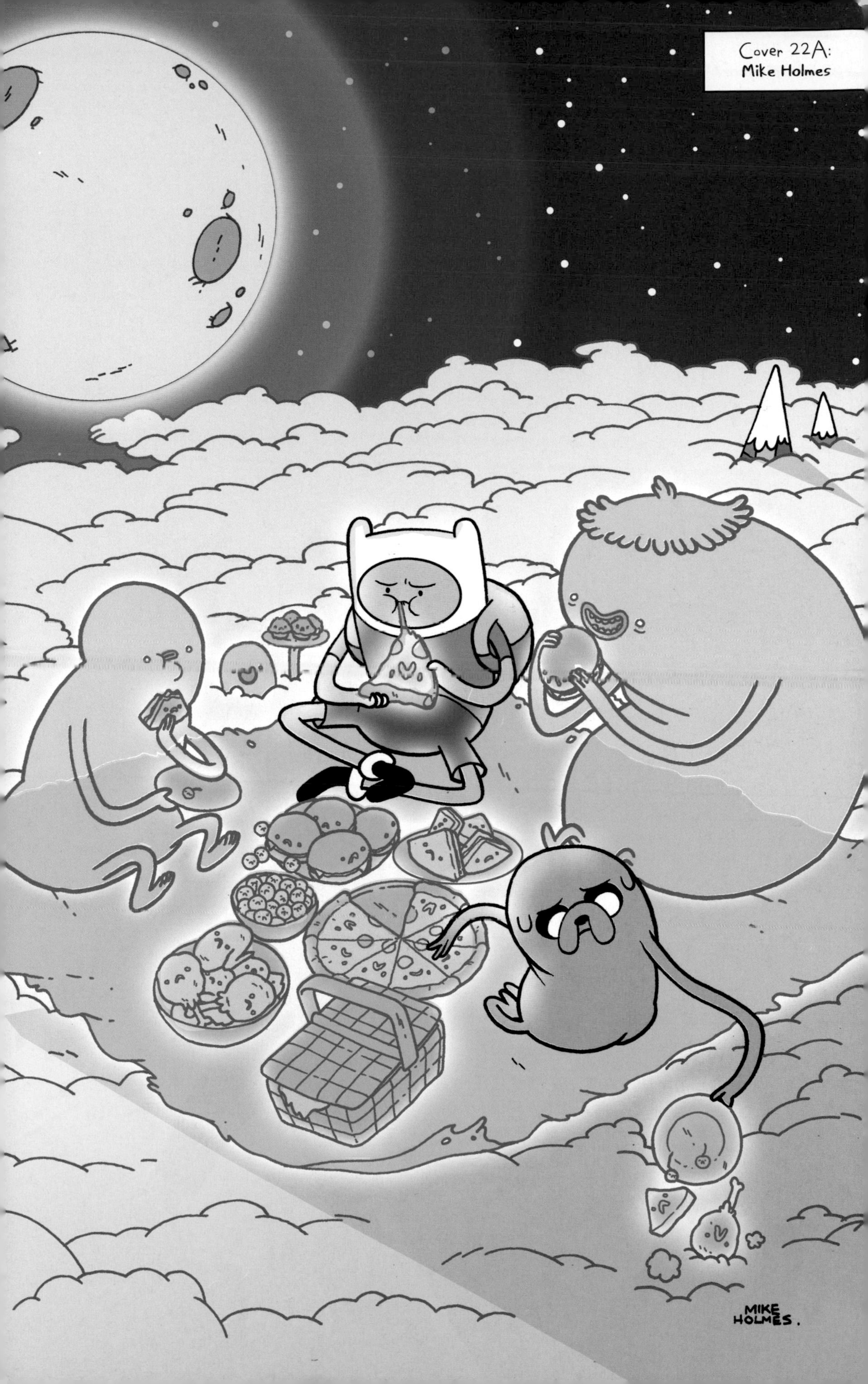
MIKE
HOLMES.

Cover 22A:
Mike Holmes

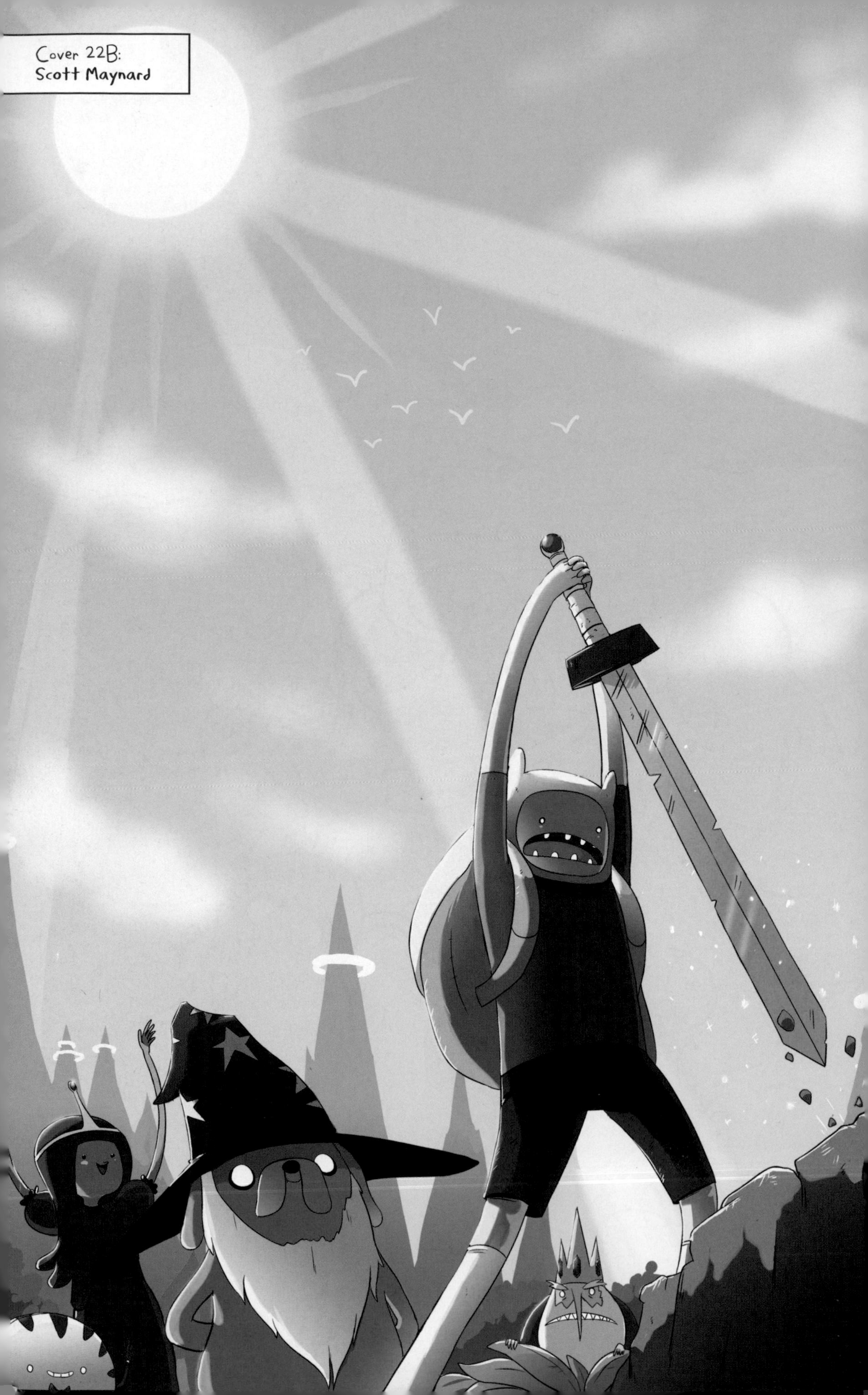

Cover 22B:
Scott Maynard

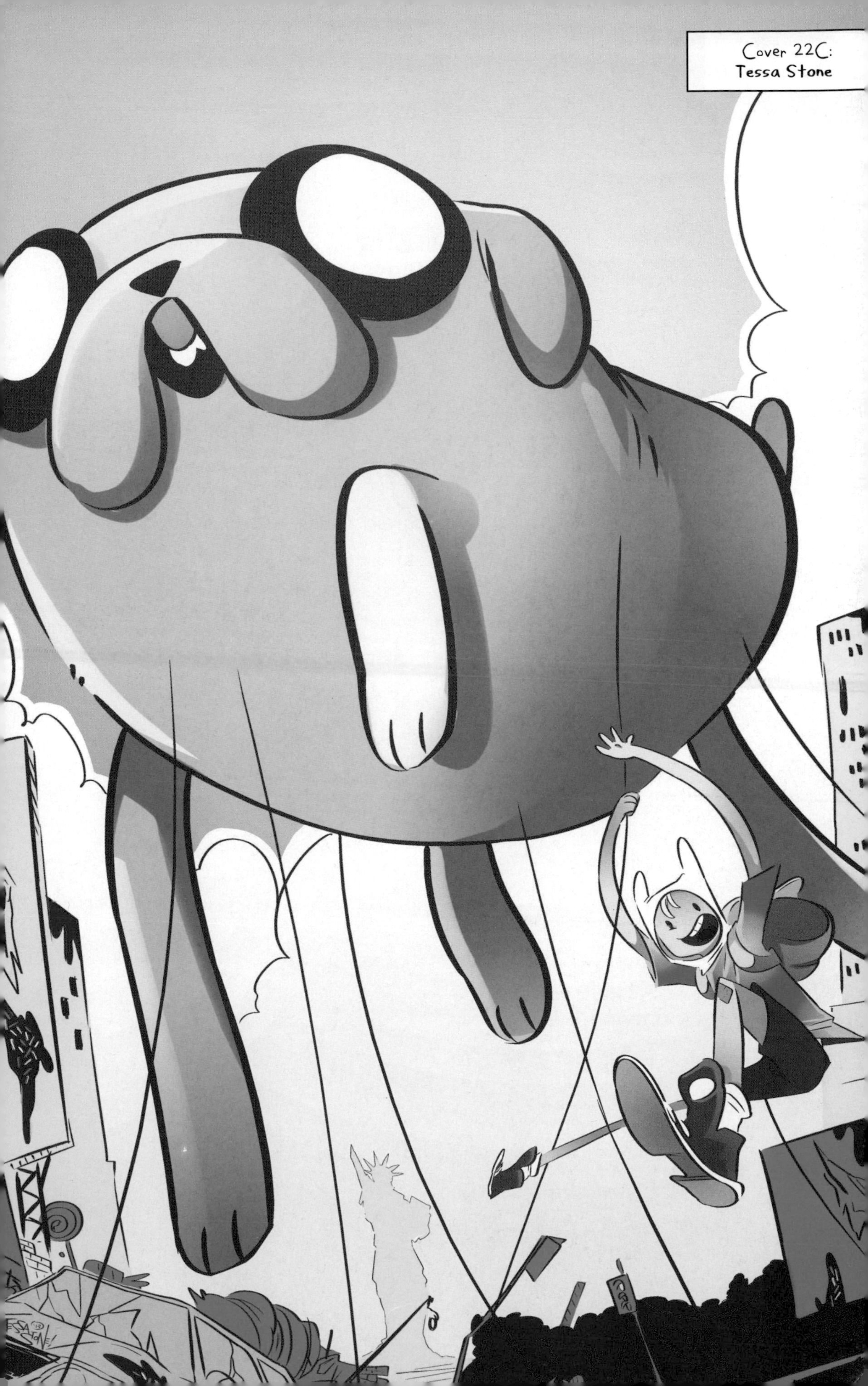

Cover 22C:
Tessa Stone

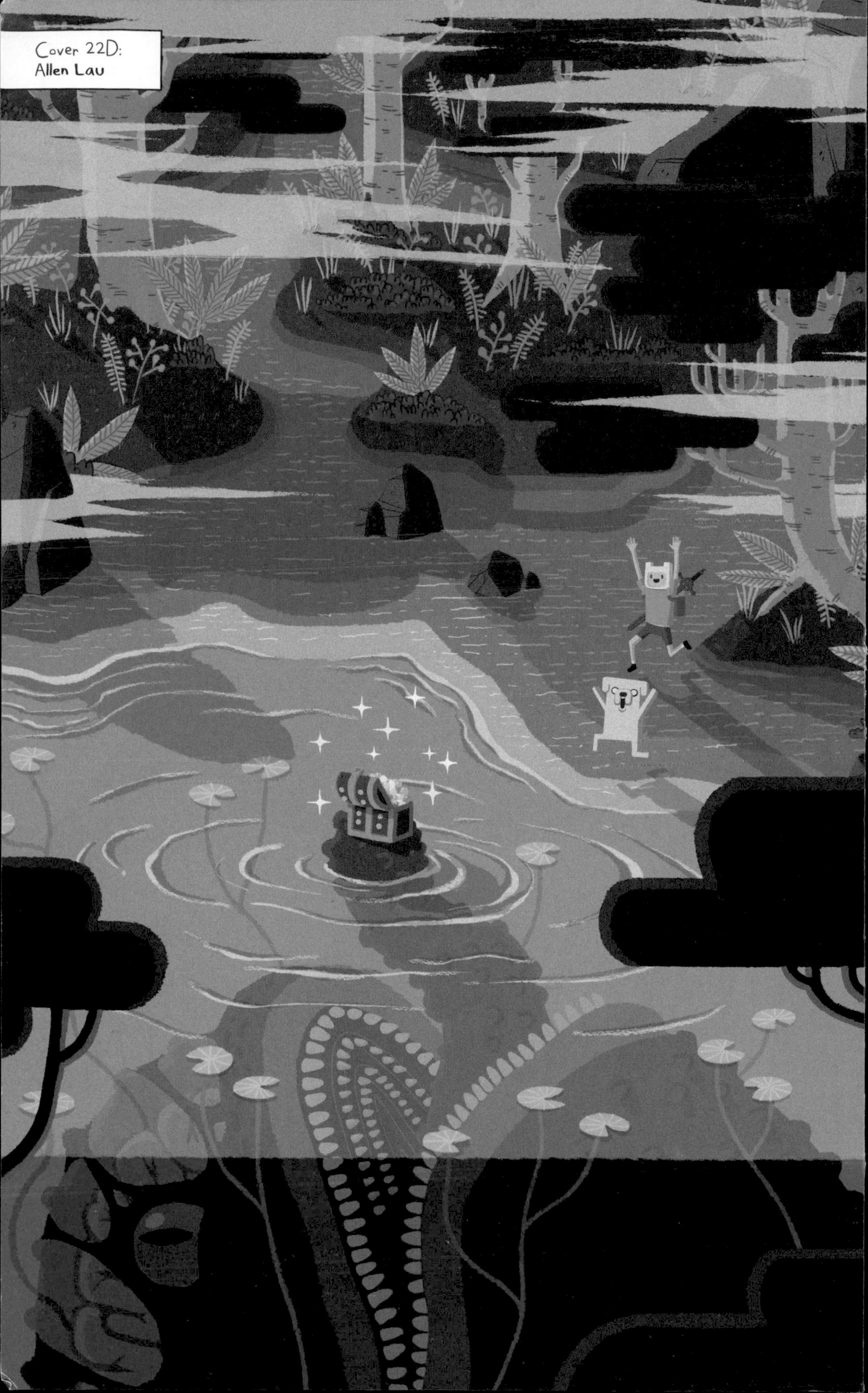

Cover 22D:
Allen Lau

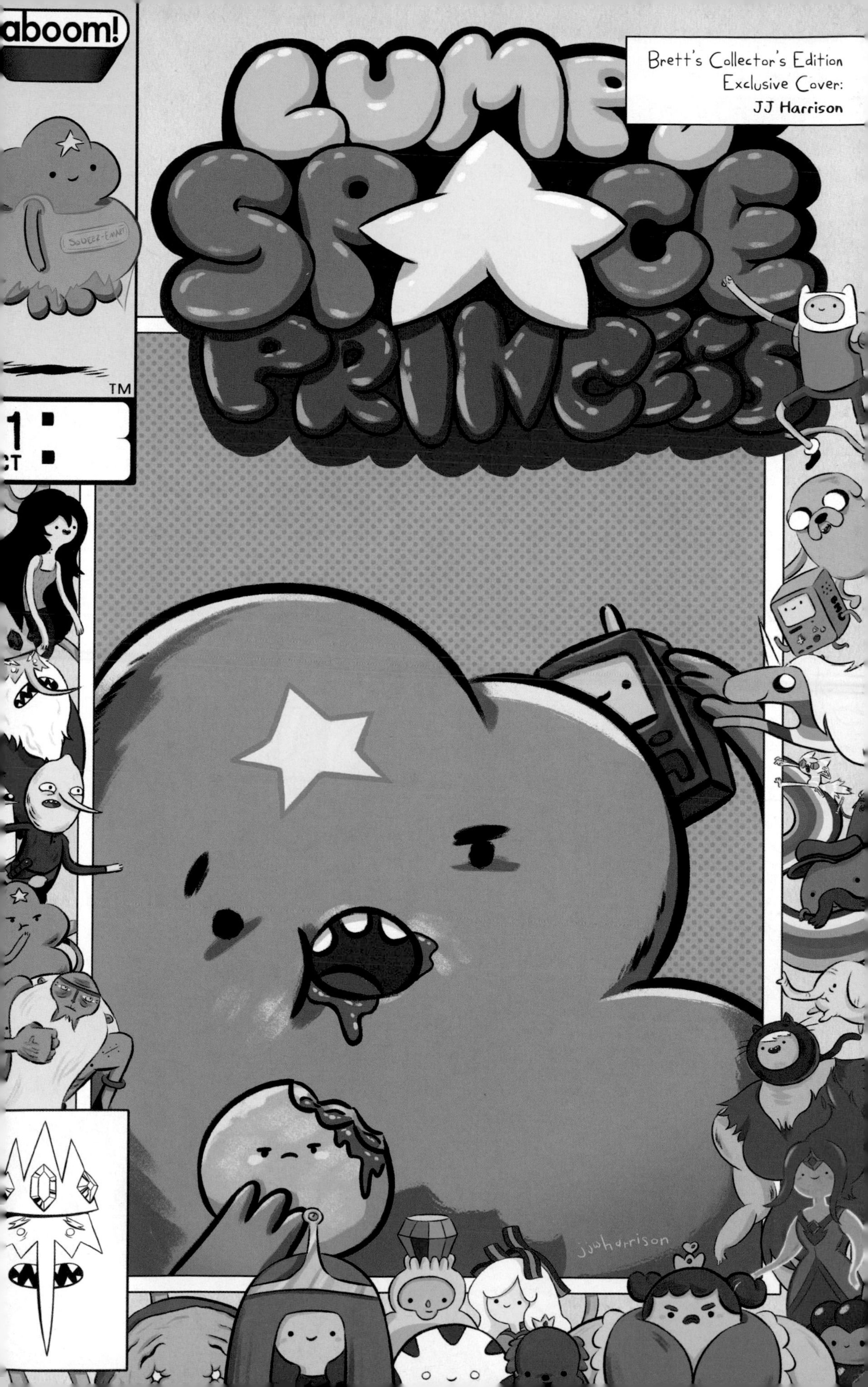
aboom!
Brett's Collector's Edition
Exclusive Cover:
JJ Harrison
TM
jjwharrison

Cards, Comics & Collectibles Exclusive Cover:
John Gallagher

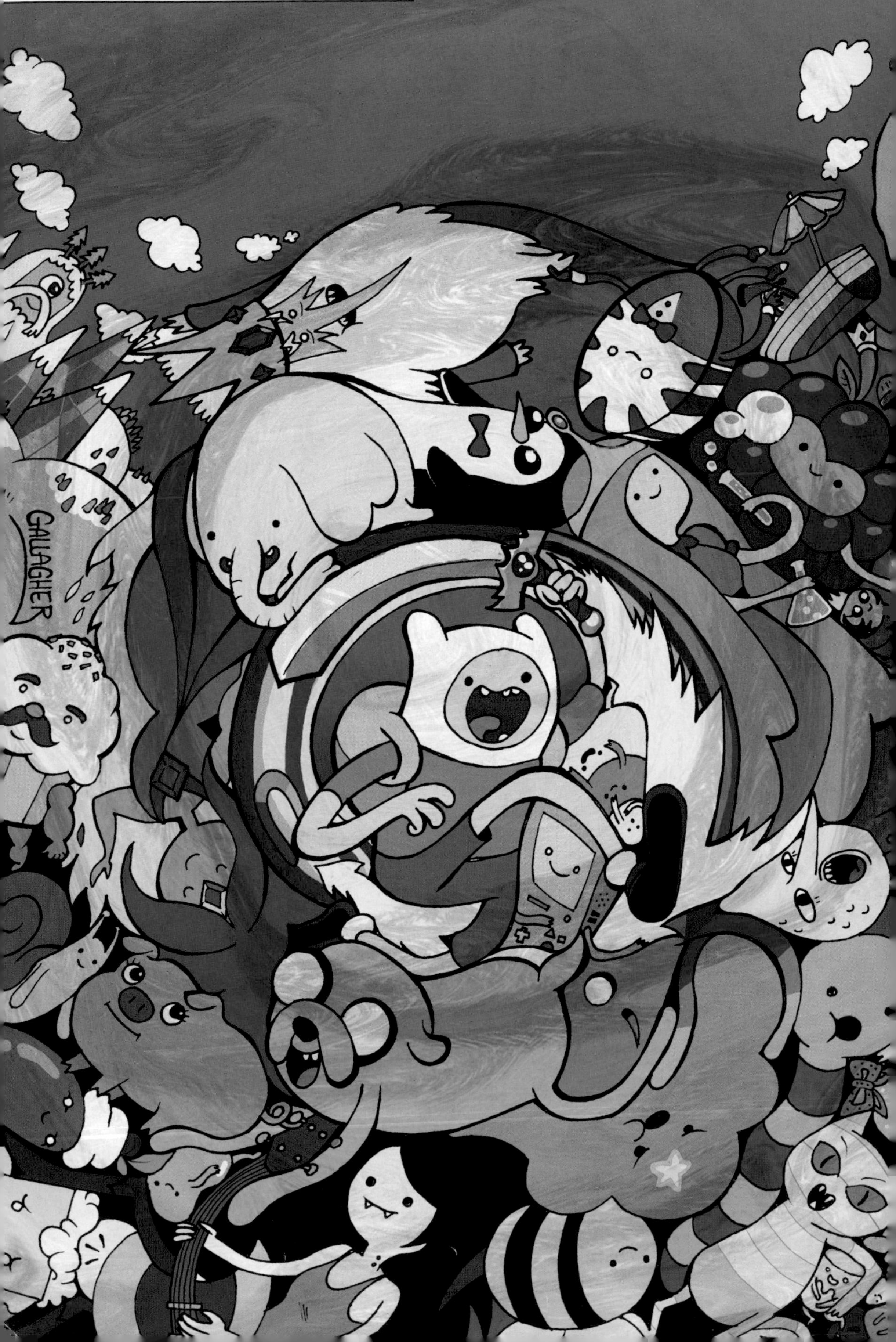

Cover 23A:
Mike Holmes

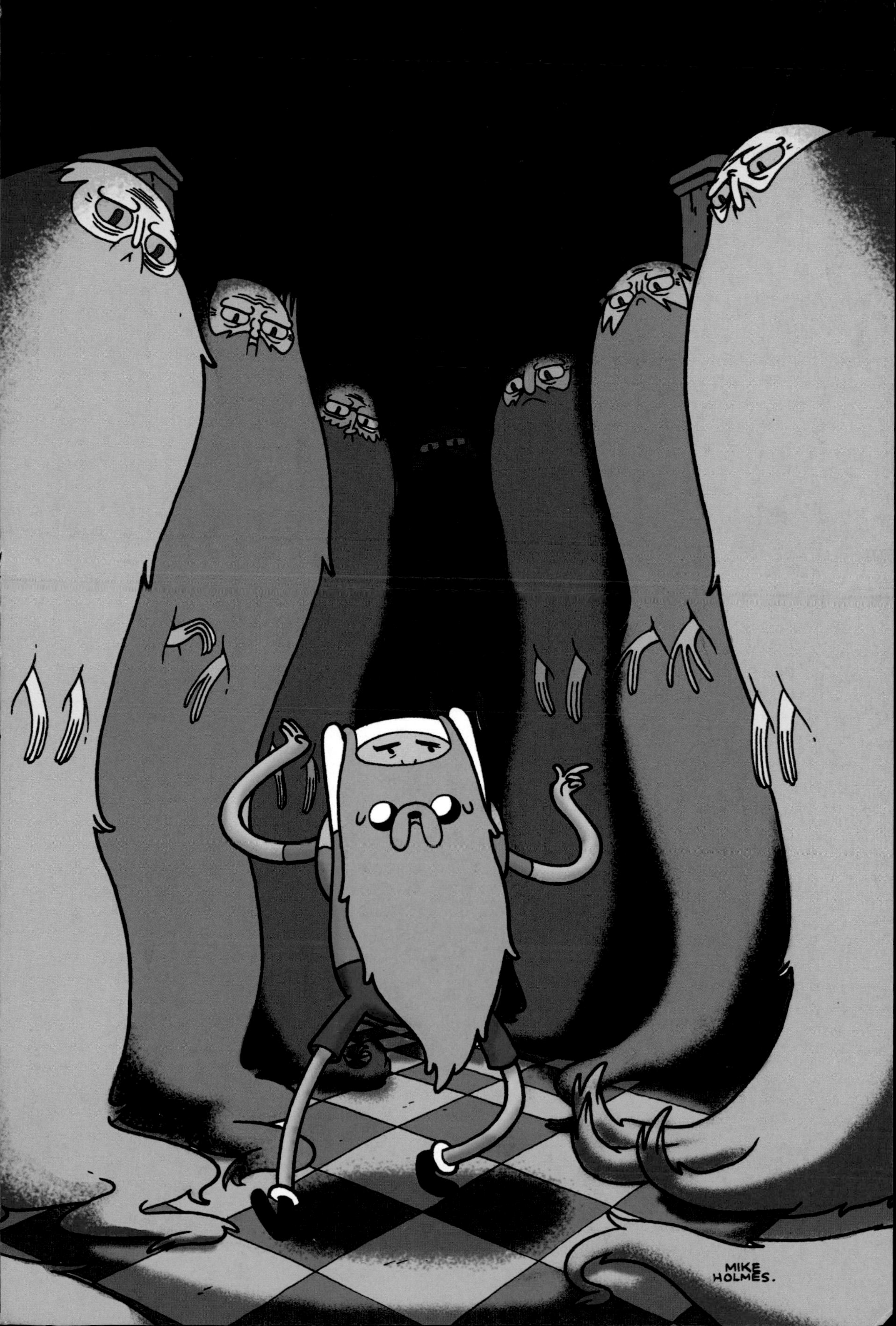
MIKE HOLMES.

Cover 23B:
Seo Kim

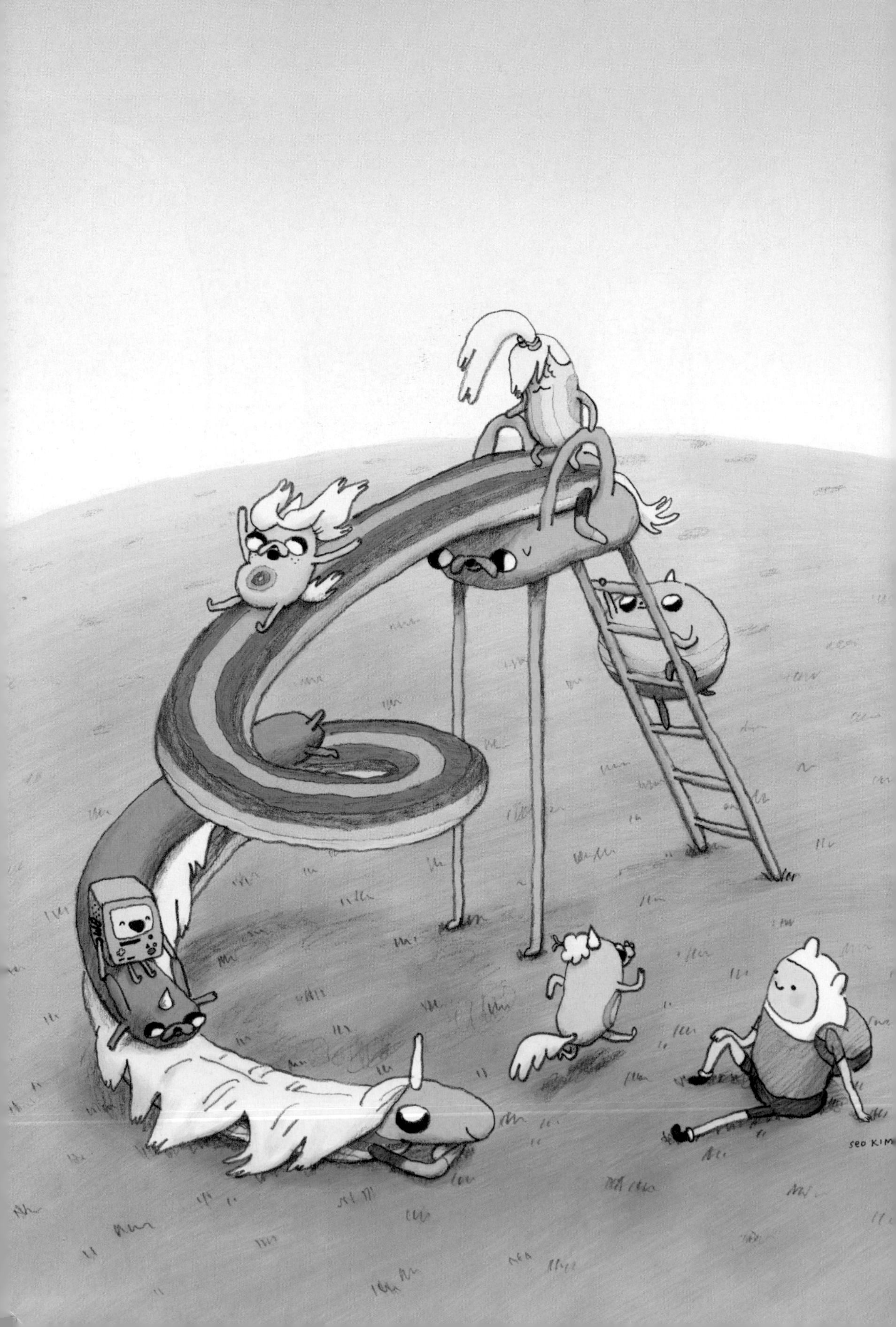
SEO KIM

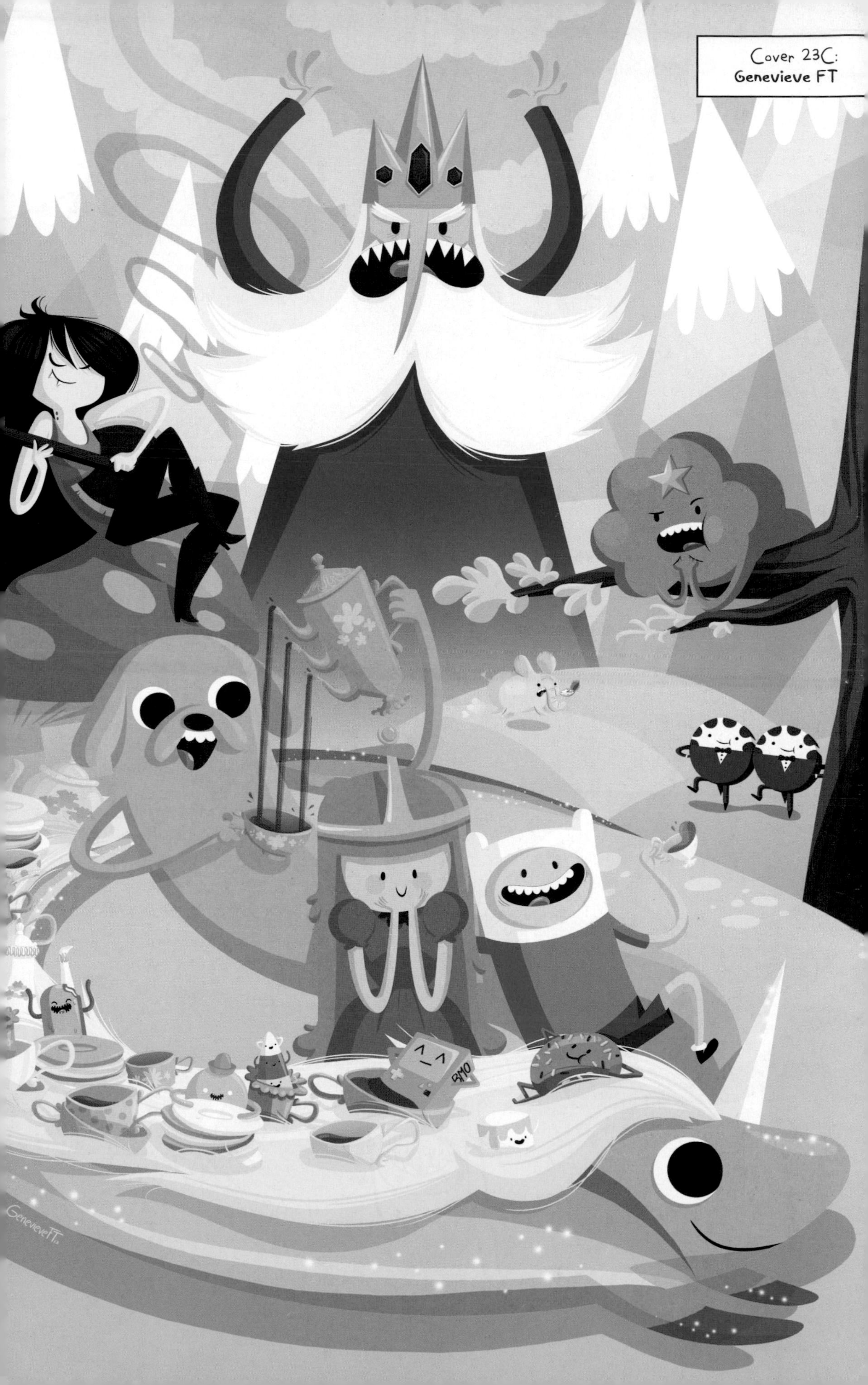
GenevieveFT

Cover 23C:
Genevieve FT

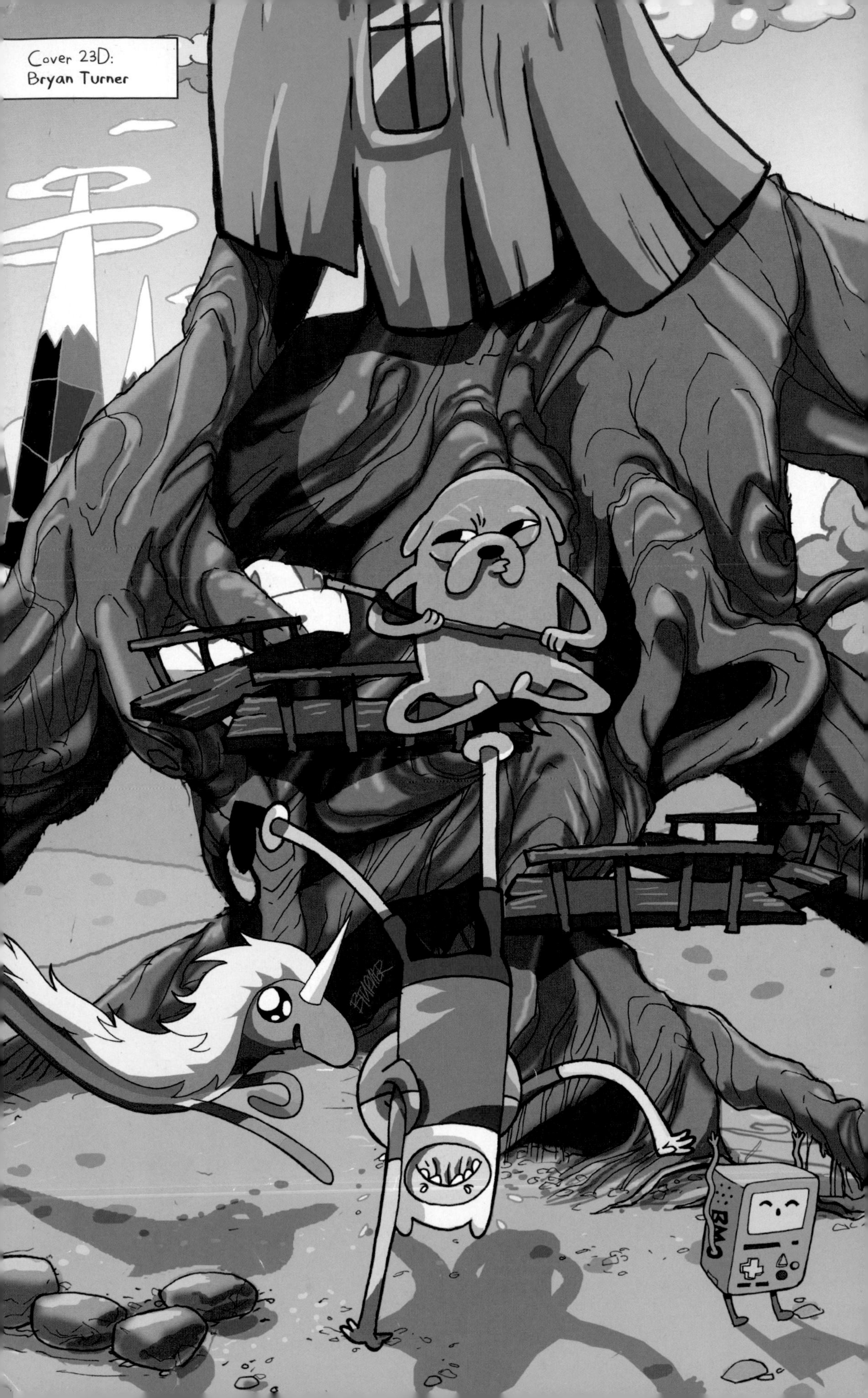
BMO
Cover 23D:
Bryan Turner

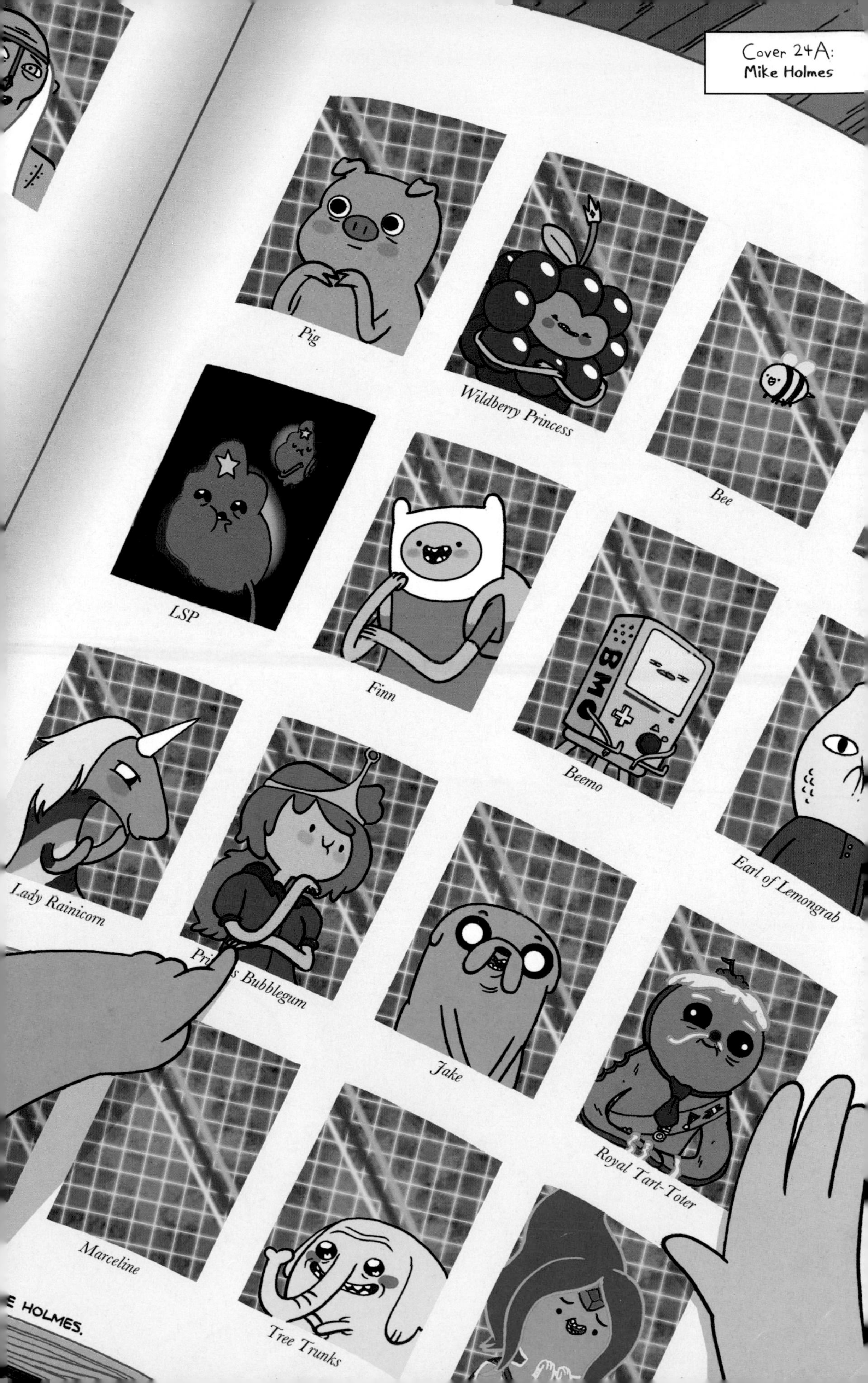

Cover 24A:
Mike Holmes
Pig
Wildberry Princess
Bee
LSP
Finn
Beemo
Earl of Lemongrab
Lady Rainicorn
Pri s Bubblegum
Jake
Royal Tart-Toter
Marceline
Tree Trunks
E HOLMES.

Cover 24B:
Brad McGinty

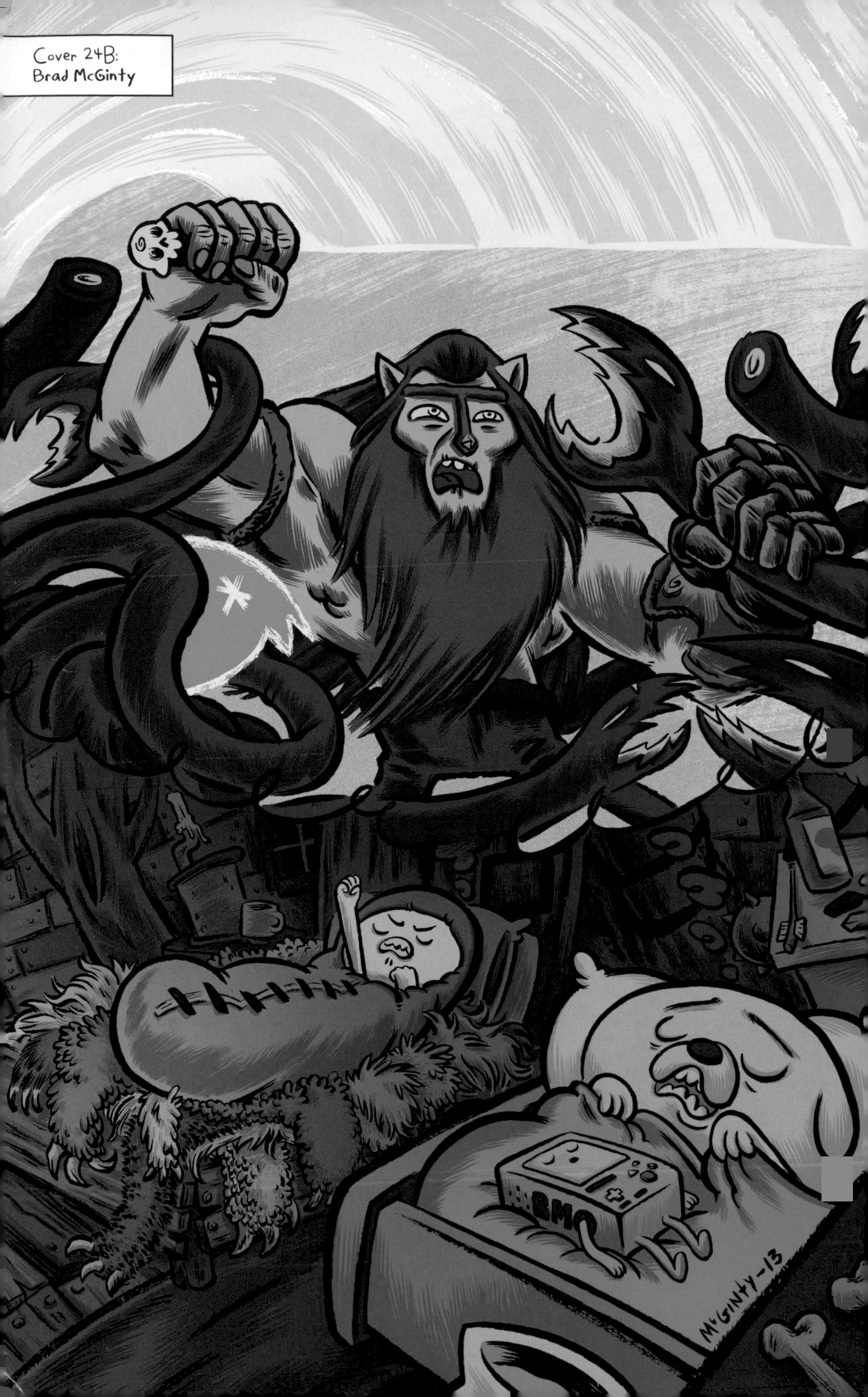
BMO
McGINTY-13

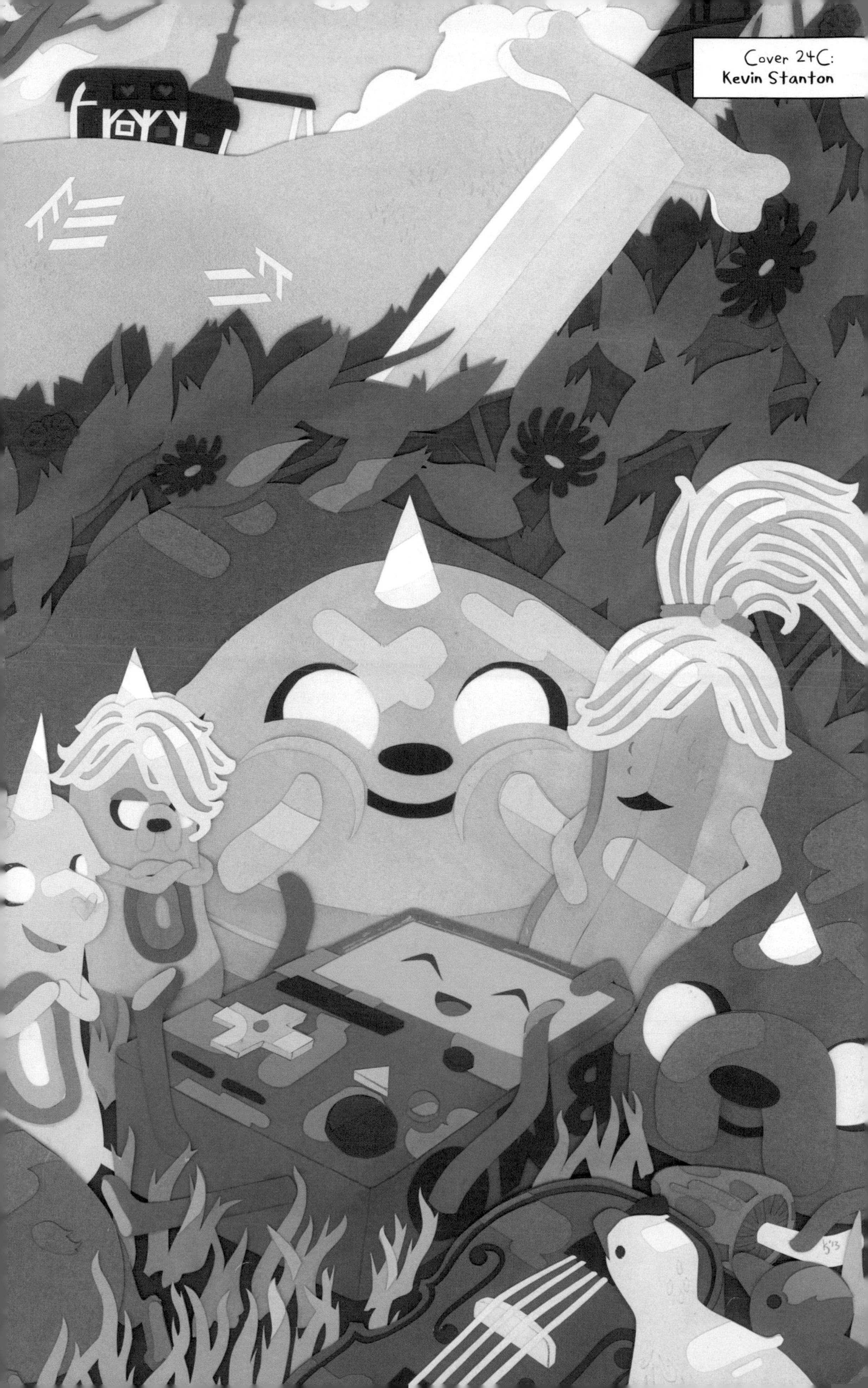

Cover 24C:
Kevin Stanton

Cover 24D:
Eva Cabrera

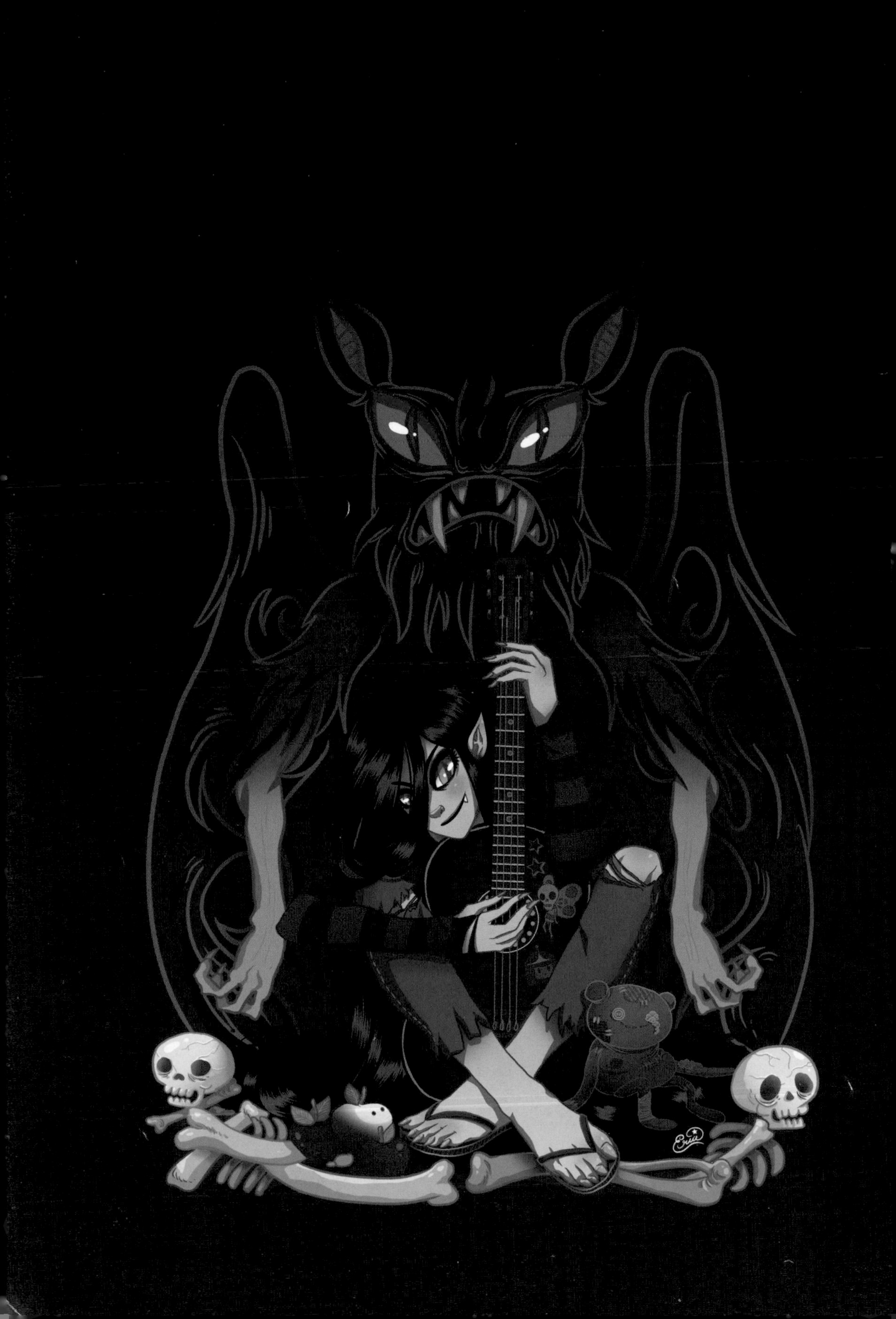

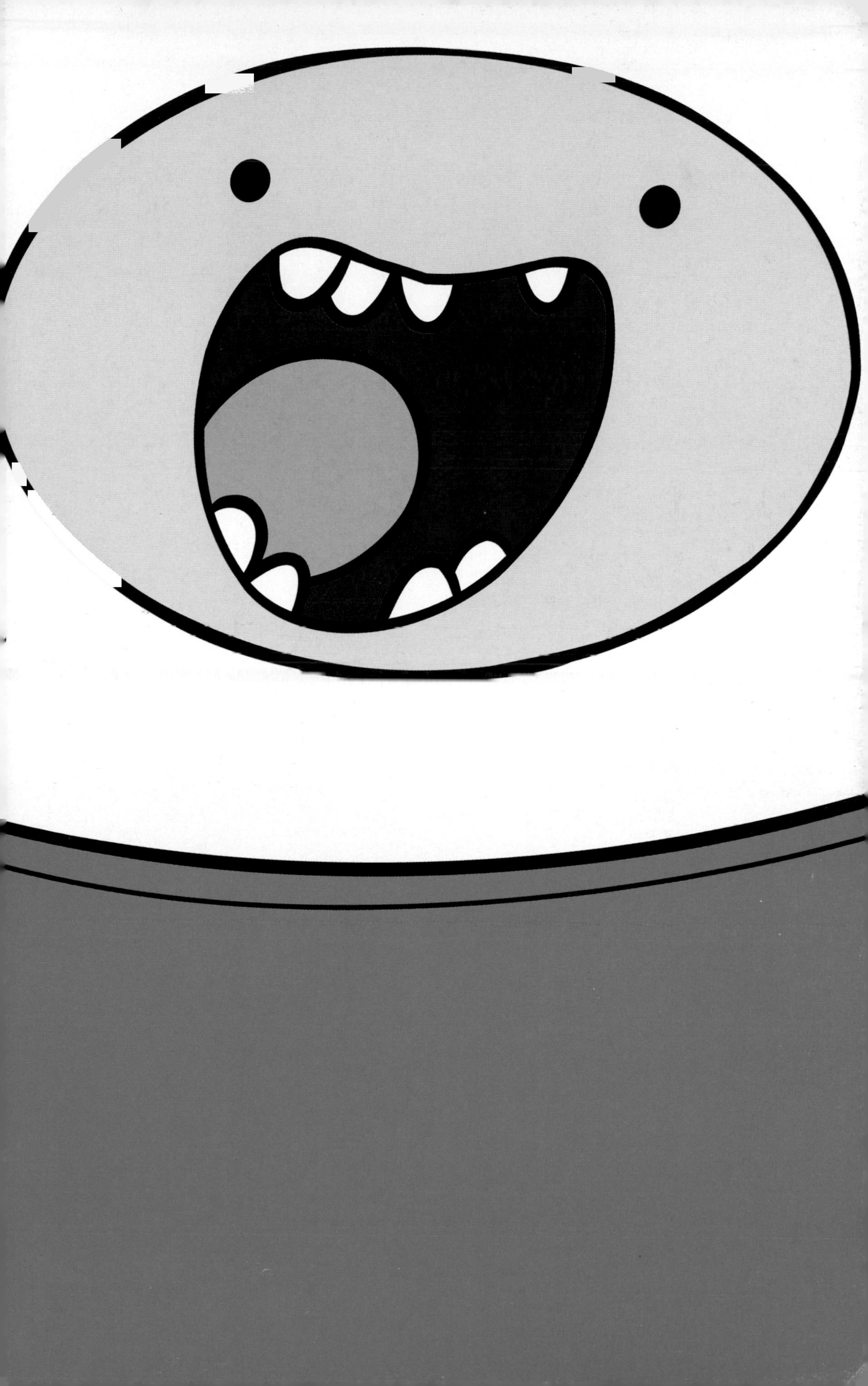

31901064365994